AN OUTWARD SHOW

**Recent Titles in
Contributions to the Study of Music and Dance**

AN OUTWARD SHOW

Music for Shakespeare on the London Stage, 1660–1830

RANDY L. NEIGHBARGER

Contributions to the Study of Music and Dance, Number 27

GREENWOOD PRESS
Westport, Connecticut • London

Library of Congress Cataloging-in-Publication Data

Neighbarger, Randy L.
   An outward show : music for Shakespeare on the London stage,
1660-1830 / Randy L. Neighbarger.
      p.   cm.—(Contributions to the study of music and dance,
   ISSN 0193-9041 ; no. 27)
   Includes bibliographical references and index.
   ISBN 0-313-27805-9 (alk. paper)
      1. Music—England—History and criticism. 2. Theater—England—
   History. 3. Music in theaters. 4. Shakespeare, William,
   1565-1616—Knowledge—Music.   I. Title.   II. Series.
   ML1731.N44 1992
   781.5'52—dc20   92-5423

British Library Cataloguing in Publication Data is available.

Library of Congress Catalog Card Number: 92-5423
ISBN: 0-313-27805-9
ISSN: 0193-9041

First published in 1992

Greenwood Press, 88 Post Road West, Westport, CT 06881
An imprint of Greenwood Publishing Group, Inc.

Printed in the United States of America

The paper used in this book complies with the
Permanent Paper Standard issued by the National
Information Standards Organization (Z39.48-1984).

10 9 8 7 6 5 4 3 2 1

Copyright Acknowledgements

The publisher and author are grateful to the following for granting use of their material:

"Walsingham," transcribed by F. W. Sternfeld in "Ophelia's Version of the Walsingham Song," *Music and Letters* 45 (1964): 111, appears by permission of Oxford University Press.

The following excerpts from Matthew Locke, *Dramatic Music*, Michael Tilmouth, ed., *Musica Britanica*, vol. 51: p. 32, [Masque of Devils], mm. 1-8; p. 53, "Dry Those Eyes," mm. 1-4; and pp. 74-5, [Masque of Neptune], mm. 78-90, are reproduced by permission of Stainer & Bell Ltd., London, England.

Excerpts from the Purcell *Tempest* score are reproduced from *The Works of Henry Purcell* (Purcell Society Volume 19, edited by Edward J. Dent) by permission of Novello and Company Limited.

Excerpts from Charles Burney, *A General History of Music*, edited by Frank Mercer, 1957, are courtesy of Dover Publications.

In addition, various libraries must be acknowledged for their permission to quote from the following unique manuscript and rare print materials:

Excerpts from Additional MSS 12219, 24889 and Egerton MSS 2493 and 2957 are quoted by permission of the British Library Department of Manuscripts.

An excerpt from Johan Ernst Galliard, "The Four Chorus's in the Tragedy of Julius Caesar," music manuscript M. Cab 1. 15, appears courtesy of the Trustees of the Boston Public Library.

MS Mus. d. 14 and MS. Mus. c. 3 are quoted by permission of the Bodleian Library, Oxford.

Excerpts reproduced from rare print material appear by permission of the British Library.

For Richard Burgwin

Contents

Contents

Acknowledgements

I would like to acknowledge the assistance I received during the research for this book from the staffs of various libraries and collections, including the British Library; the Royal College of Music; the Bodleian Library, Oxford; the Fitzwilliam Library, Cambridge; the Folger Shakespeare Library; The University of Michigan Libraries; and the Boston Public Library.

Research on this project originally was funded in part by a grant from the Horace H. Rackham School of Graduate Studies at The University of Michigan. I must acknowledge the important contributions of several Michigan faculty members: H. Don Cameron, Richard Crawford, Peggy Daub, and Dale Monson.

Andrea Ball generously read the text in its final stages. Her discerning eye solved many problems.

My cats, Meat Loaf and Buxtehude, logged nearly as much desk time on this project as I did. They calmly supervised.

I have saved my greatest debt to the end. Richard Burgwin, professor emeritus in theatre and drama at The University of Michigan, introduced me to the practical side of making music on the Shakespearean stage. It was while working on a production with him that I first became interested in the topic. Professor Burgwin has subsequently spent hours reading this work in progress and, even more importantly, provided invaluable advice and support. He has more than earned this volume's dedication.

Prologue

So may the outward shows be least themselves.

The Merchant of Venice III, 2

Shakespeare's plays have, in one form or another, held a place on the English-speaking stage from the time of their first productions. Theatre historians consider the tradition of Shakespearean performance a thread of continuity running through the seasonal changes of dramatic fashion. Music has long been recognized as part of that continuing heritage. This book looks at a period in the history of Shakespearean production when the plays, revised to accommodate tastes of the times, were often not themselves. At the same time, music and spectacle became an increasingly important feature in the presentation of the plays. Like the external trappings of Portia's gold, silver, and lead caskets, the music often became an outward show obscuring the play within.

Shakespeare intended music to be important in contemporary performances of his plays; many of the aesthetic ideas concerning musical dramaturgy, performance practices, and musical sources known to Elizabethan dramatists have been reconstructed. Shakespeare's own use of music has been studied with particular attention to the function of music and musical allusion in the plays. Collectors have attempted to recover the original tunes accompanying his dramatic lyrics. Yet while the music used in Shakespeare's own time has been the subject of much research, the music used in productions from later times has not been as systematically studied.

The effect of the Commonwealth on English drama is well known. The Puritan government closed the playhouses in 1640, and most theatrical activity stopped for the next twenty years. British poets and impresarios in French exile were then exposed to neoclassical Continental productions; these models were more influential than they might otherwise have been. When theatres reopened after the restoration of the monarchy in 1660, dramatists and audiences found pre-Commonwealth plays (including those by Shakespeare) unacceptable, so they were updated to appeal to new expectations. From 1660 through the first third of the nineteenth century (approximately 1830) the alteration of Shakespearean texts to comply with the transformation of contemporary dramaturgy was a normal occurrence. Such reworkings were judged on their own literary and dramatic merits, not according to how closely they followed older models.

The need to revise Shakespeare for the stage generated music of a kind quite unlike that envisioned by the playwright. The impetus behind the revisions, the nature of the revisions, and the resulting music did not remain static through the 170 years following the Restoration; rather, the practice of revision continued to follow changing dramatic and literary fashion. A renewed interest in Shakespeare's original texts and a concern for his characterization resulted in the decline of such revisions by 1830. It is the aim of this book to describe the music produced through this process of dramatic adaptation in its variety of forms and uses and to see how this repertoire developed as the practicalities of stage production, the literary reputation of Shakespeare, and the composition of theatrical audiences changed through the eighteenth century.

This study describes the music in productions of Shakespeare on the London stages from 1660 to 1830; Continental, North American, and provincial English productions have not been considered. This period begins with the fanciful reworkings of Davenant and Dryden. It closes with Henry R. Bishop's semi-operatic comedies, direct descendants of eighteenth-century pastiches despite their tendency to pre-Victorian sentiment. Only Shakespeare music used for stage productions is discussed in depth. This includes settings of Shakespeare's song lyrics, other original texts from the plays or poetry, and added non-Shakespearean texts, as well as incidental music, masques, operas, and afterpieces that used the plays as source works. While only one independent dance production based on Shakespeare is known from this period, stage directions in texts and playbills indicate that dancing was often included in the operas and plays. Surviving music for these dances is rare, suggesting it was not included in prints and manuscripts with other music from these productions and was in some way generic. Dance music is not considered at length here.

This book is a broad survey of Shakespearean music and its productions through the period. Many of these scores have been intensively studied by modern scholars. Their work will be identified and discussed in succeeding chapters. Other previously undiscussed repertoire and related information are brought together here for the first time. In total, this work is a concise overview of contemporary musical theatre practice as it was applied to Shakespeare.

This book also explores the different ways music was used in drama. The function of music in Shakespeare's time has been the subject of numerous studies; this function differed from that underlying the revisions that appeared shortly after the Restoration. As literary and theatrical aesthetics changed in the eighteenth century, so did the nature of the dramatic revisions. Influenced by several musico-dramatic models (Continental and domestic), English composers provided music representative of many musical genres and dramatic intents. By investigating how music was used in specific productions, it is possible to arrive at generalized conclusions about the developing role of music in Shakespearean productions.

Finally, because of the persistent popularity of this repertoire, the examination of these scores can be considered a case study in the history of English theatre music. Shakespearean revision and the resultant music were not only by-products of the assimilation of Continental literary influence into a powerful native tradition. They were also indicative of the drastically altered relationship of music and the spoken word. This dramatic and musical literature represents a large portion of the period's production activity. Between 1701 and 1800, Shakespearean performances made up 7,214 of the total 40,664 recorded London performances.[1] The repertoire's size and continuity make the scores for these productions, even if they are not always representative of other contemporary theatre music, the best examples of the variety in late seventeenth- and eighteenth-century dramatic music.

Three types of contemporary sources have been most valuable in tracing Shakespeare music through the age of revision. First are the extant musical sources themselves. The frequent fires suffered by theatre libraries—not to mention the assumption on the part of those who kept libraries that much of the material in their charge was ephemeral—resulted in a meager manuscript inheritance. Prints make up the largest part of the surviving music, and they have generally been accurately dated and attributed to their composers. The prints provide an unusual number of clues for verifying dates, provenance, and usage. Although sometimes undated, the prints often give the names of the theatre in which the music was performed and the names of the singers. Records from the daily theatrical advertisements help connect the clues in the prints to specific performances.

The major problem with printed music has been the incompleteness of the material it contains. For example, printed opera scores omit recitatives, which a student of the drama would be eager to see. The representation of scoring is inconsistent. Some provide complete instrumental scores and vocal parts, while others only include melodies, or at best two-stave reductions containing vocal melody and continuo (with occasional instrumental cues in the upper staff). Late in the eighteenth century piano/vocal scores were introduced.

Compared to the prints, the extant manuscript scores present complex problems of provenance, some of which are yet to be resolved. Fortunately, the performance circumstances for many sources have been positively identified. Manuscripts were cre-

ated as theatre copies (often complete with performance indications), study or souvenir copies, or private copies belonging to
the composer; however, neither manuscripts nor prints alone
give a complete view of the music and its performance for a
given production. Theatre scores typically were composed either
in a collaborative fashion or were assembled using some pre-existing material. Since publications as a rule represented the work
of specific composers, collections of popular melodies, or music
for a specific medium, they rarely contained the entire score for a
single play. Often only the collation of several sources reveals
all the music for one production. In weakly documented cases,
often the norm, it is likely that some of a given production's music is now lost.

Second, the textual sources also contain information on the
music. Printed play texts (often published in connection with
specific productions) are the major source, but a few manuscript
plays, work lists, and promptbooks also exist. These sources describe how the music was incorporated into the action, ascribe
music to various characters, include cast lists, and offer other information unavailable in musical sources. These texts are especially valuable when the musical sources are lost.

Third, insights into the creation and reception of eighteenth-
century Shakespearean music are derived from daily theatrical
advertisements, critical commentary, and personal memoirs and
correspondence. While some musical items are known only
through these contemporary commentaries, there is nothing to
suggest that the surviving musical source materials represent less
than a significant proportion of the total repertoire.

Quotations in this book taken from contemporary play scripts,
advertisements, and correspondence will be reprinted with original spelling, capitalization, and (when possible) typography. The
use of *sic* will be limited to circumstances where an error in the
original source may confuse meaning. References to Shakespeare's original plays will usually refer to the "folio" text, the
first complete edition of Shakespeare's plays (1623) and the basis
of most modern editions. Act and scene indications are given in
shortened form. Thus, act III, scene 2 is indicated as III, 2.

When comparisons are made between an original Shakespearean scene and its analogue in a later revision, the act/scene designation for the original text will bear the "folio" designation. For example, Shakespeare's *Macbeth* act III, scene 5 is the basis for act III, scene 8 in a Restoration revision of the play. In shortened form they are called folio III, 5 and III, 8.

The amount and complexity of information found in these sources defy a consistent depth of discussion in prose. To make source information easily accessible, chapter reference charts listing important productions in chronological order are included in Appendix C. These charts, keyed to the music and text source lists in the Bibliography, specify production date, the name of the source play if the altered version was retitled, the existence of musical and textual sources, and notes on the performance or the condition and reliability of the source material. Charts outlining scene analyses of John Christopher Smith's Shakespearean operas *The Fairies* and *The Tempest* are also included in Appendix C. Complete musical items appear in Appendix A. Appendix B is a guide to the source material for Thomas Arne's important Shakespeare music.

The chronological division of this book into five chapters is based on the dynamic created by the changing status of Shakespeare's reputation and the changing musical climate. As succeeding generations valued different aspects of Shakespeare's dramatic and poetic accomplishments, the preferred repertoire changed. Music for Shakespearean productions mirrored other musical theatre trends. A chronological organization helps provide a narrative line; however, a few topics span such temporal divisions. These discussions, placed in chapters where their evidence is most pertinent, will make free use of information from all periods.

The first chapter (covering the period 1660–95) discusses the initial inspiration for the revisions, the introduction of neoclassical dramatic models from France, and the operatic stimulus that accompanied the imported literary forms. The double models of Corneille and Molière/Lully help to explain how part of the

Shakespearean repertoire was altered with little or no musical elaboration while other plays were transmuted into semi-operas.

The second chapter (1695–1720) describes the decline of these revisions as the neoclassical ideal subsided at the beginning of the eighteenth century. The growing popularity of Italian opera contributed to a fiscal and artistic crisis, which led to the reorganization of London theatres. It also reshaped the theatrical repertoire. During this period Shakespeare production dropped to its lowest level ever. The music created for the few plays remaining in the repertoire was indicative of the growing influence of Italian compositional style.

The third chapter (1720–50) explores the revival of Shakespeare's romantic comedies, absent from the stage since the Restoration. These plays and their accompanying musical traditions were reinterpreted in the age of ballad opera and pantomime by Thomas Arne and others.

The powerful influence of David Garrick on all aspects of Shakespearean production is the focus of the fourth chapter (1750–70). Garrick, the foremost actor and theatre manager of the century, was responsible for many of the textual revisions and musical elaborations that contributed to the dramatic variety of mid-century England.

The final chapter (1770–1830) looks at the years when the Shakespearean repertoire, standardized during Garrick's tenure and stable through the last years of the eighteenth century, first came under the influence of the Romantic literary movement. Musical Shakespeareana continued to be influenced by conservative eighteenth-century musical traditions rather than by literary concerns. By the 1770s, comic opera had become a significant part of the theatrical repertoire. To capitalize on opera's popularity, managers incorporated operatic features into Shakespeare's comedies. The tragedies, too, received some musical elaboration. The turn of the century saw a new breed of actor/manager who questioned the position of music as a near-equal of the text. The elevation of Shakespeare to cultural icon, and the resultant interest in textual authenticity, historical detail, and stage characterization began by the 1830s to limit play alterations and musical elaborations.

Perhaps because of a lack of true literary genius among the lesser English talents working in these years, Shakespeare (altered though he was) provided the stage with a dramatic energy contemporary playwrights were hard pressed to match. Composers played a similarly ancillary role while creating a sizable and diverse body of music. Spanning 170 years, representing various musical genres, and with artistic aspirations both high and low, this musical Shakespeareana provides a look into the untidy musico-dramatic history of the English stage in the years between the return of Charles II and the end of the Georgian era.

NOTE

1. Charles Beecher Hogan, *Shakespeare in the Theatre, 1701-1800*, 2 vols. (Oxford: Clarendon Press, 1952), 2:715.

AN OUTWARD SHOW

1

Shakespeare Reinvented: Shakespeare Music in the Restoration, 1660–1695

Shakespeare's plays were subjected to extensive revision during the last half of the seventeenth century. The literary criteria by which plays were judged, the audiences who watched the plays, even the theatres where the plays were produced were drastically different from what they had been in Shakespeare's time, less than a century before. The plays were updated to fit these new expectations and performance conditions.

English theatre had practically disappeared from 1640 to 1660, the years leading up to and encompassing the Common-wealth. Because of this lack of native theatrical activity, European dramatic influence was especially strong when the play-houses eventually reopened. Music was a prominent part of many (but not all) of the Continental performances that English dramatists used as models after 1660, and much of the rewriting of Shakespeare involved musical elaboration. The influence of different French and Italian theatrical genres over the English writers who updated older plays resulted in a range of musical and nonmusical adaptation. Some plays were treated operatically. Some retained vestiges of Elizabethan and Jacobean tradition. In others music played little part.

The Shakespearean transformation was an indicator of the literary and dramatic changes taking place during the closing years of the seventeenth century, and it attested to the uneasy balance between music and the spoken word on the Restoration stage. This volatility contrasted with the relative stability of production and musical values in the Elizabethan and Jacobean theatres.

SHAKESPEAREAN MUSIC ON THE ELIZABETHAN AND JACOBEAN STAGE

Shakespeare considered music to be an important ingredient in the production of his plays. In the 37 plays written between 1590 and 1613 there are more than 60 songs and over 300 musical stage directions.[1] Poetic allusions to music are common in the texts. Shakespeare was not alone among his contemporaries in his attention to music. It was an integral part of Elizabethan stagecraft. However, important as it was, music was confined to limited and conventional placement and usage.

Music played two basic functions on the Elizabethan stage. It provided a realistic touch of pageantry and excitement in those scenes where music would normally be found in real-life situations, such as secular and religious ceremonies, battles, and banquets. Music also played a commentarial role, communicating to the audience some aspect of the unfolding story. This would include establishing the mood of a scene, the foreshadowing of action yet to happen, and the representation of the supernatural. Elizabethan musical attitudes reflected both classical concepts of music's power and medieval ideas concerning its cosmic and mystical significance.

It was not part of Elizabethan stage tradition for central characters to express their emotions in song at moments of crisis. Songs were usually restricted to characters outside the main action of the play—for example, fools, minstrels, and low comics. It does not necessarily follow that a noncentral character is unimportant. While some of Shakespeare's lyrics are sung by minor figures introduced for just that purpose (e.g., *Measure for Measure* IV,1), others are sung by important bystanders and commentators. The main events of the plot of *King Lear* are not directly concerned with the fool. Yet the role is of considerable length, the character moralizes in a fashion not unlike a Greek chorus, and the relationship between Lear and his fool provide some of the play's most moving moments.

Part of the restriction on singing characters may have been a reflection of the social taboo observed by the upper classes against singing in public.[2] Noble characters did not sing on stage in part because in real life the musical activities of nobles were constrained by social rules. Central characters could sing if they were outside the realm of normal human limitations. In *The Tempest*, Ariel is a creature of the supernatural, a realm described by music. The songs of the mad Ophelia in *Hamlet* IV, 5 indicate the depth of her distraction, which brings her to ignore courtly proprieties. Desdemona's "Willow Song" (*Othello* IV, 3) is perhaps the most superficially operatic scene in Shakespeare. Even here, Desdemona only sings in the privacy of her own chamber, and the song fulfills one of the major functions of Elizabethan stage music, foreshadowing her death.

In the examples above from the tragedies, dramatic qualities overshadow the musical element. In *Lear* and *Hamlet* most of the songs only appear in fragments and snatches to avoid impeding the dramatic progression. Songs and music to accompany dance were more often features of the comedies, perhaps through the influence of the Plautine comedies, which were themselves well dressed with song.

During Shakespeare's lifetime most performances of his plays took place in the public theatres, such as the Globe. These buildings, open wooden amphitheatres with platform stages, housed a variety of theatrical entertainments and gaming activities, which attracted socially heterogeneous audiences. In contrast, the private theatres were enclosed and catered to a more affluent audience. The private theatres (e.g., Blackfriars) were home to the companies of young boy actors attached to the singing schools of St. Paul's and the Chapel Royal at Windsor. The adult companies played the public houses.

For the most part the songs heard in the public theatres represented vernacular practice rather than cultivated artifice. Shakespeare often used or alluded to songs of popular origin. While

some of Shakespeare's lyrics were set as art songs (Robert Johnson's settings of "Full Fathom Five" and "Where the Bee Sucks,"
believed to be from the first production of *The Tempest*, being the
best known of these), folk music and popular song made up the
bulk of theatrical repertoire. The most highly developed Elizabethan musical forms—the madrigal and the instrumental fancy—
had no place on the public stage because such offerings neither
added to the plays' dramatic developments nor appealed to the
mixed audiences in the public houses.

The Elizabethan public theatres did not maintain well-devel-
oped musical establishments. The instrumental forces usually
consisted of a broken consort of plucked, bowed, and blown instruments—lutes, viols, recorders—supplemented by cornetts,
brass, keyboards, and percussion as required by the plays. This
variety reflected the unsettled nature of instrumental music, still
largely dependent on vocal models for repertoire and with sys-
tematic instrument groupings yet to develop. Songs were performed by musically talented members of the acting company.
Since women were not allowed on stage the adult companies used
boy actors in female roles. They supplied the only treble voices.
The musicians could be variously placed behind the scenes in a
music room above or at the back of the stage platform, on the
stage if the play required, or in unusual locations (e.g., under the
stage) for special effects. The orchestra pit, a later Continental
development, was not part of the Elizabethan stage layout.

The private theatres had more ambitious music programs in
keeping with their choir school affiliations. Instrumental music
was commonly played between acts, a feature missing in the
Elizabethan public theatres. The boys, trained as choristers,
were capable of sophisticated musical performance. For dramatic
purposes, however, the complete range of voices available to the
adult companies in the public theatres (taking into account the
treble voices of the boys in women's roles) must have been more
useful.

The adult companies occasionally performed by command at
the royal court, playing to more sophisticated audiences than in
the public houses and having a larger musical contingent at their

disposal. When Shakespeare wrote or adapted a play for court performance he not only included more opportunities for song and dance but incorporated musical symbolism and allusion even more deeply into the text than usual. *A Midsummer Night's Dream* (ca. 1595) and *The Tempest* (ca. 1611), from opposite ends of the playwright's career, both display the influence of court performance or the court masque in the practical and poetic presence of music in the scripts. Shakespeare required more musical forces in these plays than in any other.

Between Shakespeare's death in 1616 and the rise of Puritan control over the theatres in the 1640s, theatrical practice did not drastically change.[3] However, two developments of the period were to influence Shakespearean production. First, the practice of performing instrumental music during the intervals, always customary in the private theatres, moved to the public theatres by 1610.[4] Plays that had been performed without break, including those by Shakespeare, were now divided into acts to accommodate musical entertainments. Second, features of the court masque tradition were adopted by the public theatres. The influence of the rhetorical and mythological features of court masques on the organic structure of Shakespeare's plays is debatable, but the playwright clearly embraced opportunities to introduce music, dance, and spectacle into later plays like *The Tempest*. In the 1620s and 1630s the theatres achieved technical capabilities for creating spectacular scenes that had been available to Shakespeare only when he worked at the court.[5]

RESTORATION THEATRE: THE MIXING OF NEW AND OLD

The Resumption of Acting

The years of civil strife preceding the Commonwealth and the tenure of the Cromwellian government disrupted the English theatrical community. Puritanical censure closed the theatres in the early 1640s, bringing dramatic activity almost entirely to a close.

Writers and actors attempting to practice their craft were actively persecuted by the government, which believed "plays were invented by the Devil; therefore are execrable and unlawful."[6] Some acting continued, occasionally under the guise of musical concerts, but the theatre ceased to be a viable livelihood. The return of Charles II from Paris cleared the way for the reopening of the theatres.

Before the Commonwealth, the monarch controlled drama in London and throughout Britain by granting theatrical monopolies and licensing plays. Charles II reclaimed this right and in 1660 issued two monopolies. One was given to William Davenant (1606–68), a principal writer of court masques for the Stuarts and a collaborator of Inigo Jones and Henry Lawes. The other went to Thomas Killigrew (1612–83), who had stayed with the English court during the years in France. Davenant's troupe was known as the Duke's Company, Killigrew's as the King's Company. Both men had been playwrights before 1642, both had experience with the pre-Commonwealth private theatre, and both were familiar with Corneille and the vogues of the Parisian stage. The men who had almost complete control of the London theatres knew both their native heritage and the *à la mode* ideas from France. The companies held the exclusive rights to perform plays in London until 1682, when financial problems prompted the merger of the two troupes into the United Company. This single monopoly would last until the 1694-95 season, when a splinter group of actors were granted playing rights, restoring the two-company system.

When the theatres reopened in 1660, the first problem facing the new companies was rebuilding a repertoire. For a time the theatres relied on pre-Commonwealth plays, including Shakespeare's. It was not long before the work of Shakespeare and other pre-Commonwealth playwrights began to be replaced by new scripts, both serious and comic. The most important of the serious styles was the heroic drama, which was written in rhymed couplets. In these stories, often based on French or Spanish models, the hero and heroine usually find themselves in a situation where the recognition of their mutual love brings about their ruin or dishonor. Events often work out to a contrived happy ending. The heroic drama was later displaced by a form in blank verse. More popular with contemporary audiences were the comedies of humors, intrigues, and manners, in which the activities, entertainments, and values of the upper classes were explored and enjoyed.

The development of new dramatic genres, the rise of new standards of literary taste, and a new audience brought about a devaluation of Shakespeare's reputation and influence. Some of his plays simply disappeared from the repertory. Many of the remaining ones were extensively changed to accommodate dramatic principles shaped by French neoclassicism. Contemporary literary tastes and new musical attitudes would shape the Shakespearean repertoire and its music for the remainder of the century.

Shakespeare and the Neoclassical Ideal

Restoration drama was a product of compromise.[7] At its base was a reverence for English theatrical tradition as represented by Shakespeare and Jonson. Yet the expansive tendencies of Elizabethan drama were at least partially restrained by newer Continental influences.

The English court had been in exile during a time when the Parisian theatres were strongly influenced by neoclassical dramatic ideals imported from Italy. In the last half of the sixteenth century Italian *literati* found in Horace and especially Aristotle the basis for a dramatic theory that posited verisimilitude, the appearance of truth, as a fundamental goal. The Renaissance notion of dramatic neoclassicism was first completely stated by Lodovico Castelvetro (1501–71) in his 1570 translation and gloss of Aristotle's *Poetics*. While French interest in classical tradition was fired by the increased French-Italian exchanges after the marriage of Henri II and Caterina de' Medici in 1560, this interest was limited to a small, educated group who put their theory into practice in private situations. Not until the 1620s would sufficiently talented playwrights and Italian scenic innovators come together on the public stage to solidify the power of Renaissance classicism over French drama. By the time the mature works of Pierre Corneille were being performed, members of the exiled English court were frequent visitors to the Parisian theatres. Corneille's influence on English dramatists—both as a playwright of heroic dramas and as a theoretician in his three treatises on dramatic construction (1656–60)—was considerable.

According to the French *littérateurs* there were two principal tenets of neoclassical drama. First, the purposes of drama were to teach and to please. Secondly, the "three unities" had to be observed. It was thought that by observing the unities of time, place, and action the verisimilitude of the play would be sustained. Ideally, the time of the supposed action would be equal to the drama's playing time. Since the stage was in reality but one place, it should represent only one imaginary locus. The action should be limited to one plot, since the addition of subplots would actually be a division of the original play into a multiplicity of plays. This integrity of plot was also related to the concept that the two basic forms of drama, tragedy and comedy, should not be mixed.

When English playwrights influenced by Continental neoclassicism began to write after the Restoration they tended to obey the limits of the unities in a more casual manner than their French counterparts. Many, but by no means all, of the plays were confined to a twenty-four-hour time limit. As for subplots, English drama had always been rich in contrast, comic relief, and the use of individual stories combined in an effective climax. Unity of place was often stretched to include any place within traveling distance in a twenty-four-hour period.[8]

The different application of these restrictions implied a different definition of verisimilitude. The Continental concept encompassed the nature of the action and the logical cause and effect of acts of passion, greed, and other characteristics. That is, the outcome of a given act had to be a believable result of that act. It was not so much the truthfulness of the stage conception that was in question as the veracity of the symbol wherein the moral resided. For the English playwright, it was not just the result of the action, but the action itself that had to be above question. It was the goal of the dramatist (and by extension, of the others involved in the dramatic production) to suspend the disbelief of the audience by making the action not just believable, but convincingly real.

Restoration critics damned Shakespeare's tragedies for their failure to meet neoclassical standards, while still recognizing their importance in English theatre history. In his 1693 essay "A Short View of Tragedy," Thomas Rymer was more extreme than most in his censure of Shakespeare: "In Tragedy he appears quite out of his Element; his Brains are turn'd, he raves and rambles, without any coherence, any spark of reason, or any rule to controul him, or set bounds to his phrenzy."[9] Judging the Shakespeare canon according to strict neoclassical rules, especially when Restoration dramatists were not above bending the unities themselves, did not seem inappropriate to those sharing Rymer's views.

While other critics, including Dryden, might profess that Shakespeare's genius was beyond convention, the reality of the wholesale revision or avoidance of his plays indicates that Rymer's harsh judgment reflected the feelings of many of his contemporaries:

We find so much farce and *Apochryphal Matter* in his Tragedies. Thereby un-hallowing the Theatre, profaning the name of Tragedy; And instead of representing Men and Manners, turning all Morality, good sence, and humanity into mockery and derision.[10]

Plays were changed to conform to the spirit if not the exact letter of neoclassicism. This could mean the reordering or omission of scenes to reshape Shakespeare's overlapping and cumulative temporal and locational shifts into a more continuous time frame, the addition of totally new roles to provide a balance between character types, or the complete rewriting of entire plays.

The plays of Shakespeare met with no more approval from theatre audiences than from the critics. Restoration theatres did not cater to the wide spectrum of social classes that the pre-Commonwealth houses had seen. The new houses assumed the function and upper-class audiences of the earlier court theatre and the private theatres. This new audience enjoyed seeing its world mirrored in contemporary comedies, and the shows of cleverness that passed for daily conversation were echoed in the witty dialogues of the plays. The pastoral comedies of Shakespeare were too foreign to the courtier's world, and they all but vanished from the repertoire. One theatre analyst of the day commented, "There was not much of comedy known before the learned Ben Jonson, for no man can allow any of Shakespear's Comedies, except *The Merry Wives of Windsor*."[11]

Restoration Stage Music Practices

Continental influence was not limited to aesthetic rules regulating how drama should be written. English stage managers copied visual and musical aspects of European productions as well. The advances made in stagecraft by the Italians and French appealed to an English aesthetic familiar with the Stuart court masque. The British response to French and Italian operatic practices was ambivalent. The Continental relationship between music and drama both fascinated and repelled the British dramatic sensibility. The Elizabethan and Jacobean stage conventions, which had maintained a working dramatic balance between the spoken word and music, changed as Continental operatic practice merged with the more restrained musical usage of the pre-Commonwealth stage. Even considering the long connection between the spoken drama and music in England, the amount of music used before, during, and between the acts of late seventeenth-century English plays was extraordinary. More than 600 plays are known to have been performed on Restoration stages, and nearly all of them specified some kind of music.[12] Determining the function of that music caused problems for dramatists, musicians, and theoreticians.

In England, where the tradition of spoken drama was strong, the aversion to having main characters sing was a major factor in the development of Restoration stage music practices. The sixteenth-century Italian humanists, heirs to a less developed dramatic literature than England, could more freely imagine a new blend of music and poetry based, however mistakenly, on an antique ideal. The French had long considered their tongue a musical language and their poesy a kind of music, so the combination of music and drama was not outside the realm of the *Pléiade*. The English were not as willing to accept the theories that led to the creation of opera in Italy and France. "The Grecians were for . . . Musick as mad as any Monsieur of 'em all; yet their musick kept within bounds; attempted no metamorphosis to turn the Drama to an Opera."[13]

Peter Motteaux, an English producer, playwright, and commentator on stylish society, outlined his countrymen's taste in such matters by comparing Italian opera with the use of music on the English stage:

Other nations bestow the name of *Opera* only on such plays whereof every word is sung. But experience has taught us that our English genius will not rellish that perpetual singing. I dare not accuse the language for being overcharged with Consonants, which may take off the beauties of the recitative part, tho in several other Countries I have seen their *Opera's* still crowded everytime, tho long and almost all recitative. It is true that their *Trio's*, chorus's, lively songs and *recits* with Accompaniments of Instrument, Symphonies, Machines, and excellent dances make the rest be born with and sets off the other: But our English Gentlemen, when their ear is satisfied, are desirous to have their mind pleas'd, and Music and Dancing industriously intermixed with Comedy or Tragedy. I have often observed that the Audience is no less attentive to some extraordinary Scenes of Passion or Mirth, than to what they call *Beaux Endriots* or the most ravishing part of musical performance. But had those Scenes, tho never so well wrought up, been sung, they would have lost most of their beauty. All this does not lessen the Power of Music, for its Charms command our attention when used in their place. . . . But this shows that which is unnatural, as are plays altogether sung, will soon make one uneasy which Comedy and Tragedy can never do, unless they be bad.[14]

Music could not be truly dramatic because it functioned differently than comedy or tragedy. Music appealed to the sense of beauty, but the intellect and emotions were challenged by the spoken word.

It was the ability to move an audience that made an actor a favorite of the audiences. That ability lay in the delivery of the text, spoken in a chant-like fashion that the great actor Thomas Betterton claimed was as controlled as singing,[15] and the use of gestures.

The Stage ought to be the Seat of Passion in its various kinds, and therefore the Actor ought to be thoroughly acquainted with the whole Nature of the Affections, and Habits of the Mind, or else he will never be able to expres them justly in his Looks and Gestures, as well as in the Tone of his Voice and manner of Utterance.[16]

Part of the illusion of the English stage was the credibility of passion. The subjugation of words or characterization to music would make it harder for the audience to identify with the passions on stage, shattering the illusion of reality. Singing may have had dramatic meaning for the Italians, but song could not replace spoken declamation for the English.

Although he was writing on the topic of extended spoken monologues, Dryden may give another clue to the reluctance of English dramatists to accept the extended conventions of song in the main dramatic action:

It cannot be denied that short speeches and replies are more apt to move the passions and beget concernment in us, than [long ones]; for it is unnatural for any one in a gust of passion to speak long altogether or for another in the same condition to suffer him without interruption. Grief and passion are like floods raised in little brooks by a sudden rain; they are quickly up; and if the concernment be poured unexpectedly in upon us, it overflows us; but a long sober shower gives them the leisure to run out as they came in, without troubling the ordinary current.[17]

Paradoxically, in spite of the resistance of critics and poets, music assumed unprecedented importance on the Restoration stage. Many of those critics rightly feared the music would overwhelm the spoken drama:

> Did Ben now live, how would he fret, and rage,
> To see the Musick-room envye the stage?
> To see the French Haut-boyes charm the listening Pitt
> More than the Raptures of his God-like wit.[18]

Differing reasons have been suggested for the theatre audience's musical preferences. John Dryden, in the epilogue to *Oedipus*, cynically suggested the increased use of music and stage spectacle camouflaged the work of inferior dramatists:

> Yet as weak states each others pow'r assure,
> Weak Poets by Conjunction are secure.
> Their Treat is what your Pallats relish most,
> Charm! Song! and Show! a Murder and a Ghost![19]

Dryden would not be the last to blame lesser talents and a frivolous audience for the incursion of musical entertainment into what he considered the rightful domain of the poet. Some writers were concerned that incidental lyrics in their plays be functional, and conventions, based in part on Elizabethan practice, evolved.[20]

Among modern commentators, Allardyce Nicoll suggested that the audience members, for the most part neither serious nor literary-minded, were not equipped to appreciate tragic drama.[21] Stoddard Lincoln suggested that the taste for more music in drama developed during the years when the playhouses circumvented Commonwealth restrictions by presenting dramatic musical productions.[22] Edward Dent noted that the masque tradition remained strong through the seventeenth century.[23] The establishment and popular acceptance of public concerts was concurrent with increased musical activity in the theatres. The musical novelty and spectacle of Continental opera might for these reasons have seemed, under certain conditions, less foreign to a potentially xenophobic audience inclined to consider music effeminate, foreign, and useful only for the representation of affects. It remained for the playwrights, musicians, and managers to decide how best to introduce music onto the stage.

MUSIC IN THE SHAKESPEAREAN REPERTOIRE, 1660–1695

Plays with Incidental Music

For the first few years after the Restoration, the acting companies performed more or less unaltered versions of plays granted to them by warrant. All of Shakespeare's plays were eventually divided between Davenant and Killigrew. Although more than half the plays were licensed to Killigrew, he rarely produced Shakespeare, preferring plays by Fletcher and Jonson. The presence in Davenant's company of Thomas Betterton (1635–1710), the foremost actor of the last half of the century, also influenced the division of plays between Davenant and Killigrew.

The historical performance record, incomplete as it is, suggests that only twelve Shakespearean plays were actually revived in the first years after the theatres reopened. From 1660 to 1665 tragedies and histories make up most of the list of confirmed performances: *Hamlet, Henry IV, Henry VI, Henry VIII, Julius Caesar, King Lear, Macbeth, The Merry Wives of Windsor, A Midsummer Night's Dream, Othello, Romeo and Juliet,* and *Twelfth Night.* Few of these plays, and none of the comedies, received more than a handful of performances.

Working texts for these productions may have been taken from pre-Commonwealth sources (print or manuscript), as no printing of a Shakespearean play from the years 1660 to 1667 is known to exist. The theatre managers would have known the musical stage directions in plays printed before 1640, and veteran actors would have probably remembered their songs. But little evidence survives from the plays in which music is an important component—*Hamlet, Lear, Dream, Othello,* and *Twelfth Night*—to describe how they were treated on the Restoration stage.

Only the barest core of a Shakespearean repertoire established itself in the last years of the seventeenth century. The comedies, especially rich in song, were to practically disappear from the theatres for nearly seventy years. Any opportunity for the Jacobean tradition of Shakespearean musical practice to bridge the gap of the Commonwealth years was lost.

It is possible that Ophelia's songs in *Hamlet* IV,5 are the only melodies that have been transmitted from Shakespeare's time through use in Restoration productions. The Davenant *Hamlet*, first performed in the 1660s but not printed until 1677, became the standard text for many decades.[24] Davenant's cuts were extensive, but he avoided profound changes. The song lyrics survived in the Restoration texts.

Later, when early nineteenth-century English historians made the first collections of Shakespeare music, they paid special attention to Ophelia's songs. Most of these editors believed that the tunes were from Shakespeare's time. For William Linley, this judgment was at least in part an aesthetic one:

Of the wild and pathetic melodies of Ophelia, the Author can give no account. He has introduced them as he remembers them to have been exquisitely sung by the late Mrs. Forster when she was Miss Field, and belonged to Drury Lane Theatre; and the impression remains too strong upon his mind to make him doubt the correctness of the airs, agreeable to her delivery of them. The tunes were never, he believes, published before, and were probably detached compositions of different authors. The words which Shakespeare has introduced are not all his own; some may be found in Percy's old ballads.[25]

Early nineteenth-century song collectors could not check the validity of a traditional claim for the *Hamlet* songs, at least not against theatre holdings. Charles Knight described how the songs came to be in his edition of Shakespeare:

The music, still sung in the character of Ophelia, to the fragments of songs in the Fifth Scene of Act IV, is supposed to be the same, or nearly so, that was used in Shakespeare's time, and thence transmitted to us by tradition. When Drury Lane theatre was destroyed by fire in 1812, the copy of these songs suffered the fate of the whole musical library; but Dr. [Samuel] Arnold noted down the airs from Mrs. Jordan's recollection of them.[26]

The songs were published variously by Linley (1816), Caulfield (1815), Knight (1835), Nicks (1839), and Chappell (1840, 1855).

This type of "traditional" citation on the part of Linley and the others must be greeted with skepticism. In the eighteenth century two of the most important Shakespearean scores for other plays were to be misattributed only a few years after their composition, and this in the name of "tradition."[27] While there is little question that these tunes were in use at Drury Lane by the time Arnold set them down, there is no direct evidence that these tunes were the original ones.

Peter J. Seng rightly questioned the validity of the "traditional" claim, but posits an overly-strict chain of events which would need to be fulfilled for such transmission:

To suppose, however, that those tunes could have originated in Shakespeare's Globe Theatre requires uncritical acceptance of the following hypotheses: that Shakespeare was the natural father of Sir William D'avenant, that the "son" possessed the musical scores from the Globe, that he passed them on to his protege Thomas Betterton, and that Betterton brought them to Drury Lane. Some sort of case can be made for each step in the argument—even for the antique scandal on which the whole is founded—but taken in its entirety, the argument is too tangential to be credited.[28]

Seng ignored other routes of oral transmission. The small size of London's acting community (both before and after the Restoration), the popularity of Shakespeare's plays in his own time, and the relation of the Shakespeare songs to popular tunes and text analogues already in widespread circulation all allow for much more likely scenarios in which the melodies and the text settings could be passed along. Some comparisons can be made between the "traditional" songs in Linley's collection and earlier music. It seems almost too much of a coincidence that the only continuous music tradition for a Shakespeare play is connected with one of the few scripts that retained its song lyrics through the late seventeenth century.

Contemporary versions of two of Ophelia's songs exist. "How Should I Your True Love Know" is altered from a tune known as "Walsingham."[29] Both the text and the music exist in multiple versions and must have been popular. Among the musical versions, which include keyboard elaborations in the Fitzwilliam virginal manuscript and other collections, is one in William Barley's *A New Book of Tablature* (1596) for lute, orpharion, and bandora. Not as elaborately figured as the keyboard settings, the melody of the bandora setting has been transcribed with the Shakespearean text by Sternfeld.[30]

Ex. 1. "Walsingham" (1596).

by permission of Oxford University Press

This compares closely with the version given by Linley.

Ex. 2. "How Should I Your True Love Know" as in Linley, 2:50.

Despite some differences, most notably rhythmic shifts, the contour, range, and cadence structure suggest both songs come from the same model. Had the tune been brought back into use after a mid-eighteenth-century rediscovery, it would likely have been in a form closer to the original (i.e., a form found in an old printed or manuscript source) than that actually in use. The tune for "Bonny Sweet Robin" survives in a number of contemporary prints and manuscripts, titled variously "Bonny Sweet Robin," "Robin," or "Robin Is to the Greenwood Gone."[31] Once again, this is a match with the tune offered by Linley.

The provenance of the other tunes given by Linley is questionable. The melody for "Tomorrow Is St. Valentine's Day" was in theatrical use in the early eighteenth century in *The Cobbler's Opera* (1729) and *The Quaker's Opera* (1730), and it appeared in D'Urfey's *Songs Compleat* (1720), in all cases with different texts. Chappell compared Linley's melody for "And Will He Not Come Again" with a melody called "The Merry Milkmaids" in Playford's *The English Dancing Master* (1651), suggesting they were both variants of the same tune.[32] Finally, Linley claimed that Ophelia's lines "they bore him bare-faced on the beere, / and in his grave rain'd many a tear" were not spoken or sung in productions in his memory.[33]

Only one other play, *Othello*, was performed more or less unaltered through the end of the seventeenth century. Curiously, unlike *Hamlet*, it acquired no similar music tradition. A "Willow Song" from the 1670s by Pelham Humfrey was reprinted in J. S. Smith's *Musica Antiqua*. Concerning other music for *Othello*, it would be interesting to know what Restoration dramatists concerned with temporal integrity made of the extraordinarily short time it takes for Cassio to become drunk in II,3. The song texts Shakespeare used to cover this temporal abbreviation are in Restoration copies of the play.

Whatever Ophelia's and Desdemona's music had been in the early Restoration performances, one important change in acting practice between the pre-Commonwealth and the Restoration stage would have enormous musical repercussions, not just for *Hamlet* and *Othello*, but for any play with vocal music. Women were given the right to act by some of the licensing agreements.[34] One contemporary theatre goer noted that, "Upon our stages we have women actors, as beyond seas."[35] From this time on, treble singing voices would not be restricted to boy actors, and the singing complement would represent the entire range of adult voices.

The licenses granted the acting companies not only performing rights but also permission to alter the plays. The Lord Chamberlain noted that Davenant was "to reform and make fitt for the Company of Actors appointed under his direction and command" those plays assigned to him. Davenant was personally responsible for some of these alterations, the first of the Shakespearean revisions being *The Law against Lovers*, a conflation of *Measure for Measure* and *Much Ado about Nothing* that appeared in 1662. Davenant's urge to improve Shakespeare was not unique to him. Over the next forty years Shakespeare would be represented on the stage primarily in revisions reworked in the neoclassical image.

One of the paradoxes of Restoration Shakespearean revision is that the altered plays contained fewer musical allusions, stage directions, and opportunities for song at a time when music was being played increasingly during and between the acts. The model of serious French drama represented by Corneille, in which songs were allowed only for the raising and lowering of machines,[36] may have been responsible. The Restoration urge to simplify Shakespearean plots and language caused songs, musical cues, and even major characters to be excised from tragedies. The unmusical nature of the revisions as they appeared in print ran contrary to stage music practice.

The printed text of Davenant's *The Law against Lovers* includes none of the Shakespearean song texts from either source play. The music for the printed texts of Davenant's new songs and dances has not survived. In IV, 1 a character named Viola (only the name comes from *Twelfth Night*) enters an ensemble scene "dancing a Saraband awhile with Castanietos." In his diary entry for 18 February 1662, Pepys recorded that the actress "Moll Davis Sings and Dances." The song, "Wake All the Dead," leads into a dance for the company. Although Viola's song is without Shakespearean precedent, the final scene of *Much Ado about Nothing* concludes with an ensemble dance. More unusually, in *The Law against Lovers* V, 1 there is another dance, this time to texted music, where singing main characters foretell Angelo's downfall.

The single-mindedness of neoclassically inclined adapters affected the opportunities Shakespeare provided for music in the tragedies and histories. To avoid mixing comic and tragic elements, Nahum Tate removed the fool from his version of *King Lear* (1681). The comic distance that allowed the fool to sing and joke about the unfolding tragedy was inappropriate to the contemporary conception of tragic form. Poor Tom's mad songs are also missing.

In his revision of *Troilus and Cressida* (1679) Dryden included one song text, "Can Life Be a Blessing," as a serenade provided by Pandarus for the title couple's off-stage tryst in III, 2. Anonymous "Musick" enters for the song and immediately exits after. Thomas Farmer's music survives in the third book of *Choice Ayres and Songs.*

According to *A New Collection of Songs and Poems*, Simon Pack's song "The Larks Awake the Drowsy Morn" was from the King's Company production of *The Injur'd Princess*, Thomas D'Urfey's revision of *Cymbeline.* D'Urfey either did not write the song text or did not consider it important enough to include in the printed play.

The production of Tate's *Richard II* by the King's Company in 1680 included two new lyrics. The first, with unknown music, was printed at the beginning of the play's text, but was probably sung in act III by an attendant to Richard's queen to distract her from the deposition threat against the King. The folio version of the scene (folio III, 4) does not include a song. The prison scene in folio V, 5 is strikingly different from the corresponding revised scene. In the folio text, music is the stimulus for an extended metaphor in this speech by the imprisoned Richard.

> Music do I hear?
> Ha, Ha! keep time! How sour sweet music is,
> When time is broke and no proportion kept.
> So it is in the music of men's lives.
> And here have I the daintiness of ear

To check time broke in a disordered string;
But for the concord of my state and time
Had not an ear to hear my true time broke.
I wasted time, and now doth Time waste me. . . .
This music mads me; let it sound no more. . . .
Yet blessing on his heart that gives it me!
For 'tis a sign of love. . . . (lines 41-49, 61, 63-65)

Tate omitted this speech in his revision. The poignant torture of self-realization mixed with gratitude for a show of love is replaced by a torture scene in which Richard is tantalized with a table of food that "sinks down" as he tries to eat. The song that accompanies the scene is itself a kind of torture, for in response, Richard exclaims: "Ha, Musick, too! Ev'n what my Torturers please."[37] This song was one of the earliest attempts at stage music by the young Henry Purcell. Appropriately melancholy, its strictly strophic form displays little of the descriptive qualities common in the composer's mature theatre music.

The Masque in *Timon of Athens*

Masques, which had been courtly entertainments before the Commonwealth, were brought to the public stages after the Restoration. They were included as spectacles in full-length plays or presented independently as part of the evening's entertainment. Masques that were not structurally bound to their original texts would sometimes be used in other plays. In all the primarily nonmusical adaptations of Shakespeare made before 1695, only one called for an independent masque. *Timon of Athens*, as altered by Thomas Shadwell, was first played in 1678. Shadwell added a subplot that included not only a love interest for the title character but also a startling contrast of character between Titus's faithful lover Evandra and his coquettish betrothed, Melissa. The play was successful. Contemporary stage historian John Downes recalled, "'Twas very well acted, and the Musick in't well Perform'd; it wonderfully pleas'd the Court and City; being an excellent Moral."[38]

The folio stage directions indicate a masque is to be performed. Timon's banquet in I, 2 is interrupted by a group of ladies, one dressed as Cupid, who come to perform for the guests. After gaining permission to enter, Cupid exits to summon her companions. Then the stage directions call for a dance of Amazons with lutes. This brief display, with no indication of spoken verse or song lyric, suggests a truncated court masque.

In Shadwell's version the banquet scene and its masque are moved to II, 2. The addition of the subplot is responsible for the shift, but the resultant central location does give the entertainment more weight. To satisfy the expectations of a Restoration audience, Shadwell expanded Shakespeare's dumbshow into a mythological debate between the followers of Cupid and Bacchus on the respective powers of love and wine. When Bacchus commands the end of the argument ("Hold, Hold our Forces are combin'd, / And we together rule Mankind") he gives an allegorical presentiment of Timon's inability to choose between Melissa and Evandra ("I can love two at once, trust me I can").[39]

The vocal music for the 1678 production was by Louis Grabu, a French composer who was master of the king's music for Charles II. Only the opening song, "Hark! How the Songsters of the Grove," has been preserved in Playford's *Choice Ayres and Songs, II.* The four act tunes attributed to James Paisible (another French musician working in London) in the British Museum Additional MS 35043 may have been the original act tunes. These are in French overture and dance forms. All are in F major and have four completely independent string parts.

The text of the masque was altered for the 1695 revival, the second half of Shadwell's text being replaced by new verse, some of which was written by Peter Motteaux.[40] Henry Purcell provided the overture, "courtin" tune, and masque for the new production. Four D major act tunes, also attributed to Purcell, exist. Jack Westrup disputes the attribution because "the part-writing is clumsy and [the tunes] show no signs of imagination."[41]

So little of Grabu's music survives that direct comparison between it and Purcell's music is impossible; however, the new text, with expanded parts for Cupid and Bacchus, obviously gave

Purcell a greater opportunity to create a small drama. The somberness and complexity of the music for the followers of Cupid contrasts with the boisterous simplicity of that for the Bacchanalian chorus.

The major/minor contrasts of the pleasures of wine and love (D minor for Cupid, B-flat for Bacchus) continue through the solos. F major is well established at the beginning of the masque, and other key areas are closely related. If the masque is an allegory for Timon's inability to choose between devotion and profligacy (i.e., Evandra and Melissa), the B-flat conclusion—in a key associated with Bacchus—is a musical enhancement of this lack of resolve. Thus the *Timon* masque helped to integrate Shadwell's subplot of Evandra and Melissa into the Shakespearean plot.

The Dramatic Operas

A "dramatic opera" (not a contemporary term but one used by later commentators) was a play in which the masques, now of notable length, had an important dramatic function. Much, if not all, of the action was still in spoken prose or verse, but the musical and dance interludes were now incorporated into the fabric of the plot. Dialogue was sometimes interspersed among the musical numbers of the masques. Despite the occasional experiment with completely sung opera, this was the most significant inroad that operatic principles would make in the English theatres through the end of the seventeenth century.

Three Shakespearean plays would be turned into dramatic operas in the last half of the century—*Macbeth, The Tempest*, and *A Midsummer Night's Dream*. The plays' origins and performance histories suggest they were conceived for a more ambitious musical environment than the public theatres could provide. *Dream* had probably been intended for the celebration of a noble wedding, conjecture supported by the play's subject and masque-like qualities, musical requirements best satisfied by facilities at court, and textual references to events of 1594–95.[42]   The origins of

Macbeth are less clear, but the addition of spurious musical scenes into the play began even before Shakespeare's death. In 1612, musical sections of Thomas Middleton's *The Witch* were interpolated into an imperfect *Macbeth* text, perhaps for a private theatre production.[43] This version, complete with added songs, was printed in the 1623 folio and remains the earliest textual authority. *The Tempest* first played in London's private theatres.[44] It was later performed at court during the celebration of Princess Elizabeth's wedding in the winter season, 1613-14. The version of the play in the 1623 folio may be an elaborated form used in the marriage festivities, and the unusually complete stage and music directions are thought to be from Shakespeare's hand.[45]

William Davenant created the Restoration operatic versions of *Macbeth* (1663-64) and the first *Tempest* (1667), launching two of the English stage's most colorful performance histories. From the first these productions prompted contemporary commentators to describe the plays as operas. The scripts, rewritten for late seventeenth-century tastes and dressed in a variety of scores, were to hold the stage for decades. In the eighteenth century, as Shakespeare's original texts began again to be the source for acting versions, Restoration musical scenes with their non-Shakespearean texts would remain in the productions. The Restoration *Macbeth* and *Tempest* exemplified how scenic and musical innovations from the Continent were integrated into English drama. Their longevity attests to the importance of this Continental influence.

Davenant had experience with both the older English tradition and new Continental styles, which he brought to bear in reshaping older plays to new tastes. In 1634, he had entered the service of Charles I, assuming both writing and production responsibilities for the court masques.[46] After the Civil War, Davenant spent five years in French exile. During these years, the plays of Corneille and new Italian scenic technology held sway in the public theatres in Paris. It is also probable that Davenant saw Italian opera in France. Beginning in 1645, opera was performed with some regularity for the French court, and the exiled English royalty is known to have been in attendance.[47] Although Davenant's presence at these affairs is not recorded, his role in the English court-in-exile and his interest in theatrical affairs make it likely that he would have seen at least some of the operas.

Davenant returned to England and for a time was imprisoned by the Puritans. After his release in 1654, Davenant attempted to revive theatrical activity in London by offering musical presentations. These, unlike plays, were less subject to government prohibition. In the fall of 1656, *The Siege of Rhodes*, considered to be the first completely sung English opera, was performed. Davenant, who wrote the text, connected the more elaborate musical numbers with recitative, probably as a subterfuge rather than an operatic experiment. When *The Siege of Rhodes* was revived after the Restoration, it was as a play rather than as an opera.[48]

Davenant's *Macbeth*

Both *The Tempest* and *Macbeth* were among the plays granted by royal warrant to Davenant after the Restoration. *Macbeth* was the first to be adapted for the Duke's company. It was described by John Downes as:

The Tragedy of *Macbeth*, alter'd by Sir *William Davenant*; being drest in all its Finery, as new Cloaths, new Scenes, Machines, as flyings for the Witches; with all the Singing and Dancing in it: The first compos'd by Mr. *Lock*, the other by Mr. *Channell* and Mr. *Joseph Priest*; it being all Excellently perform'd, being in the nature of an Opera, it Recompenc'd double the expense; it proves still a lasting play.[49]

Downes specifies no date for the first production but says that it took place at the Lincoln's-Inn-Fields theatre.[50] Pepys saw *Macbeth* there for the first time on 5 November 1664.

In the first printing of Davenant's *Macbeth*, "with all the alterations, amendments, additions, and new songs, as it is now acted at the Dukes Theatre,"[51] there are three masques. In II, 5, an added scene, the witches foretell the future to Macduff and Lady Macduff. Two songs and a dance are interspersed with dialogue. Davenant's III, 8 closely follows folio III, 5, both of which include the Middleton song text "Come Away, Hecate." As in the folio version, Hecate assumes the guidance of Macbeth's destruction, promising a magical illusion to confound the usurper. This masque, the penultimate scene in folio act III, ends act III in Davenant's version. This change of position provides continuity of action, since act IV opens with the illusion scene. It is also an early example of the tendency for masques to be used as act finales.

Davenant's fourth act masque is similar to its folio model. Both have the song "Black Spirits, and White," the procession of the kings, and the witches' dance. The main differences are a slightly enlarged speaking part for Hecate and more elaborate stage directions in the revision.

The amount of music in Davenant's *Macbeth* is small compared to that in later dramatic operas. Downes's description of this *Macbeth* as an opera suggests that the operatic masques increased in size gradually over the years. None of Channel's instrumental music for the 1663–64 production survives, and only fragments of Matthew Locke's music have come down in corrupt form in John Playford's collection *Musicks Delight, or the Cithern* (1666).

The Tempest

Davenant once again turned his attention to Shakespeare for the 1667-68 season. The classicism of *The Tempest,* Shakespeare's last play, would have appealed to Davenant and his audiences. Neoclassical concepts were not unknown in Shakespeare's time, having been systematically described in Philip Sidney's *An Apology for Poetry* (1583). Perhaps challenged in some way by his classically inclined colleague Ben Jonson, Shakespeare was more observant of classical rules in *The Tempest* than in any other of his plays. *The Tempest* strictly adheres to the unity of time, all action taking place in about three hours. Shakespeare also observed the unity of place more closely. He still combined a number of subplots working toward a climax in a particularly nonclassical way.

Davenant also must have recognized the play's operatic potential, as Shakespeare's use of music in *The Tempest* is extraordinarily rich. Music is used to enhance the effect of the enchanted isle. Caliban explains in folio III, 2 that "The isle is full of noises, / Sounds and sweet airs, that give delight and hurt not." Much of Ariel's intervention in human affairs is accomplished by musical means, as witnessed by the enchantment of Ferdinand (I, 2) and the awakening of Alonzo (II, 2). The masque of blessing on the young lovers in IV, 1 is presented by the island's spirit inhabitants. Like *Macbeth, The Tempest* offers a number of scenes appropriate for scenic and musical elaboration, as well as the opportunity to insert new ones.

Davenant chose John Dryden as his co-adapter. The resulting text has little of Shakespeare's poetry, theatricality, or textual musicality. The subplot concerning the treason of the low comic sailors against Prospero becomes more important, while the character of Prospero is reduced to little more than an expedient. In the prologue to the printed play, Dryden credits his co-adapter Davenant with the changes prompted supposedly for balance of character types. Later in the prologue, he credits Davenant with the new "saylor" subplot as well. The vulgarity of the new low comic material and the petty jealousy subplot concerning the adolescents, which Davenant must have thought would appeal to audiences more than Shakespeare's scenes for Miranda and Ferdinand, make Dryden's praise read rather like a disclaimer:

Sir William Davenant, as he was a man of quick and piercing imagination, soon found that somewhat might be added to the design of Shakespeare . . . and therefore to put the last hand to it, he design'd the Counter-plot to Shakespear's plot, namely that of a Man who had never seen a Woman; that by this means those two Characters of Innocence and Love might the more illustrate and commend each other. . . . I must likewise do him that justice to acknowledge, that my writing received daily his amendments, and that's the reason why it is not so faulty, as the rest which I have done without the help or correction of so Judicious a friend.[52]

In the new version, Miranda has a sister, Dorinda. She too "never saw man." The young boy Hippolito, "one that never saw woman, right heir of the Duke of Mantua," has been reared, separated from the girls, by Prospero. Ariel has a spirit-mate, Milcha; and Caliban is given a monster-sister-consort named Sycorax. The usurpation plot against the king of Naples is omitted. After seeing this version of the play Pepys thought it had "no great wit."[53]

There were musical additions to the Dryden-Davenant script. A masque of devils ("Pride, Fraud, Rapin, Murder" incarnate) was inserted into act II. A new song for Ariel, "Dry Those Eyes," and an echo duet between Ariel and Ferdinand were added to act III. The duet, with its repeated phrases and explicit dynamics, was especially successful. Pepys was so "mightily pleas'd" with it that he "got Mr. Bannister to prick down the notes"[54] and the singer Mr. Harris to "repeat the words while I [Pepys] writ them down."[55] "Mr. Bannister" was John Banister (d. 1679), a composer in the king's service who wrote most of the songs for the play.

The echo duet was Banister's most ambitious contribution, musically and dramatically. (The duet appears here complete in Appendix A.) The extended canon between Ariel and Ferdinand, although a musical curiosity, is dramatically in the tradition of enchantment music; it finds precedent in songs such as the original Ariel lyrics from this scene, "Come Unto These Yellow Sands" and "Full Fathom Five." These songs not only symbolize the effect of the supernatural over the mortal realm but also move the characters to action.

The Dryden/Davenant text goes further. When Ariel tells Ferdinand (and the audience) that "Kind Fortune Smiles," the enchanted island's benevolent quality is revealed and expectations are raised for a happy ending. The song is no longer static, neither symbol nor prop. An important moment in the drama has moved into the song text. Banister represents this moment by moving back from a distant harmony (reached at Ferdinand's greatest distraction) closer to the original key. The vocal line reaches its highest point (f', f an octave and a fourth above middle c) at the moment of revelation. The song was printed only for two voices and bass, so the only indication of textural change is a reduction to one vocal part. The score may omit instrumental parts (or a change of bass instruments if this was indeed a continuo song) that highlighted the dramatic transition. The echo duet and Banister's other songs, along with "Dry Those Eyes" by James Hart, and Pelham Humfrey's "Where the Bee Sucks, Sung in the Machines by Ariel's Spirits," are preserved in a small addendum, inserted in a few copies of Playford's *Select Ayres and Dialogues*.[56]

Despite the musical additions, the musical imagery in the Dryden/Davenant script is less pervasive than in the original. Prospero's island is described as a musical realm in the original text, while much of the poetic imagery that alludes to this fact (e.g., Caliban's lines in folio III, 2) is cut from the revision. The masque of Ceres and Juno, also cut by Dryden, celebrates coming of age and loss of innocence, major themes in *The Tempest*. The interruption of the dance by the denouement of Prospero's plan is an effective use of the masque to develop urgency, one that incidentally puts the masque in dramatic perspective:

Enter certain Reapers, properly habited: they join with the Nymphs in a graceful dance; towards the end whereof Prospero starts suddenly, and speaks; after which, to a strange, hollow, and confused noise, they heavily vanish.

> *Prospero:* I had forgot that foul conspiracy
> Of the beast Caliban and his confederates
> Against my life. The minute of their plot
> Is Almost come. [*To the Spirits*] Well done! avoid. No More!
> (folio IV, 1; lines 139-43.)

In contrast, Dryden's masque of two devils in the 1667 version relies more on machines and spectacle, the likes of which Davenant probably admired in Paris. The devil masque may have been more spectacular, but contributed little to plot development or Shakespeare's image of the island as a place of "sounds and sweet airs that give delight and hurt not."

Davenant died in 1668, and control of the Duke's Company passed to Betterton. Five years later Betterton's company presented another musical revision of *The Tempest*, the origin of which is confused, despite Downes's specific attribution:

The Tempest, or the Inchanted Island, made into an Opera by Mr. *Shadwell*, having all New in it; as Scenes, Machines, particularly one scene Painted with *Myriads* of *Ariel* Spirits; and another flying away, with a Table furnish't out with "Fruits, Sweet meats, and all sorts of Viands" just when Duke *Trinculo* and his Companions were going to Dinner; all things perform'd in it so Admirably well, that not any succeeding Opera got more Money.[57]

Playwright Thomas Shadwell (1642?–92) has generally been accepted as the adapter of the operatic version first produced in the 1673–74 season. It has been suggested that Thomas Betterton, among others, was actually the principal adapter,[58] but in the absence of convincing evidence to the contrary, the Shadwell attribution seems probable. The Dryden/Davenant script underwent minor changes, including added musical scenes and some further "updating" of the lines.

The first stage direction in the opera's printed text shows how elaborately music is intertwined with spectacle:

The Front of the Stage is open'd, and the Band of 24 Violins, with the Harpsicals and Theorbo's which accompany the Voices, are plac'd between the Pit and the Stage. While the Overture is playing, the Curtain rises, and discovers a new Frontispiece, joyn'd to the great Pylasters, on each side of the Stage. This Frontispiece is a noble Arch, supported by large wreathed Columns of the Corinthian Order. . . . Behind this is the Scene, which represents a thick Cloudy Sky, a very Rocky Coast, and a Tempestuous Sea in perpetual Agitation. This Tempest (suppos'd to be rais'd by Magick) has many dreadful objects in it, as several Spirits in horrid shapes flying down amongst the Sailers, then rising and crossing in the Air. And when the ship is sinking, the whole House is darken'd, and a shower of Fire falls upon 'em. This is accompanied with Lightning, and several Claps of Thunder to the end of the storm.[59]

The unusual size of the orchestra, and its placement in the pit, show the influence of French and Italian practice. Charles II, impressed with the sound and precision of Lully's *Vingt-Quatre Violons*, had a similar group formed after he returned to London. The use of the Twenty-four Violins suggests this production was a significant occasion.[60] It is also indicative of the standardization of musical forces in the theatrical musical establishment. The replacement of the Elizabethan music room with the orchestra pit was another Continental device. This upper music room remained a usable option in the Restoration theatres,[61] but the more prominent pit location eventually became standard. The use of the pit is concurrent with the adoption of the proscenium stage as opposed to the platform stage of Shakespeare's time.

The next explicit music cue is in II, 1 where the drunken Trinculo sings two short, bawdy songs. At the scene's close, Caliban sings of his supposed freedom from Prospero. The texts are nearly identical with those in folio II, 2. The characterization of low comics through ridiculous or suggestive songs was an Elizabethan practice carried over into the Restoration. Unlike the art songs performed by trained singers or talented singer-actors, the comic songs were usually popular ballads or catches. They were performed unaccompanied, and the singer was chosen for his comedic acting skills rather than his voice. Shakespeare's childish song for Caliban identifies him with the low comics.[62]

The first fully developed masque comes at the end of act II. It is sung and danced by the spirits of the island, whom Prospero has sent to torment his overthrowers. A "flourish of Voyces under the stage" prompts one of the mortals to wonder, "What horrid Masque will the dire Fiends present?"[63] His question is answered by a chorus of demons and mortal sins. The music is interspersed with dialogue among the mortal observers. A song and "Dance of the Winds" end the masque. There is no dialogue at its conclusion, but the stage directions do not indicate whether the final action takes place during the music of the dance or after it is finished.

Shakespeare's songs "Come Unto These Yellow Sands" and "Full Fathom Five" (III, 1; folio I, 2) remain basically unchanged in text and usage, save that "Full Fathom Five" is sung by Milcha instead of Ariel.

The dance sequence in the third scene of act III, unlike the second-act masque, has a Shakespearean precedent. The folio directions are as follows:

Solemn and strange music; and Prospero on the top invisible. Enter several strange shapes, bringing in a banquet; and dance about it with gentle actions of salutation; and inviting the King, etc. to eat, they depart. When Alonzo and his companions move forward to the table, Thunder and Lightning. . . . Enter Ariel, like a Harpy; claps his wings upon the table; and with a quaint device, the banquet vanishes.

The 1674 scene begins with an interpolated song for Ariel and Milcha, followed by a "Dance of Fantastic Spirits" who bring in the table. The banquet is flown away almost immediately by two spirits, leaving the king and his companions in confusion.

Ariel and Ferdinand sing Banister's "celebrated Echo Song" in III, 5 as Ariel uses music to lure Ferdinand further into Prospero's plot. In a brief diversion in IV, 2, Caliban sings a short incantation to the island's dark devils. A dance follows.

In the first scene of act V, the final masque is a display of Prospero's magical powers, which in this version he does not relinquish. Shakespeare's blessing from Ceres and Juno was excised to make room for a new masque of Neptune and Amphitrite. Presumed to be Shadwell's most significant addition to the script, this masque would stay with various acting versions of *The Tempest* into the nineteenth century. After songs and dances from the sea deities, Ariel "and the rest" sing the Shakespeare lyric "Where the Bee Sucks." The text changes from folio V, 1 are minor ("cowslips bed" for "cowslip's bell" and "swallows wing" for "bat's back"). The changed position and choral treatment of the words make the song a general description of the aerial spirits rather than Ariel's anticipation of promised freedom.

The *Tempest* music attests to the primary importance of French influence in the first introduction of operatic principles to

English drama.   The apology for the production indicates that music, plot, and staging had all been shaped by this influence.

> From [France] new arts to please you, we have sought
> We have machines to some perfection brought,
> And above 30 Warbling voyces gott.
> Many a God & Goddesse you will heare
> And we have Singing, Dancing, Devills here.[64]

Matthew Locke (ca. 1630–77) provided the act music for Shadwell's production.   The new masques were by Pelham Humfrey (1647–74).   Both composers were well acquainted with French music.   Locke had been a member of the court musical establishment since 1660, when Charles had brought a number of French musicians back to England.   Humfrey was actually sent to Paris by the king to study French ways.[65]   Similarly, both Shadwell and Betterton (who was probably involved in the mounting of the production if not directly responsible for the conversion) were familiar with Parisian techniques.   The composers were willing, however, to incorporate techniques they had learned through their knowledge of other Continental music.

The pre-Commonwealth practice of playing "act music" before the play and between the acts was revived after the Restoration, and the form was standardized.   Typically, act music consisted of the "first and second music," which was used in a manner similar to the warning bells of our own time; the overture, played between the prologue and the first act; and the act tunes, music played between the acts.   The relationship of the overture and act tunes to the drama offered the composer an opportunity to reflect some mood or activity of the play.   Dryden noted another purpose for this music: "A Scene of mirth mix'd with Tragedy has the same effect upon us which our Music has betwixt the acts, and that we find a relief to us from the best Plots and language of the Stage if the discourses have been long."[66]   Act tunes were used to contrast with and give relief from the spoken text.   Its presence "betwixt the acts" aided in the demarcation of sections of the drama.

Locke's overture and act tunes for *The Tempest* are the most ambitious examples of Restoration act music to survive. The composer's ability to draw on English and Italian models as well as French contributed to the dramatic quality of the music. The descriptive curtain tune is a striking example.

Ex. 3. Locke. *Tempest.* "Curtain Tune," mm. 17-26.

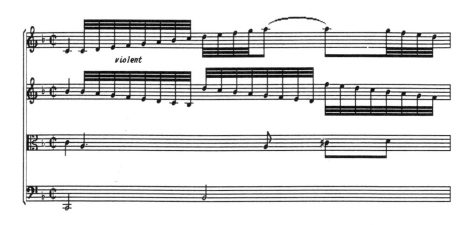

by permission of the British Library

Unusual harmonic progressions, often the result of surprising suspension resolutions, give much of the curtain tune an unsettled modulatory effect. Sevenths, either as fleeting passing tones or more sustained harmonic factors, are often resolved in an unorthodox fashion (e.g., the rhythmically weak resolution in the second half of m. 18). The chromaticism, cross-relations, and semi-tonal clashes within a framework of free polyphony are reminiscent of earlier English viol music. Locke also used increasingly active string figurations and explicit dynamic markings in his description of the blossoming storm.

Locke took advantage of the dramatic potential of the interval music in a way few other composers of his time did.[67] The "rustic air" at the end of the first act is appropriate to the pastoral scene with which the act closes. Similarly, "martial music" follows the scene in which an army of devils chase and torment the low comics. Unlike the curtain tune, the interval music more clearly shows its debt to its French model, displaying regular phraseology, less complex homophonic harmonies, and dance forms. Locke returned to contrapuntal complexity in the last act tune, a double canon. The first violins and basses in canon at the octave, with the inner voices also in canon at the octave with different material, produce novel vertical sounds. Influenced by several styles, Locke achieved an instrumental music of dramatic intensity rarely achieved even in opera. Locke's description of the operatic version of *The Tempest* as a "Grand Design"[68] helps explain this unusual expansiveness.

Humfrey's contributions were more consistently in the French style than Locke's. "The Masque of the Three Divells" in act II, with a text only slightly altered from Davenant, alternates solo numbers with choral sections. The solos are mostly in triple meter over a bass with a harmonic rhythm of one harmony per measure or slower. In spite of this inactive bass, the regular phraseology and the recurrence of various dotted rhythms in the vocal line suggest the influence of Lullian arioso. Sections in declamatory style, both duple and triple meter, seem not to be related to any textual differentiation. (Meter shifts sometime occur with the introduction of new characters, but Humfrey was not consistent with this device.) If Humfrey was not following the Lullian tendency to reserve duple meter for specifically declamatory texts, perhaps such shifts were more useful for setting the changing word patterns peculiar to English.

Ex. 4. Humfrey. *Tempest.* [Masque of Devils], mm. 1-8.

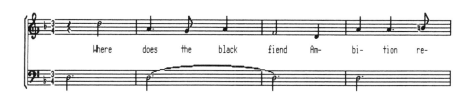

by permission of Stainer & Bell Ltd., London, England

The choral sections are unrelievedly homophonic. The rhythms suggest that they (like their counterparts in the *comédie-ballets*) may have been danced.

In the opening of the fifth-act masque of Neptune and Amphitrite, Humfrey broke with the French model. The first part of the masque displays the Italianate distinction between recitative and song styles. The declamatory sections come to full cadences before the more lyrical sections in triple meter, as shown in Example 5. The concluding section of the masque returns to the alternating airs and choruses reminiscent of the *comédie-ballets*. This music by Humfrey and his collaborators was used for *The Tempest* into the first years of the eighteenth century.

Ex. 5. Humfrey. *Tempest.* [Masque of Neptune], mm. 78-90.

by permission of Stainer & Bell Ltd., London, England

The Fairy Queen

The dramatic opera based on *A Midsummer Night's Dream*
did not become a basic part of the seventeenth- and eighteenth-
century Shakespearean repertoire as did *The Tempest* and
Macbeth. In the 1662-63 theatre season, *Dream* received its one
unsuccessful Restoration revival. The play's romantic fancy was
too unlike the sharp witticisms and modish plots that appealed to
contemporary audiences. Pepys thought it to be "the most insipid

ridiculous play that ever I saw in my life."[69] It would be thirty years before *Dream*, much changed, renamed, and bedecked with music and spectacle, would again be performed.

The Fairy Queen, with music by Henry Purcell, was first performed in May 1692 at Dorset Garden. The production was revived there in February 1693 with some text changes and additional music. The design made a special impression on Downes, who compared it favorably with those for two other operas with music by Purcell, *Dioclesian* (1690) and *King Arthur* (1691):

The *Fairy Queen*, made into an Opera, from a Comedy of Mr. *Shakespears*: This in Ornaments was superior to the other Two [operas]; especially in Cloaths for all the Singers and Dancers, Scenes, Machines, and Decorations, all most profusely set off; and excellently perform'd chiefly the Instrumental and Vocal part Compos'd by the said Mr. *Purcel*, and Dances by Mr. *Priest*. The Court and Town were wonderfully satisfy'd with it; but the Expense in setting it out being so great the Company got very little by it.[70]

If Downes is correct about the opera's reception, Purcell's music might have made *Dream* a play to rival *Macbeth* and *The Tempest* at the box office had it not been for the expense of keeping the play in repertory. *The Fairy Queen* was not revived after the second run, and the expensive scenery, which had cost the extraordinary amount of £3,000 Restoration sterling,[71] was broken up for use in other plays.

The adapter of *The Fairy Queen* is unknown. Claims have been made for Dryden,[72] and, more widely accepted, for Elkanah Settle.[73] Neither attribution has been backed up by indisputable evidence. Whoever was responsible for the revision cut Shakespeare's text heavily, while adding little to the spoken dialogue. The masque interpolations, however, are extensive. Shakespeare's musical scenes for the fairies and the low comics were replaced by four long masques, one each for acts two through five. In 1693 the first act was changed and fitted with its own masque.

The characters in the spoken dialogue of *The Fairy Queen* do not participate in the masques, which is not the case with

Macbeth or *The Tempest.* There was no shortage of singing actors in the United Company (The Duke's and King's Companies merged in 1682) had there been a desire for Titania, Oberon, Bottom, or other of the fairies and low comics to be singing roles. The increasing amount and complexity of theatre music in the last part of the seventeenth century helped create a double corps, one of actors and one of musicians.

The opera's dichotomy has caused modern commentators to question the importance of the musical sections to the dramatic action. Westrup called *The Fairy Queen* "a succession of masques, which have so little connection with the play that no one who merely heard the music would have the remotest suspicion that it was an adaptation of Shakespeare's *Midsummer Night's Dream.*"[74] Literary scholar Hazelton Spencer declared that the "embellishments" of music and spectacle "do not call for serious criticism."[75] While it is true that the masques neither fulfill conventionally dramatic or operatic (in an Italianate sense) function, nor do they parallel closely the function of musical scenes in the folio version, they do create a special atmosphere quite different from that of the original.

In *Dream,* music is used according to basic Elizabethan conventions. It is associated with the supernatural, it is used to characterize the low comics, and—most importantly for the action—it is used to induce sleep (folio II, 2 and 5) or to awaken (folio III, 1). The representation of interaction between the worlds of mortals and the supernatural is enhanced by the songs and sing-song verse.

Purcell and his unknown collaborator were charged with the task of taking an unpopular play, adding an extravagant amount of music, and turning it into a successful offering. Rather than a disjointed hybrid, as Westrup and others have charged, the result was a symbiosis of the masques and the drama. This was achieved by changing the relationship of the mortals and fairies and expanding the function of music. In Shakespeare, the mortals and fairies meet on a kind of common ground, both being equal participants in the night's strange events. In *The Fairy Queen* the music and scenic display, which in performance would

take up at least half of the entire performance, change the focus
of the play with little structural alteration to the text.[76] Since
music is almost the exclusive domain of the fairies, the mortals
are interlopers—if eventually welcomed guests—in the exotic
"Fairy Land." Even the play's title was changed to stress this
emphasis.

Music for the stage was sometimes perceived as simply ornamental rather than constantly functioning within a dramatic context. Playbills enticed audiences with "musick and all the other
ornaments proper to the play." Referring specifically to *The
Fairy Queen*, Motteux observed, "The Drama is originally
Shakespears, the Musick and Decorations are extraordinary."[77]
By the 1690s, the ornamental use of music had often become a
way to make unpopular or mediocre plays acceptable. Con-
versely, some plays were thinly veiled excuses to string together
the masques that were the real center of the evening's entertainment. Shakespeare's pastoral romance was successfully converted to an exotic extravaganza so that it could justifiably
accommodate the weight of the required musical ornaments.

The alterations to the play required one major structural
change, the moving of the low comic business out of the fifth act.
With the Pyramus and Thisbe play moved to the third act, now as
a rehearsal being watched by Puck, all of the mortal actions are
played out in relation to the fairies. The fifth act was opened up
for the final masque, in which Oberon displays the fairy realm to
the mortals to "cure [their] incredulity."

Purcell's masques mirror and extend the analogous musical
sections in *A Midsummer Night's Dream*.[78] The second act
masque replaced folio II, 2, in which the fairies sing Titania to
sleep. The long masque is in two sections. The first, in C major, is in response to Titania's charge, "All shall change at my
command, / All shall turn to Fairy Land." The first five numbers (9-13 in the edition of Purcell's works) accompany a change
of scene to "a Prospect of Grotto's, Arbors, and delightful
walks." In the 1692 version, this is also the first internal music
and the first major scene transformation. The C major tonality
introduced at the beginning of the masque becomes increasingly

chromatic, foreshadowing a shift to C minor for the second section, in which Titania is lulled to sleep. The soft and sustained night music is colored with dissonances and suspensions. The new text and music act as an expanded paraphrase of Shakespeare's original scene.

Titania's offer of music for the entertainment of Bottom as ass (and the music's description in the accompanying stage direction) is expanded from its form in folio IV, 1:

Titania: What, wilt thou hear some music my sweet love?
Bottom: I have a reasonable good ear in music. Let's have the tongs
  and the bones.

The intrusion of Bottom's "rural music" into the fairy realm, thus economically described, grew into an expansive entertainment at the hands of the unknown adapter and Purcell. A discovered scene of fawns, dryads, and naides is suddenly interrupted, first by an antimasque of four savages who frighten the spirits away, then by a rustic dialogue between a milkmaid and her swain.

The remaining masques in *The Fairy Queen* are less directly related to Shakespeare's use of music in *A Midsummer Night's Dream.* In the fourth act, the music that sends the sleeping mortals in folio IV, 1 into an even deeper sleep is transformed into a pageant of the seasons in celebration of the reunion of Titania and Oberon and the "Nuptial Day" of the still-sleeping lovers. The final masque, musically the most diffuse of all, is created by Oberon to convince the mortals of the reality of all that has happened. This final masque may have a Shakespearean precedent in a song (for Oberon, Titania, or both) and dance of blessing now missing from the preserved text of folio V, 1.[79]

Why the first-act masque was added in 1693 is a question that has not been satisfactorily answered. A drunk, stuttering poet is led on and tormented by the fairies. In return for his release, he promises to write a sonnet in honor of his fairy captors. It had long been thought this allusion was to Thomas D'Urfey, a writer known as "Poet Stutterer" because he suffered from the affliction.[80] It has also been suggested that the poet represented the unknown adapter making an on-stage apology for his additions to Shakespeare.[81] Restoration Shakespeare was often changed to suggest (or avoid the embarrassing suggestion of) topical comparison with contemporary political or cultural figures. Explanation or defense of play revisions was also common, but this was usually reserved for the prologue. Whatever the textual reference, this masque seems intrusive when compared to the dramatic effectiveness or neutrality of *The Fairy Queen*'s other musical entertainments.

While Purcell used a number of techniques to give the individual masques a kind of unity, for example organizing large tonal blocks or using solo song and choral arrangement pairs, he does not seem to have made an attempt to give the piece an overall structure. The music was still subservient to the five-act drama and conformed to its structure. While the length and placement of the masques and scenic spectacle would influence the pacing and shaping of the acts, they were still enclosed by spoken dialogue. The scenes that included large musical entertainments ended not with music, but with spoken dialogue.

SUMMARY

Two influences transpired to make the repertoire of Shakespearean music at century's end different from what it had been in the early seventeenth century. First, the repertoire of Shakespeare's plays presented on stage was limited by contemporary taste. Most of the plays were not performed with any regularity, and those that were often became the subject of drastic alteration. Much of the pre-Commonwealth musical tradition that may have survived the mid-century disruption of acting, either in print, memory, or oral transmission, was irrelevant to the Restoration representation of Shakespeare. Subsequent theatre fires and lack of concern for theatrical records would complicate rediscovery of Elizabethan practice for later generations of a more historical bent. The second influence toward change was music's increasing importance in the Restoration theatre. The experience of

Continental opera, the increasing standardization of instrumental ensembles, the transferral of the court masque tradition to the public theatres and the reinforcement of that native tradition by European scenic development, the rising popularity of the concert halls—all led to the situation where musical entertainment challenged the primacy of the spoken word in the English theatres.

The expansion of the musical elements in late seventeenth-century Shakespeare productions such as *The Fairy Queen* and *Timon of Athens* was indicative of this increased use of music during the last years of the century. Purcell's ability to create effectively integrated dramatic music was atypical if not unique. Most large musical entertainments from the 1690s had only the most incidental connection to their parent plays. The aesthetic conflict between dramatists and musicians and the financial burdens expansive musical and scenic efforts brought on the companies would come to crisis in the early years of the next century. This crisis ripened when Italian opera came to London.

NOTES

1. E. W. Naylor, *Shakespeare and Music*, 2d ed. (London: J. M. Dent & Sons, 1931), p. 3.

2. This quotation from an Italian manual of behavior for the nobility, a volume that had sold well in its English translation, indicates that the kinds of public musical displays that would suggest a person to be a professional musician were unseemly:

Therefore let a courtier come to shew his musick as a thing to passe the time withall, and as he were enforced to doe it, and not in the presence of noble men nor of any great multitude. . . . Now as touching the time and season when these sortes of musick are to be practised: I believe at all times when a man is in familiar and loving company, having nothing else adoe.

Baldassare Castiglione, *The Book of the Courtier*, tr. Thomas Hoby [1561] (London: J. M. Dent & Sons, 1928), pp. 100-101.

3. Martin Butler considered the continuation of popular dramatic tradition at the Globe and other theatres through the 1630s "perhaps

the single most underrated fact in the history of English theatre."
Theatre and Crisis, 1632-1642 (Cambridge: Cambridge University Press, 1984), p. 181.

4. R. Hosley, "Was There a Music Room in Shakespeare's Globe?" *Shakespeare Survey* 13 (1960):116-17.

5. See Allardyce Nicoll, "Shakespeare and the Court Masque," *Shakespeare Jahrbuch* 94 (1958):51-62.

6. Richard Baker, *Theatrum Redivivum, or the Theatre Vindicated* (London: Francis Eglesfield, 1662), p. 5.

7. Robert Etheridge Moore, in *Henry Purcell and the Restoration Theatre* (Cambridge, Mass.: Harvard University Press, 1961), p. 32, wrote that the English approach to all the arts in the late seventeenth and eighteenth centuries was "a combination of forces part accident and part compromise." Not only English dramatists but visual artists and musicians excelled at the combination of disparate influences and purposes.

8. John Dryden believed that English playwrights achieved a "lively imitation of nature" by an irregular application of the unities:

By their servile observations of the Unities of Time and Place, and integrity of scenes, they [French writers] have brought on themselves that dearth of plot, and narrowness of imagination, which may be observed in all their plays. How many beautiful accidents might happen naturally in two or three days which cannot arrive with any probability in the compass of twenty-four hours? Farther, by tying themselves strictly to the Unity of Place and unbroken scenes, they are forced many times to omit some beauties which cannot be shown where the act began.

Of Dramatic Poesy and Other Critical Essays, 2 vols., ed. George Watson (New York: E. P. Dutton, 1962), 1:64.

9. "A Short View of Tragedy "[1693], in *The Critical Works of Thomas Rymer*, ed. Curt A. Zimansky (New Haven: Yale University Press, 1956), p. 169.

10. Ibid., p. 145.

11. Charles Gildon, *The Life of Mr. Thomas Betterton* (London: R. Gosling, 1710),p. 173.

12. Curtis A. Price, *Music in the Restoration Theatre*, Studies in Musicology, no. 4 (Ann Arbor: UMI Research Press, 1979), p. xiv.

13. Rymer, "A Short View of Tragedy," p. 117.

14. *The Gentleman's Journal: or the Monthly Miscellany* 1 (Jan. 1692):7.

15. Gildon, *Life of Betterton*, pp. 32-33.

16. Ibid., p. 40.

17. Dryden, *Of Dramatic Poesy*, 1:60.

18. "Prologue at the Fox, When a Consort of Hautboyes Were Added to the Musick," anonymous manuscript, quoted in Robert Gale Noyes, "A Manuscript Restoration Prologue for *Volpone,*" *Modern Language Notes* 52 (1937):198. Noyes suggested that the undated manuscript was written in the mid-1670s.

19. Dryden, *Of Dramatic Poesy*, 1:237.

20. Robert Gale Noyes, in "Conventions of Song in Restoration Tragedy," *PMLA* 53 (1938):162-88, noted six functions performed by music in Restoration tragedy: opening a play (common to all plays, not just tragedy); acting as a diversion for characters in the play; breaking up episodes within a scene; between the acts; inducing sleep; and relaying action important to the plot (this last very rare).

21. Allardyce Nicoll, *World Drama* (New York: Harcourt, Brace & Co. [1955]), p. 337.

22. Stoddard Lincoln, "Eccles and Congreve: Music and Drama on the Restoration Stage," *Theatre Notebook* 18 (1963–64):7.

23. Edward J. Dent, *Foundations of English Opera* (Cambridge: Cambridge University Press, 1927; New York: Da Capo, 1965), pp. 18-42.

24. Hazelton Spencer, *Shakespeare Improved* (New York: Frederick Unger, 1927; 1963), p. 174.

25. William Linley, *Shakespeare's Dramatic Songs*, 2 vols. (London: Preston, 1816), 2:23-24.

26. *The Comedies, Histories, Tragedies, and Poems of William Shakespeare*, ed. Charles Knight, 2d ed., 12 vols. (London: Charles Knight and Co., 1843), 8:138.

27. The confusion over the "Purcell" music for *The Tempest* and the problems surrounding an early eighteenth-century setting for *Macbeth* are discussed in Chapter 2.

28. Peter J. Seng, *The Vocal Songs in the Plays of Shakespeare* (Cambridge, Mass: Harvard University Press, 1967), p. 136.

29. E. W. Naylor, *Shakespeare and Music*, 2d ed. (London: J. M. Dent & Sons, 1931), p. 190.

30. F. W. Sternfeld, "Ophelia's Version of the Walsingham Song," *Music and Letters* 45 (1964):111.

31. F. W. Sternfeld, *Music in Shakespearean Tragedy* (New York: Dover, 1963), pp. 76-77.

32. William Chappell, *Popular Music of the Olden Time*, 2 vols. (London: Cramer, Beale, and Chappell, [1855–59]), 1:237.

33. Linley, *Shakespeare's Dramatic Songs*, 2:24.

34. Leslie Hotson, *The Commonwealth and Restoration Stage* (Cambridge, Mass.: Harvard University Press, 1928; New York: Russell & Russell, 1962), p. 204.

35. Andrew Newport to Sir Richard Leveson, 15 Dec. 1660. In Great Britain, Royal Commission on Historical Manuscripts, *Fifth Report* [1876], Part 1, p. 158.

36. Gordon Pocock, *Corneille and Racine. Problems of Tragic Form*, (Cambridge: Cambridge University Press, 1973), p. 13.

37. Nahum Tate, *The History of King Richard the Second* (London: Richard and Jacob Tonson, 1681), p. 53.

38. John Downes, *Roscius Anglicanus. or an Historical Review of the Stage* (London: T. R., 1708), p. 37.

39. Thomas Shadwell, *The History of Timon of Athens. the Man Hater* (London: Henry Herringman, 1678), p. 33.

40. William Barclay Squire, "Purcell's Dramatic Music," *Sammelbande der Internationalen Musikgesellschaft* 5 (1903-4):558-59.

41. J .A. Westrup, "Introduction" to *Timon of Athens, The Works of Henry Purcell*, no. 2 (Burough Green: Novello, 1974), p. xii.

42. *The Complete Plays of William Shakespeare*, ed. William Allan Neilson and Charles Jarvis Hill (Cambridge, Mass.: Riverside, 1942), p. 88.

43. J. P. Cutts, "The Original Music to Middleton's *The Witch*," *Shakespeare Quarterly* 7 (1956):203.

44. In the forward to his revision of *The Tempest*, John Dryden mentioned the play "had been acted with success at the Black-Fryers." Dryden, *The Tempest, or the Enchanted Island*, in *Dryden: The Dramatic Works*, ed. Montague Summers (New York: Gordian Press, 1968), 2:150.

45. W. W. Greg, *The Editorial Problem in Shakespeare*, 3d ed. (Oxford: Clarendon Press, 1954), pp. 151-52.

46. Davenant was unable to take advantage of a patent granted him by Charles I in 1639, allowing him to open a public house to present "plays, scenes, and entertainments whatsoever." Arthur Nethercot, *Sir William Davenant* (New York: Russell & Russell, 1967), p. 170. Dent thought that this license to "act plays" and "exercise the musick"

may mean that Davenant intended productions that may have been more operatic than the court masques. Dent, *Foundations of English Opera*, p. 43.

47. Ibid., pp. 44-45.

48. Downes, *Roscius Anglicanus*, p. 20.

49. Ibid., p. 33.

50. Ibid., p. 31.

51. William Shakespeare, *Macbeth, a Tragedy* (London: P. Chetwin, [1674]), [title page].

52. Dryden, *The Tempest, or the Enchanted Island*, in *Dramatic Works*, 2:152-53.

53. Pepys, *Diary*, 7 May 1668.

54. Ibid.

55. Ibid., 11 May 1668.

56. The dating of the small insert "The Ariels Songs in the Play call'd the Tempest," printed by Playford, has been variously argued. The earliest dating, 1670, would place it before the operatic production.   See J. Greenhill, W. A. Harrison, and Frederick J. Furnwall, eds., *A List of All the Songs and Passages in Shakespeare Which Have Been Set to Music* (London: New Shakespeare Society, 1884;   Folcraft, Pa.: Folcraft Library Editions, 1974), p. xiii. Peter Dennison associates the insert with the 1675 edition of *Select Ayres and Dialogues* which was published by Playford after Shadwell's version, and thus was responsible for the survival of the only music from the 1667 production.   Dennison, *Pelham Humfrey*, Oxford Studies of Composers, no. 21 (Oxford: Oxford University Press, 1986), pp. 106-7.

57. Downes, *Roscius Anglicanus*, pp. 34-35.

58. The Downes attribution and literary stylistic evidence prompted W. J. Lawrence to agree that Shadwell was the operatic adapter; "Did Thomas Shadwell Write an Opera on *The Tempest?*" *Anglia* 27 (1904):205-17.   Dryden was suggested later as the adapter of his original work, in part because the preface to the 1669 printing of the Dryden-Davenant script was mistakenly reprinted in the 1674 operatic text. G. Thorn-Drury, "Shadwell and the Operatic *Tempest*," *Review of English Studies* 3 (1927):204-8. Charles Ward conjectured that Betterton, most likely to have the legal rights to *The Tempest* after Davenant's death, made the operatic changes. "*The Tempest*: A Restoration Opera Problem," *ELH* 13 (1946):19-30.   In summing up these various arguments, W. M. Milton, in "*Tempest* in a Teapot,"

ELH 9 (1942):207-18, agreed with Lawrence on the Shadwell attribution.

59. [William Dryden], *The Tempest, or The Enchanted Island* (London: Henry Herringman, 1674), p. 1.

60. Peter Dennison has suggested that only a fraction of the twenty-four actually played, a practice customary in the Chapel Royal. *Pelham Humfrey*, pp. 99-100. By 1679 the Lord Chamberlain required twenty-four violins to be used in productions for the Court. *The London Stage, A Calendar of Plays 1660-1800* (Carbondale: Southern Illinois University Press, 1960-68), pt. 1, p. cxv.

61. R. Hosley suggests the survival of the music room into the late seventeenth and early eighteenth centuries on iconographic evidence. "Was There a Music Room in Shakespeare's Globe?" p. 114.

62. J. P. Cutts believed Caliban's song might be an adaptation of the nursery rhyme "Johnny Shall Have a New Master." "Music and the Supernatural in *The Tempest*," *Music and Letters* 39 (1958):351.

63. [Dryden], *Tempest* (Henry Herringman, 1674), p. 27.

64. British Library, Egerton MS 2623, fol. 55.

65. Peter Dennison believes Humfrey studied with Lully in France. *Pelham Humfrey*, p. 6.

66. Dryden, *Of Dramatic Poesy*, 1 : 58.

67. R.E.M. Hardy contends the act tunes published with Locke's music for *The Tempest* were not intended for that play. *A Thematic Catalogue of the Works of Matthew Locke* (Oxford: Alden and Mowbry, 1971), p. 115.

68. Matthew Locke, *The English Opera, or the Vocal Musick in Psyche . . . to which is adjoyned the instrumental musick in the Tempest* (London: Ratcliff and Thompson, 1675), p. [2].

69. Pepys, *Diary*, 29 Sept. 1662.

70. Downes, *Roscius Anglicanus*, pp. 42-43.

71. Roger Savage, "The Shakespeare-Purcell *Fairy Queen*—A Defence and Recommendation," *Early Music* 1 (1973):202.

72. W. Carew Hazlitt, *Bibliographic Collections and Notes on Early English Literature*, 2d series (London: B. Quaritch, 1882), p. 185.

73. F. C. Brown, *Elkanah Settle: His Life and Works* (Chicago: University of Chicago Press, 1910), p. 96.

74. J. A. Westrup, *Purcell*, rev. Nigel Fortune (London: Dent, 1980), p. 137.

75. Spencer, *Shakespeare Improved*, pp. 323-24.

76. A performance at Edinburgh University in 1972 lasted approximately four hours, of which just slightly over two hours was music. Savage, "The Shakespeare-Purcell *Fairy Queen*," p. 209.

77. *The Gentleman's Journal*, 5 (May 1692):1.

78. Extensive musical analyses can be found in Dent, *Foundations of English Opera*, pp. 217-34; Moore, *Henry Purcell*, pp. 110-21, and Price, *Purcell*, pp. 320-57. Dent viewed *The Fairy Queen* from a musical perspective, judging it on operatic terms. Moore and Price considered the music an adjunct to the spoken text.

79. Shakespeare, *A Midsummer Night's Dream*, ed. Harold F. Brooks, The Arden Shakespeare (London: Methuen, 1971), p. cxxiii.

80. Henry Purcell, *The Fairy Queen*, in *The Works of Henry Purcell*, no. 12 (London: Novello, 1968), p. xii.

81. Savage, "The Shakespeare-Purcell *Fairy Queen*", p. 211.

2

Shakespeare in Eclipse: Shakespeare Music in the Age of Italian Opera, 1695–1720

The first fully mounted Italian opera was presented in London in 1705. That production brought to a climax an artistic and financial crisis, developing in the London theatre community over the previous decade, in which the primacy of spoken drama was challenged by music. Opera's commercial success radically changed the balance between these two arts on London's stages. In response theatre managers were forced to restructure their dramatic organizations between 1706 and 1709. These reorganizations were among a variety of transformations visited on the theatres in the years of upheaval between 1695 and 1720.

These twenty-five years were a period of feverish stage activity that came not out of dramatic or literary fomentation, but rather from political intrigues and economics based in a popular desire for nonliterary entertainment. It was not a fertile time for contemporary dramatists; nor was there an increased appreciation or rethinking of the older dramatic repertoire. The new theatrical environment had two effects on the Shakespearean repertoire. First, Shakespeare's plays, or rather their later seventeenth-century manifestations, began to disappear from the stage. Second, English theatre composers found themselves increasingly squeezed out of their own theatres by the reorganizations of 1706–9. With few successful additions to the Shakespearean repertoire and a working environment hostile to native musicians,

1710 through 1720 were indeed years of eclipse for Shakespeare and Shakespearean music.

THE THEATRES, 1695–1710:
ITALIAN MUSIC, CHANGING AUDIENCES,
AND REORGANIZATION

The United Company, the only organization licensed to perform in London since the merger of the Duke's and King's Companies in 1682, was again divided into two groups in 1695. Ongoing disagreements between United Company manager Christopher Rich and his actors over pay and part assignments erupted into open warfare. Thomas Betterton and many of his fellow actors abandoned the company, and William III granted the splinter group a license to perform. Betterton's troupe began playing at Davenant's old Lincoln's-Inn-Fields theatre.[1]

After the division of the United Company, actors shared more and more of their stage time with musicians as two companies once again competed for the London audience. Missing from the scene was Henry Purcell, who had died in November 1695. Purcell's expanded musical additions to *Timon of Athens* and *The Fairy Queen* attested both to his skill as a dramatic composer and to the increased use of music in the final years of the seventeenth century. His absence was keenly felt, for few musicians were able or willing to follow Purcell's example and work with poets to create musical scenes contributing to a play's dramatic or atmospheric development.

Contemporary observers often used combative rather than collaborative terms to describe music and drama's combined presence on stage:

Our stage is in a very indifferent condition. There has been a very fierce combat between the Haymarket and Drury Lane, and the two sisters, Music and Poetry, quarrel like two fishwives at Billingsgate.[2]

Most contemporary writers addressing the relationship between music and drama shared a literary bias and felt the need to assert the superiority of the written and spoken word. Some couched their objection to stage music in moral arguments. John Dennis stressed neoclassical drama's didactic purpose over its other function, delight:

Musick may be made profitable as well as delightful, if it is subordinate to some nobler art and subservient to reason. . . . It belongs to poetry only to teach public Virtue and public Spirit.[3]

But music would not be subordinate. Theatre managers resorted to musical entertainments when, as a contemporary observed, plays alone were not enough to bring audiences to the theatres:

The present plays with all that shew, can hardly draw an Audience, unless there be the additional invitation of a *Signor Fideli*, a *Monsieur L'abbe*, or some such foreign Regale expresst at the bottom of the Bill.[4]

In addition to music, theatre managers presented grotesques, rope tricks, and other nonmusical variety acts with increasing frequency. A newspaper columnist wrote in the 7 November 1699 *Post Boy*: "We hear that Monsieur Nivelong, the Famous Grotesque Dancer, is lately arrived from Paris and that he designs to appear shortly on one of our English Stages." Christopher Rich acquired a very special attraction for the theatre at Drury Lane and advertised in the *Daily Courant* on 18 June 1703:

The famous Mr. Clynch will for this once, at the desire of several Persons of Quality, perform his Imitation of an Organ, with 3 Voices, the Doubel Curtel, and the Bells, the Huntsmen with his Horn and Pack of Dogs; All which he performs with his Mouth on the open Stage, being what no man besides himself could ever yet attain to.

Such offerings are indications of drastic changes in the makeup and taste of theatre audiences between 1695 and 1705. The traditional view of modern theatre scholars, based on contemporary description and theatre records and receipts, has been that the aristocratic audiences of 1660–90 became more socially varied in the 1690s and into the eighteenth century. London's burgeoning population contributed to audience diversification.[5] The influx of a new merchant middle class came at a time when Royal enthusiasm for and patronage of theatre was nonexistent.

As early as 1702, John Dennis believed this broadening audience to be a threat to the quality of theatrical presentations:

Several people, who made their Fortunes in the late Wars; and who from a state of obscurity, and perhaps misery, have risen to a condition of distinction and plenty. I believe that no man will wonder, if these People, who in their original obscurity could never attain to any higher entertainment than Tumbling and Vaulting and Ladder Dancing, and the delightful diversions of Jack Pudding, should still be in love with their old sports and encourage these noble Pastimes still upon the stage.[6]

Perhaps because of the audience's declining interest in serious drama, Shakespearean plays and revisions made up a smaller part of the total theatrical offerings between 1695 and 1705 than in previous years. In the first five years of the eighteenth century, only *Hamlet*, Betterton's abridgement of *Henry IV, Part 1*, Tate's *Lear*, Davenant's *Macbeth* and *The Tempest*, and Shadwell's *Timon of Athens* remained active in the repertoire.[7] Tragedies and histories were most frequently performed. The comedies (other than *The Tempest*) were scantily represented by grossly revised versions of *Measure for Measure*, *The Taming of the Shrew*, and *The Merchant of Venice*. In the 1705–6 season (the first that can be reconstructed with some semblance of completeness) only ten of Shakespeare's plays were produced, accounting for just 19 performances in a season of at least 339 performances.[8] The international trade behind the new British middle class prosperity also brought foreign nationals, including musicians, to London. In the last years of the seventeenth century and the first years of the eighteenth, musicians from Italy and France appeared regularly at the public concerts and, increasingly, in the theatres. By 1700 the concert rooms were seriously competing with the theatres, and both used Italian musicians as major attractions.   Audiences that had first been entertained by theatre music modeled in part after Lully's now seemed more interested in Italianate music performed by Italian musicians.

Playwrights had been able to incorporate effectively a limited amount of instrumental music, songs with English texts, and dance into a dramatic scheme; however, as the required entertainments grew larger and imported attractions appeared more frequently, the connection between music and drama was weakened.   Violin sonatas and Italian opera excerpts may have been attractive enticements in the theatre advertisements, but such entertainments (e.g., the new sonatas by Gasparini in the 1703 Drury Lane performances of *Timon of Athens*)[9] could be included in a play only in the most tenuous way, discouraging attempts at integrated dramatic music.

There were fiscal as well as artistic implications, as Downes noted in 1706:

In the space of ten years past, Mr. *Betterton* to gratify the desires and Fancies of the Nobility and Gentry; procur'd from Abroad the best Dances and Singers as Monsieur *L'Abbe*, Madam *Sublini*, Monsieur *Balon*, *Margarita Delpine*, *Maria Gallia* and divers others; who, being Exorbitantly Expensive, produc'd small profit to him and his Company but vast Gains to themselves.[10]

In spite of the questionable economics, both Betterton at Lincoln's-Inn-Fields and Rich at Drury Lane felt it necessary to maintain Italian singers in their resident companies.

The Italian singers who first appeared in the playhouses in the 1690s were just the vanguard for the invasion of fully mounted Italian operas.   In January 1705, Christopher Rich produced the first complete Italian opera in London.   *Arsinoe, Queen of Cypress*, an Italianate pasticcio with an English text, successfully played twenty-five times.   At the newly built Haymarket theatre, which replaced the facility at Lincoln's-Inn-Fields, the inaugural production (9 April 1705) was another opera, Greber's *Loves of Ergasto*.   It failed.   Not even Italian singers could salvage the venture.   Downes archly noted that *Ergasto* was "performed by a new set of singers, arriv'd from Italy; (the worst that e're came from thence). . . . and they being liked but indifferently by the Gentry; they in a little time marcht back to their own country."[11] The next season, both theatres mounted successful musical productions.

Actors and playwrights might soon have found themselves permanently relegated to a secondary position on their own stages. Economics, not artistic considerations, prevented this. Because of the enormous amount of music used in the theatres in the 1690s and the first years of the eighteenth century, the two theatres developed what were in effect double companies. One group was made up of actors, and the other of singers and instrumentalists. It was soon apparent that the audience was not large enough to support such an elaborate structure. Over a period of just four years, the organizational hierarchies of the two theatres were changed three times in attempts to divide profits and responsibilities.[12]

The first reform, affecting the 1706–7 season, restricted the performance of Italian opera and dramatic opera to Drury Lane under Rich. The Haymarket retained Betterton (who retired from management in 1705) and the other distinguished actors for spoken plays only. Dances and songs were not allowed. The Haymarket retained only enough instrumental musicians to provide overtures and act tunes. Rich produced revivals of three Shakespeare musicals this season—*Macbeth, The Tempest*, and *Timon of Athens*[13] —but new productions were exclusively Italian opera.

The second reorganization took place in January 1708. The Lord Chamberlain transferred all the singers and musicians from the control of Rich back to the Haymarket, and the actors were moved back to Drury Lane. The Haymarket was now strictly an opera house. Drury Lane produced nonmusical plays. Italian opera now had a permanent venue, and the actors were once again the center of attention on their own stage. English musicians who had worked within the musico-dramatic conventions of the late Restoration were displaced. Composers who might have continued working in the theatres (e.g., Daniel Purcell and Eccles) turned to other forms of composing or retired.[14]

A final regrouping occurred in the summer of 1709. Rich was removed as manager of Drury Lane. The Haymarket retained its monopoly on Italian opera, but could do plays as well. Drury Lane could use any kind of musical entertainment save opera. In practice, the Haymarket abandoned spoken plays, leaving Drury Lane as London's sole purveyor of spoken drama for several seasons. With the exception of *The Tempest* and *Macbeth*, the reorganization effectively brought an end to Restoration dramatic opera and curtailed the amount of music inserted into all plays.

SHAKESPEARE MUSIC, 1695-1720

Altered Plays with Masques

Between 1700 and 1703, Lincoln's-Inn-Fields presented adaptations of three long-neglected Shakespearean comedies: *Measure for Measure, The Merchant of Venice,* and *Twelfth Night.* Each play was changed to include at least one large musical entertainment. These entertainments were not incorporated into the story as in the earlier dramatic operas. Unlike Purcell's masque for *Timon of Athens,* the musical scenes for the comedies are not allegorical. The masque scores used with the comedies are lost; however, the published versions of the plays and some surviving incidental music provide details of the productions.

Gildon's *Measure for Measure*

The authorship of the 1700 adaptation of *Measure for Measure* is not indicated in the published script, but it was attributed to Charles Gildon at an early date. The attribution has never been challenged.[15] The title page indicates more was involved than Shakespeare:

Measure for Measure, or Beauty the Best Advocate. As it is Acted at the Theatre in Lincolns-Inn Fields. Written Originally by Mr. Shakespeare; And now very much Alter'd With Additions of several Entertainments of Musick. London . . . 1700.

The prologue identifies the "several Entertainments":

> Hold; I forgot the business of the Day:
> No more than this, we for ourselves need say,
> 'Tis Purcels Musick, and 'tis Shakespeares Play.[16]

"Shakespeares Play" was *Measure* filtered through Davenant's 1661 *The Law against Lovers*, with that adapter's most extravagant flights of fancy and the additions from *Much Ado about Nothing* stripped away to restore the script's basic outline. "Purcels Musick" was *Dido and Aeneas*, abridged and rearranged into three entertainments. These were introduced at various points in the play, ostensibly as offerings to calm Angelo's "ruffled soul." The music for a fourth entertainment, a mythological spectacle called "Phoebus Rises in His Chariot over the Sea," is unknown, but the text is preserved in the printed script. Shakespeare's story was cut to a bare minimum, as a framework for the unrelated musical scenes.

The Jew of Venice

In the epilogue to his 1701 revision of *The Merchant of Venice*, George Granville Lansdowne's apology for his musical additions invoked a distinguished precedent:

> How was the scene forlorn, and how despis'd,
> When Tymon, without Musick, moraliz'd?
> Shakespear's sublime in vain entic'd the Throng,
> Without the charm of Purcell's Syren Song.[17]

The Jew of Venice was possibly the first stage presentation of *Merchant* since Shakespeare's time. Granville Lansdowne, influenced by neoclassical principles and theatrical necessity, eliminated the play's tragicomic qualities and inserted a large musical entertainment. The masque "Peleus and Thetis" is a self-contained mythological diversion curiously devoid of scenic devices and dances. It appears in II, 2, a new scene introduced only as a venue for the masque. The music by John Eccles is lost. *The Jew of Venice* was performed through the 1730s, but later productions were performed without the masque. In his complete published works, Granville Lansdowne included "Peleus and Thetis" in the poetry volume, separate from the play. When William Boyce set "Peleus and Thetis" to music in 1736, it was no longer connected to *The Jew of Venice*.

Love Betray'd

No music was ever written for the masque in the 1703 adaptation of *Twelfth Night*, retitled as *Love Betray'd, or The Agreeable Disappointment*. Adapter William Burnaby acknowledged: "Part of the Tale of this Play I took from Shakespeare, and about 50 of the Lines."[18] Incomplete parts exist for an overture, act tunes, and dance music by William Corbett,[19] and Eccles set two non-Shakespearean lyrics, now lost. The masque in this play was, like that in *The Jew of Venice*, completely unrelated to the story. But an accident of production, reported by Burnaby in his preface to the printed edition, befell *Love Betray'd*.

The Conduct of the Drama I broke by design to make room for a Mask that is Mention'd in the last Act, but the House neglecting to have it set to Musick, the Play came on like a change of Government.[20]

Either the lack of music or the quality of Burnaby's prose caused *Love Betray'd to* disappear almost immediately after it opened.

Burnaby's description of breaking "the Conduct of the Drama" for the masque indicates the degree to which music had become the near equal of drama on the English stage. Most contemporary writers addressing the music-drama relationship shared a literary bias. Like John Dennis, they believed music should be subordinate to the text. At least one contemporary observer, Roger North, discussed the unusual way the theatres went about the "mixing of 2 capitall entertainments" and the audience's reaction.[21]

Some that would come to the play hated the musick, and others that were very desirous of the musick, would not bear the interruption that so much rehearsal gave, so that it is best to have either by itself intire.[22]

Measure for Measure, The Jew of Venice, and *Love Betray'd* were among the last of such late Restoration revisions. The musical additions they contained became impossible after the mid-decade theatrical reorganization divided musical and dramatic functions between the theatres.

Incidental Music

Incidental songs and instrumental music continued to be included in Shakespearean productions, both in plays with more organized musical entertainments and those without. The script revisions had eliminated almost all the original Shakespearean song lyrics. Newly added songs were often ephemeral, and their texts were not included in printed copies of the play. A number of act tunes and overtures from this time do survive.

The happiest result of Gildon's revision of *Measure for Measure* was the restoration of Shakespeare's "Take, O Take Those Lips Away" to act IV. The setting by John Weldon was published in his *Collection of New Songs* (1702). This song, reminiscent of Purcell at his most expressive, deserves to be counted among the best of the eighteenth-century Shakespeare songs. The song (printed complete in Appendix A) is in two sections, the form most frequently used by Weldon. The melodic leap with which the song delivers the opening imperative is intensely dramatic. Contrast between the sections responds to the shift of mood in the text. A rising line that provides the musical equivalent of a sunburst for "the break of day" is a compelling example of text painting. The irregularity of phrase is also reminiscent of Purcell.

Gildon's revision of the text immediately following the song provides an interesting insight into his view of music. In

Shakespeare's original text, the disguised Duke interrupts the melancholy Mariana as she listens to music:

> *Mariana:* I cry you mercy, sir: and well could wish
> You had not found me here so musical.
> Let me excuse me, and believe me so,
> My mirth it much displeas'd, but pleas'd my woe.
>
> *Duke:* 'Tis good; though music oft hath such charm
> To make bad good, and good provoke to harm.
> (IV, 1; lines 10-15)

The song intensifies Mariana's unhappiness, giving her a kind of pleasure from her pain. Shakespeare's scene represents a concept of music's power and function "drawn from Renaissance musico-medical lore."[23] Gildon's account of Mariana's response to the song reflects an eighteenth-century musical philosophy:

> *Mariana:* I cry you Mercy, and cou'd wish you had not
> Found me here so Musical, it sooth'd my Griefs,
> But bred no Mirth.
> *Duke:* Musick, my good Daughter,
> Has power to soften Woe, refresh the Mind,
> And make it fit for its more strenuous Duties.[24]

Gildon wrote from a moralistic viewpoint. Music is valued more for its useful, restorative power than for its ability to please. It is also suggested that music falls lower in the hierarchy of human activity than other "more strenuous Duties."

In the decade between 1696 and 1706, a limited number of plays with new music were revived in new productions. *Hamlet* (Lincoln's-Inn-Fields, 1695–96) included a new song written by John Eccles and "sung by Mr. Knapp":

> A swain long slighted and disdained
> Of Cruel Cinthia's scorn and pride
> To an old trusty Friend Complain'd
> Who well and wisely thus Complain'd.

By long experience have I known
And tell you that you need not fear;
The Town that Parlys will be won,
And she will yield that once will hear.[25]

The generic pastoral text suggests that Eccles may not have written the song specifically for *Hamlet.* No script from this production exists, so the placement of the song and the role played by Mr. Knapp are not known. The song may come from a scene early in the play involving Hamlet's wooing of Ophelia; however, if the song was related to Gertrude's hasty remarriage (for example, in the play within the play), the diffuse cynicism of the text would become specifically caustic.

The song's bipartite form is articulated by changes of meter and key signature. Eccles preserved the text's iambic stress pattern in both the duple and triple sections of the song; however, text repetition obscures the tetrameter. The inverted dotted rhythm of the Scotch snap follows a stress variation in the text.

Ex. 6. Eccles. "A Song..." (*Hamlet*), mm. 1-6.

by permission of the British Library

A song from *Macbeth*, written by Daniel Purcell, shows more Italianate influence than Eccles's *Hamlet* song. The consistently elaborate vocal line and the ground bass suggest little attempt was made to preserve English speech rhythm.

Ex. 7. D. Purcell. "A Song..." (*Macbeth*), mm. 3-9.

by permission of the British Library

It is hard to guess how the song was introduced into the play. The "Mr. Mason" named as the singer on the broadsheet was one John Mason, a singing member of the musical establishment at Drury Lane.[26] He did not play a major role in the production. Connecting the text with the plot of the play, as was possible with the song by Eccles, is difficult. Perhaps the song was introduced as an entertainment in the banquet scene.

Because of the efforts of music publisher John Walsh, more act music from Shakespearean productions survives from the decade 1695–1705 than from previous years.[27] Some complete sets—usually a French overture with seven to eleven act tunes—were saved, often in parts printed by Walsh. In other cases, single items were preserved in manuscript.

The popularity of the character Falstaff prompted frequent performances of *Henry IV, Parts 1 and 2*. The plays were considered comedies rather than historical dramas with potentially tragic overtones. James Paisible's music for Betterton's revision of *Henry IV, Part 2* (Lincoln's-Inn-Fields, ca. 1700) may be an unusual example of a composer matching act tunes with the content of the play. The inclusion of several "trumpett aires" (melodies typical of idiomatic trumpet style, not necessarily played on a trumpet) emphasizes the play's martial setting. The dynamic markings in Walsh's print lie only in the treble part, thus suggesting the addition of a trumpet to the first violins in the "loud" sections.

Ex. 8. Paisible. *Humours of Sir John Falstaff* (*Henry IV, Pt. 2*). "Trumpett Aire," mm. 1-8.

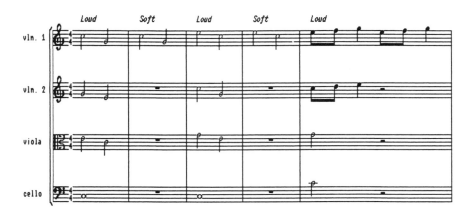

by permission of the British Library

In comparison to Paisible's music, the act tunes for the Lincoln's-Inn-Fields version of *Henry IV, Part 1* are dance movements seemingly unrelated to the play.

Composers writing act music for Shakespearean tragedies showed a preference for G minor.[28] Since the music performed the same prefatory and entr'acte function in both tragedies and comedies, the format—overtures with dance movements—was the same. The concluding act tune written by John Lenton for a turn-of-the-century revival of *Othello* is typical: a binary movement (the first half of which appears below in Example 9) with its French dance heritage evident in the saraband rhythms. The G-minor tonality and (possibly) the tempo indication reflect the sombre nature of the play.

The surviving Shakespearean act music shows no attempt at the kind of graphic visual description seen in Locke's *Tempest* overture of some thirty years before. Such music, if it did exist for theatre use, may not have been printed in collections because of its limited usefulness. It is possible that basic cues of different kinds (e.g., for storms, chase scenes, or apparitions) were used in a number of plays rather than being written anew for each production. Such music cues, if they existed, were lost; however, the absence of such items from surviving manuscripts made specifically for theatre use suggests that graphic description of stage action in instrumental music was still rare.

Ex. 9. Lenton. *Moore of Venice.* Act Tune 8, mm. 1-10.

by permission of the British Library

The Dramatic Opera Revivals

By the end of the seventeenth century Davenant's operatic *Macbeth* (1664) and Shadwell's *The Tempest* (1674) had become permanently established in the repertoire of both companies.[29] Revivals of both plays prompted the composition of new music. The music written for revivals of these plays would become the most important Shakespeare music of the first third of the eighteenth century.

Macbeth

At some point around 1700, Locke's *Macbeth* music fell from fashion. John Eccles wrote an elaborate setting of the Davenant masques. The music survives in several manuscripts, including the autograph (Add. MS 12219) in the British Library. None of the sources indicate the exact date or the theatre for which the music was written.

Eccles's second act masque is in a very diatonic C major, to modern ears an unusual choice for "witch music." In the masque's opening "symphonie," the ornament sign under the serpent part, reminiscent of the similar marking in the frost scene (II, 2) of Purcell's *King Arthur*, may represent a series of trills or a vibrato effect.

Ex. 10. Eccles. *Macbeth.* "Symphonie," mm. 1-8.

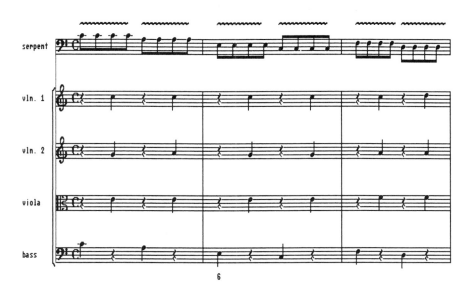

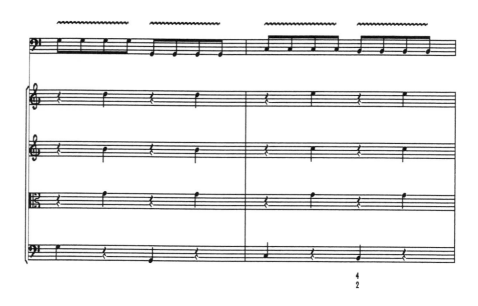

by permission of the British Library

In later vocal sections, such as that in Example 11, the melodic content of recitative in the manuscript is restricted to outlines of primary diatonic chords, sometimes filled in with passing notes. This simplicity may have been in response to the short lines of the text. Dissonances and chromaticism are absent. Changes of meter are related to word accents, not to changes in dramatic action or rhetorical purpose. The time changes provide a conversational continuity rather than highlighting contrasting textual sentiments.

Ex. 11. Eccles. *Macbeth.* Act II Masque, opening.

A- bove twelve glas- ses since have run.

goe, long a- goe.

Mr. Spalding

There are no discrete numbers for soloists. Rather, the recitative/air interludes connect the three large choral sections, in which the soloists also participate. The three sections are variously constructed. The first is an ABB form, with closing symphony, in which A and B are each elaborated antecedent/consequent phrase pairs. The second begins with a homophonic section for double SATB chorus (the only eight-part section in the masque).The closing measures of this section are contrapuntal and reduced to a four-voice texture. The third and final section of the masque is a short strophic song with choral conclusion.

by permission of the British Library

The regular phrasing and antecedent-consequent structure of the opening measures of the third-act masque seem at odds with the manuscript's description of the passage as recitative. In moments of heightened expression, both French and Italian recitative could momentarily become more melodic; however, that is not an issue with this text. The passage does connect smoothly with the following choral section. The short intro-ductory quality of this "recitative" may have been sufficient to earn the label. The chorus introduces the main section of the masque, a rondeau. The choral section with concluding symphony acts as refrain, solo sections as couplets.

The fourth-act masque is less ambitious than its predecessors. The rising motive that runs throughout the bass line of the opening symphony suggests the witches may have entered on ascending machinery. The incantation scene is simply treated, and no music is provided for the procession of the kings

Drury Lane opened a new "*Mackbeth*" on 21 November 1702, with music "vocal and instrumental, all new compos'd by Mr. Leveridge, and performed by him and others."[30] Richard Leveridge (ca. 1671-1758) was a talented bass for whom Purcell had written some of his most challenging vocal music. Besides being a singer, stage personality, and well-known fellow of good cheer, he was also a composer.[31] While his earlier music showed Purcell's influence, Leveridge was an adaptable craftsman, and in later years his music was influenced by Italian opera and ballad opera.[32]

The text used by Leveridge was only slightly expanded from Davenant's version. The music is in many ways similar to that of Eccles, though technically simpler. It is naive, unabashedly major-key, and rhythmically active. The choral texture is usually homophonic, with soprano and alto moving as a pair against an only slightly more independent bass. Even with limited means, Leveridge was still able to write a climax of almost Handelian intensity.

Leveridge's solo sections are longer than those by Eccles. Eccles moved between recitative and song, duple and triple meter. The weighty, often contrapuntal choruses, not the solos, were his architectural substance. Leveridge's songs, on the other hand, were his focal point. The song excerpted below in Example 12, nearly forty measures long in its entirety, even has its own brief instrumental introduction and conclusion. Eccles used smaller sections, combining them into larger units. Leveridge's sections were longer, each number thus gaining a certain amount of independence. Leveridge was here influenced by more contemporary Italian models, while Eccles had continued to observe mid-seventeenth-century styles.

Ex. 12. Leveridge. *Macbeth.* "Let's Have a Dance," mm. 2-10.

by permission of the British Library

Certain similarities between Eccles's and Leveridge's settings have prompted commentary. It has been suggested that the harmonic and melodic simplicity, the unrelieved major tonality, and the repeated sixteenth note patterns (which to modern ears seem incongruous with the fantastical subject) somehow symbolized witchery to a Restoration audience.[33] Direct modelling following the Johnson-Locke-Eccles-Leveridge line has also been proposed.[34]

The shared text itself must not be overlooked as a source of rhythmic similarity. The lines of verse are short, often falling into a regular rhythmic pattern. There is little action, and that limited to situations that are appropriate for terse expositions, such as the spirit roll call in act III and the incantations in act IV.

The text does not offer the kind of contrasting imagery that would suggest bipartite song form or (had either Eccles or Leveridge been so inclined) a *da capo* form.

Two questions remain concerning the *Macbeth* music. First, when (and for what theatre) did Eccles write his setting? Second, why, with a reasonably new and admirable setting already available, did Leveridge reset the text?

One theory is that Lincoln's-Inn-Fields did not have the facilities or the personnel for the Eccles version.[35] According to this view, the difficulty of the music, the double chorus, and the performance of some of the music "aloft" would have required the Eccles music to be performed at Dorset Garden in the 1694 season or before. The evidence does not rule out the possibility of an Eccles performance prior to the division of the companies, but it does suggest performances took place at Lincoln's-Inn-Fields after Betterton's group separated from the United Company. Since the double chorus is used only once, it could be performed with limited personnel either with temporary *divisi* singing or even the temporary addition of the soloists.

The Lincoln's-Inn-Fields theatre was a substantial facility, although some thirty-five years passed between Davenant's re-modelling and the Betterton troupe's move into the building. The remodelled tennis court at Lincoln's-Inn-Fields was a theatre suitable for technically complex productions. A letter by Giovanni Salvetti, dated 27 January 1661, indicates the building was refitted precisely for this purpose: "The Duke of York showed me the design of a large room he has begun to build in the Italian style in which they intend to put on shows as they do there in Italy with scenes and machines."[36] There were traps for risings and sinkings, space in front of the apron for musicians, and probably an Elizabethan-style music loft above the stage.[37]

The Eccles autograph indicates parts for the following soloists: Messrs. Sherburn, Curco, Bowman, Wiltshire, Spalding, and Lee; Mrs. Willis and Mrs. Hodgson. Most of these singers are known to have gone with Betterton to Lincoln's-Inn-Fields.[38] Mr. Spalding is mentioned in no other source, and a singing Mr. Lee is mentioned only in the Lincoln's-Inn-Fields company for 1702–3.[39]   Another manuscript copy, British Library Add. MS 31454, notes that Mr. Wiltshire was replaced by a Mr. Cook, the only record of whom is at Lincoln's-Inn-Fields in 1702.[40]

If Eccles made his setting for Lincoln's-Inn-Fields, it would follow that Rich and Leveridge would replace Locke's music with something more up-to-date to draw audiences away from Betterton's *Macbeth*.   When, after several theatrical reorganizations, Eccles was forced into retirement a few years later, there was no one in London to champion his music.   His *Macbeth* fell into disuse.   Leveridge, on the other hand, remained active in the theatres as a composer, actor, and singer for decades, promoting his own music.

The "Purcell" *Tempest*

The attribution of the best-known *Tempest* score to Henry Purcell has been questioned by nineteenth- and twentieth-century musicologists.   As early as 1903, Barclay Squire emphasized that there was no contemporary reference to a *Tempest* setting by Purcell.[41]   In addition, the music shows more Italianate influence than any other of Purcell's stage works; however, some modern commentators have considered the Italianate style of the *Tempest* music as evidence of Purcell's adaptability rather than an argument against his authorship.   Westrup called *The Tempest* "the full flowering of Purcell's gift as a composer for the stage.[42]   For Moore *The Tempest* was Purcell's valediction: "He takes farewell of one style . . . and experiments with a new Italian manner."[43]   On the basis of tradition dating from the middle of the eighteenth century, the work continued to be attributed to Purcell into the twentieth.

The earliest sources include a manuscript (now lost) which Barclay Squire dated ca. 1720,[44] and British Library Additional MS 37027, about the same age as Barclay Squire's manuscript.[45] Tenbury MS 1266 at St. Michael's College (ca. 1750) is the first source to claim authorship for Purcell.   When Harrison and Co. first published the music in 1786, the attribution was maintained.

Only one song for *The Tempest* can be definitely attributed to Purcell. "A New Song in the *Tempest,* Sung by Mis *Cross* to her Lover, who is supposed Dead" ("Dear Pretty Youth") was first printed in *Deliciae Musicae III* (1695). Letitia Cross joined the Drury Lane company during the 1694–95 season.[46] The song text indicates she played Dorinda, Prospero's second daughter in the Davenant subplot. Purcell died a few months after "Mis Cross" came to Drury Lane, so there must have been a 1695 revival of *The Tempest.* Purcell had already written one semi-opera (*The Indian Queen*) for the theater that year and probably contributed a single song to be added to the *Tempest* music by Humfreys, et al., still in use.

Margaret Laurie has argued persuasively that John Weldon, not Purcell, was the composer of the *Tempest* music in Additional MS 37207 and later scores.[47] Laurie relies on stylistic and documentary evidence to reach her conclusions. The source manuscripts do include Purcell's "Dear Pretty Youth"; however, the lack of any other *Tempest* music in collections of Purcell's music published shortly after his death and the failure of theatres to advertise such music if it did exist (and at a time when his name was frequently invoked in advertisements) are surprising if the famous score is by him. The single song by Purcell may simply have been carried over into a production with an otherwise new score, one which according to Laurie lacks both the tonal organization and sophisticated orchestration typical of Purcell.[48] An advertisement for the play in the *Daily Courant,* 30 July 1711, boasts of "All the musick compos'd by Mr. Weldon and perform'd compleat, as at the revival of the play." This Drury Lane revival may have been the first performance after the 1709 reorganization once again allowed the theatre to mount elaborate musical entertainments. The dramatic effect of this music also suggests a composition date following the public's first acceptance of Italian opera.

The so-called Purcell setting differs from that by Humfrey and his collaborators in two important ways that would affect how the music works in the play. First, the individual sections are larger and disrupt the progress of the action for a longer time. Second, the formal regularity of the final masque is at odds with the original scenic and atmospheric purpose of the scene.

In Davenant's III, 1, when Ariel lures Ferdinand further into the island by song, Banister's setting is tuneful, syllabic, and direct. The "Purcell" setting is some three times as long. Part of the musical expansion comes through word repetition and florid word settings. The movement ends with a chorus.

Ex. 13. Purcell, attrib. *Tempest.* "Come Unto These Yellow Sands," mm. 10-16.

by permission of Novello and Company Limited

Shakespeare's (and perhaps Davenant's) intent here was to use music as a magical prop. The ambitious scale of the later arrangement slows the pace of the action. Interest shifts away from the drama and toward the music. What was in earlier versions a magical scene enhanced by music became in the "Purcell" version a musical scene introduced on magical pretext.

Non-Shakespearean additions were similarly expanded. A comparison of the Banister and "Purcell" musics for the scene in act III where Ariel comforts the band of usurpers shows that a brief song of succor was changed to a fully developed aria.

Ex. 14. Banister. *Tempest.* "Dry Those Eyes," mm. 1-4.

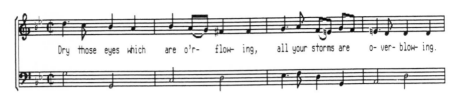

by permission of Stainer & Bell Ltd.

Ex. 15. Purcell, attrib. *Tempest.* "Dry Those Eyes," mm. 10-16.

by permission of Novello and Company Limited

The shift of emphasis from text to music is even more apparent in the treatment of the Grand Masque (Shadwell's, not Shakespeare's). The "Purcell" text is a severely shortened paraphrase of the 1674 version; however, the music is much expanded. Shakespeare's lyric "Where the Bee Sucks," a famous part of the 1674 *Tempest* because of its spectacle and Humfrey's popular music, was omitted in the later setting. Robert Moore believed Humfrey's setting of "Where the Bee Sucks" may have been included in the original production of the "Purcell" score, but this assumes a 1695 production.[49] If Add. MS 37207 dates from 1709 or later, "Where the Bee Sucks," had it been included in the production, would probably have been added to the score, as was "Dear Pretty Youth."

Shakespeare's masque in *The Tempest* was as much a dramatic device as a musical one. The Shadwell interpolation was primarily concerned with scenic spectacle, to which the music was an adjunct. In the "Purcell" masque setting, text and spectacle have become subsidiary to the music. Italianate structural devices create an architectural, if dramatically static, cantata.

"Purcell" *Tempest*, Act V

1. Recitative, Soprano and Bass 1
2. Chorus
3. Recitative and Bipartite Air, Bass 1
4. Recitative and Da Capo Air, Bass 2
5. Da Capo Air, Soprano
6. Da Capo Air, Bass 1
7. Duet (Soprano and Bass 1) and Chorus

The recitative lacks the linear dramatic progression that (at least in theory) was part of Italian opera. The arias do not provide the kind of scenic atmosphere or sense of tension, achieved by variety of form and technique, as seen in *The Fairy Queen* or *Timon of Athens*. Its dramatic function aside, the masque became a standard part of most *Tempest* productions for the rest of the eighteenth century and was still in occasional use into the nineteenth.

Shakespearean Operas

Ambleto

The first Shakespeare-related Italian opera came not from England but Italy. In 1705 Francesco Gasparini's *Ambleto* (*Hamlet*) premiered at Venice's Teatro S. Cassiano, to a libretto by Apostolo Zeno. There is no hint of Shakespeare's poetry in Zeno's Italian text. Charles Burney believed that Zeno modeled the libretto more on Shakespeare's own source for the story, the Danish history by Saxo-Grammaticus, than on the play.[50] The castrato Nicolino Grimaldi, known professionally as "Nicolini," brought the opera to London, where he sang the title role when the production opened at the Queen's Theatre on 27 February 1712. It ran for seven performances, and a collection of "favorite airs" was published in score. The opera did not return in later seasons.

The libretto unfolds perfunctorily; however, Burney, who had little else to say in praise of the opera, wrote that Zeno avoided "all the absurdities and improprieties which critics . . . had leisure to find in former opera."[51] Whatever the source, the opera displays none of the ensemble drama of *Hamlet.* The soliloquies might have presented a special opportunity for a librettist/translator, but the aria texts are traditional affective statements. The musical highlight of the score belonged not to Nicolini but to a Signora Girardeau, who had what Burney called a "noisy" vengeance aria that included impressive parts for obbligato horns and oboes.

The Comick Masque of Pyramus and Thisbe

When Richard Leveridge adapted the Pyramus and Thisbe scene from *A Midsummer Night's Dream* for a lampoon of Italian opera, he did not stray far from his model. Shakespeare had written his play within a play as a parody of the choir-school boy-actor productions, the absurdities of which must have bemused

Elizabethan audiences as the conventions of Italian opera puzzled some eighteenth-century listeners.

The preface to the printed libretto is a tongue-in-cheek apology for what is to follow:

As our present Encouragers of this Part of Theatrical Labours, have for some late years been chiefly regaled with high *Recitative* and *Buskin* Airs; I have here endeavored the quite Reverse of those exalted performances; and hope I may challenge some small Excuse for this Exotic Essay, from no less than Example and Precedent. If the first Founders, the Italians, in the Grandest of their Performances have introduced Lions, Bears, Monkies, Dragons, & c. as their Doughty Fables require: I know no reason why I may not turn Moonshine into a Minstrel; the Lion and Stone Wall into Songsters.[52]

The Comick Masque of Pyramus and Thisbe opened at Lincoln's-Inn-Fields 29 October 1716. The comparison of the practitioners of Italian opera with Shakespeare's "rude rustics" must have found some sympathetic ears, since the play returned to the stage for several seasons. What part Leveridge's music may have had in the show's success is unknown, as the music is lost.

The play opens with an abridgement of the rehearsal scene in folio III, 2. For the play within the play, the "audience" is no longer the Athenian court, but a Mr. Semibreve, Mr. Crotchet, and Mr. Gamit, who comment on the proceedings:

Semibreve: Here come two noble beasts, a Man and a Lion.
Crotchet: I wonder whether the Lion be to sing?
Semibreve: Never wonder at that, for we that have Study'd the Italian opera may do any thing in this kind.[53]

The libretto does not specifically indicate just what part of the script was set to music, but the entire play within the play was probably sung. The airs are set off by typography, and Leveridge's mention of recitative (a device many audience members would have considered ripe for parody) suggests the remainder of the rustic presentation may have been sung as recitative.

After the final theatrical regrouping of 1708 had restored musical plays to the domain of the acting company, the theatre management rebuilt its musical organization. When John Rich assumed his father Christopher's license and opened the new theatre at Lincoln's-Inn-Fields in 1714, the two-house rivalry began anew. Once again, both houses had double companies: a drama troupe and a music ensemble. The cast list printed in the edition of *Pyramus and Thisbe* indicates that roles were divided among members of the Lincoln's-Inn-Fields double company in strict fashion. The short rehearsal scene at the beginning of the play was not musical, and members of the nonsinging company played Bottom and the other rustics. For the musical portion, the low comics (now singing roles) were played by Leveridge and the other singing actors. Actors who had performed in the opening scene came back as Mr. Semibreve and the other members of the nonsinging, on-stage audience.

While the character of Leveridge's lost music can not be known, the libretto suggests that the music may have had an element of burlesque. However, the problems of adapting a full-length Shakespearean play for a serious Italianate opera in English would have been analogous to difficulties encountered by the Restoration play adapters. The theory of opera as brought from Italy, firmly based in Italianate literary models, did not readily suggest that older English drama such as Shakespeare's plays would make good librettos. Restoration dramatists and audiences had been significantly challenged by spoken Shakespeare without the addition of musico-dramatic elements.

Another, more practical, obstacle to such a project was the result of theatrical reorganization. Although by 1715–16 the musical activities had again increased at both Drury Lane and the new Lincoln's-Inn-Fields, opera—in Italian—was the domain of the Haymarket theatre. Knowledge of Shakespeare was not widespread on the Continent, and Italian librettists whose work appeared at the Haymarket very likely had little or no exposure to the plays.[54] Even if English librettists and composers had wanted to create a Shakespearean opera and their audiences had been able to accept it, the theatrical establishment in the first part of the eighteenth century was not organized to make the production of such fare possible.

SUMMARY

Around 1700 a financial and artistic crisis resulted from the increasing use of music, novelty acts, and Italian entertainers in the English theatres. Such attempts on the part of theatre managers to attract a more diverse audience would contribute to an uneasy balance between music and drama on the English stage for the rest of the century. By 1706 the fiscal burden of fully staged Italian opera made necessary the reorganization of repertoire and resources among the houses.

Paradoxically, the regrouping of theatrical forces had also ended much native theatre music activity. The curtailment of musical entertainments in spoken drama temporarily ended grand musical elaboration of spoken plays, including Shakespeare's. Only *The Tempest* and *Macbeth* had been incorporated into the repertoire deeply enough to survive dramatic opera's demise. With fewer native composers working at the theatres and increasingly elaborate entr'acte musical entertainments, the practice of providing act music for specific plays decreased. The growing body of published music—much of it Italian—was used instead between the acts.

Changes in management at Drury Lane resulted in the strengthening of the Shakespeare repertoire that had not developed an extensive musical tradition during the Restoration period. When Betterton died in 1710, three actors—Colley Cibber, Barton Booth, and Robert Wilks—achieved control of Drury Lane. They were not only successful managers, but actors of sufficient stature to assume Betterton's leading position. The three dominated the stage and chose the plays in which they appeared. Their talents were fitted for the histories and tragedies, plays that did not lend themselves to musical elaboration. Some of these plays were altered by Cibber and the others for their own use. The Shakespeare repertoire expanded between 1710 and 1720,[55]

but neither the plays nor the conditions in which they were produced encouraged the creation of new music.

NOTES

1. See *The London Stage   1660-1800 : A Calendar of Plays*, 11
vols. (Carbondale: Southern Illinois University Press, 1960–68), pt.
1, pp. xliii-xliv; also Judith Milhous, "Company Management," in
The London Theatre World, 1660-1800, ed. Robert D. Hume
(Carbondale: Southern Illinois University Press, 1980), pp. 6-12.
2. Anonymous letter, ca. 1705, cited in Percy Fitzgerald, *A New
History of the English Stage*, 2 vols. (London: Tinsley, 1882), 1:240.
3. "Essay on the Opera's" [1706] in *The Critical Works of John
Dennis*, ed. Edward Niles Hooker, 2 vols. (Baltimore: Johns Hopkins
Press, 1943), 1:385.
4. James Wright, *Historia Histrionica, an Historical Account of the
English Stage* (London: G. Croom, 1699), p. 6.
5. Harry William Pedicord, "Changing Audience," in *London
Theatre World, 1660-1800*, p. 242.
6. "A Large Account of the Taste in Poetry" [1702], in *The Critical
Works of John Dennis*, 1:293-94.
7. Charles Beecher Hogan, *Shakespeare in the Theatre, 1701-1800*,
2 vols. (Oxford: Clarendon Press, 1952), 1:2-4, 460-61.
8. *London Stage*, pt. 2, 1:101-28.
9. Ibid., pt. 2, 1:36.
10. John Downes, *Roscius Anglicanus, or an Historical Review of
the Stage* (London: T. R., 1708), p. 46.
11. Ibid., p. 48.
12. It is not necessary to detail here the managerial changes or
political maneuverings that took place during these years. The most
often cited contemporary account is Cibber's version, *An Apology for
the Life of Colley Cibber* [1740], ed. B.R.S. Fone (Ann Arbor:
University of Michigan Press, 1968), chap. 9.   A more objective and
succinct version is in George C. D. Odell, *Shakespeare from Betterton
to Irving*, 2 vols. (New York: Charles Scribner, 1920; New York:
Dover, 1966), 1:15-16. Curtis Price has clearly outlined the results of
the reorganizations with charts in *Music in the Restoration Theatre*,
Studies in Musicology, no. 4 (Ann Arbor: UMI Research Press,
1979), pp. 120-21, 126, 131.

13. Hogan, *Shakespeare in the Theatre*, 1:5.

14. According to John Hawkins, Eccles left London in disgust and "retired to Kingston in Surrey for the conveniency of angling, a recreation of which he was very fond." *A General History of the Science and Practice of Music* [1776], 2 vols. (London: Novello, 1853; New York: Dover, 1963) 2:787. Daniel Purcell finished his career as a church organist.

15. Hazelton Spencer, *Shakespeare Improved* (New York: Frederick Unger: 1927; 1963), p. 329.

16. Charles Gildon, *Measure for Measure, or Beauty the Best Advocate* (London: D. Brown and R. Parker, 1700), p. [iv].

17. George Granville Lansdowne, *The Jew of Venice* (London: Tonson, 1701), p. [47].

18. William Burnaby, *Love Betray'd, or the Agreeable Disappointment* (London: D. Brown, 1703), p. [1].

19. William Corbett, "Mr. Corbett's Musick in the Comedy called The Agreeable Disappointment," in *Harmonia Anglicana*, series 5 (London: J. Walsh, 1703).

20. Burnaby, *Love Betray'd*, p. [ii].

21. *Roger North on Music*, ed. John Wilson (London: Novello, [1959]), p. 353.

22. Ibid., pp. 353-54.

23. Peter J. Seng, *The Vocal Songs in the Plays of Shakespeare* (Cambridge, Mass.: Harvard University Press, 1967), p. 180.

24. Gildon, *Measure for Measure*, p. 31.

25. John Eccles, "A Song, set by Mr. John Eccles, Sung by Mr. Knapp in the Tragedy of Hamlet, Prince of Denmark" ([London]: Tho. Cross, [ca. 1700]).

26. Philip H. Highfill, *A Biographical Dictionary of Actors, Actresses, Musicians, Dancers, Managers, and Other Stage Personnel in London, 1660-1800*, 12 vols. (Carbondale: Southern Illinois University Press, 1973–), s.v. "Mason, John."

27. John Walsh (d. 1736) founded an important music publishing firm. His periodical music prints were influential. Later in the century the firm published many of Handel's works. See William C. Smith, "Introduction" to *A Bibliography of the Musical Works Published by John Walsh During the Years 1695-1720* (London: Oxford University Press, 1948; The Bibliographical Society, 1968), pp. v-xxix.

28. Curtis Price has noted that Restoration composers associated G minor with the subject of death.   "Music as Drama," in *London Theatre World*, p. 222.

29. Hogan,   *Shakespeare   in   the   Theatre*,   1:268-69,   423. Performances may have been even more numerous than the incomplete records suggest.

30. *Daily Courant*, 21 November 1702.

31. John   Hawkins   had   a   low   opinion   of   Leveridge's   social behavior: "Being a man of rather coarse manners, and being able to drink a good deal, [Leveridge] was by some thought to be a good companion." *A General History of the Science and Practice of Music*, 2:827.

32. See Olive Baldwin and Thelma Wilson, "Richard Leveridge, 1670–1758," *Musical Times* 111:592-94, 891-93, 988-90 for a discussion of Leveridge's compositional style.

33. Roger Fiske, *English Theatre Music in the Eighteenth Century*, 2d ed. (London: Oxford University Press, 1986), p. 27.

34. Robert Etheridge Moore, "The Music to *Macbeth*," *Musical Quarterly* 47 (1961):33-34.

35. See *London Stage*, pt. 1, p. 441.

36. British Library Add. MS 27962 Q, fol. 33r, quoted in John Orrell, *The Theatres of Inigo Jones and John Webb* (Cambridge: Cambridge University Press, 1985), p. 168.

37. Richard Leacroft, *The Development of the English Playhouse* (Ithaca: Cornell University Press, 1973), p. 81.

38. A list of acting company members, based on known documentary evidence, is at the beginning of each seasonal calendar in *London Stage*, pts. 1 and 2.

39. *London Stage*, pt. 1, p. 36.

40. Ibid., pt. 2, 1:26.

41. William Barclay Squire, "Purcell's Dramatic Music," *Sammelbande der Internationalen Musikgesellschaft* 5 (1903–4):553.

42. J. A. Westrup, *Purcell*, rev. Nigel Fortune (London: Dent, 1980), p. 140.

43. Robert Etheridge Moore, *Henry Purcell and the Restoration Theatre* (Cambridge, Mass.: Harvard University Press, 1961), p. 178.

44. Barclay Squire, "Purcell's Dramatic Music," p. 554.

45. Add. MS 37027 is the main source for the Purcell Society edition.

46. *London Stage*, pt. 1, p. 441.

47. Margaret Laurie, "Did Purcell Set *The Tempest?*" *Proceedings of the Royal Musical Association* 40 (1963–4):43-57.

48. Ibid. pp. 48-49.

49. Moore, *Henry Purcell*, pp. 202-3.

50. Charles Burney, *A General History of Music* [1789], ed. Frank Mercer, 2 vols. (New York: Dover, 1957), 2:679.

51. Ibid.

52. Richard Leveridge, *The Comick Masque of Pyramus and Thisbe* (London: W. Mears, 1716), pp. [i-ii].

53. Ibid., p. 9.

54. Shakespeare was not widely known on the Continent until the late eighteenth century. See Oswald LeWinter, "Introduction" to *Shakespeare in Europe* (Cleveland: Meridian, 1963), pp. xi-xxxiii.

55. There were at least sixty performances of Shakespeare at Lincoln's-Inn-Fields and Drury Lane in the 1719–20 season. Hogan, *Shakespeare on the Stage*, 1:18-20.

3

Shakespeare Rediscovered: Shakespeare Music in the Age of Ballad Opera, 1720–1750

Shakespearean production was an important part of theatrical activity in the 1720s and 1730s; however, only a limited part of the canon was represented on stage. The plays that did appear were repeated often and worked their way into the basic repertoire. Music was not an important part of these productions. Instead, theatre composers were putting their efforts into pantomime, dances, and venues other than full-length plays. Yet in the years when the Shakespearean repertoire was stable and (for the most part) unmusical, the theatre was the scene of literary, social, and musical developments soon to transform the playhouse offerings. In the 1730s the revival of a long-neglected group of Shakespeare's comedies—and the need to create an eighteenth-century musical style to complement them—proved to be the basis for Shakespearean stage revision and its accompanying music through the remainder of the century.

SHAKESPEARE ON STAGE AND IN PRINT

A few of Shakespeare's plays had become part of the standard theatrical fare by 1730. Cibber and other serious actors had made *Henry IV, Part 1; Hamlet; Macbeth; Julius Caesar; Othello;* and *Henry VIII* popular favorites.[1] Of the comedies, only *The Tempest* and *The Merry Wives of Windsor* were regularly offered. The public image of Shakespeare was as a tragic dramatist. During the Cibber years comedies outnumbered serious plays in the general repertoire by more than three to one.[2] At the same time Shakespeare was represented primarily by tragedies in the updated versions by Tate, Cibber, and others.

While the theatres presented a narrow view of the Shakespearean canon, literary activity began to refocus critical attention on all of the plays. An important factor in the rebirth of interest was the availability of affordable printed versions. Nicholas Rowe, the first modern editor, released his set in 1709. Editions by Alexander Pope (1725) and Lewis Theobald (1733) followed. Theobald, concerned with text transmission and source reliability, has been recognized as the originator of modern Shakespearean scholarship.[3]

The reprinting of Shakespeare and concern for textual history was itself symptomatic of a gradual abandonment of neoclassical standards as the criteria for judging Shakespeare. Alexander Pope articulated this new view:

Homer himself drew not his art so immediately from the fountain of nature. . . . [Shakespeare] is not so much an Imitator, as an instrument of Nature; and 'tis not so just to say that he speaks from her as that she speaks thro' him.[4]

While Restoration Shakespeare apologists such as Dryden had considered the playwright a "rough and rude" genius, the Augustans accepted Shakespeare's expansiveness of style and viewpoint: "Whether we view [Shakespeare] on the Side of Art or Nature, he ought equally to engage our attention."[5]

This shift in critical judgment affected stage activity more slowly than had seventeenth-century neoclassicism. Immediately after the Restoration, the theatre had been under the control of intellectuals connected with the court. The patronage ties between court and theatre had been severed by 1700. After the turn of the century, the economic influence of an increasingly upper middle-class audience became a deciding factor in what appeared on the stage.[6]   Literary figures such as Pope continued to work for a limited aristocratic audience who shared standards of education and taste, standards that were different from the audience tastes that shaped theatrical repertoire.

MUSIC IN STAGE PRODUCTIONS, 1720–1736

Afterpieces and Processionals

No musical Shakespeareana on the scale of the operatic *Tempest* or *Macbeth* was created between 1720 and 1736. This was not just the result of the limited representation of Shakespeare in the theatres. Most dramatic musical activity was channeled into pantomimes, which made up a significant part of the theatre schedule after 1715. Lincoln's-Inn-Fields actor-manager John Rich found there was a large audience for his wordless comic performances in which action was detailed by gestures. Not surprisingly, pantomimes were eventually added to the Drury Lane schedule. These entertainments usually shared an evening's bill with a full-length play and became known as "afterpieces." (Similarly, the play was called the "mainpiece.")   Much of the music written for the patent houses around 1720 was for pantomime.[7]

The use of afterpieces with Shakespearean mainpieces during the 1720s varied between the two major companies.   At Lincoln's-Inn-Fields, Rich's pantomimes had become the main attraction, and programs were often built around them. Rich frequently paired Shakespearean mainpieces with   light or farcical afterpieces. For example, in 1725 *The Merry Wives of Windsor* was performed with a Harlequin pantomime,[8] and *Hamlet* was offered with French dances in the intervals.[9] Lincoln's-Inn-Fields presented one short Shakespearean farce, Christopher Bullock's *The Cobler of Preston*, a loose adaptation of *The Taming of the Shrew*. A printed playbook includes three song texts.[10]

Drury Lane, still dominated by Cibber and his colleagues, gained a reputation as the "serious house," a distinction it would maintain through the century. Colley Cibber suggested that Drury Lane was more careful than Lincoln's-Inn-Fields with such pairings. When Drury Lane finally presented its first pantomime in 1724, Cibber felt it necessary to explain:

If I am asked (after condemning these Fooleries, myself) how I came to assent, or continue my Share of Experience to them? I have no better Excuse for my Error than confessing it. I did it against my Conscience! and had not virtue enough to starve by opposing the multitude. . . . we generally made use of these Pantomimes but as Crutches to our weakest Plays: Nor were we so lost to all Sense of what was valuable as to dishonour our best Authors in such company. . . . If therefore we were not so strictly chaste, in the other part of our Conduct, let the Error of it stand among the silly Consequences of Two Stages.[11]

The play records show that Shakespeare was not on his own as often as Cibber suggested, but there was some attempt to choose afterpieces of a less farcical nature for more substantial plays. For example, a notice in the *Daily Courant* of 30 October 1724 noted that *The Tempest* was paired with Handel's *Acis and Galatea*, company of no dishonor for any author.

A special kind of Shakespearean "entertainment" was introduced in the 1720s: the ceremonial procession with music. If a play offered the least excuse for any civil or religious pageantry, a procession could be introduced into the action with little effort. Unlike a masque, a procession required absolutely no dramatic content, yet it offered opportunity for music and visual display.

Colley Cibber was not displeased with the first procession added to *Henry VIII* on 26 October 1727:

Now, sirs, though the Menagers are not all of them able to write Plays, yet they have all of them been able to do (I won't say as good, but at least) as profitable a thing. They have invented and aborn'd a Spectacle, that for Forty Days together has brought more Money to the House than the best Play that ever was writ. The Spectacle I mean, sir, is that of the Coronation-Ceremony of Anna Bullen: and though we allow a good Play to be the more laudable Performance, yet, Sir, in the profitable Part of it, there is no comparison.[12]

The coronation spectacle was so successful at drawing audiences that it was later used more frequently as an independent afterpiece than in its original context.[13] Anonymous music for a processional with a chorus using an added text for the *Henry VIII* coronation survives in a set of part books in the British Library (RM 21.c 43-45), but, as *Henry VIII* was in the repertoires of both companies, it is not certain that this score was the one used at Drury Lane.

Songs and Incidental Music

Surviving scores and textual evidence suggest little music was written specifically for Shakespearean plays between 1720 and 1736. One production that did include dramatically integrated music was *Love in a Forest*, Charles Johnson's adaptation of *As You Like It* (Drury Lane, 9 January 1723). Johnson made some topical changes to the text and introduced the Pyramus and Thisbe comedy, spoken, into the last act. Two of the five song lyrics by Shakespeare in the folio text were retained in *Love in a Forest*. No music for "Under the Greenwood Tree" survives, but Henry Carey's setting of "What Shall He Have That Killed the Deer" was preserved in two prints under the title "The Huntsman's Song".

Carey (1690-1743) was primarily a writer, but he was also a musician of some modest skill. In "The Huntman's Song" he found an appropriate expression for the feigned rusticity of the duke and his court, exiled in the forest of Arden. The use of a *rondeau*-like musical structure for a strophic verse-and-chorus text provided unexpected variety. The song was eventually performed apart from the play as an entr'acte and listed in the *Daily Courant* playbill for 12 May 1724 as a major attraction. The advertisement mentioned the song was "accompany'd with French Horns," still something of a novelty in the theatre. The published copies of the song have no horn parts.

Typographical evidence in the printed text of *Love in a Forest*
suggests that a monologue verse Shakespeare had intended to be
spoken was used by Johnson as a song text.   In the wedding
masque in *As You Like It* (folio V, 4), Hymen descends accompanied by "soft music" to bless the lovers with two verses, one of
which is labeled a song. (The folio stage direction for music with
"Then There Is Mirth in Heaven" was to cover the noise of the
machine used for Hymen's entrance.)[14]   In *Love in a Forest*,
Johnson shortened the masque to accommodate the Pyramus and
Thisbe scene.   The song lyric "Wedding Is Great Juno's Crown"
was cut, but the verse "Then There Is Mirth in Heaven" was retained.   In the published play text, this verse and the earlier songs
"Under the Greenwood Tree" and "What Shall He Have That
Killed the Deer" are printed in italics.   Spoken verse (e.g., the
poems to Rosalind in act III) are not in italics.   This suggests
Hymen sang "Then There Is Mirth in Heaven" in the 1723 production.   Moreover, Hymen was played by "Miss Lindar," a
singing actress whose other roles included Ariel in the operatic
Tempest.[15]   No music for "Then There Is Mirth in Heaven" is
known.

Two Shakespeare songs by Richard Leveridge were published
in the 1720s.   A simple setting of "The Cuckoo Song" ("When
Daisies Pied," *Love's Labour's Lost* III, 2) appeared in a broadside dated 1725.   "Who Is Silvia?" (*Two Gentlemen of Verona*
IV, 2) was included in a 1727 collection of Leveridge's music.
The song, which appears complete in Appendix A, displays an
unusual rhythmic variety.   There is no performance record for
either *Love's Labour's Lost* or *Two Gentlemen of Verona* during
the 1720s.   A newspaper notice for a 1735 performance of *Two
Gentlemen* at the York Buildings Theatre confirms the play had
not been staged in London for 73 years.[16]   The page headings on
both songs fail to mention any production, singer, or theatre;
however, Leveridge's continuing stage career would indicate the
songs were either interpolated into other plays or used as
entr'acte entertainment.   These are the first known eighteenth-
century settings of Shakespeare song texts as poetry divorced
from their dramatic contexts.   A mountain of such settings, for

concert or amateur use, would be produced in the last third of the century, but in the 1720s the practice was unique.

Unfortunately, much of the Shakespeare-related music of this time is known only through handbills and newspaper advertisements. Purcell's music for *Timon of Athens* was replaced at both theatres. In 1729 Drury Lane substituted an all-dance masque that included a concerto by Corelli.[17] A "new Grand Overture" by Johann Christoph Pepusch opened a Covent Garden production of *Timon* on 1 May 1733. It included a new masque, "addressed to Timon . . . in Honour of Flora, the Goddess of Spring," by Thomas Roseingrave.[18] In 1730, Lincoln's-Inn-Fields advertised two new songs sung by Richard Leveridge in the character of the first gravedigger in *Hamlet*.[19] The *London Daily Post and General Advertiser* announced "New Musick proper to" *Hamlet* by Carey (29 February 1736) and an overture for *Richard III* by a Mr. Bellear (18 March 1734), part of the completely unknown repertoire from the maverick theatre at Goodman's Fields. Given the limited resources of the upstart stage and the tendency for the same composers to work at all the theatres, it is unlikely that Goodman's Fields produced significant unknown Shakespeareana.

The Sheffield/Galliard *Julius Caesar* Choruses

John Sheffield, Duke of Buckingham, altered and expanded Shakespeare's *Julius Caesar* into two plays: *The Tragedy of Marcus Brutus* and his own *Julius Caesar*. Sheffield arrived at a unique solution to the problem of pairing musical entertainments with serious mainpieces in his *Julius Caesar* plays. To each he added four poems, which were to be set as "choruses"; however, Sheffield considered these texts as choruses in a commentarial rather than a musical sense.

The duke died in 1721, but his widow Katherine went forward with plans to stage the plays privately. Giovanni Bononcini, a composer recently arrived from Italy, was chosen to set the *Marcus Brutus* choruses, while Johann Ernst Galliard, a German

established in London, provided the *Julius Caesar* music.
Marcus Brutus, with Bononcini's choruses, was performed only
once at Buckingham House 11 January 1723; however, the
Duchess of Buckingham, a Jacobite who feared retribution for the
political content of the plays, postponed the appearance of *Julius
Caesar*.[20]

Although the early nineteenth-century theatrical chronicler
Genest claimed at least one eventual production, it is unclear
whether Galliard's music was ever performed in Sheffield's
play.[21] A printed acting copy of a relatively unaltered *Julius
Caesar* includes the text of the Sheffield choruses and suggests a
performance around 1729.[22] Galliard was "attached to Rich"[23] at
Lincoln's-Inn-Fields, which might have been the source of the
acting copy. In addition to any performances the music may have
received with some form of *Julius Caesar*, the choruses were
performed detached from the play during the 1730s at the King's
Theatre, Lincoln's-Inn-Fields, and Hickford's Rooms.

Two manuscript sources for Galliard's music survive: the
1723 autograph dated and annotated by the Duchess of Buckingham (Boston Public Library M. Cab. 1.15) and a working copy
with corrections and performance indications (British Library
Add. MS 25484). The latter identifies the tenor soloist as "Mr.
[John] Beard," who sang in the performances in the 1730s. The
annotations in the score were made at the time of the independent
performances.[24]

Sheffield's attempt to control the companion musical piece to
provide an evening's entertainment with a single focus was
unique. The version of Sheffield's *Julius Caesar* published in
1723 indicates the verses are to be sung after the fifth and final
act. The segregation of music into the pantomimes, companion
pieces, and intervals that had arisen after the theatrical reorganizations was still the norm into the 1720s. By providing texts that
could be set as discrete cantatas, Sheffield encouraged music that
would contribute to the affect and moral of the play while having
no purely dramatic function.

Galliard's setting—the largest Shakespeare-related score since
the dramatic operas—stands in sharp contrast to the theatrical

miniatures produced at the same time; however, the musical resources required—chorus, soloists, and orchestra (four-part strings, alternating oboes and flutes, continuo)—were well within the means of the theatres presenting pantomimes and orchestral works. The four choruses together last well over an hour. Each is a clearly organized unit of five to seven movements showing a tonal arch form. (The six-movement first chorus is the exception: F, d, F, a, d, B-flat.) Four-part choral movements alternate with arias, duets, and accompanied recitative. Some of the arias segue into the following choruses, strengthening the structural unity. The third chorus, "Representing Two Ariel Spirits after Much Thunder and Lightning," is a cantata for two soloists.

Galliard was well versed in the Italian style and had written two operas for London. He had also worked as an orchestral player under Handel. The two composers were on friendly terms and subscribed to each other's published works.[25] Handel's influence is apparent in the operatic nature of the solo vocal numbers and, in choral movements such as that shown in Example 16, the use of contrapuntal lines building to homophonic climaxes.

Yet music written for the provinces, not the London opera stage, may have been a model for Galliard. Handel wrote the serenata *Acis and Galatea* and the oratorio *Esther* for the Duke of Chandos. The works were performed at the duke's country residence. Neither was performed in London until after 1730.

In both pieces, the function of the chorus was novel. Italian operas and other musico-dramatic forms typically emphasized the role of the solo singer. Choruses were small-scale, dramatically unimportant movements. In *Acis and Galatea* and *Esther*, the chorus assumes an active role in the proceedings, and the choral movements are substantial constructions. Moreover, Handel avoided a strict adherence to a recitative/aria sequence in *Acis and Galatea*, creating series of musical numbers with a greater sense of musical continuity.

These features are also seen in the Galliard score. The chorus assumes a persona capable of delivering the Sophoclean gestures of Sheffield's poetry. Paul Henry Lang noted a parallel between the French revival of the classic chorus in drama and Handel's increased use of the chorus in oratorio.[26] The French model may have also been an influence on Sheffield. Galliard's use of segues between solos and ensembles without recitative (especially in the first chorus) again resembles technique used by Handel in *Acis*. If the two expatriates were indeed on amicable terms, Galliard could very well have known and been influenced by Handel's example in these works.[27]

Ex. 16. Galliard. *Julius Caesar.* Fourth chorus, mm. 5-16. Chorus parts only.

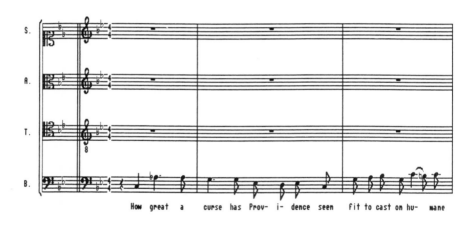

by permission of the Boston Public Library

It is difficult to draw conclusions about the Shakespeare-related music of the 1720s and early 1730s when so much of it is known only through newspaper notices and references in printed texts. The surviving music and the descriptions of lost works represent little in the way of actual dramatic music. This limited musical repertoire can be attributed only in part to the restricted play offerings. Those songs and masques that do occur, such as those in *Love in a Forest*, are isolated incidents, reduced from

Shakespeare's intentions and without the length or elaborate structures of their Restoration counterparts. Most of the music—processions, interval music, the lost overtures—has no direct textual referents. The connection, however tenuous, that Restoration theatre composers had built between play and music had disintegrated. However, in the final years of the 1730s, composers would begin to create a new repertoire of dramatic Shakespearean song.

THE THEATRE IN THE 1730s

The practice of using music in Shakespearean plays had become moribund by the late 1720s, but the 1730s brought three important changes. First, conventions of music in plays were transformed by the popularity of a new musico-dramatic genre, the ballad opera. Second, waning popularity of Italian opera allowed more British composers opportunities to write significant dramatic music. At the same time, the Shakespeare literary revival that began with the play editions by Rowe, Pope, and Theobald finally influenced play selection in the theatres.

The Beggar's Opera (Lincoln's-Inn-Fields, 29 January 1728) startled London audiences familiar with the omnipresent Italian opera. Theatre-goers who "used to sit together like an Audience of Foreigners in their own country, and to hear whole Plays acted before them in a Tongue which they did not understand,"[28] were presented with a story of English origin and in English. This was the first representative of a new theatrical genre, the ballad opera. The twentieth-century scholar W. L. Lawrence has provided a working definition: "Broadly speaking, 'ballad opera' . . . signified a play of humorous, satirical, or pastoral order intermixed with simple song, the music for which was for the most part derived from popular ditties of street-ballad type."[29] Ballad opera's success was based in the ways it differed from Italian opera. It was in English, not Italian. The plots were topical rather than classical. The songs were either popular tunes or newly composed melodies in a popular idiom, and the music was interspersed throughout the play's action amidst spoken dialogue.   One characteristic ballad opera acquired from its Italian counterpart, in contradiction to previous English musico-dramatic practice, was the assignment of principal characters to singing roles.   Ballad opera itself would hold the stage for scarcely a decade, but the format would affect other theatre offerings.

Only one Shakespearean play was adapted as a ballad opera for London. *The Taming of the Shrew* and Lacy's *Sauny the Scot* were the sources for *A Cure for a Scold*, written by Jeremy Worsdale.[30] The opera opened at Drury Lane in February 1735. The printed play book gives the text for 23 songs, but no score survives.

At the same time ballad opera was making inroads into the theatrical repertoire, an attempt was made to revive interest in serious, completely sung English opera. The backer of this venture was Thomas Arne, father of Thomas the composer. The group included musicians and librettists who worked for the theatres in various capacities: Henry Carey, the younger Arne, J. F. Lampe, and John Christopher Smith. In the spring of 1732 the group opened a season at the Haymarket. The effort was short-lived because of the inadequacies of the group's librettists and the inexperience of the two young composers of promise, Arne and Smith. Burney considered the attempted competition with Handel "the contention of Infants with a Giant."[31] The project did provide an opportunity for these composers to work in a more ambitious dramatic format than was possible in the regular theatrical season, even if what they produced was "an humble and timid imitation of Handel's style of composition."[32]

In 1737 the new Licensing Act went into effect, strengthening the crown's control over theatrical presentations. Clearly a gagging bill, the act silenced political satire.[33] It also put an end to the unsanctioned theatres that for some years had operated illegally in competition with the two patent houses. Less competition and closer censorial regulation brought about a decline in the number of new scripts. Older plays were revived to fill gaps in the repertoire.

A group of aristocratic women of letters, known only as Shakespeare's Ladies, took advantage of this situation. These "Ladies of Great Britain were so earnest to prop the sinking State of Wit and Sense that they form'd themselves into a Society and revived the memory of the forsaken Shakespeare."[34] The identities of the group's members are unknown, but they must have been women of high social position to have had such influence on theatrical management. Advertisements for the new Shakespeare productions claimed the plays were presented "At the desire of several Ladies of Quality."[35]

Shakespeare performances increased at both theatres, but Rich was more daring in reviving long-neglected plays. In the 1737–38 season Covent Garden played *Hamlet, Macbeth, Lear, Cymbeline, Much Ado about Nothing, Richard II, Henry IV (Parts 1 and 2), Henry V, King John*, and *The Merry Wives of Windsor*. The loss of music for these performances is particularly frustrating. None of the music appears to have been published or even mentioned in the daily advertisements. Fortunately, when the Drury Lane company turned its attention to long-neglected plays, the music from these productions survived to become the core of the Shakespeare repertoire for nearly the next century.

SHAKESPEARE MUSIC, 1737–1750

Arne's Shakespeare Music

In 1740 Drury Lane patentee Charles Fleetwood and actor Charles Macklin began to add long-ignored Shakespearean plays to the theatre's schedule and to withdraw some of the adaptations already in the repertoire in favor of more accurate texts (e.g., *As You Like It*).[36] In the process, they inherited a number of song lyrics absent from the stage for a century. The Elizabethan tunes had long been disregarded and may have been unknown to eighteenth-century performers. Thomas Arne the younger was now main resident composer at Drury Lane. The eleven songs and one masque he provided for Macklin's productions are the first major eighteenth-century response to authentic Shakespeare lyrics. The songs, written by a composer attuned to the music and dramatic conventions of Italian opera and the English stage, are themselves a mixture of Italian and English styles.

Relatively few Arne manuscripts survive because of fires at theatres and churches where Arne worked. Most of Arne's Shakespeare music is known only though contemporary prints. The scoring and length of the individual items show the influence of Italian and ballad opera on songs inserted into spoken plays. The songs are modestly scored for theatre orchestra: violins (sometimes in unison), a bass line with figures, and occasional obbligato flute.[37] Even this light scoring implies the use of a pit orchestra. The realistic introduction of on-stage instrumentalists in incidental songs is here replaced by the orchestral convention of Italian and ballad opera.

Although the songs are shorter than comparable arias in Arne's masque *Comus* (1738) and his *Tempest* masque (1746), they are longer than incidental songs from earlier periods. A vocal solo of fifty measures or more was an unusual digression from the play's action. The average length of solo songs in *Comus* is seventy-one measures. The longest song has 168 measures, the shortest 30. Arne's Shakespeare songs average 52 measures, with a high of 84 and a low of 30. Most Elizabethan settings fall between 20 and 24 measures. All figures disregard repeat signs.

Burney described Arne's melodic style as "easy, natural, and agreeable."[38] Many of the songs are in six-eight or three-eight meter, not just for a pastoral or rustic effect,[39] but to accommodate the regular rhythmic stress pattern of the text without disturbing the metric regularity of the music. The occasional cross relation between text stress and musical stress (e.g., on the word "merry" in Example 17) does not destroy the song's metric pattern but simply adds variety. The alteration of stressed and unstressed syllables does not interfere with the flow of the larger units (e.g., the dotted eighth note in six-eight).

None of the Arne songs approach the simplicity of the slighter tunes that had been used in productions earlier in the century.

Example 18, an anonymous epilogue tune for *The Merry Wives of Windsor* (Lincoln's-Inn-Fields, ca. 1720), is an extreme example of how textual stress patterns raise the potential for monotony.

Ex. 17. Arne. "Under the Greenwood Tree," mm. 13-18.

by permission of the British Library

Ex. 18. [Epilogue Song], *Merry Wives of Windsor.*

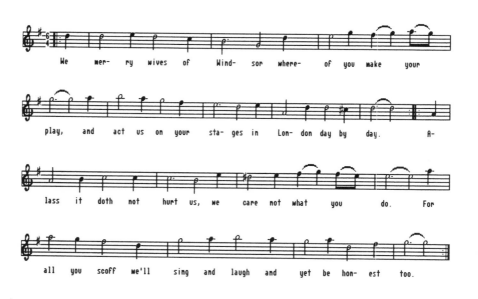

by permission of the British Library

Arne's songs are longer and more elaborately phrased than many of the ballad tunes used in other contemporary productions.[40] "Tell Me Where Is Fancy Bred" (*The Merchant of Venice* III, 2) is Italianate in its vocal range, word repetition, melisma, and ornamentation.

Ex. 19. Arne. "Tell Me Where Is Fancy Bred," mm. 7-18.

by permission of the British Library

Ex. 20. Arne. "Where the Bee Sucks," mm. 21-25.

by permission of the British Library

Most often, Arne avoided instrumental vocal lines, large leaps, passage work, melisma and ranges of over an octave. "Tell Me Where Is Fancy Bred," however, has a range of almost two octaves. One leap covers the octave and a sixth from tenor c# to a above middle c.[41] Melisma was used sparingly to illustrate images in the text, such as Ariel's reference to flying in "Where the Bee Sucks" (Example 20.) In the opening measures of the first setting of "Come Away, Death" from *Twelfth Night* II, 4 (complete in Appendix A), Arne made effective use of melodic leaps, but the result here is more reminiscent of Purcell than of Italian opera.

Arne used *da capo* form infrequently in the songs. Occasionally he used a written-out *da capo* if the text permitted (e.g., "Under the Greenwood Tree"). Rather than force strophic lyrics into a tripartite form, Arne more commonly used binary (or rounded binary) form. The repeat of both halves extended the length of the song and destroyed the impression of a verse/chorus structure. The parallel structure of the verses in the strophic "Come Away, Death" is retained while the musical repetition at the beginning of the second verse (mm. 42-48) is disguised by harmonic alteration of the opening phrase. Each vocal phrase is echoed by a short instrumental refrain, which further disguises the song's two stanzas by giving the impression of a continuous ritornello-like structure.

Arne used limited orchestral resources cleverly. The instrumental introductions, rather than simply anticipating the vocal line, display melodic independence. The phrasing, articulation, and dynamics of the printed scores are unusually explicit for such sources. The flute parts are treated with variety and rarely double the strings. In two of the songs, "Under the Greenwood Tree" and "When Isacles Hang by the Wall" ["The Owl"], the flute is used in imitation of birdsong. The flute, rather than the violins, doubles the voice in "Where the Bee Sucks." The voice, strings, and flute participate in a charming echo effect in "Under the Greenwood Tree."

Most of the songs were appropriate to the plays in which they were used and were introduced according to Shakespeare's stage directions. In addition, some lyrics from other plays and by other authors were used. These additions were intended for major characters, notably Celia in *As You Like It* and Lorenzo in *The Merchant of Venice*. The placement of the added songs varied. Some were inserted where Shakespeare gave a simple stage direction for music. Other examples indicate that the songs were beginning to take on a more picturesque, less realistic function.

In the Drury Lane *Merchant of Venice* elopement scene (II, 6), Lorenzo was given a serenade to sing outside Jessica's window. Some half-century later Genest found the inclusion of this song absurd to the point of offensiveness.[42] According to Restoration and Elizabethan practice, this was precisely the wrong place to introduce a song, especially with a main character suddenly bursting into song at a most inappropriate moment. Mid-eighteenth-century audiences had been prepared for the insertion of such songs by *The Beggar's Opera* and its progeny, now making additions such as Lorenzo's serenade acceptable. While the relaxation of the taboo against singing main characters was important, the actual dramatic value of the change should not be overstated. In a 1759 revival of *Merchant* , for instance, a nonsinging actor took the part of Lorenzo, and the songs were assigned to a singer, possibly in the role of a servant.[43]

Arne worked on two productions of *The Tempest* for the Drury Lane theatre. An advertisement for the 1740 revival of the

Dryden/Shadwell version claims Arne provided only two songs, probably added to the "Purcell" score.[44] For a production opening 31 January 1746, John Lacy revived Shakespeare's original text, adding Shadwell's Neptune and Amphitrite masque to the last act.[45] A manuscript score for this second production is the most problematic of Arne's Shakespeare sources.

Additional MS 29370 was acquired by the British Library in 1876. It includes three separate sections bound together. The first is a collection of Arne's Vauxhall songs in single-sheet prints dating from the 1760s and 1770s. Added to this are several pages of manuscript music with no apparent watermark. This manuscript includes music from *The Tempest* and the opera *Rosamund* (dated in the manuscript 1746 and 1733, respectively). Three rare Arne autograph scores (non-Shakespearean music) are bound in at the end of the volume. The manuscript score that includes the *Tempest* music is not in Arne's hand. The calligraphy is unusually neat, and there are no indications of performance details. The volume is possibly a reference copy. The source from which the copyist worked appears to have been incomplete at the time MS 29370 was made. The original was possibly a theatre copy lost during the Drury Lane fire of 1809. If all three parts of the volume were assembled at the same time, MS 29370 dates from 1770-1800.

The *Tempest* score includes the following numbers:

1. "Come unto These Yellow Sands"
2. "Behold Your Faithful Ariel Fly"
3. "Ere You Can Say Come and Go"
4. The Wedding Masque
   a. "Ceres, Most Bounteous Lady"
   b. "Thou with Thy Saffron Wings" (incomplete)
   c. [". . . Play with Sparrows"] (incomplete)
   d. "High Queen of State"
   e. "Honour, Riches, Marriage Blessing"
   f. "Ye Nymphs Called Naiads"
   g. "You Sunburnt Sicklemen"
5. "Wide o're This Bright Ariel Scene"

The absence of "Where the Bee Sucks" from MS 29370 and the text's inclusion in the Shadwell version suggest the song may have been one of the two Arne wrote for the 1740 revival; however, the manuscript's incompleteness and the song's first publication date of 1747 keep such speculation inconclusive. In the 1746 production, a setting of "Where the Bee Sucks" by William Defesch may have been used.[46]

Arne's work for *The Tempest* was more ambitious than his other Shakespeare music. The string writing is in four parts. Indications for alternating flutes suggest oboes were intended but not indicated. The arias are more operatic than the earlier songs. Most surprising is the inclusion of the fourth-act masque of Iris, Ceres, and Juno, missing from the play since Davenant's time. The Neptune and Amphitrite masque, attributed to Arne in the newspaper announcement, is lost.

Some of the texts set by Arne were not originally intended as song lyrics. In the fourth act, Ariel's poetic response to Prospero's command to lead in the low comics became an aria:

> Before you can say come and go
> And breathe twice and cry so, so
> Each one tripping on his toe
> Will be here with mop and mow. (IV: 1, lines 44-77)

Even though the text differs from the surrounding verse by having a strict rhyme scheme and scansion, Arne (or perhaps Lacy) felt the need for a buffer between the play and the song. A short recitative to an added text, "Behold Your Faithful Ariel Fly," prefaces the aria.

The nuptial masque, also in folio IV, 1, includes only two music directions: the blessing song and a dance of nymphs and reapers. Arne set the entire masque to music. Like Ariel's song before, the rhyme scheme and scansion of the goddesses' speeches are quite regular. There is a certain amount of narrative not directly related to the play's main action in these lines. Arne wrote a series of arias, one for each goddess, and a concluding trio with chorus, all connected with recitative. The text was slightly altered to allow the recitative/aria pairs. Unfortunately, the missing pages fell across some of this text.

Ceres's aria text is set off by changing a descriptive dependent clause into an independent address. A few measures are missing from the end of this bipartite aria (an A, A' form where the first section cadences in the dominant and the second section—similar to the first in melodic material and treatment—ends in the tonic). Only a fragment remains of Iris's aria. All of the preceding recitative is missing as well. The blessing, a duet in the folio text, becomes a *da capo* solo for Juno. A choral dance concludes the masque.

The Arne songs from the 1740s were important in reviving the popularity of Shakespeare's lyrics. The composer combined the simpler characteristics of the English ballad and the artifice of Continental music to achieve a melodic style suited to Shakespeare's poetry. Arne almost always retained a semblance of the poetry's original meter, and the text was not lost in a flurry of notes. The music was commercially successful. Two collections were published shortly after the first productions, and the songs appeared frequently in periodicals. Arne's songs were to be the model for almost all of the settings, theatrical and nontheatrical, that would follow in the next half-century.

Only a few years after Arne wrote his settings for Drury Lane, Thomas Chilcot, organist at Bath Abbey, turned his attention to Shakespearean lyrics. In 1750 Chilcot published a set of "Songs with their Symphonies . . . the Words by Shakespeare and Other Celebrated Poets." Although Chilcot had no connections with the London theatres, the list of subscribers to the volume was lengthy and included Handel and Boyce.[47] Chilcot's songs are reminiscent of Arne's, mostly binary in form and carefully orchestrated. They are more elaborate than Arne's, being scored for four-part strings and an occasional obbligato instrument. The vocal writing is consistently more Italianate. Some have motto beginnings. The songs were not intended for the stage, but their wide distribution may have led to their use, especially in productions of *Henry VIII* and *Antony and Cleopatra* in the late 1750s. The music attests to the influence of Arne's model. Chilcot's songs were important and ambitious settings, circulated widely enough to be influential.

Operatic Shakespeare

Pyramus and Thisbe

Johann Friedrich Lampe, a colleague of Arne's in the opera venture of the 1730s, produced a burlesque on the Pyramus and Thisbe plot for Covent Garden in 1745. The title page of the score calls the piece a "mock opera," and indeed a good deal of mocking by word and tune takes place. The libretto (Bodleian Malone MS 151) was rewritten and shortened from Leveridge's version. The introductory rehearsal scene was eliminated, and the spoken interjections of Mr. Semibreve and his companions were cut to a minimum. Except for these comments, the opera was entirely sung. The recitatives were not included in the printed score.

The work is a curious mix of spirited melodies and broad musical humor. It is a piece of some ambition, scored for four-part strings and horns and oboes in pairs. The overture, in four movements, begins boisterously, turning to an *affetuoso* in the minor that leads into the opening scene.

Lampe's score lampooned a number of operatic practices, including nonsensical word repetition to sustain a musical line.

Ex. 21. Lampe. *Pyramus and Thisbe.* "The Wall's Song," mm. 34-45, string parts condensed.

by permission of the British Library

The misuse of instrumental figuration in vocal lines was targeted, and even an entire aria type (the "rage" aria) was caricatured. There are a number of passages, such as that below in Example 22, that seem to parody overuse of the Scotch snap. English composers had used the Scotch snap since the seventeenth century to facilitate the setting of short, accented syllables of dissyllabic words, a characteristic more common in English than French or Italian.   However, Lampe's setting of "But Shall I Go Mourn for That" from *The Winter's Tale* (Covent Garden, 1742) in Example 23 suggests English composers were attracted to rhythmic device for its own affective quality as well.

Ex. 22. Lampe. *Pyramus and Thisbe.* "And Thou, O Wall," mm. 13-18.

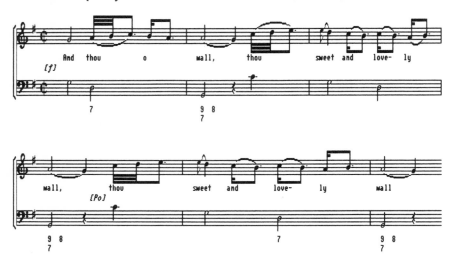

by permission of the British Library

Ex. 23. Lampe. "But Shall I Go Mourn For That," mm. 7- 14.

by permission of the British Library

Although Lampe's harmonic construction within individual numbers in *Pyramus* is conservative, the keys of the individual movements display a use of arch form that mirrors the rising and falling action of the script.

1. Overture   F; F; F; f
2. "The Wretched Sighs and Groans"   g
3. "And Thou O Wall"   G
4. "O Wicked Wall"   e
5. "Fly Swift Good Time"   D
6. "Not Cephalus to Procris"   G
7. "I Go Without Delay"   c
8. "Ladies Don't Fright Ye"   c
9. "The Man in the Moon Am I Sir"   G
10. "Where Is My Love"   a
11. "Approach Ye Furies Fell"   B-flat
12. "Now Am I Dead"   g
13. "These Lily Lips"   g
14. "This Folding, Beholding"   F

Tonal relationships had been used to unify dramatic compositions since Purcell's time. Here the organization may have been influenced by the plot. The symmetry of the plan is maintained while introducing the half-step relationships (A minor and B-flat) at numbers 10 and 11. The slapstick among the Lion, Pyramus, and Thisbe that occurs between numbers 9 and 10 is the climax of the stage business. The lost recitative for these sections must have provided modulatory tonal preparations for the items in A minor and B-flat. The spoof of serious opera's obligatory happy ending returns to the opening F major.

Rosalinda

Unlike Zeno's *Hamlet*, Paolo Rolli's libretto for *Rosalinda*, taken from *As You Like It*, is unquestionably a Shakespearean adaptation; however, many of the incidents in Shakespeare's plot were omitted in the simplification. The plot was reduced to its barest essentials, leaving only the characters equivalent to Rosalind, Celia, Orlando, Frederick, and the Duke. The removal of the acerbic Jacques and the rude comics highlights the differences between a Shakespearean pastoral and the Italian genre. Francesco Maria Veracini wrote the music for *Rosalinda*. It opened at the King's Theatre 31 January 1744 and played for only twelve performances. Burney wrote unfavorably of the work:

The first Air that presents itself in the printed copy of the favorite songs is "The Lass of Patie's Mill," which Monticelli condescended to sing, and Veracini to set parts and ritornels to, in order, as they imagined, to flatter the English. But as few of the North Britons, or admirers of this national and natural Music, frequent the opera, or mean to give half a guinea to hear a Scots tune, which perhaps their cook-maid Peggy can sing better than any foreigner, this expedient failed of its intended effect. Veracini's own music in the opera is wild, aukward, and unpleasant; manifestly produced by a man unaccustomed to write for the voice.[48]

Despite Burney's comments, the song is in fact a considerable reworking of the popular air and goes far beyond the simple addition of "parts and ritornels."[49] Burney was correct about the opera's London reception; *Rosalinda* did not enter the regular repertoire at the King's Theatre.

SUMMARY

The Shakespearean stage presence changed between 1720 and 1750. The literary renaissance of interest in the plays began with the publication of Rowe's edition in 1709. By 1720 this revival was yet to affect the theatres, where Shakespeare was still represented by a few Restoration adaptations and a limited number of tragedies and histories in varying degrees of revision. The theatrical musical establishments turned much of their attention to the popular pantomimes and supplemental entertainments rather than spoken plays. From 1720 to the mid 1730s, there is little documentation of music written specifically for Shakespearean production, and only a fraction of the music survives. Then two major theatrical events influenced Shakespearean production and its music.

The success of *The Beggar's Opera* in 1728 and the resulting series of ballad operas presented by the theatres helped to redefine the function of music within spoken plays. In the late 1730s and the 1740s, Rich at Lincoln's-Inn-Fields and Macklin at Drury Lane expanded the Shakespearean repertoire with long-ignored plays and restored texts of plays already in the schedule. Thomas Arne's music for the Drury Lane productions in the 1740s reflected not only contemporary musical styles but the beginnings of operatic conventions in songs created for otherwise all-spoken plays. Unlike much of the music inspired by the Restoration revisions, the new songs were often based on Shakespeare's own texts and stage directions. True operatic treatment of Shakespeare remained a rarity.

In 1747, David Garrick, a member of the Drury Lane company, became co-manager of the theatre. Over the next quarter of a century, Garrick would prove himself the eighteenth century's most important actor and a powerful manager with a shrewd sense of public taste. He also exercised significant literary skill tailoring plays according to his artistic and business instincts. Garrick's influence on London's theatre community and its offerings was profound, and his actor-manager's view of Shakespeare contributed to the next phase in the eighteenth century's attitude toward the playwright.   Garrick's influence on theatrical music was to be no less profound.

NOTES

1. Discussing the formation of the general theatre repertoire, George Winchester Stone suggested "dramatic impact comes not so much in the number of play titles as in the frequency of play performances." "The Making of the Repertory," in *The London Theatre World, 1660-1800*, ed. Robert D. Hume (Carbondale: Southern Illinois University Press, 1980), p. 183.   In the same passage he noted that the frequency and quantity of comments by spectators suggests the impact made by the plays. Stone counted the performances of plays in what he called "the Cibber period," ending ca. 1730. Nine of Shakespeare's works were among the most-repeated plays, each receiving at least seventy performances. Ibid., p. 197.

2. Ibid, p. 95.

3. Textual variants suggest Rowe did not consult folio sources. Arthur Sherbro, *The Birth of Shakespeare Studies* (East Lansing, Mich.: Colleague Press, 1986), p. 2.   Theobald's attack on the suspect sources for Pope's edition caused a vicious, highly publicized dispute between the two writers. Beverly Warner, *Famous Introductions to Shakespeare's Plays* (New York: Bert Franklin, 1968), p. 50.

4. Alexander Pope, "Preface to the Edition of Shakespeare" [1725], in *Eighteenth-Century Essays on Shakespeare*, ed. D. Nicoll Smith (New York: Russell & Russell, 1962), p. 48.

5. Lewis Theobald, "Preface to the Edition of Shakespeare" [1733], in *Eighteenth-Century Essays on Shakespeare*, p. 64

6. Harry William Pedicord, "Changing Audience," in *London Theatre World*, p. 241.

7. Roger Fiske, *English Theatre Music in the Eighteenth Century*, 2d ed. (London: Oxford University Press, 1986), pp. 67-93.

8. *The London Stage, 1660-1800: A Calendar of Plays*. 11 vols. (Carbondale: Southern Illinois University Press, 1960–68), pt. 2, 2:709.

9. Ibid., 719.

10. Christopher Bullock, *The Cobler of Preston.   and the Adventures of Half an Hour* (London: T. Corbett [1723]), pp. 3-4, 11, 16.

11. Colley Cibber, *An Apology for the Life of Colley Cibber*, ed. B.R.S. Fone (Ann Arbor: University of Michigan Press, 1968), pp. 280-81.

12. Ibid., p. 293.

13. Theophilus Cibber took credit for the independent staging of the *Henry VIII* processional, claiming he needed "to bring Wilks to consent that the Coronation should be added to other plays as a detached entertainment." *The Life and Character of the Excellent Actor Mr. Booth* (London, 1753), as quoted in John Genest, *Some Account of the English Stage from the Restoration in 1660 to 1830*, 10 vols. (Bath: for H. E. Carrington, 1832), 3:200.

14. Peter J. Seng, *The Vocal Songs in the Plays of Shakespeare* (Cambridge, Mass.: Harvard University Press, 1967), p. 92.

15. Philip H. Highfill, *A Biographical Dictionary of Actors, Actresses, Musicians, Dancers, Managers, and Other Stage Personnel in London, 1660-1800*, 12 vols. (Carbondale: Southern Illinois University Press, 1973–), s.v. "Lindar, Miss."

16. *London Daily Post and General Advertiser*, 6 October 1735.

17. *Daily Post*, 23 April 1729.

18. *Daily Journal*, 1 May 1733.

19. *Daily Journal*, 15 April 1730.

20. Johann Ernst Galliard, "The Four Chorus's in the Tragedy of Julius Caesar" [1723], Boston Public Library manuscript M. Cab. 1. 15, fol. [1v].

21. Genest, *Some Account of the English Stage*, 3:89-93.

22. *Julius Caesar, a tragedy* (London, 1711), pp. 87-90. A copy is held in the library at the University of Michigan, Ann Arbor. The Sheffield texts are also included in *Julius Caesar, a Tragedy as it is now acted by His Majesty's Servants* (London: J. Tonson and J. Darby, 1729).

23. Charles Burney, *A General History of Music* [1789], ed. Frank Mercer. 2 vols. (New York: Dover, 1957), 2:989.

24. Sheffield's text was printed in the playbook for the larger entertainment *A Serenata (in Three Interludes) call'd Love and Folly . . . as it is performed at the King's Theatre* (London, 1739), pp. 8, 13-16. Galliard also wrote the music for *Love and Folly*.

25. Paul Henry Lang, *Handel* (New York: W. W. Norton, 1966), p. 117.

26. Ibid., pp. 373-77.

27. Handel never wrote any Shakespeare music for the stage. Although Handel's music was often used in the theatres, especially as interval entertainment, the composer did not work for the dramatic companies. Being his own impresario provided him both financial benefits and freedom from requirements of employers. Besides, the theatre was primarily the domain of the English musicians, fairly or unfairly considered to be less well trained. The only Shakespearean texts known to have been set by Handel are a few lines from *Antony and Cleopatra*, incorporated into *Alexander Balus* by librettist Thomas Morell. Winton Dean, *Handel's Dramatic Operas and Masques* (London: Oxford University Press, 1959), p. 484.

28. Joseph Addison, *The Spectator*, 21 March 1711.

29. W. J. Lawrence , "Early Irish Ballad Opera and Comic Opera," *Musical Quarterly* 8 (1922):398.

30. Although Worsdale is named as the author of *A Cure for a Scold* in the published play, the attribution has been questioned. Edmund McAdoo Gagey, *Ballad Opera*, Columbia University Studies in English and Comparative Literature, no. 130 (New York: Benjamin Blom, 1937), p. 121. Another *Shrew*-based ballad opera, modelled on Bullock's *Cobler of Preston*, was performed by a children's company in Dublin in January 1731. Lawrence, "Early Irish Ballad Opera," p. 403.

31. Burney, *General History*, 2:781.

32. Ibid.

33. Genest, referring to the bill some three-quarters of a century after its enactment, claimed that the power given by the act had been "Scandalously abused." *Some Account of the English Stage*, 3:521.

34. *Grub Street Journal*, 3 March 1737, quoted in Emmet L. Avery, "The Shakespeare Ladies Club," *Shakespeare Quarterly* 7 (1956):155-56.

35. Ibid., p. 154.

36. The Macklin playbooks are lost. *Bell's Edition of Shakespeare's Plays*, 8 vols. (London: John Bell, 1774) is thought to represent the Macklin promptbooks for the comedies. William Appleton, *Charles Macklin, An Actor's Life* (Cambridge, Mass.: Harvard University Press, 1960), p. 250.

37. Roger Fiske, after studying ballad opera scores, concluded that violas, when present in the theatre orchestra, doubled the bass. This copied common Italian practice. *English Theatre Music*, p. 117.

38. Burney, *General History*, 2:1029.

39. Since the late sixteenth century the English pastoral tradition had included comic and rustic tendencies that would have been out of place in the elevated Arcadia of the Italian pastoral. Music was one of the ways of portraying rusticity. Ellen T. Harris, *Handel and the Pastoral Tradition* (London: Oxford University Press, 1980), pp. 94-95.

40. It is an oversimplification to suggest that all street ballads, especially those with rural or narrative origins, display rhythmic inflexibility. Neither the model stress pattern of 4+3; 4+3 nor iambic pentameter is inescapable. Nevertheless, it was not uncommon for these songs to become conventionalized in their popular urban versions, partly through their use as dance tunes. This standardization made it easier to dress familiar tunes in new lyrics. Claude M. Simpson, *The British Broadside Ballad and Its Music* (New Brunswick, N.J.: Rutgers University Press, 1966), pp. xii-xiii.

41. The actors most closely associated with the Arne Shakespeare songs are Kitty Clive, Thomas Lowe, and John Beard. Clive (1711-85) was best known as a comic actress. Her lack of serious musical training did not keep her from success in ballad opera, but her attempts at more demanding musical roles met with less favor. Tenor Lowe (d. 1783) also lacked a thorough musical education. Burney considered Lowe a natural talent who squandered his ability through lack of industry (*General History*, 2:986). Of the three, only Beard (trained as a chorister in the King's Chapel) was primarily a musician. His career included both concert and theatrical appearances, some of them for Handel.

42. Genest, *Some Account of the English Stage*, 3:644-45.

43. *Public Advertiser*, 13 December 1759.

44. *London Daily Post and General Advertiser*, 28 November 1740.

45. *General Advertiser*, 31 January 1746.

46. Irena Cholij, "Defesch's *Tempest* Songs," *Musical Times* 67 (1986):325-27.

47. Thomas Chilcot, *Twelve English songs, with their Symphonies* (London: John Johnson, 1745), p. [ii].

48. Burney, *General History*, 2:843.

49. John Walter Hill has compared the aria with the original tune in *The Life and Works of Francesco Maria Veracini*, Studies in Musicology, no. 3 (Ann Arbor: UMI Research Press, 1979), pp. 45-46.

4

Shakespeare Ascendant: Shakespeare Music in the Age of Garrick, 1750–1770

In the fall of 1741 David Garrick, a young wine merchant and aspiring actor from Lichfield, made his London stage debut at Goodman's Field, an illegitimate theatre that attempted to circumvent the Drury Lane and Covent Garden patents by presenting plays as free interval offerings in concerts that were ostensibly the main event. Despite the inauspicious venue, Garrick's debut as Richard III was an immediate success. Within the year Garrick joined the company at Drury Lane. His early roles there included Hamlet, Lear, Macbeth, and of course Richard III. In 1747 he joined the Drury Lane administration, where one of his goals as manager was to make Drury Lane, always considered the serious theatre, the "House of Shakespeare."[1] Garrick was to dominate the London theatre community for over thirty years. From this position he was the single most important influence on contemporary attitudes toward Shakespearean stage production through the middle third of the century.

GARRICK THE SHAKESPEAREAN

During the Garrick years, Shakespeare, his reputation already enhanced by various printed editions and stage revivals, would become the symbol of the English dramatic and literary tradition.

This gradual transformation was underway in the 1730s, when the Shakespeare Ladies Club could speak, with only a little exaggeration, of "the memory of the forsaken Shakespeare." Up to that time Shakespeare's plays had been incompletely and inaccurately represented in the theatres; however, the publication of editions by Pope in 1725 and Theobald in 1733 (not to mention the furor caused by their varying interpretive and editorial viewpoints) kept the canon near the center of contemporary literary thought. The Shakespeare Ladies' Covent Garden revivals and the Drury Lane productions of the early 1740s were signs of renewed interest in staged Shakespeare. The 1740s also saw the publication of new editions by Thomas Hamner (1744) and William Warburton (1747). Shakespearean studies acquired a new academic authority when William Hawkins, a literature professor at Oxford, brought Shakespeare's poetics to the classroom for the first time with a series of lectures begun in 1751.[2]

The role of Garrick and his theatrical compatriots in this reshaping of Shakespeare's image was to popularize and personalize the plays and their characters. Garrick also amended the long-held perception of Shakespeare as primarily a tragic author. During Garrick's management, 27 percent of Drury Lane's tragic offerings and 16 percent of the comedies were Shakespearean.[3] Critics increasingly accepted Shakespeare as a central figure in English cultural history. It remained for the theatres, and especially for the commanding figure of Garrick, to make the case for Shakespeare's supremacy to a wide, general audience.

Garrick's power came from his involvement in every aspect of the theatrical process. Actor, *littérateur*, and manager, he transformed dramatic offerings. As an actor, only Betterton had rivaled his command of the stage. Garrick was a playwright and text editor, providing new plays and transforming old ones (even those by the revered Shakespeare) to best display his own skills and those of his actors. As manager, Garrick supervised an unusually wide range of production activities. His interest in scenic design and technical stagecraft contributed to increased sophistication in stage lighting, painting, and machinery.

Garrick also appreciated the value of money and was happy when a show turned a profit. His commemorative verse for the opening of the 1750 season at Drury Lane suggests a cold practicality on the subject of attracting audiences:

> Sacred to Shakespeare was this spot design'd
> To pierce the heart and humanize the mind.
> But if an empty house, the actor's curse,
> Shews us our *Lears*, and *Hamlet's*, lose their force;
> Unwilling, we must change the noble scene,
> And, in turn, present you Harlequin;
> Quit poets, and set carpenters to work,
> Shew gaudy scenes, or mount the vaulting *Turk*
> For, tho' we actors, one and all, agree
> Boldly to struggle for our—vanity;
> If want come on, importance must retreat;
> Our first, great, ruling passion is—to eat![4]

All of Garrick's knowledge—dramatic, literary, and technical—was practical and directed at pleasing an audience.

As an actor, Garrick professed the deepest admiration for Shakespeare and "wished to lose no drop of that immortal man."[5] Familiar with early Shakespearean texts and contemporary scholarship, he restored much of Shakespeare's original language to the stage. Yet as a manager and actor, Garrick wanted to define staged Shakespeare in his own image. The mid-eighteenth century was not yet an age of historical accuracy in play texts, and Shakespeare had not yet become an inviolable literary icon. Garrick was free to follow the example of nearly a century's worth of adapters when it suited his purpose.

The Shakespearean revisions made for and by Garrick differ from earlier transformations. Restoration adapters had sought to bring to the plays order and consistency, which conformed to contemporary ideals. The Augustans continued to rewrite Shakespeare's poetry in the belief that older verse was inferior to their own. Through all this time the revisions (like the original plays of the day) focused on social interaction rather than characterization. Restoration and Augustan plays "emphasize permanent patterns of human relationships with less attention to the depths of individual experience."[6]

Garrick's revisions shifted this focus to the nature and expression of individual characters, a view that transformed Shakespearean literary criticism in the second half of the century.[7] His skills as a versifier are frequently questioned; however, he edited Shakespeare according to his own practical experience as an actor, his sense of audience reaction, and the nature of the character portrayed. Accordingly, his scripts were a mix of restored texts, portions retained from earlier adaptations, and new additions.[8] The visual arts, music, dance, and Garrick's own personal magnetism were also integral to the Drury Lane Shakespeare.

SHAKESPEARE MUSIC UNDER GARRICK

Garrick made the expected protestations against the trespasses of music, dance, and pantomime on the legitimate stage, yet no theatre manager since Davenant had been so actively involved in the musical components of his productions.[9] Garrick's education did not include formal music study, but he acquired considerable knowledge on his own and was able to discuss music intelligently with no less a figure than Charles Burney.[10] He personally sought out musical scores for Drury Lane.[11] The major English composers of the time (including Thomas and Michael Arne, Charles Burney, Charles Dibdin, William Boyce, Theodore Aylward, Jonathan Battishill, and William Shield) worked at Drury Lane and were on good terms with Garrick.[12] During his tenure at Drury Lane, Garrick increased by 43 the number of singers on the payroll.[13] He supervised the theatre's dancing program and hired his own dancers.[14]

Garrick used musical spectacle, the eighteenth-century descendent of the Restoration masques. He knew that incidental music and songs could contribute to spoken drama, and he was an active participant in the development of English comic opera. Many of his Shakespearean productions would bear witness to this musical preoccupation.

Romeo and Juliet and Other Processionals

As the dominant theatrical figure of his time, Garrick influenced all of London's dramatic community, not just Drury Lane. But on one occassion he clearly followed his competitor's lead. The ongoing rivalry between Drury Lane and Covent Garden broke into head-to-head competition on 28 September 1750 when both theatres opened productions of *Romeo and Juliet*. Garrick played Romeo for Drury Lane opposite Anne Bellamy. He also rewrote the play, giving the lovers a final meeting in the Capulets' tomb. At Covent Garden the celebrated Spranger Barry and Susanna Cibber took the title roles. The atmosphere of competition was "more than a clash of stars, it was a battle of planets."[15]

It must have been a matter of some chagrin to Garrick that Rich's production enjoyed special public acclaim for "an additional Scene of the Funeral Procession of Juliet, in which was introduced a solemn Dirge (the words by Shakespeare) set to music by Mr. Arne."[16] Ironically, this kind of procession had first been successful for Colley Cibber at Drury Lane a quarter-century earlier in *Henry VIII*. Not to be outdone, Drury Lane responded just three days after the première with "an additional scene representing the funeral procession to the monument of the Capulets . . . the Music of the Funeral Procession composed by Dr. Boyce."[17]

Arne gave Covent Garden a colorful, if slight, accompaniment for getting the funeral procession on and off the stage. His text was, despite the *Gentleman's Magazine* attribution, not by Shakespeare.

Ah, hapless Maid doom'd to the gaping Jaws
Of a cold comfortless and dreary Tomb,
Thy Marriage Song is chang'd to mournful Dirge
Thy bridal bed to a black Fun'ral Hearse.
Hark, Hark, how with awful Pause and Solemn Bell
In death like Sounds Tolls her untimely Knell.

She was her Parents' Sole Delight.
They had but one and only Child.
Since Death has torn her from their Arms
With Grief and Sorrow they are Wild.
Their Grief and Sorrow ev'ry Bosom Shares
Witness our Sighs and Groans and falling Tears.[18]

Two trumpets, muffled kettledrum, and a tolling bell sounded a cadence while the procession moved on stage, then fell silent for the remainder. The choral dirge, accompanied only by strings and a pair of flutes, included vocal solos, a brief cello solo, and a section repeated *ad libitum* "till all the Procession is over."[19]

Not everyone was impressed with Covent Garden's staging. One German visitor to London was particularly displeased: "The newly added scene, the burial of Juliet, is stupid and ridiculous. A bell is actually tolled on the stage. The costumes are mediocre and the decorations positively bad."[20] However, the speed with which Garrick added a procession to his own production indicates this was a minority opinion.

So many parallels exist between the two dirges that Garrick and Boyce must have been inviting comparison.[21] Garrick inserted the procession at the beginning of the fifth act, the fourth having closed with the discovery of the "dead" Juliet. Garrick's lyrics were no less melodramatic than those used at Covent Garden, but the text did provide a formal pattern, which Boyce observed when writing the music.

Rise, Rise!
Heart-breaking sighs,
The woe-fraught Bosom swell,
For Sighs alone
And Dismal Moan
Should echo Juliet's Knell.

She's gone—the sweetest flow'r of May
That blooming blest our sight;
Those eyes which shone like breaking day
Are set in endless Night!

Rise, Rise! (etc.)

She's gone from Earth, nor leaves behind
So fair a Form, so pure a Mind;
How coulds't thou, Death, at once destroy,
The Lover's hope, the Parents Joy?

Rise, Rise! (etc.)

Thou Spotless Soul, look down below
Our unfeigned sorrow see;
Oh give us Strength to bear our woe,
To bear the Loss of Thee!

Rise, Rise! (etc.)[22]

Boyce appropriated some musical devices used by Arne, but his more conservative nature made him downplay their theatrical quality. The one exception was the tolling bell, used throughout a five-section piece of considerable length. Certain features of Arne's dirge were mimicked in Boyce's, including introductory choral statements accompanied by solo winds and vocal solos accompanied by solo strings. The soprano and alto solos (sung by Kitty Clive and Miss Norris) were doubled by boys' voices for ecclesiastical color. Avoiding the filler Arne used to cover stage exits and adopting the *rondeau* structure suggested by the verse, Boyce created a substantial musical accompaniment for this spurious scene.

Later Shakespeare processions remained primarily visual spectacles, like the original Cibber processional in *Henry VIII*. In the 1754–55 season both houses were again competing, this time with productions of *Coriolanus*. The Drury Lane version opened nearly a month before Covent Garden's, perhaps because, as one contemporary observer suggested, Garrick did not want to get involved in matching Covent Garden's extravagance:

Mr. Garrick was eager to get the start of the rival theatre, where it was preparing with infinite pomp and splendour. The very idea of a triumphal procession at Covent-Garden struck terror to the whole host of Drury, however big they looked and strutted on common occasions. [23]

Covent Garden's "pomp and splendor" was catalogued in a printed copy of the play:

Underneath is the order of the Ovation, as it was exhibited.
But, previous to that, there was a civil procession from the Town. . . .
These walked to the sound of flutes and soft instruments. . . .   The ovation was performed to the sound of fifes and trumpets, in the following order:

> Six Lectors
> One Carrying a small Eagle
> Six Incense-bearers
> Four Souldiers
> Two Fifes
> One Drum
> Two Standard-bearers
> Ten Souldiers
> Two Fifes
> One Drum
> Two Standard-bearers
> Six Souldiers
> Two Standard-bearers
> Four Serpent Trumpets[24]

By this time, all the musicians were on stage, although the list describing the other participants continues for almost another page. The order of the ovation, independent of the civil procession, included 118 people. Unfortunately, no music survives.

Although Garrick chose not to compete with the Covent Garden *Coriolanus* procession, Drury Lane's 1762 *Henry VIII* was again revived with the coronation of "Anne Bullen." Drury Lane's procession was not quite as large as Covent Garden's *Coriolanus* spectacle, but it boasted more musicians: nine trumpets, one fife, five drummers, and nine choristers. [25] The music, possibly popular or generic martial fare, is unknown.

Songs and Incidental Music

Shakespearean musical practice from the Restoration on did not change completely with the passing of theatrical seasons. New music was added to the familiar as the growing play repertoire required. Older scores, palimpsest-like, were retained with additions representative of new musical styles. The "Purcell" *Tempest* and Leveridge's *Macbeth* , for example, were occasionally challenged but never completely displaced. Arne's songs from the 1740 Drury Lane productions continued in use. Masques and processions continued as important musical additions. Source material for much of the music used in mid-century is lost. The existence of some songs and incidental music is known only through the playbills and periodical advertisements. Surviving prints and manuscripts from two Drury Lane productions from the 1750s give clues to Garrick's dramatic use of incidental music.

Garrick followed his paradoxically divergent inclinations toward textual revision and restoration in a production of *The Winter's Tale* (21 January 1756). The play, retitled *Florizel and Perdita, a Dramatic Pastoral*, was much cut, reduced to half an evening's entertainment.[26] Garrick shortened the story of Leontes and Hermione, leaving Shakespeare's pastoral subplot as the main action. All six songs and a dance from *The Winter's Tale* IV, 3 and 4 appear in the printed book of Garrick's adaptation, as does an additional song text. Shakespeare grouped all the songs and dances into the pastoral scenes in act IV, creating the effect of a musical interlude. In Garrick's shortened version the effect must have been even more pronounced.

William Boyce provided music for this production. Three songs attributed to Boyce appear in William Linley's 1816 collection *Shakespeare's Dramatic Music*: "When Daffodils Begin to Peer," "Will You Buy Any Tape," and the trio "Get You Hence, for I Must Goe!" There is, however, a discrepancy between the text of the songs in Linley and the printed playbook. The text in Linley's "Jog-on, Jog-on" (I, 3; folio IV, 3) has been intermingled with "When Daffodils Begin to Peer." One explanation is that Garrick, a zealous trimmer of plays, shortened the song texts, which were then not reproduced in the printed *Florizel and Perdita*. Several of Garrick's Shakespeare productions contained disclaimers to the effect that "It was impossible to retain more of the Play and bring it within the Compass of a Night's Entertainment."[27]

At least one song text in another play edited by Garrick was abridged to shorten a scene. In the *Cymbeline* of 28 November 1761, the 24-line, four-stanza dirge in act IV was reduced to:

Fear no more the Heat o' the Sun,
Nor the furious Winter's Blast;
Thou thy worldly Task hast done,
And the Dream of Life is past.
Monarchs, Sages, Peasants must
Follow thee and come to dust.[28]

The song text from *The Winter's Tale* in Linley's collection would allow the telescoping of the scene (and the omission of an intervening song, which, according to Linley, Boyce did not set). Such a change would be typical of Garrick's editing. Linley was connected with Drury Lane and had first-hand knowledge of its productions. His personal acquaintance with Boyce gives further credence to the attribution.

Shakespeare himself had directed that music be used for the animating of the statue in *The Winter's Tale* V, 3. Garrick retained this episode and Shakespeare's stage indication in *Florizel and Perdita*. The music Boyce wrote for this scene, complete in Appendix A, is an unusual example of background music structured and paced around stage action. A gradual quickening of harmonic rhythm and melodic figuration grows out of opening stasis. At one point the music is interrupted for Paulina's command to the statue:

'Tis time; descend—be stone no more—approach;
Strike all that look on you with marvel![29]

Garrick's awareness of music's potential to contribute to a scene's dramatic impact was also brought to play in his use of background music to heighten the pathos of the reunion of Lear and Cordelia in *King Lear*.[30]

The Winter's Tale had already been altered for Covent Garden two seasons earlier. MacNamara Morgan cut even more aggressively than Garrick, leaving little more than the last two acts of Shakespeare's play. Arne supplied the music for three Shakespeare texts, two additional ones, and a pastoral dance. Only one of the songs survives, a setting of the non-Shakespearean text "Come let us be blithe and gay" in the 1762 *Winter's Amusement* collection.

The *Tempest* Masque

In 1756, Garrick yet again commissioned Boyce, this time to provide music for *The Tempest*.[31] All the original song texts were retained. The masque was severely cut and rewritten. Only Ceres and Juno appear, joined by Hymen. The introduction of the goddesses and the tale of Cupid were replaced by a brief introduction sung by Juno. If Garrick had thought the unedited text of the masque, set for Drury Lane in 1746 by Arne, too digressive, it is peculiar that he approved Boyce's lengthy setting of the shortened text. The new masque may have had more to do with Garrick's opinion of Arne as a composer. (Some years later, Garrick would write to Arne, "Our theatrical connections have not yet been serviceable to either of us."[32]) Garrick had not provided text for recitative, so Boyce anticipated song texts to give the masque a "song-recitative-song-recitative-song" structure. The final song was in gigue rhythm to accommodate the masque's concluding dance.

The True Shakespearean Operas:
The Fairies and *The Tempest*

The most unusual musical products of Garrick's Shake-spearean revisions were two Italianate operas with English librettos based on actual play texts. Two previous Italian operas seen in London, *Ambleto* and Veracini's *Rosalinda*, had been only remotely related to the Shakespearean plots on which they were supposedly based. Although greatly changed, Drury Lane's *The Fairies* (3 February 1755, based on *A Midsummer Night's Dream*) and *The Tempest* (11 February 1756), both in English, retained much of Shakespeare's poetry.

The extent of Garrick's involvement with the operas is unclear. In a letter to a colleague the actor denies authorship of the librettos:

I received your letter, which is indeed more facetious than just—for if you mean that *I* was the person who altered the *Midsummer Night's Dream* and *The Tempest* into operas, you are much mistaken.[33]

Modern literary critics, suggesting Garrick's stylistic hand is evident in the librettos, have been unwilling to accept this disclaimer. The high quality of *The Fairies*[34] and musico-dramatic similarities between *The Tempest* and *Florizel and Perdita*[35] are among the arguments offered in support of Garrick's authorship. This letter was written after the failure of the second of the two works, at a time when Garrick would have been eager to disassociate himself from the project. Whether or not he was the author, as a manager active in the day-to-day theatre operations he was at least responsible for approving projects and must at one time have considered them potential successes.

The Fairies

Garrick definitely wrote the prologue to *The Fairies*, which he spoke at all performances. He suggested that there were literary and nationalistic reasons for attempting the opera:

Excuse us, first, for foolishly supposing,
Your Countryman could please you in composing;
An op'ra too!—play'd by an English Band,
Wrote in a Language which you understand—
I dare not say, WHO wrote it—I could tell ye,
To soften Matters—Signor Shakespearelli:
This aukward Drama—(I confess th' Offense)
Is guilty too, of Poetry and Sense
And then the Price we take—you'll all abuse it,
So low, so unlike Op'ras—but excuse it,
We'll mend that Fault, whenever you shall chuse it.
Our last Mischance, and worse than all the rest,
Which turns the whole Performance to a Jest,
Our Singers all are well, and all will do their best.[36]

For the music, Garrick turned to John Christopher Smith, the younger. Smith had not composed for the theatre since his youthful involvement with the English opera project. His conservative musical personality, shaped by sporadic studies with Handel and Pepusch, resulted in the first of the operas being more Italianate than Arne or even Boyce might have provided in the circumstance. Garrick was willing to capitalize on the connection between Smith and Handel, inviting what Dogberry might have called "odorous" comparisons:

Struck with the wonders of his master's art
Whose sacred dramas shake and melt the heart,
Whose heav'n born strains the coldest breast inspire,
Whose chorus thunder sets the soul on fire!
Inflam'd, astonish'd, at those magic airs,
When Samson groans, and frantic Saul despairs,
The pupil wrote--his work is now before ye.[37]

The libretto for *The Fairies* is different in effect from the original play and profoundly different from Purcell's *The Fairy Queen*. Almost all changes were accomplished by cutting rather than rewriting. What remains is the basic outline of the plot, almost exclusively in Shakespeare's verse. Whoever the libretto's

author was, he skillfully managed to reshape the play while retaining much of the original poetry.

While Shakespeare had been rewritten during the Restoration
to comply with neoclassical rules, such attempts were less common by the middle of the eighteenth century. Supposed faults in
the construction of Shakespeare's plays were no longer an issue
with contemporary literary critics. The superimposition of certain neoclassical conventions on the libretto for *The Fairies* was
the result of a librettist conforming to the operatic format. The
"classicization" of the plot was second-hand, not the direct result
of altering the play for literary reasons.

Shakespeare's original scenic structure was based on changes
of time and place. Continental scenes were usually defined by
patterns of entrances and exits. By dividing the play in the Continental manner, the librettist more easily allocated different parts
of the text as either recitative or air. This kind of scene division
is not to be found in any of Garrick's other Shakespearean
adaptations. Whether or not Garrick was the author of the libretto, the opera text is more the result of the requirements of the
operatic form than the need to impose order on the text.

Textual cuts are various. The low comic material is completely eliminated. (Shakespeare's scene between Titania and
Bottom is replaced with a report from Puck: "My mistress with a
patch'd fool is in love.")[38] Other cuts reflect the librettist's
skepticism about opera's ability to capture the play's ensemble
dialogue. The rapidly paced lines about the misplaced affections
of Demetrius (*Midsummer Night's Dream* I, 2) are typical of
these cuts:

> *Hermia:*   I frown upon him, yet he loves me still.
> *Helena:*   O that your frowns would teach my smiles such skill.
> *Hermia:*   I give him curses, yet he gives me love.
> *Helena:*   O that my prayers could such affection move.
> *Hermia:*   The more I hate, the more he follows me.
> *Helena:*   The move I love, the more he hateth me.

Only one such rapid interchange, much abridged, survives in the libretto in the recitative sections of III, 5.

The most surprising feature of the libretto is the limited role of the fairies. They provide neither the earthiness of Shakespeare's sprites nor the exotic pomp of *The Fairy Queen*. These fairies are barely on stage long enough to perform their function in the plot concerning the four lovers. The lovers, rather than being participants in the meeting of foreign spheres (those of the noble mortals, the low comics, and the supernatural beings), are here the center of attention. They have become the first and second couples of opera seria. The final word on the cuts comes from the printed libretto:

Many Passages of the first Merit, and some whole Scenes in the *Midsummer Night's Dream*, are necessarily omitted in this Opera, to reduce the Performance to a proper length; it was feared that even the best Poetry would appear tedious when only supported by *Recitative*.[39]

Of the twenty-seven airs, ten were settings of Shakespeare texts, seven from *Dream* and three from other plays. Of the others, "where Shakespeare has not supplied the Composer with Songs, he has taken them from Milton, Waller, Dryden, Lansdown, Hammond, &c. and it is hoped they will not seem to be unnaturally introduced."[40] Four of the seven song texts taken from *Dream*—"You Spotted Snakes," "Now until the Break of Day," "Flower of This Purple Dye," and "Up and Down"—were either original lyrics or were separated from the main text as incantations. The three remaining lyrics come from act I, scenes 4 and 5 (folio I, 1). These reflective passages of monologue include:

Love looks not with the eyes but with the mind,
And therefore is wing'd Cupid painted blind:
Nor hath love's mind of any judgement taste;
Wings, and no eyes, figure unheedy haste,
And therefore is love said to be a child,
Because in choice he often is beguiled.

In the prologue Garrick overboasted of his English cast. The singers were a mixed group of English and Italian performers, including John Beard as Theseus, Jenny Vernon as Helena, a Signora Passerini as Hermia, Mr. Atkins as Demetrius (singing only recitative), and the castrato Gaudagni as Lysander.[41] Hippolyta was mute. The fairies were portrayed by children, including as Oberon "Master Reinhold," a chorister from St. Paul's.

There is no discernable pattern to the key sequence of the opera's various numbers, save that the opera begins and ends in D. The vocal range of the cast may have played the largest part in Smith's tonal choices. As was common for the time, the recitatives were not included in the printed score.

The opera begins with a French overture taken from Smith's 1744 pastorale *Daphne*.[42] A minuet follows, during which Garrick was to "enter—interrupting the Band of Music" to speak the prologue.[43] The first act opens with an instrumental march for the entrance of Theseus and his court.

Almost every item in the score is a *da capo* or *dal segno* aria with a similar tonal pattern. The "A" section moves without significant digression to the dominant, then back to the tonic. The "B" sections are much shorter. The first phrase typically cadences on the mediant. Tonal variety is restricted to the central sections, which sometimes move to the parallel minor and its minor dominant. Some remain entirely in one key. None includes lengthy modulations. The texts are limited to a single line (sometimes repeated) or a couplet, with repetition of the final words at the closing cadence.

If the aria format and tonal layout are not varied, the instrumentation and orchestral textures are. The orchestra includes four-part strings, horns and oboes in pairs, trumpet, transverse flute, and continuo. The horns and trumpet are limited to court scenes. In Helena's aria in act I, scene 5, the first violins alone do little more than double the voice over a figured bass. The arias for the big-voiced Mr. Beard were scored for all orchestral resources.

Whether by coincidence or in response to a less rigid metric scheme, Smith's music for the song texts taken from *Dream's* original dialogue is less patterned and more irregularly phrased than those using non-Shakespearean texts. Word repetitions are not used to provide strictly regular text rhythms, but for melodic extension.

Ex. 24. Smith. *The Fairies.* "Love Looks Not with the Eyes," mm. 7-18.

by permission of the British Library

Lyrics transferred from other plays receive varyingly successful treatment. "Where the Bee Sucks" (Example 25) is particularly problematic because its duple-meter text is at odds with a triple-time melody.

Ex. 25. Smith. *The Fairies.* "Where the Bee Sucks," mm. 1-6.

by permission of the British Library

The songs for the child singers were modest in format and reminiscent of theatre ballads. Smith's fairy music, exemplified in Oberon's air "Flowers of This Purple Dye" in Appendix A, characterizes the spirit world with a *galant* simplicity that contrasts with the more operatic music of the lovers. This characterization continues into the orchestral numbers. The unison marcato strings in the sinfonia to the act I fairy scene are almost Mendelssohnian. Otherwise, Smith made only simplistic attempts at descriptive or pictorial music, such as the act III, scene 5 "hunting sinfonia" (complete with horn calls), or brief rustic musical references within arias.

The librettist's tendency to cut dialogue from the text discouraged Smith from writing extended musical numbers that furthered dramatic action. The act II duet for Lysander and Hermia, a *da capo* song in which both singers share the same text, is the only ensemble number among the principals. Only one chorus was included in the printed score, another *da capo* movement based on a call-and-response pattern.

The short run of *The Fairies*—nine performances in one season—suggests the opera was not well received.[44] Burney, however, remembered it as a special, if limited, success:

I can recollect no English operas in which the dialogue was carried on in recitative, that were crowned wtih full success, except *The Fairies*, set by Mr. Smith in 1755, and *Artaxerxes*, by Dr. Arne in 1763; but the success of both was temporary, and depended so much on the singers . . . that they never could be called stock pieces, or, indeed, performed again, with any success, by Inferior singers.[45]

Another theatre-goer offered limp praise, remembering, "It was performed and with good success, aided not a little by an excellent prologue, and as excellently spoken, by Mr. Garrick."[46]

The Tempest

Public opinion would not be so kind to the operatic *Tempest* Drury Lane presented the next season. Trimming this play to provide a libretto posed problems the adapter did not solve. The four separate plots that Shakespeare had molded together could not be separated without leaving scars. The Caliban/Stephano/Trinculo story was discarded and replaced by a simpler low comic affair loosely based on Dryden's adaptation. The plot against the king of Naples was entirely omitted. The remaining stories—Prospero's recovery of his dukedom and the Ferdinand/Miranda match—were rearranged in an attempt to reduce the numerous location shifts in the play. The division of Shakespeare's larger scenes into smaller ones was accomplished less systematically than in *The Fairies*. In spite of attempts to solve the problem of locale shifts, the scene changes could only be reduced, not eliminated. Entrances and exits occurred frequently within scenes. The musical organization in the scenes was correspondingly irregular and failed to show the traditional ordering seen in *The Fairies*. Some scenes contained only recitative; others had as many as four arias or ensemble numbers.

While several of the air texts in *The Fairies* had been taken from its source play's dialogue, only one of the *Tempest* arias was so supplied. The precedent for Ariel's singing the "Before you can say come and go" speech (III, 2; folio IV, 1) had been established at Drury Lane by Arne a decade before. Three original song lyrics were retained: Caliban's "No More Dams" and Ariel's "Come unto These Yellow Sands" and "Full Fathom Five." ("Where the Bee Sucks" had already been appropriated for *The Fairies*.) The rest of the texts came from various sources. Some were taken from Dryden's adaptation. "Arise, Ye Subterranean Winds" was taken from the 1674 Shadwell version. The rest came from other Dryden plays or were newly written for the opera.[47]

Smith's return to the theatre prompted him to temper his more severe style with popular elements in *The Tempest*. Most of the solos in *The Fairies* had been *da capo* or *dal segno* arias, with more modest theatre tunes and rococo elements limited primarily to the music for the child-fairies. *The Tempest* had four more musical items (38, compared to 34 in *The Fairies*), but more of these were shorter, being either through-composed or in bipartite (A, A'). There was little attempt at distinguishing different character strata through musical style. Some of Prospero's songs are ballad tunes. On the other hand, Stephano, one of the low comics, has an extended aria.

The opportunity for stage spectacle was uncharacteristically reduced in the libretto. The storm scene (folio I, 1) was cut entirely. Only one of the spirit apparitions was retained. The wedding masque was omitted. Perhaps in response, some of Smith's music is unusually picturesque. In Ariel's first song (folio I, 2, lines 196-206, changed to future tense), while the spirit describes the storm he is about to create, the orchestra rages with storm effects. The song is through-composed, taking its shape from Smith's conception of the storm, first furious, then fading quickly into the distance.

Smith used more ensemble numbers in *The Tempest* than in *The Fairies*. The sailors' drinking song is a more developed dramatic piece than any of the ensemble numbers in *The Fairies*. The combat duet between Trincalo and Mustacho (I, 5) is more like the short, concluding "choruses" to Restoration comic entertainments than Italian comic opera ensemble finales.

> *Trincalo:* Whilst blood does flow within these veins,
>   Or any spark of life remains,
>   My right I will maintain.
> *Mustacho:* Whilst I this temper'd steel can wield
>   I'll ne'er to thee, thou braggard, yield,

> Thy threats are all in vain.
> *Trincalo:* I defy thee.
> *Mustacho:* I'll not fly thee.
> *Trincalo:* Braggard, come.
> *Mustacho:* —Braggard?
>> Thy boasted courage not I'll try;
>> I see thou art afraid to die.
> *Trincalo:* Not I.
> *Mustacho:* That's a lye.
> *Trincalo:* Lye, Sir?
> *Mustacho:* Ay, Sir.
> *Both:* Behold, I conquer, or I die.[48]

Other ensembles in the opera include Smith's updated setting of Dryden's "Echo Duet."

Recitative was not printed in the published score, with the exception of Prospero's great speech when he abandons his magical powers (folio V, 1). Smith set this text (III, 4) as an elaborate accompanied recitative. Although the recitative soliloquy had been common in Italian opera in the seventeenth century, it was an uncommon solution for the English.[49] This recitative was included in the printed score either for its dramatic importance or its musical interest. Accompanied recitative was nothing new to English composers, who had been using it since the Restoration. But on the basis of surviving examples, this was the first and only recitative presentation of one of the great Shakespearean scenes performed on the eighteenth-century English stage.

The speeches and dialogues that were used as texts for arias and other musical numbers tended to be rhythmically circumscribed verses with simple rhyme schemes. The aria text that follows Prospero's recitative is a rhymed paraphrase of the original text.

> I'll break my staff,
> Bury it certain fathoms in the earth,
> And deeper than did ever plummet sound
> I'll drown my book. (Shakespeare, *Tempest*, V, 1; lines 54-57.)

> Deep in the earth, where sun shall never shine
> This cloud-compelling war [*sic* - "bar"?] I place;
> This book the unfathom'd ocean shall confine,
> Beyond the reach of mortal race. ([Garrick], *Tempest*, p. 38).

The opera was performed six times (11, 13, 18, 20, and 26 February and 16 March 1756).[50] Smith borrowed the overture from his unperformed Italian opera *Il ciro riconosciuto* for *The Tempest*.[51] Several well-known singers were in the lead roles, with the double casting of John Beard as both Prospero and Trincalo exacerbating the script's lack of character development. The script was not the successful adaptation *The Fairies* had been. The play's basic themes of innocence and experience were lost through the cuts. Much of the dialogue was still Shakespeare, but rearranged and diluted with scenes from Dryden's version.

It is also true that this all-sung *Tempest* lost much of its musical imagery. The isle is not "full of noises, sounds, and sweet airs." With the masques—Shakespeare's, Dryden's, and Davenant's—removed, most of the mystical connection between music and the supernatural that Shakespeare had made a large part of the play (and that his Restoration adapters had to some degree preserved) was lost. Ariel's enchantment of Ferdinand ("Come unto These Yellow Sands") is the only musical/magical symbolism that was retained.

The opera was not well received. Criticism targeted the text, not the music. Theophilus Cibber, Garrick's chief theatrical rival and perhaps not the most dispassionate of critics, complained *The Tempest* had been "castrated into an opera."[52] A contemporary Garrick biographer, presumably more kindly disposed to his subject, could muster little enthusiasm for the piece:

Garrick ought not to have suffered such a play to dwindle into an opera: The harmony of the versification wanted no aid from music. He had said in a former prologue that, "He wished to lose no drop of that immortal man," and here he has lost a tun of him. Had he revived the *Tempest* as it stands in the original, and played the character of

Prospero, he would have done justice to the God of his Idolatry, and honour to himself.[53]

The argument citing "the Harmony of the versification" recalls Betterton's comparison of music and recited verse. Garrick took these criticisms seriously, and the following season he staged a much-restored, spoken version of *The Tempest* in which he played Prospero (20 October 1757, the same production for which Boyce supplied the masque). Despite his lack of success in the ventures with Smith, Garrick was still not finished with his attempt to operatize Shakespeare.

The 1763 *Midsummer Night's Dream*

During the 1760s, Covent Garden, now under the control of John Beard, substantially increased its operatic programming. Garrick, who had been responsible for an operatic repertoire at Drury Lane in the years of competition with Rich, now added more musical entertainments to the schedule. All-sung English opera, afterpiece opera, and comic opera with spoken dialogue (the musico-dramatic descendent of ballad opera as well as the parallel of the French *opéra-comique*) made up a large part of both houses' offerings.[54] Among Garrick's new productions was yet another musical version of *A Midsummer Night's Dream.* This time, the dialogue was spoken, since Garrick wanted "to avoid the dullest part of Musick, w[hich] is ye Recitative."[55] Remembering this production some years later, Genest would call it "a sort of opera."[56]

The new *Dream* was conceived as a pastiche comic opera. Garrick's autograph worksheet for the first draft of the song distribution survives in a manuscript, W. B. 469, at the Folger Library in Washington, D.C. The worksheet lists the songs Garrick intended to use and their planned location in the dialogue. Some songs were to be borrowed from *The Fairies*. Garrick also intended to commission the rest from John Battishill, Michael Arne, Theodore Aylward, and Charles Burney. Other songs in the layout were simply described as "new." The distribution of songs among the characters was like the earlier opera's—the four lovers (Demetrius now having songs), Oberon, Titania, and Puck. Seven songs were intended for act I, seven in act II, four in act III, six in act IV, and only two, including a "finishing piece for all," in the last act. Despite operatic precedence, the mock play of Pyramus and Thisbe was not musical.

Garrick's plans changed considerably by the time the production opened. There were thirty-three songs in the play, five more than in Smith's opera. Fifteen of those songs came from *The Fairies.* (It is impossible to tell from the playbook if any of the instrumental numbers from the opera were also used.) The remainder were newly written for the production. The *opera seria* song distribution that Garrick had at first intended to retain was not carried over into the final production.

There is no consistent pattern to the placement of the airs in the spoken dialogue. Some come at the end of lengthy reflective or descriptive passages. Others are placed at a point in the plot where a character makes a major decision, as when Hermia refuses to obey the Duke's command to marry Demetrius.

> So will I grow, so live, so die my Lord
> Ere I will yield my virgin heart and hand
> Unto his Lordship, to whose unwish'd yoke
> My soul consents not to give sov'reignty.
> > AIR
> With mean disguise let others nature hide,
> And mimick virtue with the paint of art;
> I scorn the cheat of reason's foolish pride,
> And boast the graceful weakness of my heart.[57]

The text and music of this air were retained from *The Fairies.* Two of Smith's airs with texts taken from the play's dialogue were also retained in the opening dialogue between Hermia and Helena in I, 1.

Of the several duets newly written for the production, the argument duet in act II is the only one with a dramatic exchange in the text:

Queen:	Away, away,
	I will not stay,
	But fly from rage and thee.
King:	Begone, begone,
	You'll feel anon
	What 'tis to injure me
Queen:	Away, false man
	Do all you can,
	I scorn your jealous rage.
King:	We will not part;
	Take you my heart!
	Give me your favourite page.
Queen:	I'll keep my page!
King:	And I my rage!
	Nor shall you injure me.
Both:	Away, away, &c.[58]

This dialogue, written by Garrick, is reminiscent of the battle duet text in Smith's *Tempest*.

The show ran for only one night; it was considered "a bad alteration of the original."[59] No book of airs from the ill-fated full-length show was published, but Battishill and Aylward published their contributions separately. To salvage something of the production it was converted to an afterpiece. This time Garrick and his partner George Colman omitted the lovers, Theseus, and Hippolyta, leaving the fairy story and the low comics in a script called *A Fairy Tale*. Michael Arne's songs were retained in *A Fairy Tale* and later published. The failure of *A Midsummer Night's Dream*, the first full-length English comic opera version of a Shakespearean text, at last dissuaded Garrick from further attempts to operatize the plays.

The Jubilee

In 1769 Garrick and a number of supporters in Stratford-upon-Avon mounted an ambitious festival in celebration of Shakespeare. This Shakespeare Jubilee has since been recognized as a turning point in critical and popular awareness of

Shakespeare: "It marks the point at which Shakespeare stopped being regarded as an increasingly popular and admirable drama- tist and became a god."[60] Garrick's service to "the God of his Idolatry" had contributed to widespread recognition of the play- wright's domination of English literary tradition. The Jubilee was Shakespeare's coronation.

Months of planning in Stratford and back at Drury Lane cul- minated in a three-day festival that opened 6 September 1769. Ironically, the event's speeches, processions, and musical texts included not a word of Shakespeare. Charles Dibdin and Thomas Arne were among the composers supplying music. Bad luck and worse weather plagued the festival, which was a financial disap- pointment.   However, when later that autumn Garrick took a scaled-down version of the pageant (appropriately titled *The Ju- bilee*) back to London, its success rivaled Drury Lane's most popular Shakespearean productions.

The parade of characters from Shakespeare's plays that ended *The Jubilee* was especially popular:

The last scene is a magnificent Transparent one in which the Capital characters of Shakespeare are exhibited at full length with Shake- speare's Statue in the middle crowned by Tragedy and Comedy, fairies and Cupids surrounding him, and all the banners waving at the upper end.[61]

Shakespearean processions representing a historical event or cer- emony that could be inserted into a play with some dramatic jus- tification had been a staple at Drury Lane since 1725. The *Ju- bilee* procession was profoundly different, representing characters whose natures and motivations were raised to iconic stature by memorable performances of Garrick and his colleagues.   Dib- din's processional tunes were to be used as background music while the actors paraded in costume.

The processionals, along with glees and songs from *The Ju- bilee* (encomiums to Shakespeare not directly related to the plays or characters), were published in a volume called *Shakespeare's Garland.* Dibdin's uncomplicated music was printed in an even more simplified keyboard score to make it attractive to prospective buyers who could then play these pieces in their own homes. While Dibdin's processionals fell far short of being true musical character sketches, they insinuated Shakespeare's characters into middle-class drawing room culture.

SUMMARY

Shakespeare's place in dramatic and literary history changed radically during Garrick's domination of the London theatre community. Garrick, Rich, and Beard strove to create a staged Shakespeare immediately recognizable as the product of their own houses. In this milieu, the musical representation of Shakespeare was multifaceted. Much of the late seventeenth- and early eighteenth-century repertoire and practice was retained, albeit changed by the requirements of play repertoire and musical fashion. Surviving incidental music and songs written for Garrick, such as Boyce's music for animating the statue in *The Winter's Tale*, suggest he was sensitive to the dramatic possibilities of music in Shakespearean production.

Whether as impresario or librettist, Garrick was uniquely involved in creating operatic versions of *A Midsummer Night's Dream* and *The Tempest*. The precedence of earlier "operas"— the Restoration versions that were products of the masque tradition and the eighteenth-century *Pyramus and Thisbe* afterpieces— did not prepare the way for the all-sung works of Smith or the 1763 comic opera version of *Dream*. The mediocre showing of these productions raises questions about the lack of a significant opera tradition in Shakespeare in eighteenth-century England.

Perhaps the answer lay in the lack of a first-rank musical talent. Perhaps the inherent "music" of Shakespeare's verse, cited by Betterton, was too strong to be successfully subjugated to a more exacting meter and melody. Or perhaps mid-eighteenth century librettists and musicians were incapable of reconciling the contemporary image of Shakespeare—with its pre-Romantic emphasis on character and a growing "Masterwork" status—with either the Italian operatic tradition's different narrative movement and emphasis with the developing farcical and sentimental contemporary comic opera. Stage musicians in the years immediately following Garrick's tenure were to find the challenge no less daunting.

NOTES

1. Edward Wagenknecht, *Merely Players* (Norman: University of Oklahoma Press [1966]), p. 15.

2. J. W. Binns, "Some Lectures on Shakespeare in Eighteenth-Century Oxford: The *Praelectiones poeticae* of William Hawkins," in *Shakespeare: Text, Language, Criticism: Essays in Honour of Marvin Spevack,* ed.   Bernard   Fabian   and   Kurt   Tetzeli   von   Rosador (Hildesheim: Olms-Weidmann , 1987), pp. 19-33.

3. Gary Taylor, *Reinventing Shakespeare* (New York: Weidenfeld & Nicolson, 1989), p. 119.

4. *The Gentleman's Magazine,* Sept. 1750, p. 422.

5. Arthur Murphy, *The Life of David Garrick, Esq.,*   2 vols. (London: J. Wright, 1801), 2:302.

6. Christopher Spencer, "Introduction" to *Five Restoration Adaptations of Shakespeare* (Urbana: University of Illinois Press, 1965), pp. 11-12.

7. George Winchester Stone, "David Garrick's Significance in the History of Shakespearean Criticism," *PMLA* 65 (1950):187.

8. The Garrick Shakespeare adaptations are surveyed in George Winchester Stone, Jr. and George M. Kahrl, *David Garrick: A Critical Biography* (Carbondale: Southern Illinois University Press, 1979), pp. 249-65, 269-77.

9. Roger Fiske, *English Theatre Music in the Eighteenth Century,* 2d ed. (London: Oxford University Press, 1986), pp. 205-51; Stone and Kahrl, *David Garrick* , pp. 223-46.

10. *The Letters of David Garrick,* 3 vols., ed. David M. Little and George M. Kahrl (Cambridge, Mass.:   Harvard University Press, 1963), 1:404.

11. Garrick reported one such occasion in his correspondence. Ibid., 2:433.

12. Stone and Kahrl, *David Garrick,* p. 224.

13. Ibid., p. 223.

14. *Letters of Garrick*, 1:414-15.

15. W. J. Macqueen-Pope, *The Theatre Royal, Drury Lane* (London: W. H. Allen, 1945), p. 172.

16. *The Gentleman's Magazine*, Sept. 1750, p. 427.

17. *The General Advertiser*, 1 Oct. 1750.

18. [Thomas A. Arne], *A Compleat Score of the Solemn Dirge in Romeo and Juliet* (London: Henry Thorowgood, [1765]), pp. 1-5.

19. Ibid., p. 1.

20. Chrislob Mylius, "Tagebuch seine Reise nach England," in *Archiv zur neuren Geschichte Geographie, Natur-und Menschenkunde* (Leipzig, 1787), 23 October 1753, quoted in John Alexander Kelly, *German Visitors to English Theatres in the Eighteenth Century* (Princeton: Princeton University Press, 1936; New York: Octagon, 1978), p. 25.

21. Competition between Thomas Arne and William Boyce was not limited to this production. "Mr. Arne and Mr. Boyce were frequently concurrents at the theatres and in each other's way, particularly at Drury Lane." Charles Burney, *A General History of Music* [1789], ed. Frank Mercer, ed. 2 vols. (New York: Dover, 1957), 2:1010.

22. William Shakespeare, *Romeo and Juliet . . . with alterations and an additional scene* (London: J. and R. Tonson, 1750), p. 43.

23. Tate Wilkinson, *Memoirs of His Own Life*, 4 vols. (York: Wilson, Spence, and Mawman, 1790), 4 : 172.

24. Shakespeare, *Coriolanus or, the Roman Matron. A Tragedy Taken from Shakespeare and Thomson* (London: A. Millar, [1755]), p. [iii].

25. The order of the processional as printed in Shakespeare, *Henry VIII . . . With the coronation of Anne Bullen. . . .* (London: C. Hitch & L. Hawes, 1762), appears in George C. D. Odell, *Shakespeare from Betterton to Irving*, 2 vols. (New York: Charles Scribner, 1920; New York: Dover, 1966), 1:425-26.

26. *Florizel and Perdita* shared a bill with *Catherine and Petruchio*, Garrick's abridged version of *The Taming of the Shrew*. See *The London Stage 1660-1800: A Calendar of Plays*, 11 vols. (Carbondale: Southern Illinois University Press, 1960-68), pt. 4, 2:521.

27. Shakespeare, *Cymbeline; a Tragedy . . . with alterations* (London: J. and R. Tonson, 1762), p. [2].

28. Ibid., p. 38.

29. David Garrick, *Florizel and Perdita. A Dramatic Pastoral . . . Alter'd from The Winter's Tale* (London: J. and R. Tonson, 1758), p. 63.

30. Fiske, *English Theatre Music*, p. 205.

31. This acting edition is the source text for the 1774 Bell edition. George Winchester Stone, "Shakespeare's *Tempest* at Drury Lane," *Shakespeare Quarterly* 7 (1956):5.

32. *Letters of David Garrick*, 3:1029.

33. Ibid., 1:256.

34. George Winchester Stone, "*A Midsummer Night's Dream* in the Hands of Garrick and Colman," *PMLA* 54 (1939):470-72.

35. Odell, *Shakespeare from Betterton to Irving*, 1:358-66.

36. [David Garrick, attr.], *The Fairies. An Opera* (London: Tonson and Draper, 1755), p. A2.

37. Ibid., p. A3.

38. Ibid., p. 34.

39. Ibid., p. 6.

40. Ibid., p. 6.

41. The libretto to *The Fairies* lists Curioni as Lysander. Gaudagni is named in the printed score and in Burney's description of the opera in *General History*, 2:681.

42. Andrew P. McCredie, "John Christopher Smith as a Dramatic Composer," *Music and Letters* 45 (1964):26.

43. [Garrick], *Fairies*, p. A2.

44. *London Stage*, pt. 3, 1:cliv.

45. Burney, *General History*, 2:681.

46. Wilkinson, *Memoirs*, 4:202.

47. George Robert Guffey, "Introduction" to *After the Tempest* (Los Angeles: University of California Press, 1969), p. xvii.

48. [David Garrick, attr.], *The Tempest. An Opera* (London: J. and R. Tonson, 1756), pp. 16-17.

49. Arias had not always been the exclusive medium of solo expression. Soliloquies were common in Italian opera recitatives through the middle of the seventeenth century. Margaret Murata, "The Recitative Soliloquy," *Journal of the American Musicological Society* 32 (1979):45.

50. *London Stage*, pt. 4, 2:lix.

51. McCredie, "John Christopher Smith as Dramatic Composer," p. 26.

52. Theophilus Cibber, *Two Dissertations on the Theatre* (London: Reeves, 1756), quoted in Odell, *Shakespeare from Betterton to Irving*, 1:365.

53. Murphy, *Life of Garrick*, 2:302-3.

54. Roger Fiske has compiled a list of these English-language productions, comparing the number with a tally of spoken plays in the decade. *English Theatre Music*, pp. 342-44.

55. *Letters of Garrick*, 2:652-53.

56. John Genest, *Some Account of the English Stage from the Restoration in 1660 to 1830*, 10 vols. (Bath: for H. E. Carrington, 1832), 5:40.

57. Shakespeare, *A Midsummer Night's Dream . . . with Alterations and Additions, and Several New Songs* (London: J. and R. Tonson, 1763), pp. 8-9.

58. Ibid., p. 20.

59. Genest, *Some Account of the English Stage*, 5:40.

60. Christian Deelman, *The Great Shakespeare Jubilee* (New York: Viking, 1964), p. 7.

61. *Freeholders' Magazine*, October 1769, quoted in *London Stage*, pt. 4, 3:1430.

5

Shakespeare Deified: Shakespeare Music Enters the Romantic Era, 1770–1830

Garrick retired from the management of Drury Lane in 1776. His career had spanned the years during which Shakespeare had ceased to be one respected writer among other worthies and had become the leading figure of England's literary pantheon. Yet by the beginning of the 1770s practicality was already beginning to split the Shakespeare idolaters into two denominations—theatre people and scholars.

The theatre community recognized the plays as a central part of their heritage; however, performance practices changed slowly. The need to please a heterogeneous audience of varied tastes, the cost of new productions, and the continuing tradition of favorite productions brought a kind of conservatism to the repertoire that prevented sudden drastic change in text or presentation. Paradoxically, the theatre audience's desire for novelty resulted in a reduction in Shakespearean production during the last three decades of the eighteenth century. For example, Drury Lane under Garrick had presented an average of 55 nights of Shakespeare during the early 1760s. By the 1780s the average had fallen to 24 nights per season.[1] Newly written sentimental comedies and comic opera became staples.

It was easier for the second group of Shakespeare worshipers, scholars who were not concerned with a play's on-stage effectiveness, to remake their opinions based on studies of the original

texts. Indeed, literary critics of the late eighteenth century grew
to distrust stage presentation of Shakespeare. Samuel Johnson,
whose edition of the plays appeared in 1765, reportedly said:
"Many of Shakespere's plays are the worse for being acted."[2]
By the early years of the nineteenth century, critics such as
Samuel Taylor Coleridge and Charles Lamb, fearing stage production could deemphasize the importance of the text, contributed
to the growing concept of Shakespeare as literature to be con-
templated rather than drama to be acted. Lamb, remembered today for his prose versions of "stories from Shakespeare," went so
far as to say that "the plays of Shakespeare are less calculated for
performance than those of almost any other dramatist whatever."[3]

The plays were seen to be repositories of characterization,
fully developed philosophies, and psychological insight. Reading
Shakespeare became a required part of cultured education. Literary critics had taken the playwright's words out of the mouths of
actors and put them onto the pages of books, where they became
icons.   Not until the early 1800s would these early Romantic
views of Shakespeare influence actors and transform stage presentation.

The effect of this polarity on Shakespearean music in the final years of the eighteenth century was threefold. First, the conservative nature of Shakespearean production encouraged the
continued use of established repertoire, refurbished, updated, and
expanded in response to musical fashion rather than dramatic exi-
gencies. Second, as Shakespeare's poetry was incorporated into
literary, and thus domestic, culture, music intended not for the
stage but for concert hall and amateur use became an increasingly
growing segment of the Shakespearean musical repertoire—a
segment which would occasionally find its way back into dramatic use. Third, the study of Shakespeare's use of music became itself a field of historical study divorced from stage practicalities.

MUSICAL COMMENTARY IN END-OF-CENTURY EDITIONS

The most tangible results of the new Shakespeare scholarship were new complete editions with extensive textual annotations. Two of the more important editors, Samuel Johnson and Edmond Malone, recognized that discussion of musical issues was necessary as an adjunct to understanding the musical allusions in Shakespeare's poetry and the dramatic functions of musical stage directions. Charles Burney contributed to the musical commentary in the Johnson edition (1765, rev. 1773 and 1778). John Hawkins, a magistrate and literary commentator who was only secondarily a musician, provided similar service to Malone (1790).

Unlike Pope and some other of his editorial predecessors, Johnson was enthusiastic about Shakespeare's use of music. He recognized the symbolic and characterizational power of music in scenes such as Ariel's tuneful enchantment of Ferdinand in *The Tempest* :

The reason for which Ariel is introduced thus trifling is, that he and his companions are obviously of the fairy kind, an order of beings to which tradition has always ascribed a sort of diminutive agency, powerful but ludicrous, a humorous and frolic controlment of nature, well expressed by the song of Ariel.[4]

Johnson also noted that Shakespeare's use of masques was calculated and closely connected with spoken dialogue, citing the long-abandoned masque in *Timon of Athens*, in which the dance of the Amazons is compared to Timon's "sweep of vanity."[5]

Shakespeare included musical allusions in the play texts knowing his audience would be familiar with the popular songs and contemporary vocabulary. Much Elizabethan terminology and music would have been unfamiliar to an eighteenth-century playgoer. Offending scenes were rewritten or cut from the performing editions, but readers of complete critical texts required explanations. Variants of popular songs used by Shakespeare were of interest because of textual differences. For this reason, Johnson was the first scholar to attempt to untangle the lineage of the "Willow Song" in *Othello*.[6]

The editors were less interested in the actual music used in late sixteenth- and early seventeenth-century productions. The Appendix of Malone's 1790 edition included several songs from manuscripts identified only as being "from Shakespeare's time."[7] These had been collected by Hawkins but not included in earlier editions. Malone explained, "Not thinking them of much value I omitted to insert them, but in compliance with the wishes of a musical friend, I shall give them a place."[8] Malone shared Johnson's concern for textual evidence of Shakespeare's knowledge and use of music without being particularly interested in the music that Shakespeare used to achieve his effect.

Charles Burney thought Shakespeare's use of music merited several pages in the *General History* chapter on seventeenth-century England. He noted that almost all the comedies introduced singing; furthermore, "even in most of his tragedies, this wonderful and exquisite dramatist has manifested the same predilection for music."[9] Burney raised a number of issues that later writers would take up at greater length. He recognized the use of music in *A Midsummer Night's Dream* and *The Tempest* as a signature of the supernatural.[10] He also discussed musical allusions. Burney criticized some of Shakespeare's statements about music, considering him a kind of musical expert rather than a mirror of Elizabethan musical attitudes. Burney's interpretation of the Duke's lines in *Measure for Measure* IV, 1 may say more about Burney's own ideas on the relationship of words and music than about his knowledge of Renaissance musical attitudes:

"'Tis good; though Music oft hath such charm / To make bad good; and good provoke to harm." This is a heavy charge, which it would not have been easy for Shakespeare to substantiate, and does not very well agree with what he says in *The Tempest* of the *innoxious* efficacy of Music: "Sounds and sweet airs, that give delight and hurt not." Music may be applied to licentious poetry; but the poetry then corrupts the Music, not the Music the poetry.[11]

As a musician, Burney was more concerned than the textual editors with the music used in Shakespeare's time. He noted that a song was missing from the last act of the folio text for *A Midsummer Night's Dream.*[12]   He defined the meaning of "Rural Music" in the stage direction to *A Midsummer Night's Dream* IV, 1:   "Poker and tongs, marrow-bones and cleavers, salt-box, hurdy-gurdy, &c. are the old historical instruments of music on our Island."[13] Burney also included, in its entirety, music for the catch from *Twelfth Night* II, 3:

Ex. 26. "Hold Thy Peace" as in Burney.

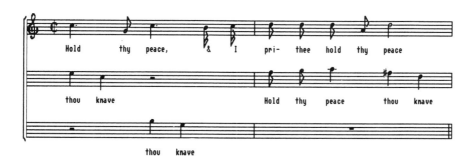

The catch first appeared in Thomas Ravenscroft's *Deuteromelia* (1609). Some scholars now believe it was not the version commonly used in Shakespeare's time.[14]

The effect of these musical concerns on theatrical offerings (or, more correctly, their lack of effect) can be seen in another series of published Shakespeare. The edition printed by John Bell in 1773–74 was a collection of the plays "as they are now performed at the Theatres Royal in London; regulated from the Prompt Books of Each House."[15]   These are the acting texts, variously from Covent Garden or Drury Lane, chosen for inclusion presumably on the basis of which productions were more popular. The edition recorded the standardization of Shakespeare texts in the last years of Garrick's tenure. The texts were representative of productions up to the time of John Philip Kemble's revisions beginning in 1789.[16] "Bell's Shakespeare" was not as profusely glossed as the scholarly editions. The notes, written by Francis Gentleman, refer to alterations and additions as well as to the original text.

The texts in Bell's edition suggest many songs and musical scenes were cut from the performing editions. Garrick's abridgement of the *Tempest* masque, with Boyce's music, was still in use as late as 1776.[17] Gentleman thought the cuts "judiciously made [the masque] half again as short as the original."[18] The masque at the end of *As You Like It* was totally omitted. The song "Then There Is Mirth in Heaven" was sung by an unspecified singer to cover Rosalind's final entry.[19] The original *Timon of Athens* masque and its dialogue were again in use, having displaced the Purcell masque, at least at Drury Lane.[20] The fourth-act masque in *Macbeth*, interestingly the one with a folio precedent, was removed. Other items missing from Bell's texts included the "Willow Song" scene, gone from the Covent Garden *Othello* since the mid-1750s,[21] the prison scene in *Richard II*, most of the songs in *As You Like It*, and "O Mistress Mine" and "Come Away Death" from *Twelfth Night*.

Some additions were indicated in the scripts as well. The two songs of Lorenzo in *The Merchant of Venice* and Garrick's text for the *Romeo and Juliet* dirge were included, as was a new song text in *Henry VIII* to replace "Orpheus and His Lute." Gentleman was mildly critical of such changes. Referring to "Blow, Blow Thou Winter Wind," an original Shakespeare text and one of the only two songs retained in *As You Like It*, Gentleman drily commented: "The song is aptly introduced here, and contains more meaning than nine tenths such compositions."[22]

Bell's Edition should not be taken as evidence that Shakespearean production from the latter part of the century was less musical than it had previously been. Such a view is not supported by theatrical observers, the individually published playbooks, or the amount of published music. Comic opera with spoken dialogue, having supplanted completely sung opera and ballad opera at both Covent Garden and Drury Lane, became an important part of the theatre season in the last quarter-century.

Of the twelve most-frequently performed offerings between 1775 and 1800, fully half were comic operas.[23] The popularity of these musicals spilled over into other productions, including Shakespeare. George Colman, a playwright who had himself revised Garrick's comic opera version of *A Midsummer Night's Dream* into an afterpiece, later mocked such musical Shakespeareana through a character in one of his plays who spoke with what was taken to be a comic caricature of an Italian accent:

Vat signify your triste Sha-kes-peare? Begar, dere
was more moneys got by de grand spectacle of de Sha-kes-peare
Jubilee, dan by all de *comique* and *tragique*
of Sha-kes-peare beside, ma, foi! You make-a de
danse, and de musique, and de patomime of your Sha-kes-peare, and
den he do ver well.[24]

Ernest Brandes, a German philosopher and theatre advocate, was a more detached and sober critic than Colman. After observing the London theatres during a trip to England in 1784, Brandes criticized the extensive use of music in Shakespeare productions. He even suspected that actresses trying out for the role of Ophelia were chosen more for their singing ability than their acting.[25] Covent Garden intimate James Boaden verified that this was true into the 1780s, when he recounted the impact the great Mrs. Siddons made in the role following a series of singers as Ophelia.[26]

Other theatre observers between 1760 and 1790, including Genest, were also impressed (not always favorably) with the amount of music in productions. If the lack of musical references in Bell is to be considered a kind of indicator, it suggests that musical episodes and their texts were frequently changed in the performances and did not merit being recorded in a permanent text. The quantity of printed music associated with specific productions and the many contemporary accounts not recorded in Bell suggest that musical additions were in fact changed frequently, depending on the availability of singers and music.

SHAKESPEARE MUSIC TO 1800

New Song Repertoire

Even after several decades of exposure to Italian opera, "the English seem at all times to have received more delight from dramas, in which the dialogue is spoken and the songs are incidental than from such that were sung throughout."[27] When Garrick called recitative "the dullest part of Musick," he recognized his audience's distrust of the musical exposition of action. Completely sung opera, Shakespearean and non-Shakespearean alike, was displaced at the theatres by comic operas with spoken dialogue.

As for the preference for comic rather than tragic plots in musical treatments, Garrick biographer and contemporary Thomas Davies offered one view:

The serious and comic happily blended, as in *The Duenna* and *Love in a Village*; or the entirely comic, as in *The Beggar's Opera*, the farcical, as in *Midas*; or even a simple fable elegantly told . . . such dramatic pieces as these are just representations of nature, humor, and passion, and will forever charm.[28]

Shakespeare's comedies, with their blend of the serious and the comic, should have been ideal for such an aesthetic; however, with the continuing exception of *The Tempest* and *Macbeth*, none of the plays became the basis for a musical production on the scale of *The Duenna*, *The Poor Soldier*, or other operas popular after 1770. Yet much of the music for Shakespearean productions from the 1760s and later, although more modest in scale than concurrent comic operas, displays musical, textual, and dramatic characteristics typical of that genre.

When the Shakespeare song repertoire began to expand in the 1740s with the revival of the comedies, original lyrics were most frequently used in play productions. By the 1760s, new song texts reminiscent of the spurious Restoration adaptations appeared with increasing frequency. There were more singers with greater

skill and more talent in the companies of both houses, an improvement Burney credited in large part to "the compositions and
instructions of Dr. Arne, who endeavoured to refine our melodies
and singing more from Italian than English models."[29]

The songs became more vocally demanding.   Some of the
singers wrote their own music to show off their particular vocal
strengths.   Michael Kelly, a tenor with a successful operatic career, wrote songs of high tessitura with wide ranges.

Ex. 27. Kelly. "To See Thee So Gentle" (*Tempest*, Drury Lane,
1789), vocal part, mm. 20-26.

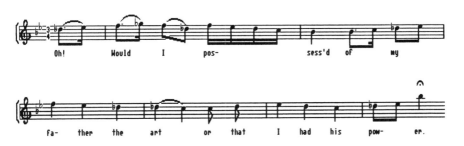

by permission of the British Library

Composers also took advantage of the opportunity to write for
more flexible voices.

Ex. 28. Baildon. "Jessica's Song" (*Merchant of Venice*, Covent
Garden, 1751), mm. 9-16.

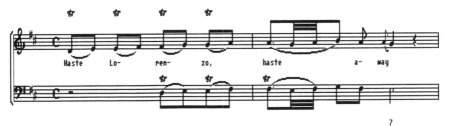

7

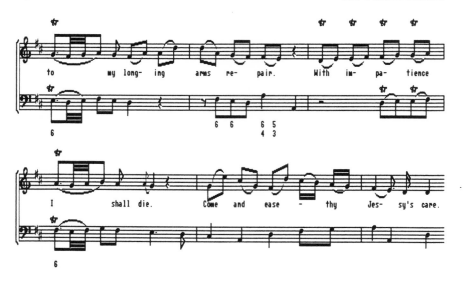

by permission of the British Library

This new concern for vocal technique may have been at least partly responsible for the turning away from Shakespearean song lyrics.

As early as 1755, in a generally favorable critique of Smith's *The Fairies*, one writer noted the restrictions Shakespeare's poetry placed on a composer:

I wish the Choice had been Words in general more Lyric, that is more bending and pliant to harmony. How far the Composer deserves, or otherwise, I leave to Connoisseurs in Music to determine.[30]

Since Arne, most composers had responded to the iambic stress patterns in many Shakespearean lyrics with either dotted patterns, triple meter, or with short-long rhythmic patterns reminiscent of the Scotch snap. The verses did not lend themselves to highly ornamented vocal lines, and such settings were rare. Even as the music for the newly added texts became more florid, concurrent Shakespeare settings retained a simpler syllabic nature, as exemplified in Vernon's "Epilogue Song" from *Twelfth Night* (Appendix A). The occasional Shakespeare lyric that encouraged elaborate treatment was set frequently. Aylward's setting of "Hark, Hark, the Lark" from *Cymbeline* (also complete in Appendix A) was one of several made since Chilcot's in 1750.

The added non-Shakespearean texts usually shared two characteristics. First, they avoided as much as possible the harder consonants, while maintaining a consistently open vowel sound.

> My soul's by Love and you subdu'd,
> Again my faith I plight.[31]

The charge made by Motteux that English was "overcharg'd with consonants" was now being applied to lines such as "where the bee sucks" and "when that I was and a little tiny boy." The second characteristic of the new song texts was an avoidance of uneven rhythms and irregular phrasing.

> O thou are source of all my pleasure,
> Treasure of my soul art thou.[32]

Words that would normally be given a trochaic stress when spoken ("pleasure" and "treasure" in the above example) were set with even stress on both syllables.

Ex. 29. Kelly. "What New Delights" (*Tempest*, Drury Lane, 1789), mm. 19-25.

by permission of the British Library

Although many writers on poetry and music were suspicious of the "monotonous parallels" in the simplicity of the new *galant* style brought to England from the Continent in the 1760s,[33] composers working with parallel period forms made a more uniform verse structure important in song lyrics. The new texts displayed both parallel phrase structure and regularity of rhythm.

Ex. 30. "Trust Not Man" (*Twelfth Night*, Drury Lane, ca. 1765), mm. 9-24.

leave you "poor de- lu- ded" to la- ment.

by permission of the British Library

Similarly, the metrical irregularities and blank verse of play text not originally intended to be sung would have discouraged musical setting even if the dramatic situation were appropriate.

Thomas Linley, the elder, a musician at Drury Lane, recognized and disapproved of such poetical simplification:

The idea of reducing poetry to verse in order to make it fit musical expression is wrong: for it is the imagery and sentiments conveyed by the words that ought to inspire the musician, and not any particular kind of verse—The variety of rhythm and poetical feet are oftener found in poetical prose, or blank verse, than in verses which rhyme.[34]

Linley was not writing specifically about Shakespearean music. Nevertheless, the methods prevalent in choosing and setting verses of all kinds had the effect of introducing new texts into Shakespearean productions and limiting new settings of Shakespeare's lyrics.

Almost without exception the new songs were concerned with a given play's romantic subplot. Shakespeare's lovers rarely had to overcome the barriers placed in the way of characters in the "comedies of tears" by Garrick and, later in the century, Frederick Reynolds and others; however, the tribulations of Jessica and Lorenzo in *The Merchant of Venice,* Miranda and Ferdinand in *The Tempest,* or Olivia and Orsino in *Twelfth Night* sufficiently resembled the sentimentalism of contemporary comedy to encourage similar textual and musical elaboration of Shakespearean roles.

> Let me then in wanton play
> Sigh and gaze my soul away.[35]

> What new delights invade my bosom,
> In every vein what rapture play
> Whilst on thee I fondly gaze?[36]

The above excerpts, from *The Merchant of Venice* and *The Tempest* respectively, reflect the generic and interchangeable qualities of the new love lyrics. The songs are truly incidental, in no way furthering the action and having only the most generalized of commentarial effects.

Antiquarian Interests

Musical antiquarianism was not an isolated phenomenon but part of a general interest in the past and a growing sense of cultural historicism. The founding of the Academy of Ancient Music in the 1750s and the Concert of Ancient Music in 1776 attested to revived interest in music from earlier times, defined by the rules of the organizations as being more than twenty years old. At about the same time, the Catch Club and the Madrigal Society were established to promote the singing of Renaissance repertoire. The membership of these societies was mixed and included both amateurs and professional members. Burney noted that the interest in older catches, canons, and madrigals had resulted in "innumerable compositions of that kind."[37] As the unaccompanied vocal pieces known as "glees" (based in spirit if not technique on the madrigal form) became increasingly popular, the Anacreontic Society, the Noblemen's and Gentlemen's Catch Club, and other groups were created for their performance. Shakespearean texts, revered as repositories of past knowledge, were perfect for this conservative musical form.

The literary interest in Shakespeare marked by the Jubilee of 1769 had resulted in an outpouring of settings of lyrics, monologues excerpted from the plays, and poems. Words that could never be sung in their dramatic context were acceptable when moved from the theatre to the pleasure garden or parlor. The growing home audience of amateurs was the intended market for many of these pieces.[38] Shakespeare's poetry, which had proved unsuitable for the increasingly complicated theatrical songs, could easily be set to the simpler melodies appropriate for a domestic audience. In addition to glees, composers also provided the amateur market with solo songs accompanied by keyboard, harp, or guitar.

Ex. 31. Kelly. "Hamlet's Letter to Ophelia," mm. 5-13

by permission of the British Library

Among the composers of glees, R.J.S. Stevens was a popular favorite in the last years of the century. A series of Shakespearean glees by Stevens, surviving in a manuscript currently at the Fitzwilliam Library, Cambridge, was published and widely circulated. Glees had been used in operatic productions prior to 1780, but one of the earliest surviving accounts of a contemporary glee's use in a staged Shakespearean production names Stevens's setting of "Sigh No More, Ladies" from a 1789 Drury Lane *Much Ado about Nothing*.[39] Although the folio text of *Much Ado about Nothing* II, 3 does not explicitly assign the song, the associated dialogue clearly indicates it is for the servant Balthasar:

Don Pedro. By my troth, a good song.
Balthasar. And an ill singer, my lord.
Don Pedro. Ha, no, no, faith; thou sing'st well enough for a
    shift.
Benedict. An he had been a dog that should have howled thus,
    they would have hang'd him; and I pray God his bad voice bode no
    mischief.

Here Drury Lane introduced a glee requiring several performers (complete in Appendix A) in place of a solo song, seemingly contradictory to its context.

The glee, crossing the blurred boundary between concert hall and theatre, became the most common ensemble type in Shakespearean productions in the final years of the eighteenth century. It remained so into the early years of the nineteenth century, when compositions by James Hook, Samuel Webbe, Benjamin Cooke, and others would be added to the repertoire. William Linley, in the preface to his 1816 Shakespeare music collection, did not unreservedly approve the dramatic use of glees:

The two beautiful glees of Mr. Stevens, viz. "It was a lover and his lass" and "O Mistress Mine" are composed for five and six voices; but how are these same words introduced in the plays from which they are taken? Why, the first are meant to be sung as a duet by two pages, in a simple quaint way, to please Touchstone the clown in *As You Like It*, and the other words as a song to be sung by the clown himself in *Twelfth Night* to gratify the two drunken knights. Not that the melody of such intended compositions should be either uncouth or vulgar . . . yet there should be a characteristic quaintness mingled with its sweetness; the glees referred to are not only elegant compositions, but distinguished for their masterly construction.[40]

Linley stated two objections, one implicit, the other explicit. First was the dramatic incongruity arising when a song lyric intended for a specific character was set as an ensemble piece. Second, the refined artifice of the eighteenth-century glee was at odds with the unsophisticated or rustic circumstances in which Shakespeare often introduced musical numbers in the action.

The drama critic Leigh Hunt, writing a few years after Linley, was even more outspoken on the dramatic inappropriateness of glees:

But for one true flight of gaiety and inspiration like Arne's "Where the Bee Sucks," we have fifty happy pieces of poetry ludicrously contradicted by doleful and pompous music; especially in those solemn personages called Glees, who play into each other's hands as gravely as old ladies at whist.[41]

An issue raised by neither Linley nor Hunt was the indiscriminate introduction of glees, with texts excerpted from any one of Shakespeare's plays or poems or by some other poet altogether, into situations Shakespeare did not single out for music. The potential for dramatic chaos in these circumstances was later to become a concern of literary writers.

Returning for the moment to antiquarian concerns, the edition of the Leveridge *Macbeth* music published in 1770 by William Boyce was another example of interest in England's musical past. Among the manuscripts in Boyce's collection while he was working on the *Cathedral Music* collection was the unattributed *Macbeth* score, now Egerton MS 2957 in the British Library.[42]

Perhaps because of the discussion of Davenant's production in *Roscius Anglicanus*, Boyce attributed the music to Matthew

Ex. 32. Arnold. *Macbeth*. "Menuetto," mm. 1-8.

Locke.[43] Thus misattributed, the music continued to be revised according to current musical fashion for use in the theatres.   In Drury Lane's 1776–78 *Macbeth*, "the original Music composed by Matthew Locke"[44] had "a proper Attention paid to it in the getting up by Mr. Linley (who composed the Additional Accompaniments)."[45]   The Locke attribution was not universally accepted.   William Linley (son of Thomas Linley, the elder, who was responsible for Drury Lane's "Additional Accompaniments") believed the score was a second version by Eccles.[46]   Later revisions to the score were made by Thomas Linley, the younger (1778) and Henry R. Bishop (1819).   Not until the twentieth

by permission of the British Library

century was a second manuscript with an attribution to Leveridge discovered.[47]

The historical authenticity of other aspects of *Macbeth* also came under scrutiny. Having been performed in contemporary English military dress for several decades, the play was acted in "the Habits of the Times"[48] and "Scotch habit"[49] for the first time in the 1770s. Taking advantage of the fashion for upcountry folk tunes and the desire to emphasize the "Scotch" theme in *Macbeth*, Samuel Arnold composed a set of "Favorite Scotch Airs" for the Little Theatre in the Haymarket.

The title page of the score, published in 1785, is the only record of this production. Most of the numbers were to be performed before the play and during the intervals. The interval tunes were settings of actual Scottish folk songs: "Berks of Endermay," "The Yellow-Hair'd Laddie," "Lochaber," and several more.[50] These source melodies were themselves anachronistic in the play's eleventh-century setting. Two numbers in Arnold's collection intended for use in the play proper (a march for Macbeth's first entrance and, in Example 32, a minuet for the banquet at which Banquo's ghost appears) do not use pre-existing tunes, but combine the Scotch snap with *galant* melodic traits in a peculiar mix.

Even though music historians had already begun to collect and study music from Shakespeare's time and before, there was no recorded attempt to revive any Elizabethan music in the late eighteenth century productions. Paradoxically, in an age that romanticized the idea of the past and claimed to create new music in the spirit of the old, much of the earlier repertoire was criticized for being unsophisticated. Malone may have held a common view of Elizabethan songs in "not thinking them of much value." Some musicians even felt such music could not work in the theatre. William Linley's experience with audiences at Drury Lane led him to conclude that Elizabethan songs were unsuitable for the Georgian Stage:

This music could merely be received as a curiosity; it could not, in the present day, be so shaped as to be rendered palatable to a refined musical ear. . . . Striking dramatic melodies, in particular, were not known until the great Purcell burst forth.[51]

Creating the musical illusion of antiquity was acceptable in glees, and Mrs. Jordan could accompany herself on the obsolete lute as she sang a newly composed "Willow Song" in a 1798 Drury Lane *Othello*. Composers and producers preferred to recreate a past redolent of contemporary sensibilities. Comprehensive concern for Elizabethan stagecraft, and the subsequent birth of serious Shakespearean musical scholarship and musical stage performance, was still nearly a century away.

Tempest Redux

When the aged Garrick retired in 1776, the management of Drury Lane passed to Richard Brinsley Sheridan and Thomas Linley, the elder. Sheridan spent more energy on his writing than in management of the theatre, while Linley was a musician who had come to London from Bath to direct the theatre's Lenten oratorio season. Neither brought an actor's perspective to the job. Among the productions mounted in honor of the new regime was a revival of *The Tempest* (4 January 1777), replacing the version introduced by Garrick in 1757. Cast lists in newspaper advertisements[52] and song lyrics in surviving musical sources indicate Garrick's text was revised for the new production. No complete playbook for this production seems to have been published; however, nineteenth-century Shakespeare bibliographer W. A. Harrison uncovered library catalogue evidence of printed song texts "altered by R. B. Sheridan," suggesting Drury Lane's new co-manager supplied textual alterations and new song lyrics.[53]

Advertisements credited the music in this production to Thomas Arne, Purcell, and Thomas Linley, the younger (1756–78). Young Thomas, a violin prodigy and acquaintance of Mozart, turned to composing late in his short life. Leader of the Drury Lane orchestra, he assisted his father at the theatre and was in part responsible for the music to the successful opera *The Duenna*. In 1776 he wrote a nondramatic *Lyric Ode on the Fairies, Aerial Beings, and Witches of Shakespeare*. The few surviving compositions by young Linley give credence to Roger Fiske's description of him as "our most promising composer between Purcell and Elgar," whose untimely death in a boating accident "changed for the worse our whole history of music."[54]

Linley's contributions to *The Tempest* , the finest music written for a Shakespearean production in the last half of the eighteenth century, are preserved in British Library Egerton MS 2493. Made by Drury Lane copyist J. S. Gaudry in 1780,[55] the manuscript contains six *Tempest* items: an opening "storm" chorus, "O Bid Your Faithful Ariel Fly," "Come unto These Yellow

Sands," "While You Here Do Snoring Lie," "Ere You Can Say Come and Go," and a choral conclusion for Arne's "Where the Bee Sucks." Selections from *The Duenna* were also included. Commemorative annotations were added to the manuscript in 1812 by Linley's younger brother William (author of *Shakespeare's Dramatic Music*).

In addition to composing new music, young Thomas was probably responsible for organizing pre-existing items, including selections by Arne, "Purcell," and possibly J. C. Smith.[56] More music was needed for two "spirit" dances in the first and third acts and for a grand ballet in act IV. [57] The unusual sounds of "the invention of Merlin,"[58] a keyboard instrument (built by the serendipitously named John Joseph Merlin) with strings at 4, 8, and 16-foot pitch activated by both piano and harpsichord actions, was heard from behind the scenes. None of this extra music is preserved in the manuscript.

The play's opening scene was omitted in this production[59], replaced by a scenic shipwreck created by the pioneer stage designer Philip deLoutherbourg. In his comments on *The Tempest* in Bell's 1774 edition, Francis Gentleman remarked on Shakespeare's opening to the play: "The name and first material incident of this piece are exceedingly contrastic to comedy; however, there is a good opportunity afforded for curious scenery and mechanism."[60] Jettisoning the text provided even more opportunity for visual show, although one observer much regretted the loss of Shakespeare's text.[61] Another playgoer found the representation of the tempest's blazing heavens all too realistic: "It is to be hoped the managers do not this evening intend again to put the audience in danger of suffocation, by repeating the shower of flammable matter during the storm in the first act."[62]

The opening chorus by Linley, with new words presumably by Sheridan, accompanied this spectacle.

> Arise, ye Spirits of the storm.
> Appal the guilty eye!
> Tear the wild waves, ye mighty winds,
> Ye blasting lightnings, fly!

Dart through the Tempest of the Deep,
And Rocks and Seas confound!

Hark how the vengeful Thunders roll!
Amazement flames around,
Behold—the fate-devoted bark
Dash'd on the trembling shore.
Mercy! the sinking wretches cry—
Mercy! They're heard no more. [63]

When the play was brought back the following season, the storm scene was moved "by desire" to the beginning of the second act,[64] presumably the desire of fashionable latecomers who did not want to miss the shipwreck.

Linley's opening chorus displays aspects of sonata-allegro construction. The gathering storm is represented in the first key area (D major) over a prolonged pedal point. After a lengthy transition to V/V, a new figuration of string arpeggios (the "tempest toss'd" sea) is introduced; however, A major is not fully confirmed before a surprising shift to F-sharp minor. A return to D major introduces what is analogous to an exposition repeat (Example 33), where the chorus appears for the first time, added to the orchestral material introduced in the opening measures.

After the transition to V/V, the A major section is this time confirmed when a full cadence ends the exposition. The beginning of a quasi-development section is announced with F-sharp in open octaves from both chorus and orchestra, recalling the emphasis of F-sharp in the expository measures. The movement's central area, divided into four clearly articulated sections, does not develop previously introduced thematic material. It is modulatory but gravitates toward F-sharp minor and major throughout. The recapitulation (announced by the return of the pedal point) brings back D major, musical material, and text ("Arise, arise, arise"). After a transition analogy, music and text first introduced in the development section return, this time in D, for a quiet close as the storm subsides.

Ex. 33. Linley. *Tempest.* Opening chorus, mm. 88-93.

by permission of the British Library

The new arias were intended for Miss Field, a child protégée of the elder Linley who was making her stage debut as Ariel.[65] Linley's musical vocabulary was more progressive than that of his musical compatriots.   Ariel's songs are substantial compositions displaying considerable lyric charm and Mozartean grace.   "O Bid Your Faithful Ariel Fly," the only song using a non-Shakespearean text, is a lengthy *da capo* movement of 163 measures.   Linley combined the operatic style current in the theatre with dramatic gestures modeled after the "Purcell" score.

Ex. 34.   Linley.   "O Bid Your Faithful Ariel," mm. 71-78.

Text repetition, extensive in all the arias, was not limited to parallelism or sequence. A single repeated word could be used to extend phrase length.

Ex. 35. Linley. "O Bid Your Faithful Ariel," mm. 116-22.

by permission of the British Library

The setting of "While You Here Do Snoring Lie" twice repeats the complete text in which Ariel warns the sleeping Alonzo of an imminent attack (II,2). The insertion of a 51-measure song into the scene of attempted assassination must have stemmed any potential for dramatic urgency, a problem in the entire play according to one writer:

From the necessary delay in the course of exhibition, too much time is afforded for recollection, an air of langour therefore prevails before the piece is nearly ended, the spur of expectation is lost, and the interest of the plot, the great point in stage exhibition, is not felt in the Theatre.[66]

The two choral movements in the manuscript are extensions of songs rather than independent movements. The choral conclusion of "Come Unto These Yellow Sands" may actually have been a separate number, separated from the solo song by dialogue. The song is in B-flat, and the following chorus is in an unprepared D major. Moreover, there is no segue indication in the score. The play ended with a scene of "ariel" spirits in the style of Shadwell. A discrepancy exists between a newspaper account of this finale and the music manuscript. The writer for *The Morning Chronicle, and London Advertiser* admiringly mentioned "Mr. Jackson's Quartetto and Chorus of Where the Bee Sucks,"[67] but the chorus preserved in Egerton MS 2493 and clearly attributed to Linley is intended for Arne's setting.

There is no evidence of a masque—either Shakespeare's goddesses or Neptune and Amphitrite—in the original 1777 production. None of the maskers are mentioned in the first newspaper playbills; moreover, a contemporary commentator, while neither confirming nor denying the original presence of a masque, definitively states that in subsequent seasons "some prejudice existed against the masque introduced by the immortal Author, and it was, therefore, omitted."[68] It seems reasonable to surmise the masque was absent from the very first. Despite this, Burney described the production as "more a musical masque than opera or play."[69] The sheer length of the individual musical numbers precluded their being simple incidental music. Perhaps Burney found the shipwreck's visual spectacle and the symbolic association of music and dance with the supernatural more suggestive of earlier masque tradition, less like either the commentarial quality or buffo ensembles of Italian opera or the mix of dialogue and music in comic opera.

In contrast, Covent Garden's *Tempest*, which opened 27 December 1776, was blasted as "an operatical mutilation."[70] Newspaper advertisements listed music by Arne, Fisher, and Smith as well as a masque. The play was contracted into three acts "on accound [*sic*] of the additional airs, etc."[71] A major feature of this production was a new setting of Garrick's verse "O Bid Your Faithful Ariel Fly" by the 66-year-old Thomas Arne.

Drury Lane's *Tempest* was revised again in 1789 by John Philip Kemble, a promising young actor who had recently assumed the daily routine of managing the theatre for the indifferent Sheridan. Kemble's *Tempest* returned much of the Dryden-Davenant material to the script. Michael Kelly, who played Ferdinand for Kemble, considered this something of a "novelty."[72] According to Kelly, most of the music was by Purcell, "got up by Mr. Linley [the elder]."[73] The romantic subplot became a major musical addition, and Kelly himself wrote new sentimental songs and duets for Ferdinand and Miranda, played by Kelly's concurrent off-stage romantic interest, Anna Crouch.

In all, fourteen musical numbers were added to the show. Much of the dialogue in the log-bearing scene was cut for songs and a duet, and Shakespeare's masque was omitted in favor of Neptune and Amphitrite. The shipwreck chorus by the younger Thomas Linley was retained in the second act. Literary commentators reacted strongly to the text changes:

The Audience were disappointed and displeased at the liberties taken by Authors and Managers with one of our Poet's most celebrated comedies. . . . It is a very Hazardous attempt to alter Shakespeare's writing for we at once lose Connection, thought, Style, and language.[74]

The audience's displeasure must have been less severe than the above critic imagined or their delight at the music and spectacle

more robust. Kemble's hybrid *Tempest* returned to the Drury
Lane stage every season until 1802.

THE EARLY NINETEENTH CENTURY: THE AGE OF KEMBLE AND KEAN

After the turn of the century, the London stages were dominated by two actors: John Philip Kemble, who left Drury Lane in
1803 to become a share holder at Covent Garden, and Edmund
Kean, a younger actor who became the leading figure at Drury
Lane. The differences between the two exemplify the shifts of
dramatic fashion as the theatre based in the traditions of Garrick
and Sheridan entered the nineteenth century.

Kemble represented a classical attitude to acting. Declamation was the actor's stock in trade, and Kemble thought far too
much emphasis was put on "the manners of familiar life in dramatic representations."[75] Kemble represented the eighteenth-
century actor/manager tradition established by Garrick. Like
Garrick, he was seen as a defender of the original Shakespearean
texts; however, also like Garrick, he freely adapted scripts if he
thought he could improve their stageability. Some of Kemble's
productions retained earlier alterations, but such retentions became rarer in later years. Cuts and altered speech assignments
were more frequent, but negligible compared to earlier abridg-
ments (e.g., Garrick's *Florizel and Perdita*). Kemble did not
make significant additions of his own or change the nature of the
plays, as Dryden, Tate, Lacy, and others did. James Boaden,
Kemble's first biographer, described the process by which the
acting versions were made:

Now this, in Mr. Kemble's notion of the business, was not to order the
prompter to write out the parts from some old mutilated prompt copy
lingering on his shelves; but himself to consider it attentively in the
author's genuine book: then to examine what corrections could be
properly admitted into his text; and, finally, what could be cut out in
the representation, not as disputing the judgement of the author, but as
suiting the time of the representation to the habits of his audience, or a

little favouring the powers of his actors, in order that the performance might be as uniformly good as it was practicable to make it.[76]

Kemble also shared with Garrick a healthy regard for novelty on the stage to keep the audience's interest. If this meant honored scripts were dressed with visual spectacle and music, so be it.

Kean, coming to prominence in 1814, some years after Kemble, represented a different concept of acting that emphasized strong personal insight, melodramatic exaggeration, and interpretive flashes of insight. Coleridge commented: "His rapid descents from the hyper-tragic to the infra-colloquial, though sometimes productive of great effect, are often unreasonable. To see him act is like reading Shakespeare by flashes of lightning."[77] The literary study of Shakespearean characterization had spawned a similar psychological and philosophical criticism of Shakespearean stage characterization, represented in the acting of Kean and the writings of William Hazlitt and (to a lesser extent) Leigh Hunt. Kean could be called a Romantic actor in that he combined the abstract conventions of stage representation with emotional expression commonly shared with his audiences: "In this forced conjunction of two realms, life and the stage . . . was a new emphasis whose time had apparently come."[78]

The traditional music repertoire for Shakespearean production was enlarged with offerings by a new generation of stage composers, names that today are less familiar than those of their earlier counterparts. John Davy went to London seeking a career as a violinist but began writing for the theatres in the 1790s. Charles Edward Horn, the son of German immigrants, was a singer (Caspar in the first London performance of *Der Freischütz*) and conductor who ended his career as director of Boston's Handel and Haydn Society. John Braham was a singer at Drury Lane. William Henry Ware was a member of one of London's minor musical dynasties.

Of the musicians associated with Shakespearean productions in the first third of the century, only Henry Rowley Bishop was primarily a composer and arranger. Remembered today for the aria "Home Sweet Home" from the opera *Clari, or the Maid of*

Milan, Bishop was in his day considered a major talent. His long-term reputation was harmed by the dissipation of his energies in too many projects, a problem Leigh Hunt recognized when he said Bishop "would not be the most unequal writer living, if he were not the musician of all-work at the theatre."[79] Bishop's potential aside, the years between 1800 and 1830 did not see a major group of talents comparable to the Arnes, Boyce, J. C. Smith, and the Linleys contributing to the Shakespeare music repertoire.

The John Philip Kemble Promptbooks

A large collection of Kemble's promptbooks, complete with his longhand notes on production details, are preserved at the Folger Library and have been published in facsimile. The promptbooks date from the years 1806–13 and represent Shakespeare during the Kemble regime at Covent Garden. They are especially valuable as examples of musical practice from their time, since fires destroyed the music libraries at Covent Garden (1808) and Drury Lane (1809).[80] Moreover, very few published scores for Covent Garden's Shakespearean productions from 1800 to 1830, and almost none for Drury Lane, are known today. The Kemble promptbooks indicate all music cues, not just songs or major instrumental movements. The plays in which large amounts of music were used include: *Coriolanus* (1811), *Henry VIII* (1806), *Henry IV, Part 2* (1808?), *Romeo and Juliet* (1811), *The Tempest* (1806—a much restored text compared to the 1789 Drury Lane version), *Macbeth* (1808), and *The Merchant of Venice* (1813).

The stage directions provided by Kemble indicate he was sensitive to the music's ability to establish the mood of a dramatic scene. These directions sometimes indicate the effect the music was to produce. "Mourning music" was played in the scene with Virgilia and Volumnia in *Coriolanus* (V, 1; folio V, 3).[81] An organ was directed to play sad music in the scene where Queen Katherine grieves over her separation from the king in *Henry*

VIII.[82] By the time both of the examples above had been staged, a number of melodramas had been presented successfully in previous Covent Garden seasons.

The term melodrama here refers not to a sensational or sentimental entertainment, but to a form of dramatic presentation arising around 1800 in which spoken text was musically accompanied throughout. While the music in comic opera had been charged with impeding the drama's flow, the music in melodrama contributed to the forward movement of the action while at the same time contributing to the expression of sentiment. According to one writer of melodrama, music would "fix the attention, rouse the passions, and hold the faculties in anxious and impatient suspense."[83] Kemble's use of music as running commentary to a Shakespearean scene had precedent in the contemporary melodrama as well as in Garrick's pioneering use of music in scenes from *A Winter's Tale* and *King Lear.*

Kemble used on-stage trumpets and drums or, alternately, the pit orchestra for entrances and exits. (He used such stage directions rather more frequently than indicated in the folio.) The on-stage musicians were regular employees retained for this purpose; however, if additional musicians were needed on stage, they were pulled up from the orchestra.[84] In the histories and tragedies, the pit orchestra sometimes joined the on-stage brass in creating a martial atmosphere. For *King John* (1804) the wind instruments in the pit were to play a march increasingly louder and louder, as if a band were approaching from a distance.[85] *Henry VIII* was to end with "The most magnificent triumphal march that can be imagined."[86] Music was also used to fill scene transitions.

Kemble used Garrick's dirge text in the 1811 Covent Garden *Romeo and Juliet.*[87] An earlier production, overseen by Kemble at Drury Lane on 17 November 1788, had included a now-lost setting of the dirge by Thomas Linley, the elder, which may also have been used later at Covent Garden.[88] However, at some point after 1811 Kemble or his successors rejected the texted version of the procession. Fanny Kemble, who acted Juliet at Covent Garden in the 1820s, recalled the processions:

The Suppression of that very dreadful piece of stage pageantry has at last, I believe, been conceded to the better taste of modern audiences: but even in my time it was still performed, an exact representation of a funeral procession, such as one meets everyday in Rome, with torch-bearers, priests, and bier covered with its black velvet pall, embroidered with skull cross-bones, with a corpse-like figure stretched upon it, marched round the stage, chanting some portion of the fine Roman Catholic requiem music.[89]

The dirge, an independent piece of music, had been replaced by Gregorian chant. (This had certainly happened by the middle of the 1820s, when Berlioz saw the Kemble production. The funeral procession in the fourth section of Berlioz's dramatic symphony is itself suggestive of chant.)

When Kemble staged *The Tempest* at Covent Garden in 1806 he removed many of the incidental songs, including all of the Ferdinand-Miranda arias and duets. Kemble's *Macbeth*, on the other hand, retained all the music then in use and restored to the fourth act the "Black Spirits and White" masque missing in Bell's edition.[90] The witch chorus was made up of 35 singers positioned around the stage in a variety of patterns.[91] Surprisingly, the banquet scene music was not played by an on-stage band but from the pit.[92]

The Merchant of Venice retained the musical elaboration of the Lorenzo-Jessica subplot. The musical texts were all non-Shakespearean. Two new duets were added to the songs (which included the still-popular Arne elopement serenade). One of the new numbers was used as the act III finale.

> *Jessica:*   With vows of everlasting truth
> You've won my captive heart, fond youth
> But, parted once, might I not find,
> That "Out of sight were out of mind?"
>
> *Lorenzo:*   Ah, do thyself no wrong, my dear!
> Away with every jealous fear
> For each fair object I might see
> Could but inspire a thought of thee.

Both: Thus absence fans to stronger flame
                The love that fires the constant soul:
                As distant points with surer aim
                The faithful needle to its darling pole.[93]

The final music is a duet between Jessica and Lorenzo inspired by the musical scene in folio V, 1. The song is inserted where Shakespeare's stage direction directs minstrels to play in the background.[94]

Pastiche technique continued to be the norm for assembling the musical part of a new production. The piano/vocal score released in association with the 1806 *Tempest* included music by Linley, Arne, and "Purcell," as well as the new overture and act symphonies by John Davy. William Henry Ware added an overture and act tunes to Leveridge's *Macbeth* music in 1805.

A worksheet from *Henry IV, Part 2*, surviving in British Library Additional MS 33570, describes some of the music by popular composers that Henry R. Bishop adapted as incidental music for the play. The overture was from Cherubini's *Anacreon*, and the first-act prelude was "Haydn's Mil.[itary] Movet. no. 12." The second act opened with the march from Handel's *Athalia*. Another second-act number, used perhaps to cover a scene change, was listed as occasional, as was the third-act overture. Bishop's early success as a comic opera composer made his increasing reliance on pastiche scores after his 1810 appointment to Covent Garden surprising, leading to speculation that he was pressured into this format by the demands of theatre management.[95]

Music was important in Kemble's Shakespeare productions. He continued to use the ceremony and spectacle of processions with music. He retained comic opera elements in some of the comedies. More interesting was Kemble's use of incidental music within the plays. The music assumed less importance as an independent entertainment and was carefully orchestrated into a primarily spoken scene to create an effect that would enhance the drama.

Elliston's Burlettas: *Macbeth* and *The Jubilee*

If the acting of Kemble and Kean represented the most elevated efforts of the patent theatres, the career of Robert William
Elliston (1774–1831) mirrored practical and popular aspects of
London theatrical life in the early nineteenth century. Elliston
acted at Drury Lane and the Haymarket and was impresario for
several seasons in the illegitimate theatres that sprang up in the
early 1800s. The two patent houses were clearly inadequate to
meet the growing London population's demand for entertainment,
but the patents were retained because the government did not
want to lose control over dramatic presentations. Although the
theatrical monopolies forbade play performances in any house
save Covent Garden and Drury Lane (and in summer the Haymarket), the upstart theatres circumvented the prohibition on spoken dialogue with musical presentations, equestrian shows, and
aquatic displays.

In 1809, Elliston gained control of the Royal Circus, St.
George's Field. That summer he added a burletta version of *The
Beggar's Opera* to the Circus's usual fare of dance and pantomime. The term burletta was first used in the eighteenth century to describe a short comic entertainment in recitative and
song. Burlettas had been part of the increased operatic activity in
the patent houses in the 1760s and 1770s; however, the alterna-
tive theatres adopted the form because it gave them a legal kind
of dramatic presentation. The *Beggar's Opera* burletta attracted
sizable audiences and ran for fifty performances.

Elliston needed a new offering to maintain public curiosity,
and on 30 August 1809 *The Times* announced the opening of a
"Ballet of Music and Action, founded on *Macbeth*: in which an
anxious and industrious effort will be made to illustrate the
scenes, machinery, imagery, and descriptions delivered to us in
that play by the immortal Shakespeare." The text, reduced to
scarcely 300 lines, was recast in rhymed recitative and supplemented with extravagantly decorated dance and pantomimed action. The music included an arrangement of the "Matthew Lock"
(i.e., Leveridge) score with the addition of a new overture and

other incidental music by Thomas Busby, organist at the Royal Circus. Elliston himself took the role of Macbeth. The burletta *Macbeth* was an overwhelming success with the audience and, surprisingly, with some critics. The 31 August *Morning Chronicle* claimed that "with the exception of the dialogue, the performance was almost exactly the play of Shakespeare."

The following summer in the remodeled Circus, rechristened the Surrey Theatre, Elliston presented a revised version of Garrick's *Jubilee*. Several scenes from Shakespeare were acted out in mime and accompanied with music. Elliston became manager of Drury Lane theatre in 1819. In his final season there, 1829–30, Elliston produced and acted in a new entertainment by William Thomas Moncrieff called *Shakespeare's Festival; or, A New Comedy of Errors*. The entertainment's second act was *The Jubilee*. As manager of a patent theatre Elliston was no longer restrained by prohibitions against spoken dialogue; however, the Shakespearean tableaux were still primarily dumbshows, accompanied by songs arranged for the occasion by Jonathan Blewett.

The Bishop/Reynolds Adaptations

Kemble was never responsible for an operatic production on the scale of Garrick's *Tempest* and *Dream* ; however, in 1816, the last year of his tenure at Covent Garden, the first of a series of Shakespearean comic operas opened to commercial success and critical damnation. Kemble's failing health limited his presence at the theatre, and the responsibility for that season's *A Midsummer Night's Dream* thus fell to the playwright Frederick Reynolds, the author of several successful sentimental comedies. Reynolds, who had been "permanently engaged as 'thinker' at Covent Garden" since 1814,[96] provided an extraordinarily truncated text that served as little more than the connective material for a series of songs, glees, and instrumental pieces. Bishop arranged a pastiche score.

The opening on 17 January 1816 of what was to be the first of several Bishop/Reynolds collaborations caused a furor. The production's popular success was matched only by the loathing of the critics. One newspaper considered the show "a dull pantomime."[97]   Genest could praise it only for its scenery and because it had fewer songs than Garrick's 1763 *Dream* :

It is evident that [Reynolds] thought this divine play would not please a modern audience, unless it were made more divine by the addition of many songs—some fine scenery—and a grand pageant—It was certainly better to have *A Midsummer Night's Dream* revived in this mangled state than not to have it at all—yet this alteration does Reynolds no credit—it is so far better than that of 1763, as he has about 16 songs instead of 33.[98]

Dream had not been staged with anything near the complete original text since that time in 1662 when Pepys found it to be "the most insipid ridiculous play."   Subsequent years saw little improvement in its reputation.   A radically revised text and music by Purcell were not enough to earn *The Fairy Queen* a place in the regular repertoire.   Garrick tried twice to turn *Dream* into an opera, never trusting the script enough to mount a fully spoken production.

Reynolds was only following precedent and continuing fashion by turning *A Midsummer Night's Dream* into a comic opera; unfortunately, his revisions were severe enough to muddle the plot. The musical opportunities provided by Shakespeare were all used, and many more were invented.   The comic dialogue for the four lovers was much cut to make room for love songs and duets.   In an unusual twist, Helena's jealous appraisal of Hermia's charms (I, 1: "Your eyes are lode-stars") was given to Lysander as earnest praise and then set to music.   To streamline the last act, the Pyramus and Thisbe scene was transferred to the middle of the play.   The play's closing scene became a masque-like celebration of Theseus's victory over Hippolyta, in which a ceremonial march for the Theban and Cretan soldiers provided a rousing, if un-Shakespearean, finale.

Bishop often chose to borrow from popular modern composers when assembling his pastiches.   His compilation for *Dream*, more retrospective because Garrick's two reworkings of the play had produced so much music, included music by Handel, Arne, John Christopher Smith, and other composers in addition to some new material by Bishop. For some reason, Bishop ignored Smith's setting of "Flower of This Purple Dye," appropriating the melody of yet another aria from *The Fairies* for Oberon's incantation. Bishop's original contributions confirm contemporary reports of his melodic gifts. His operatic style was influenced by Rossini, but he was also capable of expressing sincere sentiment in direct, uncomplicated airs.

The opening song from *A Midsummer Night's Dream*, itself borrowed from Bishop's opera *Midas*, is in a simple strophic form.

Ex. 36. Bishop. "By the Simplicity of Venus Doves," mm. 9-16.

by permission of the British Library

The play's so-called choruses are not large scale movements modelled after Handel or, considering a more contemporary model, the Wesleys. Rather, they are glees, often with only one singer per part. The simplicity of much of the music suggests that Bishop may have considered the amateur buyers for the eventual printed piano/vocal score even as he prepared the music for the theatre. The music survives in full score in British Library Additional MS 36944, one of several surviving manuscripts and promptbooks, which together suggest the Covent Garden orchestra around 1820 regularly consisted of strings, two flutes, two oboes, two clarinets, two bassoons, two trumpets, two horns, tympani, piano, and organ.

Three years later, Bishop provided new "Songs, Duets, Glees, and Choruses Selected entirely from the Plays, Poems, and Sonnets of Shakespeare" for an comic opera version of *The Comedy of Errors*.[99]   In the apology to the revised play's printed text Reynolds explained the reasoning behind this textual conglomerate:

The admirers of Shakespeare have long regretted that most of his Lyrical Compositions [emphasis Reynolds's] have never been sung in a Theatre. The *Comedy of Errors* (one of the shortest and most lively of his Comedies) has been selected as the best vehicle for their introduction. A few additional scenes and passages were absolutely necessary for this purpose; and however deficient these may be found, it is hoped they will be readily pardoned, as having served to bring on the stage, more of the "native wood notes wild" of our Immortal Bard![100]

The professed aim was the presentation of songs based on the "lyric" texts of Shakespeare, a presentation in which the play itself was a means rather than the end.

The musical items in the published score and their respective text sources attest to Reynold's anthological industry: (1) Overture; (2) "It Was a Lover and His Lass" (*As You Like It*); (3) "Beauty is but a Vain and Doubtful Good" (*Passionate Pilgrim*); (4) "Blow, Blow Thou wintry [*sic*] Wind" (*As You Like It*); (5) "The Poor Soul Sat Sighing" (*Othello*); (6) "Under the Greenwood Tree" (*As You Like It*); (7) "Saint Withold Footed Thrice the World" (*King Lear*); (8) "Come Live With Me" (*Passionate Pilgrim*); (9) "Sweet Rose" (*Passionate Pilgrim*); (10) "What Shall We [*sic*] Have" (*As You Like It*); (11) "Take, O Take Those Lips Away" (*Measure for Measure*); (12) "As It Fell Upon a Day" (*Passionate Pilgrim*); (13) "Come Thou Monarch of the Vine" (*Antony and Cleopatra*); (14) "Oh, How This Spring of Love" (*Two Gentlemen of Verona*); (15) "Lo, Here the Gentle Lark" (*Venus and Adonis*). The texts include poems, song lyrics, and play dialogue.

Had Reynolds simply mounted a fully staged musical review without attempting to gather such disparate parts into a dramatic context, he might have created a widely popular production that even a man of letters like Genest, protesting against adaptations with a reformer's zeal, might have accepted. But Genest was unwilling to accept this *Comedy of Errors*, which he called "literary murder,"[101] as a legitimate representation of Shakespeare:

Reynolds in his advertisement hopes that his additional scenes will be readily pardoned as being absolutely necessary for the sake of introducing the songs. Reynolds may be assured that the only sentiments which the real friends of Shakespeare can feel towards him are indignation at his attempt, and contempt for the bungling manner in which he has executed it.[102]

Leigh Hunt, a critic concerned less with literary authority than with theatrical effect, also felt Reynolds had profoundly diluted Shakespeare's genius:

The performance of *The Comedy of Errors* here is a curiosity. People think they are going to see a play of Shakespeare's; and so they are in one respect, for the words are chiefly his: but for the first time perhaps since the performance of one of Shakespeare's plays, the audience have little or no consciousness of the great dramatist, except occasionally perhaps a feeling of wonder at its being so little like him. The general impression is from the singing of Miss Stephens and Miss Tree, and the judicious grinning of Liston. These three things it must be allowed are excellent. It is only a pity that Liston has not still more to do, and that the ladies with their songs do a great deal more than the original gives warrant for. The original is not an opera, where everything, being to be sung, is made to be sung and the very discords become concordant. It is a play of endless puzzle and confusion, with characters anything but harmonious; a game at improbable cross purposes, which are obscure to nobody but the parties concerned; and which have neither time, nor temper, nor anything else to be dallying with duets and sostenutos.[103]

The problems with introducing songs into the script were not limited to matters of textual authenticity or dramatic pacing. Reynolds's contrived scenes were distressingly clumsy. For example, in act III the characters suddenly found themselves in a hunting party amidst snow-capped mountains, simply so that "What Shall He Have That Killed the Deer" might be introduced as a glee. (The score and printed text disagree on the song introduced here; the playbook specifies "When Isacles Hang by the Wall.") This scene prompted Genest to further tartness: "We should be obliged to Reynolds, if he would inform us in what book of Geography he met with these mountains covered with snow, in the neighborhood of Ephesus."[104]

The "opera" opened on 11 October 1819 and played a total of 27 times that season.   Hunt attributed this financial success to Bishop and the singers: "We do not wonder however that people go to see a comedy which ought only to be read, now that we have heard Miss Stephens and Miss Tree sing together."[105] Bishop appropriated music by Arne ("Blow, Blow Thou Winter Wind," "Under the Greenwood Tree"), R.J.S. Stevens, John Stevenson, and Mozart, arranging it into a collection of duets, solos, and choruses.

Reynolds and Bishop next effected a sea change on a *Twelfth Night*. The production premiered 8 November 1820. No printed copies of Reynolds's script (or of any of his later Shakespearean adaptations) survive; probably none were printed.[106] There is no way to know how Reynolds incorporated the songs into the play; however, the texts collected for the songs in *Twelfth Night* were less varied in subject matter and mood than those in *The Comedy of Errors*. Curiously, Bishop omitted "O Mistress Mine" and

"Come Away Death," while retaining Vernon's setting of the "Epilogue Song." A passage of dialogue from the end of folio III, 1 between Olivia and Viola, disguised as Cesario, became the basis for an extended duet. The score included melodies from Mozart, Winter, and Stevenson. In an unusual reference to Elizabethan music, Bishop created a pasticcio glee of "Who Is Sylvia" drawing on settings by Morley and Ravenscroft. Leigh Hunt found the operatic conversion of *Twelfth Night* more convincing because of Bishop's ability to adapt song types to the individual characters.[107] The play concluded with a masque borrowed from Covent Garden's current production of *The Tempest.*

Bishop and Reynolds collaborated on three more Shakespearean comic operas in the 1820s. The score for *The Tempest* (1820) included music by Haydn, as well as selections from Rossini's *La Gaza Ladra* and *Armida*, Mozart's *Die Zauberflöte*, and earlier *Tempest* scores by John Davy and Thomas Arne. Song texts for *The Two Gentlemen of Verona* (1821) came primarily from the sonnets and *The Passionate Pilgrim*, while the score for *As You Like It* (1824) had as its centerpiece the Arne settings of "Under the Greenwood Tree," "Blow, Blow Thou Winter Wind," and "When Daisies Pied." The tenor Charles Edward Horn, not content to limit his Covent Garden duties to singing, contributed three original songs with texts from the sonnets to the 1821 *Tempest* and a setting of "Poor Corydon" (*The Passionate Pilgrim*) to *As You Like It*. In 1824 Bishop ended his association with Covent Garden, to be replaced as music director by Carl Maria von Weber.

After Bishop left Covent Garden, Reynolds created one more Shakespearean comic opera. *The Merry Wives of Windsor*, with a score arranged by Charles E. Horn from music of Jonathan Blewett, T. S. Cooke, John Parry, Samuel Webbe, Jr., and John Braham, opened 20 February 1824. Genest, whose general disregard for theatre music might otherwise call his comments on the Shakespearean comic operas into question, provided the following evidence that Reynolds had, with *Merry Wives*, "reached the acme of dramatic infamy":[108]

The scene represented a distant view of Windsor, with a most glowing *summer* sky. . . . Fenton entered solus—he spoke to this effect—"How I love this spot, where dear Anne Page so often has met me and confessed her love—Ha! I think the sky is overcast—the wind too blows like an approaching storm—well—let it blow on—I am prepared to brave its fury"—he then began to sing—"Blow, blow thou *winter's* wind."[109]

The continued critical disgust at the "vile and degrading . . . system of travestie"[110] by which Shakespeare had been "operatized" was based in part on the concept of Shakespeare's inviolable worth as England's greatest literary and cultural icon, a concept that would have been inconceivable to dramatists in the late seventeenth century. In more general terms these critics were also distressed by the nondramatic entertainment—animal acts, juggling, even opera—that the patent theatres were required to graft onto plays in order to compete with the growing number of upstart theatres that had sprung up in the early years of the nineteenth century.

Such complaints had been leveled against the theatres at regular intervals since the Restoration between intermittent periods of reform. At least one editorialist realized that these productions had been as much about money as they were about music and words: "The system of making Tragedies operas, and singers actresses, is an absurd one, and only serves to show how much in the way of combination is required, in these times, to make a house."[111] The theatre was facing another crisis of direction. The Reynolds and Bishop operas were the last examples of a performance tradition in which Shakespeare's texts were used as a supporting skeleton for the outward show.

SUMMARY

By the time Garrick retired in 1776, Shakespeare's reputation as England's leading literary and dramatic figure was confirmed. The Shakespearean stage repertoire had become standardized through the acting versions of the 1750s and 1760s, as represented in Bell's 1773–74 edition. It remained stable through the century. Older music for the plays—for example, the "Purcell" *Tempest*, the "Locke" (i.e., Leveridge) *Macbeth*, and the Arne music from the 1740s—remained in the repertoire and was periodically updated according to musical fashion. New music for the plays was often influenced by the popularity of the operatic repertoire then sharing the stage with spoken plays. Literary and historical scholars began to study Shakespeare's own use of music, but antiquarian interests had little immediate effect on stage music except for the introduction of newly composed glees and partsongs nominally modeled after earlier madrigals.

Theatrical change in the early years of the nineteenth century came about through the introduction of Romantic concepts of acting and play interpretation. Texts were altered less frequently and many non-Shakespearean musical scenes were removed from acting copies of the plays. The promptbooks of John Philip Kemble indicate music was used with increasing frequency to establish the mood of dramatic scenes. At the same time, the competition from an increasing number of illegitimate theatres, which were restricted by law to nonspoken offerings, continued to keep musical extravagance high in the priorities of the patent houses.

Much of this Shakespearean musical activity involved the creation of pastiche scores rather than the creation of significant new compositions. The operatic adaptations by Frederick Reynolds and Henry Bishop represent the end of a Shakespearean comic opera tradition begun in the middle of the previous century. The popular approval and critical disgust at the Reynolds/Bishop productions were indicative of the cross purposes at which actors, musicians, theatre managers, and dramatists worked in the years leading up to 1830. The theatre community was in an artistic and organizational crisis reminiscent of the first decade of the eighteenth century.

NOTES

1. Charles Beecher Hogan, *Shakespeare in the Theatre. 1701-1800,* 2 vols. (Oxford: Clarendon Press, 1952), 2:25-36, 71-78.

2. James Boswell, *Boswell's Life of Dr. Johnson,* ed. G. Birkbeck Hill, 6 vols. (Oxford: Clarendon Press, 1934), 2:31.

3. Charles Lamb, "On the Tragedies of Shakespeare considered with Reference to their Fitness for Stage Representation," in *The Works of Charles Lamb,* ed. William Macdonald, 12 vols. (London: J. M. Dent & Sons , 1903), 3:20.

4. *The Plays of William Shakespeare,* ed. Samuel Johnson, 8 vols. (London: J. and R. Tonson, 1765), 1:25-6.

5. Ibid., 8:28.

6. Ibid., 8:609.

7. *The Plays and Poems of William Shakespeare,* ed. Edmond Malone, 10 vols. (London: H. Beldon, 1790), 10:558.

8. Ibid.

9. Charles Burney, *A General History of Music,* ed. Frank Mer-cer, 2 vols. (New York: Dover, 1957), 2 : 269.

10. Ibid., 2:270.

11. Ibid., 2:271.

12. Ibid., 2:270.

13. Ibid.

14. Peter J. Seng, *The Vocal Songs in the Plays of Shakespeare* (Cambridge, Mass.: Harvard University Press, 1967), p. 103.

15. *Bell's Edition of Shakespeare's Plays,* 8 vols. (London: John Bell, 1774), 1:title page.

16. George C. D. Odell, *Shakespeare from Betterton to Irving,* 2 vols. (New York: Charles Scribner, 1920; New York: Dover, 1966), 2:16-19.

17. Robert Dale, "Dramatic Music of William Boyce" (Ph.D. dissertation, University of Washington, 1975), p. 227.

18. *Bell's Edition,* 4:47.

19. Ibid., 1:145.

20. Ibid., 5:94.

21. See also William Shakespeare, *Othello. the Moor of Venice* (London: T. Witford, 1755).

22. *Bell's Edition,* 1:108.

23. Roger Fiske, *English Theatre Music in the Eighteenth Century,* 2d ed. (London: Oxford University Press, 1986), p. 412.

24. George Colman, *New Brooms!* (London: T. Roberts, 1776), quoted in Allardyce Nicoll, *A History of English Drama. 1600-1900*, rev. ed., 4 vols. (Cambridge: Cambridge University Press, 1952), 3:112.

25. Ernst Brandes, *Bermarkungen Über das Londoner, Pariser, and Wiener Theater* (Göttingen, 1786), cited in John Alexander Kelly, *German Visitors to English Theatres in the Eighteenth Century* (Princeton: Princeton University Press, 1936; New York: Octagon, 1978), p. 109.

26. James Boaden, *Memoirs of the Life of John Kemble. Esq.*, 2 vols. (London: Longman, Hunt, Rees, Orme, Brown, and Green, 1825), 1:329.

27. Burney, *General History*, 2:268.

28. Thomas Davies, *Memoirs of the Life of David Garrick, Esq.*, 2 vols. (London: Longman, Hurst, Rees, and Orme, 1808), 2:87.

29. Burney, *General History*, 2:1017.

30. *The Tuner*, Letter 5, 1755, quoted in Odell, *Shakespeare from Betterton to Irving*, 1:366.

31. Theodore Aylward, *Six Songs in Harlequin's Invasion, Cymbeline, and Midsummer Night's Dream* (London: Bremner, 1765), p. 9.

32. Michael Kelly, "What Wakes This New Pain in My Breast?" (Dublin: John Lee, 1790), p. 1.

33. James Anderson Winn, *Unsuspected Eloquence. A History of the Relations Between Poetry and Music* (New Haven: Yale University Press, 1981), pp. 251-59.

34. *The Private Correspondence of David Garrick*, ed. James Boaden, 2 vols. (London: S. Bently, 1831–32), 2:99, quoted in George Winchester Stone, "The Prevalence of Theatrical Music in Garrick's Time," in *The Stage and the Page: London's "Whole Show" in the Eighteenth-Century Theatre*, ed. George Winchester Stone (Berkeley: University of California Press, 1981), p. 119.

35. Joseph Baildon, "Haste Lorenzo, Haste Away" (London, [1776]).

36. Michael Kelly, "What New Delights" (Dublin: John Lee, 1790), p. 1.

37. Burney, *General History*, 2:1022.

38. Charles Cudworth, "Song and Part Song Settings of Shakespeare's Lyrics, 1660–1960," in *Shakespeare in Music*, ed. Phyllis Hartnoll (London: Macmillan, 1964), pp. 66-74.

39. *Public Advertiser*, 9 Dec. 1789.

40. William Linley, *Shakespeare's Dramatic Songs*, 2 vols. (London: Preston, 1816), 2:2-3.

41. *Examiner*, 26 Dec., 1819, p. 829.

42. Fiske, *English Theatre Music*, p. 28.

43. John Downes, *Roscius Anglicanus, or an Historical Review of the Stage* (London: T. R., 1708), p. 33.

44. *Public Advertiser*, 25 Nov. 1776.

45. William Hopkins, [manuscript diary], 25 November 1776, Folger Shakespeare Library, Washington, D. C. 25 November 1776, quoted in *The London Stage 1660-1800: A Calendar of Plays*, 11 vols. (Carbondale: Southern Illinois University Press, 1960–68). Pt. 5, 1:38.

46. Linley, *Shakespeare's Dramatic Songs*, 2:3-5.

47. Robert Etheridge Moore, "The Music to *Macbeth*," *Musical Quarterly* 47 (1961):29.

48. *Public Advertiser*, 25 Nov. 1776.

49. Hopkins, [diary], 25 Nov. 1776.

50. Some of the songs are preserved in a contemporary collection: James Johnson, *The Scots Musical Museum*, 6 vols. (Edinburgh: James Johnson, 1787–1803).

51. Linley, *Shakespeare's Dramatic Songs*, 2:1.

52. *Public Advertiser*, 4 Jan. 1777; also *Morning Chronicle, and London Advertiser*, 6 Jan. 1777.

53. Harrison saw references to the Sheridan booklet in the catalogues of two private libraries, but he never saw an actual copy. J. Greenhill, W. A. Harrison, and Frederick J. Furnwall, eds., *A List of All the Songs and Passages in Shakespeare Which Have Been Set to Music* (London: New Shakespeare Society, 1884; Folcraft, Pa.: Folcraft Library Editions, 1974), p. xx.

54. Fiske, *English Theatre Music*, p. 413.

55. Thomas Linley, the younger, "Music for The Tempest and The Duenna," Egerton MS. 2493, British Library, fol. 57.

56. The music included an "air from the Opera" for Mr. Vernon as Ferdinand. *Morning Chronicle, and London Advertiser*, 6 Jan. 1777. Announcements preserved in the Drury Lane and Covent Garden scrapbooks suggest an air for Ferdinand from Smith's *The Fairies* may have already been included in *Tempest* productions ca. 1773. Mary Margaret Nilan, "The Stage History of *The Tempest*: A Question of Theatricality" (Ph.D. dissertation, Northwestern University, 1967), p. 54.

57. *Gazetteer and New Daily Advertiser*, 4 Jan. 1777. The playbill in the same day's issue of *The Public Advertiser* places the spirit dances in acts III and IV.

58. *Public Advertiser*, 6 Jan. 1777.

59. *Morning Chronicle, and London Advertiser*, 8 Jan. 1777, cited in *London Stage*, pt. 5, 1:50.

60. *Bell's Edition*, 3:5.

61. *Morning Chronicle, and London Advertiser*, 8 Jan. 1777, cited in *London Stage*, pt. 5, 1:50.

62. *Morning Chronicle, and London Advertiser*, 6 Jan. 1777.

63. The layout of the text as it appears here comes from *Shakespeare's Tempest; or, the Enchanted Island, adapted to the stage, with additions from Dryden and Davenant* (London: Longman, Hurst, Rees, and Orme, 1807), p. 16. Linley's word repetition is not indicated.

64. *Public Advertiser*, 20 Sept. 1777.

65. *Public Advertiser*, 4 Jan. 1777.

66. *Morning Chronicle, and London Advertiser*, 6 Jan. 1777.

67. Ibid.

68. Boaden, *Kemble*, 1:268-69.

69. Burney, *General History*, 2:269.

70. *Morning Chronicle, and London Advertiser*, 28 Dec. 1776.

71. Ibid., 27 Dec. 1776.

72. Michael Kelly, *Reminiscences* [1826], ed. Roger Fiske (London: Oxford University Press, 1975), p. 163.

73. Ibid.

74. *Promoter*, quoted in Charles Harold Gray, *Theatrical Criticism in London to 1795* (New York: F. Blom, [1964]), p. 305.

75. John Taylor, *Memoirs*, ed. Richard H. Stoddard (New York: , 1875), pp. 218ff., quoted in Bernard Grebanier, *Then Came Each Actor* (New York: David McKay Co., 1975), p. 127.

76. Boaden, *Kemble*, 2:2.

77. *Specimens of the Table Talk of the Late Samuel Taylor Coleridge*, 2 vols. (London: John Murray, [1835]) 1:24.

78. Joseph Donohue, *Theatre in the Age of Kean* (Oxford: Basil Blackwell, 1975), p. 59.

79. *Examiner*, 26 Dec. 1829, p. 829.

80. Fiske discussed the effect the fires have had on knowledge of eighteenth- and early nineteenth-century English music in *English Theatre Music*, pp. 581-82.

81. John Philip Kemble, *John Philip Kemble Promptbooks*, ed. Charles H. Shattuck, 11 vols. (Charlottesville: University Press of Virginia, 1974), *Coriolanus* [1811], p. 55.

82. Ibid., *Henry VIII* [1806], p. 66.

83. "Advertisement" for Thomas Holcraft's *A Tale of Mystery*, 2d ed. (1802), quoted in Donohue, *Theatre in the Age of Kean*, p. 107. Reflection on the use of music in film scores suggests this concept is not as unfamiliar to modern audiences as might at first be thought.

84. Kemble, *Promptbooks, As You Like It* [1810], p. 27.

85. Ibid., *King John* [1804], p. 14.

86. Ibid., *Henry VIII* [1806], p. 66.

87. Ibid., *Romeo and Juliet* [1811], p. 63.

88. *London Stage*, pt. 5, 2 : 1100.

89. Frances Ann Kemble, *Record of a Girlhood*, 3 vols. (London: Richard Bentley and Son, 1878), 1:33.

90. Kemble, *Promptbooks, Macbeth* [1808], p. 45.

91. Ibid., p. 29.

92. Ibid., p. 37.

93. Ibid., *Merchant of Venice* [1813], p. 45.

94. Ibid., p. 61.

95. *The New Grove Dictionary of Music and Musicians*, s.v. "Bishop, Henry Rowley."

96. *The Dictionary of National Biography*, s.v. "Reynolds, Frederic."

97. *London Examiner*, 21 Jan. 1816.

98. John Genest, *Some Account of the English Stage from the Restoration in 1660 to 1830*, 10 vols. (Bath: for H. E. Carrington, 1832), 8:548.

99. *William Shakespeare's A Comedy of Errors . . . with Alterations . . . the selections from Dr. Arne, R.J.S. Stevens, and Mozart* (London: Sampson Low, 1819), title page.

100. Ibid., p. 3.

101. Genest, *Some Acount of the English Stage*, 9:46.

102. Ibid.

103. *Examiner*, 26 Dec. 1819, p. 828.

104. Genest, *Some Account of the English Stage*, 9:48.

105. *Examiner*, 26 Dec. 1819, p. 828.

106. Odell, *Shakespeare from Betterton to Irving*, 2 : 135.

107. *Examiner*, 12 Nov. 1820, pp. 733-34.

108. Genest, *Some Account of the English Stage*, 9:235.

109. Ibid., 9 234.
110. *Examiner*, 12 Nov. 1820, pp. 733-34.
111. *John Bull*, 27 May 1821.

Epilogue

The year 1660 is a natural line of demarcation in English theatre history. The resumption of acting and the injection of Continental influences into the interrupted native practice clearly marked the beginnings of new practices. But why is 1830 the end date for this study? Although 1830 is not as precise a temporal landmark as the Restoration reopening of the theatres, the year opened a decade in which long-evolving dramatic, literary, and musical transformations would converge and point to new directions for English drama.

The death of George IV in 1830 marked more than the end of over a century of Georgian rule. It was the official and belated rite of passage into the nineteenth century. The social and political climate, influenced by economic realities that would motivate Victorian society, led to the Reform Bill of 1832. Governmental restructuring recognized the transformation of eighteenth-century England into a nineteenth-century industrial power.

The new government was faced with yet another crisis in London's theatrical community, a crisis that was in its way as much a barometer of social change as it was an indicator of literary or dramatic fashion. The relative stability of theatrical and musical practice before 1800 had been disintegrating since the turn of the century. The patent system that had made such stability possible through the eighteenth century was by 1830 on the verge of collapse.

Since 1660 crown control through strictly limited monopolies had regulated and defined London's theatrical community. Through the eighteenth century, successful challenges to the system were rare. Government control created a stable environment in which diverse forms of expression grew out of a basically conservative and standardized tradition. By the early years of the nineteenth century, a growing number of minor theatres were successfully able to avoid patent prohibitions with burlettas, other kinds of musical entertainments, and visual spectacles while attracting varied audiences dissatisfied with the productions of the patent houses. The offerings of the minor theatres shaped early nineteenth-century English drama as the legitimate houses could not.

In 1832, with the patent houses in financial difficulties and no longer adequate to meet the entertainment demands of London's growing population, Parliament held hearings on the declining state of drama and the practicality of patent rights. A move to abolish the patents that year failed, but the system of government control had become ineffectual. The eventual abolition of the patents in 1843 was inevitable.

Another reason to choose 1830 as a terminus was the changing nature of Shakespearean stage adaptation. When, in 1660, Dryden described the re-creation of a work from the past for contemporary eyes and ears, he explained a good deal about Restoration Shakespearean adaptation:

I take imitation of an author . . . to be an endeavor of a later poet to write like one who has written before him, on the same subject; that is, not to translate his words, or to be confined to his sense, but only to set him as a pattern, and to write, as he supposes the author would have done, had he lived in our own age.[1]

Restoration dramatists and audiences, because of the twenty-year hiatus in theatrical activity, did not readily identify with older dramatic styles. Shakespeare's plays could not satisfy late seventeenth- and early eighteenth-century audiences in their subject matter, structure, or style. But Dryden's literary bias made him disregard another factor in the revision process: technical and musical activity. The replacement of the platform stage by the proscenium stage and the Italian misconception of the musico-dramatic heritage of classical literature may have been as important in Shakespearean revision as neoclassical literary concepts. Restoration adapters, neither bound to translate Shakespeare nor "confined to his sense," easily incorporated new production practices into their updated versions of the plays.

Stage managers in the middle years of the eighteenth century returned with increasing frequency to Shakespeare's original poetry. They still faced the challenge of adapting Shakespeare's poetry for a contemporary audience familiar with a traditionally musical stage. The restored texts used by Macklin and Garrick, coupled with new acting styles, were novelties to the London audiences.[2] The unfamiliarity of the texts made musical elaborations such as Smith's operas, both houses' versions of *The Winter's Tale*, and the 1763 *Midsummer Night's Dream* major representatives of these plays rather than variants.

This is very unlike the modern attitude by which "we must judge how far an opera takes the measure of the play on which it is based."[3] Today's audiences recognize that Verdi's *Otello*, Prokofiev's *Romeo and Juliet*, and even *Kiss Me Kate* are independent works. They are based on Shakespearean models, and their success may be judged in part on how closely they capture what is perceived to be the essence of the source plays; however, they are too far removed from the originals to be considered alternate versions of Shakespeare.

Audiences between the Restoration and the nineteenth century accepted the Shakespearean revisions in place of the originals. *The Tempest* and (except for very early performances) *A Midsummer Night's Dream* were known only in their musical versions. Dramatists from the middle of the eighteenth century may not have been guided by a set of theoretical rules in their reshaping of Shakespeare for the stage, but the practicalities of staging and audience expectations were much the same for Garrick as they had been for Dryden.

By the early years of the nineteenth century Shakespeare's literary reputation was firmly re-established. The play texts, rather than production values, increasingly became the central standard by which stage presentations were judged. The plays were still changed according to circumstance. Kemble altered scripts "suiting the time of the representation," but returning to "the author's genuine book" for the play's central identity.[4] The interpretation of the plays was unabashedly Romantic; however, the idea was to see Shakespeare's texts through modern eyes, not to rewrite the plays as if Shakespeare had lived in 1800.

Although production requirements would encourage new kinds of Shakespearean incidental music in the middle years of the century, a sizable amount of the seventeenth- and eighteenth-century musical repertoire for Shakespearean production would continue in use well past 1830. William Linley's 1816 anthology *Shakespeare's Dramatic Music* provided an important insider's overview of Georgian musical practice in Shakespearean plays, while Caulfield's frequently inaccurate *Collection of the Vocal Music in Shakespeare's Plays* (1815) aided the perpetuation of the music while causing attribution problems.

Musical collections published for the tercentenary of Shakespeare's birth in 1864 (*Shakespeare's Vocal Album*, a reprint edition of Caulfield, and a belated issue of *Chappell's Musical Magazine* devoted to Shakespearean music) show that settings by Arne, Stevens, Cooke, and others remained in the repertoire alongside newer music by Schubert, Arthur Sullivan, and other composers both British and Continental. The Leveridge masques for *Macbeth*, revised and reorchestrated, continued to be used off and on in London productions until 1875,[5] but Covent Garden's replacement of Kemble's Dryden-based version of *The Tempest* with the Shakespearean text in 1838 marked the demise of the "Purcell" music's dominance.

The most important mid-century change in Shakespearean incidental music would be the result of increasingly complex stage scenery to create the illusion of a proscenium window into a new reality, which would require more elaborate incidental music to cover scene changes. The connection between literary concepts and musical inspiration developed by German Romantic composers, exemplified in Mendelssohn's incidental music to *A Midsummer Night's Dream* (1826, 1842), would also become a feature of Victorian incidental music for Shakespeare.

The range of musical genres used in Shakespearean productions between 1660 and 1830 requires comment. Many songs were written for both Shakespearean and non-Shakespearean lyrics. Incidental music ranged from Restoration act tunes to Galliard's unusual *Julius Caesar* choruses and the detailed background music Boyce wrote for *The Winter's Tale*. Masques had decorated Restoration productions, and two of the three seventeenth-century dramatic operas (or their antecedent versions) remained popular through the eighteenth century. London audiences saw two Italian operas ostensibly based on Shakespeare, two English-language operas using Shakespeare's poetry as the basis for librettos, a ballad opera, a burletta, several comic operas, and two "mock operas." The formal variety of musical Shakespeareana is itself representative of the range of dramatic forms the London stages produced from the Restoration to the end of the Georgian period.

The lack of a first-rank operatic treatment by one of England's late eighteenth-century operatic talents (e.g., Stephen Storace or the younger Thomas Linley) is a curious omission in English stage and music history. Some operas based on Shakespeare's plays actually achieved some popularity on the Continent at this time, although the French and German translations through which Shakespeare was known in Europe considerably changed the plays' dramatic forms and characterizations.[6]

Stephen Storace actually wrote a Shakespearean opera, but not for London. Working in Vienna during the 1780s, Storace wrote the music for *Gli Equivoci*, an Italian libretto based on *The Comedy of Errors*. Michael Kelly, also in Vienna and singing in the character of one of the brothers, thought highly of the work:

Storace had an opera put into rehearsal, the subject of his own choice, Shakespeare's *Comedy of Errors.* It was made operatical, and adapted for the Italian, by Da Ponte, with great ingenuity. He retained all the main incidents and characters of our immortal bard; it became the rage, and well it might, for the music of Storace was beyond description beautiful.[7]

Gli Equivoci was never performed in London, but Storace used some of the individual movements in a variety of productions there. Kelly "lamented to see his beautiful Italian opera dismantled."[8] Copies of *Gli Equivoci* survive in the Sachsiche Landesbibliothek, Dresden, and the Gesselschaft der Musikfreunde, Vienna.

It was not until the end of the nineteenth century and the beginning of the twentieth that directors such as William Poel and Harley Granville Barker began reviving Elizabethan production techniques in Shakespearean productions: the continuity of action as played on a platform stage with simple scenic settings, speedy delivery of unabridged texts, and team work rather than reliance on a single star actor.[9]

At the same time—and also coincidental with the revival of interest in older music and instruments, exemplified by the work of Arnold Dolmetsch—E. W. Naylor and G. W. Cowling became the first of many music historians to seriously collect and study music for the plays from Shakespeare's time. Books by Naylor and Cowling[10] made much of this older music widely available and attempted to describe the musical activity of the Elizabethan stage.

As the new dramaturgy transformed Shakespearean stage production in the early years of the twentieth century, the rediscovered musical repertoire became the primary model that new Shakespearean scores would have to follow or reject. The music written for Dryden and Cibber, for the god of Garrick's idolatry, and for the outward shows of Rich and Elliston moved farther and farther from center stage and into the wings of obscurity.

NOTES

1. John Dryden, "Preface to the Translation of Ovid's *Epistles*" [1680], in *Essays of John Dryden*, ed. W. P. Ker, 2 vols. (Oxford: Oxford University Press, 1926), 1:239.

2. George Winchester Stone, "The Making of the Repertory," in *The London Theatre World, 1660-1800*, ed. Robert D. Hume (Carbondale: Southern Illinois University Press, 1980), p. 187.

3. Winton Dean, "Shakespeare and Opera," in *Shakespeare in Music*, ed. Phyllis Hartnoll (London: Macmillan, 1964), p. 89.

4. James Boaden, *Memoirs of the Life of John Kemble, Esq.* 2 vols. (London: Longman, Hurst, Rees, Orme, Brown, and Green, 1825), 2:2.

5. Roger Fiske, *English Theatre Music in the Eighteenth Century*, 2d ed. (London: Oxford University Press, 1986), p. 26.

6. William Barclay Squire, "Shakespearean Opera," in *A Book of Homage to Shakespeare*, ed. Israel Gollancz (Oxford: Oxford University Press, 1916), p. 81.

7. Michael Kelly, *Reminiscences* [1826], ed. Roger Fiske (London: Oxford University Press, 1975), p. 120.

8. Ibid.

9. See Robert Speaight, *William Poel and the Elizabethan Revival* (Cambridge, Mass.: Harvard University Press, 1954); Harley Granville Barker, *Prefaces to Shakespeare* (Princeton: Princeton University Press, 1963); Eric Salmon, *Granville Barker, A Secret Life* (Rutherford: Farleigh Dickinson University Press, 1983), pp. 204-33.

10. See G. H. Cowling, *Music on the Shakespearean Stage* (Cambridge: Cambridge University Press, 1913) and E. W. Naylor, *Shakespeare and Music*, 2d ed. (London: J. M. Dent & Sons, 1931).

Appendix A:
A Collection of
Shakespeare Music

List of Musical Items

Banister: "Eccho Song, 'twixt Ferdinand and Ariel"
(*The Tempest*, 1667)

Weldon: "Take, O Take Those Lips Away"
(*Measure for Measure*, 1700)

Leveridge: "Who Is Silvia?"
(*The Two Gentlemen of Verona*)

Arne: "Come Away, Death"
(*Twelfth Night*, 1741)

Boyce: "The Music for Animating the Statue in Shakespeare's
Play of the Winter's Tale" (1756)

Smith: ["Flower of This Purple Dye"] Sung by Master Reinhold
(*The Fairies*, 1755)

Aylward: "Hark! Hark! the Lark"
(*Cymbeline*, 1759)

Vernon: "Epilogue Song"
(*Twelfth Night*, 1763)

Stevens: "Sigh No More, Ladies"
(*Much Ado about Nothing*, 1789)

Eccho Song, 'twixt Ferdinand and Ariel
(*The Tempest*, 1667)

Printed by Playford, 1675   John Banister

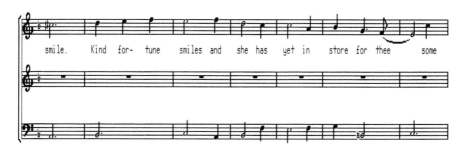

smile. Kind for- tune smiles and she has yet in store for thee some

strange fe- li- ci- tie; fol- low me, fol- low me and thou shalt see.

Take, O Take Those Lips Away
(*Measure for Measure*, 1700)

Walsh, [1702]   John Weldon

lead - - - - the

morn   But   my kis- ses   bring a- gain,

but   my kis- ses   bring   a- gain,   bring,   bring,

bring,   bring,   bring   a- gain.

But my kis- ses

bring   a- gain,   but   my kis- ses   bring   a- gain,   seals of love,

seals   of love tho'   seal'd   -   -   -

-         -   -   tho'   seal'd in   vain.

Seals of love - - - tho'

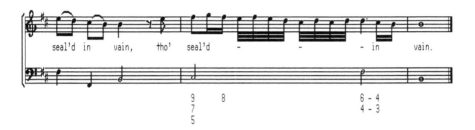

seal'd in vain, tho' seal'd - - - in vain.

Who Is Silvia?
(*The Two Gentlemen of Verona*)

Printed for the Author, 1727   Richard Leveridge

kind as she - is fair, for Beau- ty dwells - with kind- ness.

Love does to her eyes re- pair to help him of his

blind- ness and, be- ing help'd, in- ha- - bits there.

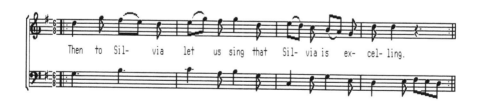

Then to Sil- via let us sing that Sil- via is ex- cel- ling.

She ex- cels all Mor- tal things up- on the dull Earth dwel- ling. To

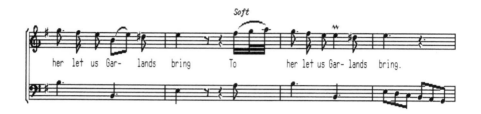

Soft

her let us Gar- lands bring To her let us Gar- lands bring.

Loud

She ex- cels all Mor- tal things up- on the dull Earth dwel- ling. To

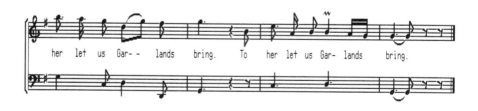

her let us Gar- - lands bring. To her let us Gar- lands bring.

Come Away, Death
(*Twelfth Night*, 1741)

William Smith, [1741]

Thomas Arne

Flow'r sweet on my black Cof- fin let there be strown.

Not a Friend, not a Friend greet my Corps, my poor Corps where my

The Music for Animating the Statue in
Shakespeare's Play of the Winter's Tale
(1756)

Bodleian MS Mus. d. 14   William Boyce

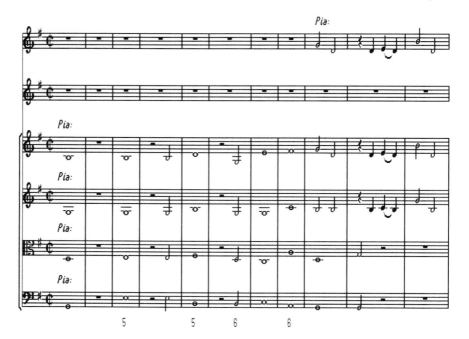

[Flower of This Purple Dye]
Sung by Master Reinhold
(*The Fairies*, 1755)

J. Walsh, 1755

John Christopher Smith

Hark! Hark! the Lark
(*Cymbeline*, 1759)

Bremner, 1755

Theodore Aylward

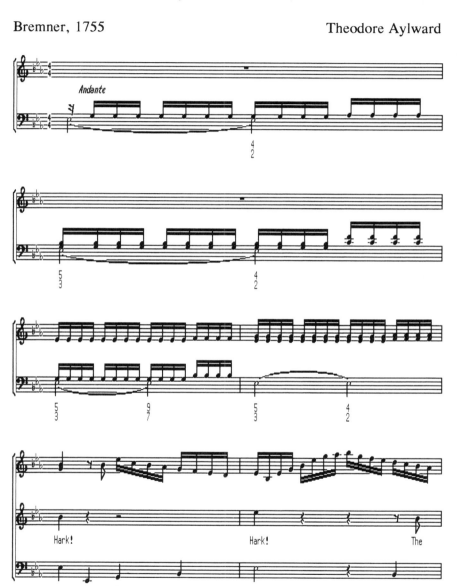

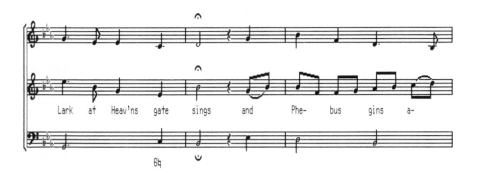

Lark at Heav'ns gate sings and Phe- bus gins a-

rise - - - - - - -

- Hark! Hark! Hark!

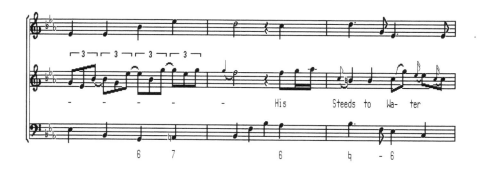

Epilogue Song
(*Twelfth Night*, 1763)

John Johnston, 1772   Joseph Vernon

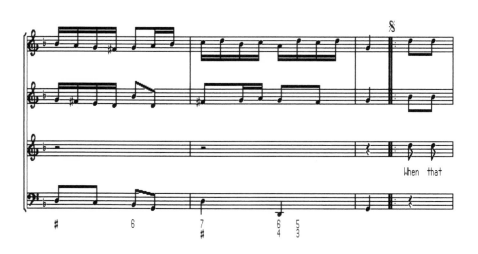

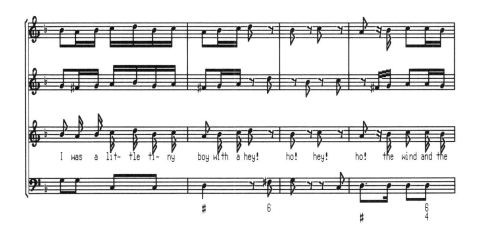

I was a lit- tle ti- ny boy with a hey! ho! hey! ho! the wind and the

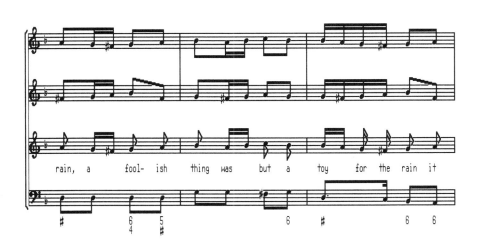

rain, a fool- ish thing was but a toy for the rain it

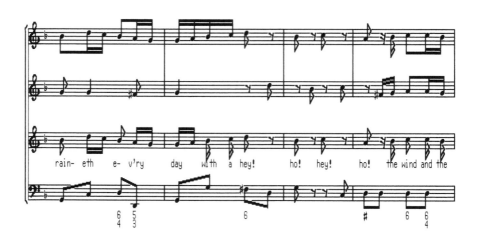

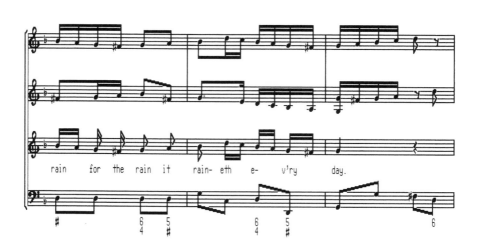

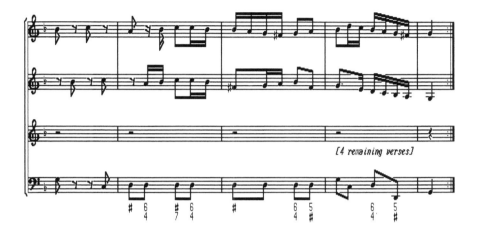

[4 remaining verses]

Sigh No More, Ladies
(*Much Ado about Nothing*, 1789)

Caulfield, 1815   R.J.S. Stevens

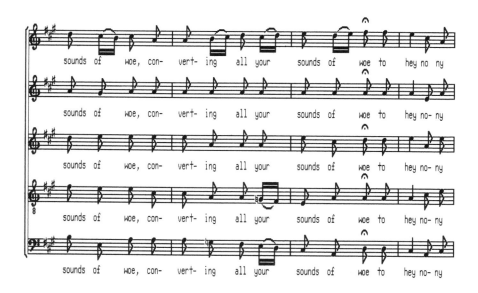

no- ny   hey no- ny   no- ny   hey no- ny   no- ny   hey no- ny   no- ny.

no- ny hey   no- ny   no- ny hey   no- ny   no- ny hey   no- ny   no- ny.

no- ny   hey no- ny   no- ny   hey no- ny   no- ny hey   no- ny   no- ny.

no- ny   hey no- ny   no- ny   hey no- ny   no- ny   hey no- ny   no- ny.

no- ny   hey no- ny   no- ny   hey no- ny   hey no- ny   hey no- ny   no- ny.

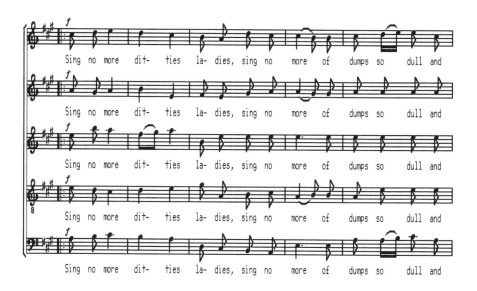

Sing no more dit- ties la- dies, sing no more of dumps so dull and

Sing no more dit- ties la- dies, sing no more of dumps so dull and

Sing no more dit- ties la- dies, sing no more of dumps so dull and

Sing no more dit- ties la- dies, sing no more of dumps so dull and

Sing no more dit- ties la- dies, sing no more of dumps so dull and

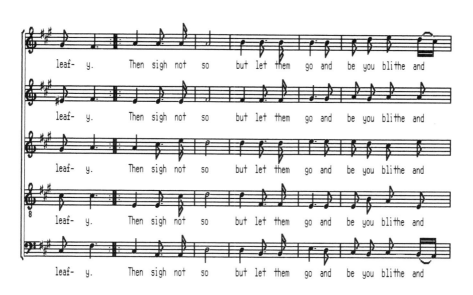

sounds of woe, con- vert- ing all your sounds of woe to hey no- ny

sounds of woe, con- vert- ing all your sounds of woe to hey no- ny

sounds of woe, con- vert- ing all your sounds of woe to hey no- ny

sounds of woe, con- vert- ing all your sounds of woe to hey no- ny

sounds of woe, con- vert- ing all your sounds of woe to hey no- ny

no- ny hey no- ny no- ny hey no- ny no- ny hey no- ny no- ny.

no- ny hey no- ny no- ny hey no- ny no- ny hey no- ny no- ny.

no- ny hey no- ny no- ny hey no- ny no- ny hey no- ny no- ny.

no- ny hey no- ny no- ny hey no- ny no- ny hey no- ny no- ny.

no- ny hey no- ny no- ny hey no- ny no- ny hey no- ny no- ny.

Appendix B:
Settings of
Shakespearean Texts
by Thomas Arne

This list of Thomas Arne's settings of original Shakespearean texts (both song lyrics and extracted dialogue) is arranged by play. The music source for each song is indicated, and a summary of sources for reference to the Bibliography follows the song list. The Drury Lane productions redistributed some of the song texts among the plays, and these shufflings are also indicated.

As You Like It

　　"Blow, Blow Thou Winter Wind" (*The Songs in . . . As You Like It*)

　　"Under the Greenwood Tree" (*The Songs in . . . As You Like It*)

Cymbeline

　　"Fear No More the Heat o' the Sun" (*Winter's Amusement*)

Love's Labour's Lost

　　"When Daisies Pied" (*The Songs in . . . As You Like It*; used in *As You Like It*)

　　"When Isacles Hang by the Wall" (*The Blind Beggar of Bethnal Green*; used in *The Merchant of Venice*)

The Merchant of Venice
   "Tell Me Where Is Fancy Bred" (*The Songs in . . . As You Like It*; used in *Twelfth Night*)

Much Ado about Nothing
   "Sigh No More, Ladies" (*Vocal Melody I*)

The Tempest
   "Ariel's Song" ["Where the Bee Sucks"] (*Lyric Harmony II*)
   "Come Unto These Yellow Sands" (Add. MS 29370)
   "Ere You Can Say Come and Go" (Add. MS 29370)
   The Masque (Add. MS 29370)

Twelfth Night
   "Come Away Death," first setting (*The Songs in . . . As You Like It*)
   "Come Away Death," second setting (*Twelfth Night*, 1785)

In addition, four songs attributed to Arne appear only in the 1815 *Collection of Vocal Music in Shakespear's Plays* by John Caulfield. Caulfield's attributions are notoriously inaccurate, and his Arne attributions are questionable:

As You Like It
   "Then There Is Mirth In Heaven"

Love's Labour's Lost
   "On a Day, Alack the Day"

Much Ado About Nothing
   "Pardon, Goddess of the Night"

The Tempest
   "While You Here Do Snoring Lie"

SUMMARY OF SOURCES

The Songs in . . . As You Like It and Twelfth Night (1741)

The Songs and Duets in the Blind Beggar of Bethnal Green . . . Merchant of Venice (1742)

Vocal Melody, Book 1 (1746)

The Second Volume of Lyric Harmony (1747)

Winter's Amusement (1762)

The Songs in Twelfth Night. . . (1785)

"Music in the Tempest," British Library Additional MS 29370 (ca. 1800)

John Caulfield, *A Collection of Vocal Music in Shakespear's Plays* (1815)

Appendix C:
Production Charts and
Scene Analysis Tables

Production Charts

Production Chart for Chapter 1, 1660-1695

Production Chart for Chapter 2, 1696-1720

Production Chart for Chapter 3, 1720-1750

Production Chart for Chapter 4, 1750-1770

Production Chart for Chapter 5, 1770-1830

Scene Analysis Tables

John Christopher Smith: *The Fairies*

The Fairies. Act I Scene Analysis of Libretto and Music

The Fairies. Act II Scene Analysis of Libretto and Music

The Fairies. Act III Scene Analysis of Libretto and Music

John Christopher Smith: *The Tempest*

The Tempest. Act I Scene Analysis of Libretto and Music

The Tempest. Act II Scene Analysis of Libretto and Music

The Tempest. Act III Scene Analysis of Libretto and Music

PRODUCTION CHARTS

The production charts collect and summarize information about musically important Shakespearean productions, 1660-1830. If the name of the performance version of a play differs from its source play, the original title is given parenthetically. Dates refer to the opening night of the production or the earliest date that can be approximated. Source indications are keyed by item number to the lists of music sources, Shakespearean texts, and modern music editions in the Bibliography. Listed sources include only those items that have definite or probable connection to specific productions. Comments include brief descriptions of music used in the productions as well as the condition and authority of the sources.

Production Chart for Chapter 1
1660-1695

Theatre abbreviations: **CG**: Covent Garden;   **DG**: Dorset Garden;   **DL**: Drury Lane;   **KT**: King's Theatre;   **LIF**: Lincoln's-Inn-Fields;   **QT**: Queen's Theatre.

PRODUCTIONS (original play)	ADAPTER	THEATRE/ DATES	TEXT SOURCES	MUSIC SOURCES	MOD. ED.	COMMENTS
Othello		Aug. 1660?		68		Humfrey "Willow Song" printed in *Musica Antiqua* (1812). Original source not identified.
Hamlet	Davenant	LIF 1661	31			Restoration texts retain Ophelia's songs in act IV.
Henry VIII		LIF Dec. 1663		86		Locke "Orpheus with his lute" in *Catch That Catch Can* (1667).
Macbeth	Davenant	LIF 1663-64	39	85		Dances by Channell and Priest missing. Instrumental arrangements of two songs by Locke in Playford collections. Some music by Robert Johnson may have been revived.

Title	Author	Theatre/Date				Notes
The Tempest	Dryden/Davenant	DG 7 Nov. 1667	5	18	3, 9	Playford print includes songs by Banister, Hart, and Humfrey.
The Tempest	Shadwell, after Dryden	DG 30 Apr. 1674	46	18, 61, 67, 83, 102	3, 9	Locke act music. Humfrey masques. Reggio "Arise ye Subterranean Winds" (attrib. in Add. MS 29397). Songs by Banister, et al. retained from 1667 DG production. Dances by Draghi lost.
Timon of Athens	Shadwell	DG Jan. 1678	22	59, 37, 97, 101	13	Songs by Grabu and Clarke. Paisable act tunes from later manuscripts. (See Purcell, *Timon of Athens, Works of Henry Purcell 2*, pp. x-xi).
Troilus and Cressida	Dryden	Duke's Theatre 1679	6	54	6	Non-Shakespearean song text set by Farmer and printed in *Choice Ayres and Songs III* (1687).
The History of King Richard the Second	Tate	DL 8 Jan. 1681	56	100	11	Purcell setting of non-Shakespearean text. Play text indicates a second song for which no music is known.
Titus Andronicus	Ravenscroft	DL 1687	19	40	7	Clarke act tune. Manuscript by theatre copyist.
The Fairy Queen (*A Midsummer Night's Dream*)	Anon.	DG 2 May 1692; revived 16 Feb. 1693	7	96, 99	10	Purcell's dramatic opera. Royal Academy of Music manuscript in various hands, partly autograph. Music added in 1693 revival also in RAM autograph.
The Tempest	Shadwell	DG 1695		98	12	"Dear Pretty Youth" is the only *Tempest* music attributed to Purcell in a contemporary source, a Playford print. This song was probably added to the music used in the DG production of 1674.
Timon of Athens	Shadwell	DG 1695		101, 95, 37, 97		Purcell curtain tune, overture, and masque. Anonymous act tunes. Masque in MS, "Jo Walter: His Book," dated 1680. Masque is a later addition in another hand. Song by Clarke.

Production Chart for Chapter 2
1696–1720

Theatre abbreviations: **CG:** Covent Garden; **DG:** Dorset Garden; **DL:** Drury Lane; **KT:** King's Theatre; **LIF:** Lincoln's-Inn-Fields; **QT:** Queen's Theatre.

PRODUCTIONS (original play)	ADAPTER	THEATRE/ DATE	TEXT SOURCES	MUSIC SOURCES	MOD. ED.	COMMENTS
Antony and Cleopatra	Sedley	DG 1696		38, 39	7	Clarke overture and act tunes in manuscript score.
Macbeth	Davenant	LIF 1696-1700		51	5	Eccles masques. Several manuscript scores in good condition. Add. MS 12219 autograph.
The Moore of Venice (*Othello*)		DL 1697		76		Lenton act tunes in manuscript parts.
Sauny the Scot (*The Taming of the Shrew*)	Lacy	DL 1698	14	88, 92, 94		Two printed continuo songs by Daniel Purcell with non-Shakespearean texts. Anon. act tunes in manuscript.
The Humours of Sir John Falstaff (*Henry IV, Pt. 2*)	Betterton	LIF 1700	33	89		Paisible act tunes in parts published by Walsh.

Play	Author	Theatre / Date				Notes
Measure for Measure	Gildon	LIF 1700	11	87, 103, 116		Purcell's *Dido and Aeneas* was divided into three parts and inserted into *Measure for Measure* as entertainments. The music for a fourth entertainment, "Phoebus Rises in His Chariot Over the Sea," is unknown. Two melodies of unknown use survive in dance collections. Weldon "Take O Take Those Lips Away" published 1702.
Hamlet		LIF ca. 1700		53		Published Eccles setting of non-Shakespearean continuo song.
Henry IV, Pt. 1	Betterton	LIF ca. 1700	32	43		Corbett act tunes in parts published by Walsh.
The Jew of Venice (*The Merchant of Venice*)	Granville Lansdowne	LIF Jan. 1701	12			Eccles music for the masque *Peleus and Thetis* is lost.
Macbeth	Davenant	DL 21 Nov. 1702		78, 93		Leveridge masques. Fitzwilliam Museum MS 87 names Leveridge as the composer. Masque texts slightly changed from Davenant. Song by Daniel Purcell (printed as a continuo song) added to the production.
Love Betray'd (*Twelfth Night*)	Burnaby	LIF 1703	2	44		Corbett act tunes in parts published by Walsh. Surviving copies incomplete. The theatre neglected to have Burnaby's masque set to music.
The Tempest	Shadwell	DL 17 July 1711?		117	12	New music for masques and songs. Several manuscript copies variously dated. Serious problems of attribution and dating. The earliest manuscript source (ca. 1720) names no composer. The Purcell attribution does not appear until ca. 1750. Purcell's "Dear Pretty Youth" retained.

Ambleto (*Hamlet*)	Zeno	QT 27 Feb. 1712	58	Italian opera by Gasparini. Libretto in Italian. Manuscript from 1705 production in Venice. Printed score from London performance excludes recitative. Some discrepancies between two sources. Burney questioned whether Zeno's libretto was in any way influenced by Shakespeare's play (*General History* 2:679).
The Comick Masque of Pyramus and Thisbe (*A Midsummer Night's Dream*)	Leveridge	LIF 29 Oct. 1716	15	The music by Leveridge is lost.
Sauny the Scot (*The Taming of the Shrew*)	Lacy	LIF 1716	79	Leveridge setting of non-Shakespearean text published in broadside.

Production Chart for Chapter 3
1720–1750

Theatre abbreviations: **CG**: Covent Garden; **DG**: Dorset Garden; **DL**: Drury Lane; **GF**: Goodman's Fields; **KT**: King's Theatre; **LIF**: Lincoln's-Inn-Fields.

PRODUCTIONS (original play)	ADAPTER	THEATRE/ DATE	TEXT SOURCES	MUSIC SOURCES	MOD. ED.	COMMENTS
Measure for Measure		LIF 8 Dec. 1720	41	57, 52		Galliard "Take O Take Those Lips Away" in published collection. Anon. incidental music Newberry MS Case VM 3.1 p985.
Love in a Forest (*As You Like It*)	Johnson	DL 9 Jan. 1723	13	35		Carey "What Shall He Have That Killed the Deer?" Version in Carey's *Works* gives full choral parts and figured bass only.
Tragedy of Marcus Brutus (*Julius Caesar*)	Sheffield	Buckingham House 11 Jan. 1723	54	29		Bononcini "Four Choruses" in manuscript. One private performance only.
Henry V	Hill	DL 5 Dec. 1723		50		Published Eccles setting of non-Shakespearean text.
Henry IV, Pt. 1	Betterton	LIF 18 March 1725		81		Non-Shakespearean song "The Play of Love" variously attributed to Leveridge and Pepusch.
Henry VIII		DL 26 Oct. 1727	35	63		Music for added coronation scene. Manuscript not positively connected with DL.
Timon of Athens	Shadwell	DL 23 Apr. 1729				Purcell masque replaced by dance with music by Corelli.
Hamlet		LIF 15 Apr. 1730				Two songs by Leveridge, sung by him in the character of first gravedigger, are unknown.
Timon of Athens	Shadwell	CG 1 May 1733				Overture by Pepusch and masque by Roseingrave both lost.

Richard III	C. Cibber	GF 18 Mar. 1734				Bellear overture lost.
Cure For a Scold (*The Taming of the Shrew*)	Worsdale	DL 25 Feb. 1735	58			Music lost. Printed play lists 23 songs.
Hamlet		GF 29 Feb. 1740				Music by Carey lost.
Julius Caesar (music only)	Sheffield	KT 14 Apr. 1739	53	56		Galliard's setting of Sheffield's "Four Choruses" performed apart from the play as independent entertainment. Printed texts suggest the choruses may have been used as entr'actes in an unaltered *Julius Caesar* at LIF prior to 1729.
The Tempest	Shadwell/ Dryden	DL 28 Nov. 1740	3		1	Two songs by Arne added to "Purcell" score. "Where the Bee Sucks," published in *Lyric Harmony II* [1747], may come from this production.
As You Like It		DL 20 Dec. 1740	7, 12		1	Songs by Arne in printed score: strings à 3, figured bass, flute, vocal solo.
Twelfth Night		DL 15 Jan. 1741	12, 14		1	Songs by Arne in printed score. 1786 version gives two versions of "Come Away Death."
Winter's Tale		CG Nov. 1741	73, 75		1	Two published songs by Lampe: "But Shall I Go Mourn For That," "Jog-on, Jog-on."
The Merchant of Venice		DL 14 Dec. 1741	11		1	Arne songs in printed score: strings à 4, figured bass, voice.
Rosalinda (*As You Like It*)	Rolli	KT 3 Jan. 1741	20	109	1	Italian opera by Veracini. Manuscript score incomplete. Italian libretto published.

271

Pyramus and Thisbe (*A Midsummer Night's Dream*)	Anon., after Leveridge	CG 25 Jan. 1744	18	74	8	"Mock opera" by Lampe. Published score omits recitatives.
The Tempest		DL 31 Jan. 1746		8, 47		Restored text. Arne songs and Act IV masque. Add. MS 29370, a study souvenir score made between 1770 and 1809 copied incomplete. Arne's setting of *Neptune and Amphitrite*, carried over from Shadwell text, is lost. Songs by Defesch (including "Where the Bee Sucks").
Cymbeline		CG 7 Apr. 1746		31		Boyce dirge with slightly altered text in autograph.
Much Ado about Nothing		DL 14 Nov. 1748		10		Arne "Sigh No More" in *Vocal Melody I.*

Production Chart for Chapter 4
1750–1770

Theatre abbreviations: **CG**: Covent Garden; **DL**: Drury Lane.

PRODUCTIONS (original play)	ADAPTER	THEATRE/ DATES	TEXT SOURCES	MUSIC SOURCES	MOD. ED.	COMMENTS
Romeo and Juliet		CG 28 Sept. 1750	45	5		Arne dirge for Juliet's funeral procession published in full score in 1765.
Romeo and Juliet	Garrick	DL 28 Sept. 1750		30		Boyce dirge for Juliet's funeral procession in autograph manuscript. Scene added to production on 1 Oct. 1750.
The Merchant of Venice		CG 16 Nov. 1751		17		Song for Jessica by Baildon.
The Sheep Shearing (*Winter's Tale*)	Morgan	CG 25 Mar. 1754	16	4		One setting by T. Arne of a non-Shakespearean text survives in printed reduced score.
Coriolanus	Sheridan	CG 10 Dec. 1754	27			Processional with on-stage musicians, music unknown.
The Fairies (*A Midsummer Night's Dream*)	Garrick?	DL 3 Feb. 1755	9	105	14	Opera by J. C. Smith. Printed score omits recitative. English libretto published.
Florizel and Perdita (*Winter's Tale*)	Garrick	DL 21 Jan. 1756	8	1, 32, 33		M. Arne. Setting of non-Shakespearean song text published in reduced-score. Boyce's "Music for animating the statue . . ." in autograph score. Songs from act IV printed in Linley, *Shakespeare's Dramatic Songs*. Text in printed play differs from songs as they appear in Linley. "Get You Hence for I Must Go" in *Lyra Britanica*.

273

Title	Attribution	Theatre / Date	No.	No.	Notes
The Tempest	Garrick?	DL 11 Feb. 1756	10	106	Opera by J. C. Smith. Printed score omits all recitative except one.
The Tempest		DL 20 Oct. 1757		34	Act IV masque by Boyce in autograph.
Cymbeline		CG 15 Feb. 1759		16	Aylward's "Hark, hark the lark" in printed collection.
Henry VIII		DL 1761	36		Processional with on-stage musicians, music unknown.
Cymbeline	Garrick	DL 28 Nov. 1761	29		Masque "with dancing" in act II.
Comedy of Errors	Hull	CG 24 Apr. 1762			M. Arne setting of non-Shakespearean text , "Stray Not To Those Distant Scenes."
Two Gentlemen of Verona	Victor	DL 22 Dec. 1762	51	110	Vernon's "Who Is Sylvia?" in print. Playbill advertises "a New Overture and Music Between the Acts."
Twelfth Night		DL 19 Oct. 1763		110	Vernon "Epilogue Song" printed in full score. Non-Shakespearean "French Air" arranged by M. Kelly.
A Midsummer Night's Dream	Garrick	DL 23 Nov. 1763	42	2, 16, 19, 105	Text indicates 33 songs, including several retained from Smith's *The Fairies*. New songs by M. Arne, Aylward, and Battishill survive in prints. Lost songs by S. Arnold and C. Burney.
A Fairy Tale (*A Midsummer Night's Dream*)	Colman/ Garrick	DL 26 Nov. 1763	3	2	1763 *Dream* abridged into afterpiece. M. Arne songs retained from earlier production.
The Jubilee (Spectacle by Garrick)		DL 14 Oct. 1769		48	The printed collection of Dibdin's music for *The Jubilee* (in a simplified keyboard reduction) includes music to accompany a mute stage representation of Shakespeare's characters.

Production Chart for Chapter 5
1770–1830

Theatre abbreviations: **CG**: Covent Garden; **DL**: Drury Lane; **HAY**: Haymarket.

PRODUCTIONS (original play)	ADAPTER	THEATRE/ DATE	TEXT SOURCES	MUSIC SOURCES	MOD. ED.	COMMENTS
Macbeth		DL 25 Nov. 1776				T. Linley, Sr.'s arrangement of Boyce's printed edition of Leveridge (from Egerton MS 2957). Linley's arrangement lost.
Macbeth		CG 1776?		55		Fisher. Act I Masque in autograph score. Performance date uncertain.
The Tempest	Sheridan	DL 4 Jan. 1777		82		T. Linley, Jr. storm chorus, songs for Ariel, conclusion in dated manuscript made by theatre copyist. Production also included music from Arne and "Purcell" scores.
Comedy of Errors	Hull	CG 22 Jan. 1779		49		Simplified printed score of non-Shakespearean text, setting by Dibdin.
Henry VIII		CG 30 Oct. 1780				William Shield's music and chorus for the Royal Christening lost.
Macbeth		Hay 1785?		15		Interval tunes, processionals, scene music by S. Arnold in printed full score.
Twelfth Night		DL 1785?		13, 72		Non-Shakespearean song by M. Kelly.
Henry VIII		DL 25 Nov. 1788				T. Linley, Sr.'s setting of "Orpheus With His Lute" lost.

Play	Adapter	Theatre / Date			Notes
Much Ado about Nothing				107	R.J.S. Stevens glee "Sigh No More Ladies."
The Tempest	Kemble	DL 27 Nov. 1789	47	70, 71	Kemble's revision used parts of the Dryden/Sheridan text. Music by T. Linley, Jr., Arne, and "Purcell" supplemented by two settings by M. Kelly of non-Shakespearean songs.
The Merchant of Venice		DL 8 Nov. 1791		104	Non-Shakespearean duet by T. Shaw.
Othello		DL 1798		64	Hook "Willow Song" in piano/vocal score.
Macbeth		CG 5 Nov. 1805	40	111, 114	Overtures and act symphonies by W. H. Ware published in piano reduction.
Coriolanus	Kemble	CG 3 Nov. 1806	28	112, 113	Overtures and act symphonies by W. H. Ware.
The Tempest	Kemble	CG 8 Dec. 1806	49	45, 46	Overture and act music by J. Davy published. Production included music by Linley, "Purcell", Arne, J. C. Smith.
Macbeth	Cross	Royal Circus 30 Aug. 1809	4		"Ballet of Action and Music" with score based on "Locke" (i.e., Leveridge) music with additions by Busby.
The Jubilee	T. Dibdin, after Garrick	Surrey Theatre 6 Aug. 1810			Scenes in mime with music.
Winter's Tale	Kemble	CG 28 Nov. 1811	52		Overture and act symphonies by H. R. Bishop.
Cymbeline	Kemble	CG 3 Jun. 1812	30	20	Dance by Bishop in manuscript.

Play	Author	Theatre/Date			Notes
Antony and Cleopatra	Kemble, after Dryden	CG 15 Nov. 1813	23	21	Bishop funeral procession for soloists, chorus, and orchestra in act V.
Macbeth		DL 5 Nov. 1814			Overture and entr'actes by C. E. Horn.
A Midsummer Night's Dream	Reynolds	CG 17 Jan. 1816	43	24	Comic opera adaptation. Bishop's music in manuscript and printed piano/vocal score.
Timon of Athens		DL 28 Oct. 1816	50		Incidental music by T. S. Cooke lost.
Comedy of Errors	Reynolds	CG 11 Dec. 1819	26	25	Comic opera adaptation. Bishop's music in manuscript and piano/vocal score.
Coriolanus		DL 25 Jan. 1820		41	"Grand Triumphal March" for chorus and orchestra by T. S. Cooke.
Twelfth Night	Reynolds	CG 8 Nov. 1820		26	Comic opera adaptation. Bishop's music in manuscript and piano/vocal score.
The Tempest	Reynolds, after Shadwell	CG 15 May 1821		27	Bishop pastiche of music by J. Davy, T. Arne, C. E. Horn, Haydn, Mozart, Rossini.
Two Gentlemen of Verona	Reynolds	CG 29 Nov. 1821		23	Comic opera adaptation. Bishop's music in manuscript and piano/vocal score.
Henry IV, Pt. 2	Kemble	CG 1821	34	22	Bishop's coronation processional in autograph score.
As You Like It	Reynolds	CG June 1824 DL 25 Nov. 1824		28, 66	Comic opera adaptation. Bishop's music in manuscript and piano vocal score. "Poor Corydon" from *Passionate Pilgrim* set by C. E. Horn.

The Merry Wives of Windsor	Reynolds	DL 20 Feb. 1824	65	Music by C. E. Horn in manuscript. Production included music by J. Blewitt, T. S. Cooke, J. Parry, S. Webbe, Jr., and J. Braham.
The Taming of the Shrew		DL 14 May 1828	42	Comic opera elaboration by Cooke and Braham, incorporating music by Rossini.
Shakespeare's Festival, or A New Comedy of Errors	Moncrieff	DL 23 Apr. 1830		A new play with an enlarged version of *The Jubilee* in the second act, songs arranged for the occasion by Blewitt.

SCENE ANALYSIS TABLES

John Christopher Smith: *The Fairies*

The "folio" column indicates each scene's source passage from *A Midsummer Night's Dream*. Act/scene/line indications in the "folio" column refer to the text as it appears in the New Cambridge Edition. Because the opera libretto retains the original sequence of action, major omissions from the play can be indicated. The "entrance/exit" column is a summary of character entrances (E) and exits (X). The "music" column describes the musical numbers in each scene (Aria types: DC—*da capo*; DS—*dal segno*; no indication—through composed), their tonality being listed in the "key" column. The scene's action is summarized in the last column.

The Fairies. Act I Scene Analysis of Libretto and Music

Character Key: TH—Theseus. HI—Hippolyta. E—Egius. HM—Hermia. L—Lysander. D—Demetrius. HL—Helena. P—Puck. F—a fairy. TT—Titania. O—Oberon.

SCENE	FOLIO	ENTRANCE/EXIT	MUSIC	KEY	ACTION
			1. Overture	D minor	
		E - Prologue (spoken) X - Prologue	2. Minuet	D major	The apology
I, 1	I, 1: 1-19	E - TH, HI	3. Sinfonia 4. Air - TH (DS)	D major D major	Court entrance
I, 2	I, 1: 20-127	E - E, HM, L, D X - TH, HI, E, D	5. Air - HM (DC) 6. Air with chorus (not in printed score)	G major	Love triangle introduced TH gives HM ultimatum
I, 3	I, 1: 128-179		7. Air - L (DS)	D major	HM, L plan escape

I, 4	I, 1: 180-225	E - HL X - HM, L	8. Air - HL (DS) 9. Air - HM (DC)	G major F major	HL told about escape plot
I, 5	I, 1: 226-251	X - HL	10. Air - HL	A major	HL goes to tell D
	I, 2	(Low comics omitted)			
I, 6	II, 1: 1-59	Scene change. E - P, F	11. Air - P (DC)	D major	Narrative of argument between TT and O
I, 7	II, 1: 60-185	E - TT, O, with trains X - TT with train X - P	12. Sinfonia 13. Air - TT (DC) 14. Air - O	B-flat A major F major	TT refuses O's demand O sends P after magic herb

The Fairies. **Act II Scene Analysis of Libretto and Music**

Character Key: TH—Theseus. Hl—Hippolyta. E—Egius. HM—Hermia. L—Lysander. D—Demetrius. HL—Helena. P—Puck. F—a fairy. TT—Titania. O—Oberon.

SCENE	FOLIO	ENTRANCE/EXIT	MUSIC	KEY	ACTION
II, 1	II, 1: 186-246	E - O E - D, HL X - D, HL	15. Air -HL (DS)	F	O becomes invisible O watches D scorn HL
II, 2	II, 1: 247-268	E - P X - O, [P]			O plans to help HL, sends P to enchant D

Scene	Measures	Stage action	Music	Key	Action
II, 3	II, 2: 1-34	E - TT with train X - train 1 E - O X - O	16. Air - TT (strophic)	C minor	TT prepares to sleep O enchants TT
II, 4	II, 2: 35-65	E - L, HM	17. Duet - L, HM (DS)	G major	L, HM sleep
II, 5	II, 2: 66-83	E - P X - P			P mistakenly enchants L
II, 6	II, 2: 84-144	E - D, HL X - D X - HL, L	18. Air - L (DC)	B-flat	D deserts HL H awakens L L pursues HL
II, 6 [sic-i.e. **II, 7**]	II, 2: 145-156	X - HM	19. Air - HM (DS)	A major	HM finds herself alone
	III, 1	(Low comics omitted)			
II, 7 [sic-i.e. **II, 8**]	new scene	E - O with train, P	20. Air - O (bipartite) 21. Dance (not in score) 22. Air - O (A-B-A)	F major D major	Fairy revels

1No exit is indicated for the sleeping TT for the remainder of the act.

The Fairies. **Act III Scene Analysis of Libretto and Music**

Character Key: TH–Theseus. H–Hippolyta. E–Egius. HM–Hermia. L–Lysander. D–Demetrius. HL–Helena. P–Puck. F–a fairy. TT–Titania. O–Oberon.

SCENE	FOLIO	ENTRANCE/EXIT	MUSIC	KEY	ACTION
III, 1	III, 2: 4-40	E - O, P			P tells O of TT's "patch'd fool"
III, 2	III, 2: 41-84	E - D, HM X - HM	23. Air - HM (DS)	A major	P discovers his mistake
III, 3	III, 2: 85-121	X - P E - P [X - O, P] [1]	24. Air - O (bipartite)	B-flat	O tries to correct P's mistake
III, 4	III, 2: 122-176	E - L, HL	25. Air - L (DC)	D major	L woos HL
III, 5	III, 2: 177-344	E - HM X - HL X - L, D X - HM	26. Air - HL (DS) 27. Air - HM (DS)	B-flat A major	L and D both woo HL, L spurns HM L and D fight
III, 6	III, 2: 348-349	E - O, P X - O X - P	28. Air - O (DS) 29. Air - P	F major G major	O plans to disenchant TT

	Measures	Stage	Number	Key	Event
	IV, 1: 1-78	(Low comics omitted)			
III, 7	IV, 1: 79-90	E - O, TT	30. Air - TT (DC) 31. Dance (not in score)	E-flat	The lovers sleep
III, 8	IV, 1: 107-185	E - TH, HI, E (L, HM, HL, D) 2	32. Sinfonia	F major	Lovers are discovered by TH's party
			33. Air - TH (DS)	F major	Lovers "correctly" paired
			34. Air - HL (DS)	A major	
			35. Chorus with solo (DC)	D major	
	IV, 2	(Remainder omitted)			
	V				

1No exit direction is given for O and P. They re-enter in III, 6.

2The lovers exit in III, 5. They do no re-enter but are discovered in III, 8.

John Christopher Smith: *The Tempest*

In this scene-by-scene description, the "source" column indicates the analogous sections of the folio text or the Dryden adaptation. Act/scene/line indications in the "source" column refer to the folio text as it appears in the New Cambridge Edition. The Dryden references are to the first printed edition: *The Tempest, or the Enchanted Island* (London: Henry Herringman, 1670). The "music" column describes the musical numbers in each scene (Aria types: DC—*da capo*; DS—*dal segno*; no indication—through composed), their tonality being listed in the key column. The scene's action is summarized in the last column.

The Tempest. **Act I Scene Analysis of Libretto and Music**

Character Key: A—Ariel. P—Prospero. M—Miranda. F—Ferdinand. S—Stephano. V—Ventoso. MS—Mustacho. T—Trincalo. AN—Anthonio. N—Alonzo, King of Naples. G—Gonzalo. C—Caliban.

SCENE	SOURCE	ENTRANCE/EXIT	MUSIC	KEY	ACTION
			1. Overture	G major	
			2. Minuet	G major	
I, 1	I, 2: 196-206	E - A X - A	3. Air - A	B-flat	A foretells storm
I, 2	I, 2: 1-188	E - P, M			
			4. Air - M (DC)	G major	M asks P to calm storm
					P tells M their history
			5. Air - P	A minor	
			6. Air - M	D minor	M sleeps

284

I, 3	I, 2: 189-94, 237-300	E - A X - A X - P, M	7. Air - A (bipartite) 8. Air - P (ABA)	G minor F major	P details tasks for A P chastises A M awakens
I, 4	I, 2: 376-406. Dryden III, p. 42	E - F, A X - F, A	9. Air - A (DC) 10. Air - A (bipartite) 11. Duet - A, F (ABA'B'CD)	G major E-flat C major	F enchanted
I, 5	Dryden II, pp. 19-22	E - S, V, MS E - T	12. Hornpipe 13. Air - S (ABA'B') 14. Duet - T, MS (bipartite) 15. Air - T, et al. (bipartite)	G major C major F major D major	All bewail their fate All lay claim to the island T, MS fight All compromise

The Tempest. Act II Scene Analysis of Libretto and Music

Character Key: A—Ariel. P—Prospero. M—Miranda. F—Ferdinand. S—Stephano. V—Ventoso. MS—Mustacho. T—Trincalo. AN—Anthonio. N—Alonzo, King of Naples. G—Gonzalo. C—Caliban.

SCENE	SOURCE	ENTRANCE/EXIT	MUSIC	KEY	ACTION
II, 1	I, 2: 408-501	F discovered, E - P, M, A			
			16. Air - G (DS)	F major	M and F meet
			17. Air - P	F major	M and F fall in love
		X - M, P, A, F	18. Air - M	D major	F challenges P
II, 2	II, 1: 1-122	E - N, AN, G			N mourns F
II, 3	Dryden III, p. 37	E - A, "Banquet"	19. Air - A (DC)	G major	N, AN, G resolve to eat
II, 4	new	X - A, "Banquet" E - A, "Strange Shapes"	20. Air - A 21. Dance (not in score)	B-flat	A frightens mortals
		X - all E - P X - P	22. Air - P (DS)	E minor	P contemplates his power
II, 5	Dryden IV, p. 51	E - F	23. Air - F (bipartite)	E major	F thinks about M

	Dryden IV, p. 52	E - M, P	24. Air - F (DC)	F major	love scene
II, 6		X - M, F, P	25. Air - M (DC)	B-flat	
II, 7	II, 2	E - C	26. Air - C (bipartite)	D major	T discovers C and gives him wine
		E - T	27. Air - C (AA')	G major	C pledges loyalty to T
	new	E - S, V, MS	28. Terzetto - T, S, C (ABC)	B-flat	S, V, MS are frightened by C and make T sole ruler of the island

The Tempest. Act III Scene Analysis of Libretto and Music

Character Key: A—Ariel. P—Prospero. M—Miranda. F—Ferdinand. S—Stephano. V—Ventoso. MS—Mustacho. T—Trincalo. AN—Anthonio. N—Alonzo, King of Naples. G—Gonzalo. C—Caliban.

SCENE	SOURCE	ENTRANCE/EXIT	MUSIC	KEY	ACTION
III, 1	IV, 1: 1-33	E - P, M, F	29. Air - F (bipartite)	G major	P blesses union of F and M
III, 2	IV, 1: 34	E - A	30. Air - A (bipartite)	D major	P enquires about N
	V, 1: 17-30	X - A			
III, 3	IV, 1: 51-56	X - F, M	31. Air - M (DS)	F major	P counsels F

				D_6 - F	P abjures his powers
III, 4	V, 1: 1-16, 31-51		32. Accomp. Recit. - P 33. Air - P (DS)	G minor	
III, 5	V, 1: 104-171	E - A, AN, N, G			P reveals himself to N
III, 6	V, 1: 172-174	F, M discovered	34. Air - F (DS)	G major	N sees F
III, 7	V, 1: 175-318	E - P, A, AN, N, G [1]	35. Air - F (bipartite)	A major	P, AN, N reconciled
			36. Air - P (DS)	C major	A freed
			37. Duet - F, M (DC)	D major	
			38. Chorus (not in score)		

[1] The stage direction here is unclear. P, A, AN, and G (already on stage) apparently enter into the cell where F and M are discovered playing chess.

Selected Bibliography

MUSICAL SOURCES

If a musical item's bibliographic main entry does not indicate its source play the play's title is parenthetically added to the listing. The location and date for the production in which the music was probably first used is given in parentheses at the end of the entry.

Abbreviations:

Lbm—British Library, London; Lcm—Royal College of Music, London; OB—Bodleian Library, Oxford

CG—Covent Garden; DG—Dorset Garden; DL—Drury Lane; KT—King's Theatre; LIF—Lincoln's-Inn-Fields; QT—Queen's Theatre

1. Arne, Michael. "Come, Come My Good Shepherd" (*Florizel and Perdita*, i.e. *The Winter's Tale*). In *The London Magazine*, 1756. (DL, 1756).
2. _____. *The Favorite New Songs and Duet in the Fairy Tale* (*Midsummer Night's Dream*). London: Charles and Samuel Thompson, 1764. (DL, 1763).
3. Arne, Thomas. "Ariel's Song" ("Where the Bee Sucks," *Tempest*). In Arne, Thomas. *The Second Volume of Lyric Harmony*. London: William Smith, [ca.1747]. (DL, 1740?).

4. _____. "Come Let Us Be Blithe and Gay" *(Florizel and Perdita,* i.e. *The Winter's Tale).* In Arne, Thomas. *The Winter's Amusement.* London: Printed for the author, [1762]. (CG, 1755).

5. _____. *A Compleat Score of the Solemn Dirge in Romeo and Juliet.* London: Henry Thorowgood, [1765]. (CG, 1750).

6. _____. "Fear No More the Heat o' the Sun" *(Cymbeline).* In Arne, Thomas. *The Winter's Amusement.* London: Printed for the author, [1762]. (DL, 1759).

7. _____. *The Music in The Comedy of As You Like It.* London: Harrison & Co., [ca. 1786]. (DL, 1741).

8. _____. "Music in The Tempest." Lbm Add. MS 29370 [ca. 1800], fols. 87-111. (DL, 1746).

9. _____. "O Bid Your Faithful Ariel Fly" *(Tempest).* In *The Syren, a New Collection of Favorite Songs.* London: Longman and Broderip, 1777. (CG, 1777).

10. _____. "Sigh No More, Ladies" *(Much Ado about Nothing).* In Arne, Thomas, *Vocal Melody,* Book I. London: I. Walsh, 1746. (DL, 1748).

11. _____. *The Songs and Duets in The Blind Begger of Bethnal Green . . . with The Favorite Songs in The Merchant of Venice.* London: W. Smith, [1742]. (DL, 1741).

12. _____. *The Songs in The Comedies called As You Like It and Twelfth Night.* London: William Smith, [1741]. (DL, 1740 and 1741).

13. _____. *The Songs in Twelfth Night in Score.* London: Harrison & Co., [1786]. (DL, 1785?).

14. _____. "To Fair Fidele's Grassy Tomb" *(Cymbeline).* In Arne, Thomas. *The Second Volume of Lyric Harmony.* London: William Smith, [1747]. (DL, 1747).

15. Arnold, Samuel. *The Favorite Scotch Airs . . . as they are performed in Macbeth.* London: W. Warrell, 1785. (Haymarket, 1785?).

16. Aylward, Theodore. *Six Songs in Harlequin's Invasion, Cymbeline, and Midsummer Night's Dream.* London: Bremner, 1765. (DL, 1759; DL 1763).

17. Baildon, Joseph. "Sung by Mrs. Chambers in the Character of Jessica in the Merchant of Venice." In *The Laurel, Book 2.* London: Walsh, 1752. Also "Jessica's Song in The Merchant of Venice" ("Haste Lorenzo, Haste Away"). London, [1776]. (CG 1751).

18. [Banister, John, et al.]. *The Ariels Songs in the Play call'd The Tempest.* London: Playford, [1675?]. (DG, 1667).

19. Battishill, Jonathan. *A Collection of favorite songs sung at the publick Gardens and Theatres* (Songs from *Midsummer Night's Dream*). London: Charles and Samuel Thompson, [1765]. (DL, 1763).

20. Bishop, Henry R. [*Cymbeline*, dance movement]. Lbm Add. MS 36963. (CG, 1812).

21. _____. *Epicedium in Shakespeare's Play of Antony and Cleopatra.* London: Goulding, D'Almaine, Potter and Co., 1813. Lbm Add. MS 36963. (CG, 1813).

22. _____. [*Henry IV.* Coronation Scene]. Lbm Add. MS 33570. (CG, 1821).

23. _____. *The Overture, Songs, Duets, Glees and Choruses, in Shakespeare's Play of the Two Gentlemen of Verona.* London: Goulding, D'Almaine, Potter & Co., [1812]. Lbm Add. MS 36953. (CG, 1821).

24. _____. *The Overture, Songs, Duets, Trios, Quartets and Choruses in Shakespeare's Midsummer Night's Dream.* London: Goulding, D'Almaine, Potter & Co., [1816]. Lbm Add. MS 36944. (CG, 1816).

25. _____. *The Overture, Songs, Two Duets, and Glees in Shakespeare's Comedy of Errors.* London: Goulding, D'Almaine, Potter & Co. [1819]. Lbm Add. MS 27714. (CG, 1819).

26. _____. *The Songs, Duets, and Glees in Shakespeare's Play of Twelfth Night.* London: Goulding, D'Almaine, Potter & Co., [1820]. Lbm Add MS 36952. (CG, 1820).

27. _____. [*The Tempest*]. Lbm Add MS 36963, Lcm MS 62. (CG, 1821)

28. _____. *The Whole of The Music in As You Like It.* London: Goulding, D'Almaine, Potter & Co., [1824]. Lbm Add. MS 27717. (CG, 1824).

29. Bononcini, Giovanni. "Four Choruses for Marcus Brutus" (*Julius Caesar*). manuscript, Nottingham University Library.

30. Boyce, William. "Dirge for Romeo and Juliet." OB. MS. Mus. c. 3 (DL, 1750).

31. _____. "A Dirge in Cymbeline of Shakespeare" ("Fear No More The Scorching Sun"). OB. MS. Mus. c. 35. (CG, 1747).

32. _____. "The Music for Animating The Statue, in Shakespeare's Play of The Winter's Tale," OB. MS. Mus. d. 14. (DL, 1756).

33. _____. [Songs in *The Winter's Tale*, act 4]. In Linley, William. *Shakespeare's Dramatic Songs*, 2:24-6. London: Preston, 1816.

34. _____. [*Tempest*, Masque]. Lcm MS 92. (DL, 1757).

35. Carey, Henry. "What Shall He Have That Killed the Deer?" (*Love in a Forest*, i.e. *As You Like It*). In *The Works of Mr. Henry Carey*. 2d. ed. London, 1726. (DL, 1723).

36. Chilcot, Thomas. *Twelve English Songs, with their Symphonies. The Words by Shakespeare and other Celebrated Poets.* London: John Johnson, 1745.

37. Clarke, Jeremiah. "Alas, Here Was the Poor Alonzo Slain, Sung by Mrs. Hodgson in the Play called Timon of Athens." In *Monthly Mask of Vocal Music*, Jan. 1704. (DG, 1696).

38. _____. "Clarke Overture in Antony & Cleopatra." Lcm MS 1172, fol. 15. (DG, 1696).

39. _____. "Lady Warton's Farewell in Antony & Cleopatra." Lcm MS 1172, fol. 20v. (DG, 1696).

40. _____. "Mr. Cl in Titus Andronicus" (act tune). Lcm MS 1172, fol. 10 v. (DL, 1687).

41. Cooke, T. S. "Grand Triumphal March in the Tragedy of Coriolanus." London: Royal Harmonia, [n. d.]. (DL, 1820).

42. [Cooke, T. S., and John Braham]. *The Taming of the Shrew, Shakespeare's revived comedy.* 2 vols. London, 1828. (DL, 1828)

43. Corbett, William. *Mr. Corbet's Musick in The Comedy call'd Hen[ry] the 4th.* London: J. Walsh and J. Hare, 1703. (DL, ca. 1700?).

44. _____. "Mr. Corbett's Musick in the Comedy called The Agreeable Disappointment" (*Love Betray'd*, i.e. *Twelfth Night*). In *Harmonia Anglicana*, series 5. London: J. Walsh, 1703. (LIF, 1703).

45. Davy, John. *The Favourite New Overture to The Tempest.* London: Turnbull, [n.d.]. (CG, 1806).

46. [Davy, John, et al.]. *The Original Music in The Tempest.* London: Birchall, [n.d.]. (CG, 1806).

47. Defesch, [William]. *The Songs in The Tempest or the Enchanted Island.* London: for Wm. Smith, [1747]. (DL, 1746).

48. Dibdin, Charles. *The Overture, Songs, Airs and Choruses, in the Jubilee or Shakespeare's Garland.* London: J. Johnston, [1770]. (DL, 1769).

49. _____. "Tarry Here With Me and Be My Love" (*Comedy of Errors*). London: S.A.P.T., 1780. (CG, 1779).

50. Eccles, John. "Fill all the glasses" (*Henry V*). London, [ca. 1725]. (DL, 1723).

51. _____. [*Macbeth*, Masques]. Lbm Add. MS 12219. Also Add. MS 31454; Lcm MSS 182 and 857; Royal Academy of Music, London, MS 26 C-E. (LIF, ca. 1700).

52. _____. "Mr. Eccles Music in the Play Measure for Measure." Newberry Library, Chicago, manuscript: Case VM 3.1 P985. (LIF, 1700).

53. _____. "A Song, set by Mr. John Eccles, Sung by Mr. Knapp in the Tragedy of Hamlet, Prince of Denmark" ("A Swain Long Slighted and Disdained). London: T. Cross, [ca. 1700]. (LIF, 1700?).

54. Farmer, Thomas. "Can Life Be a Blessing" (Dryden's *Troilus and Cressida*). In *Choice Ayres, Songs, and Dialogues Book III.* London: A. Dodbid and J. Playford, Jr., 1681. (LIF, 1679).

55. Fisher, John Abraham. [*Macbeth*, Masques]. Manuscript. Shakespeare Music Catalogue Project, University of Victoria, B.C. (CG, 1776?).

56. Galliard, Johann Ernst. "The Four Chorus's in the Tragedy of Julius Caesar." Boston Public Library manuscript M. Cab. 1. 15. Also Lbm Add. MS 25484. (LIF, ca. 1729?).

57. _____. "Take, O Take Those Lips Away" (*Measure for Measure*). In *Musical Miscellany.* London: John Watts, 1729–31. (LIF, 1722).

58. Gasparini, Francesco. "Ambleto" (*Hamlet*). Manuscript, Deutsche Staatsbibliothek, Berlin. Also *Songs in The Opera of Hamlet.* London: J. Walsh & J. Hare, 1712. (QT, 1712).

59. Grabu, Louis. "Hark How the Songsters of the Grove" (*Timon of Athens*). In *Choice Ayres and Songs . . . the Second Book.* London: Ann Godbid, 1678. (DG, 1678).

60. "Hark The Sound of The Drum. Sung by Mr. Andrews in *The Tempest.*" London, [ca. 1764]. (DL, 1760?).

61. Hart, James. "Adieu to the Pleasures" (*Tempest*). See Banister, John. *The Ariels songs.* Also in *Choice Ayres, Songs, and Dialogues, newly reprinted.* London: William Godbid, 1676. (DG, 1674).

62. [*Henry VIII*, Act tune]. Lcm MS 1172, fol. 20v.

63. [*Henry VIII*, Coronation Processional]. Lbm RM 21. c43–45. (DL, 1726?).

64. Hook James. "The Willow, a favorite air, sung by Mrs. Jordan and accompanied by herself on the lute" (*Othello*). London: J. Dale, [1798]. (DL, 1798).

65. Horn, Charles Edward. [*The Merry Wives of Windsor*]. Lbm Add. MS 33800. (DL, 1824)

66. _____. "Poor Corydon" (*As You Like It*). London: Clementi, Collard & Collard, [1825]. (CG, 1824).

67. Humfrey, Pelham. [*Tempest*, Masques]. (Also includes Reggio's "Arise ye subterranean winds.") Bibliotheque Nationale, Paris. Manuscript F1090: 51,52. (DG, 1674).

68. _____. "Willow Song" (*Othello*). In Smith, J. Stafford. *Musica Antiqua*. London: 1812. (1660?).

69. Kelly, Michael. "Hamlet's Letter to Ophelia." London: Printed for M. Kelly, 1799.

70. "To See Thee So Gentle" (*Tempest*). London: Longman & Broderip, [1789]. (DL, 1789).

71. _____. "What New Delights" (*Tempest*). Dublin: John Lee, 1790. (DL, 1789).

72. _____. "What Wakes This New Pain in My Breast?" (*Twelfth Night*). Dublin: John Lee, 1790. (DL, 1785).

73. Lampe, Johann Friedrich. "Jog On, Jog On" (*Winter's Tale*). London, [1741]. (CG, 1741).

74. _____. *Pyramus and Thisbe* (from *Midsummer Night's Dream*). London: J. Walsh, 1745. (CG, 1745).

75. _____. "Set by Mr. Lampe from Shakespear" ["But Shall I Go Mourn for that My Dear"] (*Winter's Tale*). [n. p.], [1741]. Also in Lampe, Johann Friedrich. *Lyra Britannica*. London: Ino. Simpson, [1745]. (CG, 1741).

76. Lenton, John. "The Moore of Venice" (*Othello*, Act tunes). Lbm. Add. MS 27685, fols. 6r, v; 29r, v; 54r, v; 74r, v. (DL, 1697).

77. Leveridge, Richard. "The Cuckoo" ("When Daisies Pied," *Love's Labour's Lost*). London, [1725].

78. _____. [*Macbeth*, Masques]. Fitzwilliam Museum, Cambridge: MS 87, fols. 63–96. Also Lbm Egerton MS 2957. (DL, 1702).

79. _____. "When Sawny First Did Woe Me" (*Sauny The Scot*, i.e. *Taming of The Shrew*.) London, [ca. 1716]. (LIF, 1716?).

80. _____. "Who is Silvia" (*Two Gentlemen of Verona*). In Leveridge, Richard. *A Collection of Songs*, 2 vols. London: Printed for the author, 1727.

81. [Leveridge, Richard, attrib.] ["The Play of Love"]. London, [n.d.]. (*Henry IV, Part 1* ; LIF, 1725).

82. Linley, Thomas, the younger. "Music for The Tempest and The Duenna" Lbm Egerton MS 2493. Also Lcm Mss 335, 938; Tenbury MS 742. (DL, 1777).

83. Locke, Matthew. *The English Opera; or the Vocal Music in Psyche . . . to which is adjoyned the instrumental music in the Tempest.* London: Ratcliff and Thompson, 1675. (DG, 1674).

84. _____. "A Jig called Macbeth." In *Musick's Delight or The Citern.* London: W. G., 1666. (LIF, 1664).

85. _____. "Macbeth on the Flagelet." In Greeting, Thomas. *The Pleasant Companion.* London: John Playford, 1672.

86. _____. "Orpheus With His Lute" (*Henry VIII*). In *Catch That Catch Can: or The Musical Companion.* London: Playford, 1667. (LIF, 1663).

87. "Measure for Measure." In *Twenty-Four New Country Dances.* London: J. Walsh and J. Hare, 1718. (LIF, 1700).

88. "The Musick in The Play call'd Sawney The Scot or ye Temeing of ye Shrew" (act tunes). LBM Add 35043, fols. 104r, v. (DL 1698).

89. Paisible, James. "Mr. Peasable's Ayre's in the Comedy call'd The Humors of Sir Iohn Falstaf" (*Henry IV, Part 2*). In *Harmonia Anglicana*, Series 1. London: J. Walsh and J. Hare, 1701. (LIF, 1700).

90. _____. [*Timon of Athens*, Act Tunes]. Lbm Add. MS 35043. Also Lcm MS 1144. (DG, 1678).

91. Pasquali, Nicolo. *The Solemn Dirge in Romeo and Juliet.* London: R. Bremen, 1771.

92. Purcell, Daniel. "Beyond The Desart Mountains" (*Sauny The Scot*, i.e. *Taming of The Shrew*). London: Thomas Cross, [1699]. (DL, 1698).

93. _____. "A Song Sung by Mr. Mason in Magbeth [*sic*] ("Cease Gentle Swain"). London, [ca. 1704]. (DL, 1704?).

94. _____. "Twas in The Month of May, Jo" (*Sauny The Scot*, i.e. *Taming of The Shrew*). London: William Pearson, 1699. (DL, 1698).

95. Purcell, Henry. "Courtin [i.e., Curtain] Tune in Timon of Athens." Lcm MS 1172, fol. 5r. and v. (DG, 1695).

96. _____. [*Fairy Queen*, Act tunes.] (*Midsummer Night's Dream*). In *A Collection of Ayres, compos'd for the theatre and upon other*

occasions. London: J. Heppinstall, 1697. Also Lcm MS 1172. (DG, 1692).

97. _____. "Mr. Purcell in Timon of Athens" (Overture by Purcell; anon. act tunes; act tunes by Paisible). Lcm MS 1144, fols. 54-5. Also Lbm Add. MS 35043. (DG, 1695; DG 1678).

98. _____. "A New Song in the Tempest" ["Dear Pretty Youth"]. In *Deliciae Musicae III*. London: J. Heppinstall, 1695.

99. _____. "op. Faire Queen" (*Fairy Queen*, i.e. *Midsummer Night's Dream*). Manuscript. Royal Academy of Music. Also British council MS Op. 45, Gresham College Library MS VI 5, 6, Lbm Add. MSS 30839 and 39565-7, Lcm MSS 944, 1144. Also *Some Select Songs as They Are Sung in The Fairy Queen*. London: J. Heppinstall, 1692. (DG, 1692).

100. _____."Retire'd From Any Mortal's Sight" (*Richard II*). In Playford, John. *Choice Ayres and Songs . . . the fourth book*. London: A. Godbid and J. Playford, Jr., 1683. (DL, 1681).

101. _____. [*Timon of Athens*, Masque]. In "Jo. Walter: His Book Anna Domino 1680." Manuscript. West Sussex Record Office, Chichester. Also Lbm Add. MSS 5337, 31447, 31452, and Library of St. Michael's College, Tenbury, MS 338. (DG, 1695).

102. Reggio, Pietro. "Arise ye Subterranean Winds" (*Tempest*). Lbm Add. MS 29397. Also Bibliotheque Nationale, Paris. Manuscript F1090: 51, 52. (DG, 1674).

103. "A Scotch Tune in Measure for Measure." In *Apollo's Banquet*. London: W. Pearson, 1701. (LIF, 1700).

104. Shaw, Thomas. "A New Duet introduced in the Merchant of Venice at the Theatre Royal, Drury Lane." London: Longman & Clementi, [n. d.]. (DL, 1791).

105. Smith, John Christopher. *The Fairies* (*Midsummer Night's Dream*). London: J. Walsh, 1755. (DL, 1755).

106. _____. *The Tempest*. London: J. Walsh, 1756. (DL, 1756).

107. Stevens, R.J.S. "Sigh No More, Ladies" (Glee, *Much Ado about Nothing*). London: J. Bland, [1790]. (DL, 1789).

108. "Trust Not Man, sung by Mrs. Abington in Twelfth Night." London, [ca. 1765]. (DL, ca. 1765).

109. Veracini, Francesco Maria. *Rosalinda* (*As You Like It*). Manuscript. Sachsiche Landesbibliothek, Dresden. (KT, 1744).

110. Vernon, Joseph. *The New Songs in the Pantomime of The Witches . . . 12th Night . . . Two Gentlemen of Verona*. London: John Johnston, 1772. (DL, 1762; DL, 1763).

111. Ware, William Henry. "The Favourite Act Symphonies to Macbeth." London: Hodsoll, [n. d.]. (CG, 1805).

112. _____. "The Much Admir'd Act Symphonies to Coriolanus." London: Hodsoll, [1806]. (CG, 1806).

113. _____. "The Much Admir'd Overture to Coriolanus." London: Hodsoll, [1806]. (CG, 1806).

114. _____. "The Much Admir'd Overture to Macbeth." London: Hodsoll, [n. d.]. (CG, 1805).

115. Weldon, John. "Love in Her Bosome End My Care" (*Love Betray'd*, i.e., *TwelthNight*). London, [ca. 1703]. (LIF, 1703).

116. _____. "Take O Take Those Lips Away" (*Measure for Measure*). In Weldon, John. *A Collection of New Songs*. London: I. Walsh, [1702]. (LIF, 1700).

117. Weldon, John, attrib.; formerly attrib. Purcell. [*The Tempest*]. Lbm Add. MS 37027. Also Tenbury MS 1266. (DL, 1711).

MODERN EDITIONS

1. Arne, Thomas Augustine. *Nine Shakespeare Songs.* Edited by Percy Young. London: Chappell, 1963. (Includes: "Under the Greenwood Tree," "Blow, Blow Thou Winter Wind," "The Cuckoo Song," "The Owl," "Come unto These Yellow Sands," "Ariel's Songs," "Dirge in *Cymbeline.*" Edited for performance.)

2. _____. *The Second Volume of Lyric Harmony.* London: William Smith, [ca. 1747]; facsimile ed. Music for London Entertainment, series F, vol. 2. Tunbridge Wells: Richard MacNutt, 1985. (Includes "To Fair Fidele's Grassy Tomb" and "Where the Bee Sucks.")

3. [Banister, John, et al.]. *The Ariels Songs in the Play call'd The Tempest.* London: Playford, [1675]; facsimile ed. In Music for London Entertainment, series A, vol. 5a. London: Stainer and Bell, 1989.

4. Defesch, [William]. *The Songs in "The Tempest or the Enchanted Island."* London: for Wm. Smith, [1747]; facsimile ed. Huntingdon: King's Music, [1987]. (Includes "While You Here Do Snoring Lie," "Ere You Can Say Come and Go," "Where the Bee Sucks," "O Bid Your Faithful Ariel Fly," "Ah Fancy Sick.")

5. Eccles, John. *The Music in "Macbeth".* Edited by G. O.'Reilly. London: Cathedral Music, 1979.

6. Farmer, Thomas. "Can Life Be a Blessing" (Dryden: *Troilus and Cressida*). In *Choice Ayres, Songs, and Dialogues Book II*. London: A. Godbid and J. Playford, Jr., 1681; facsimile ed. Music for London Entertainment, series A, vol. 5b. London: Stainer and Bell, 1989.

7. *Instrumental Music for London Theatres, 1690-1699: Royal College of Music, MS 1172*. Edited by Curtis Price. Withyham: Richard MacNutt, 1987. (Includes act music from *Henry VIII*, Shadwell's *Timon of Athens*, Sedley's *Antony and Cleopatra*, Ravenscroft's *Titus Andronicus*, and *The Fairy Queen*.)

8. Lampe, Johann Friedrich. *Pyramus and Thisbe* (from *Midsummer Night's Dream*). London: J. Walsh, 1745; facsimile ed. Music for London Entertainment, series C, vol. 3. London: Stainer and Bell, 1988.

9. Locke, Matthew. *Dramatic Music*. Edited by Michael Tilmouth. Musica Britanica, no. 51. London: Stainer and Bell, 1986. (Locke's act tunes for the 1674 *Tempest* and the music by Banister, Humfrey, Reggio, and Hart are arranged in performance order.)

10. Purcell, Henry. *The Fairy Queen*, Edited by J. S. Shedlock; Rev. ed. Edited by Anthony Lewis. *The Works of Henry Purcell*, no. 12. London: Novello, 1968.

11. _____. "Retir'd From Any Mortal's Sight." In *Dramatic Music, Part II*. *The Works of Henry Purcell*, no. 20. London: Novello, 1916.

12. _____. *The Tempest*. Edited by Edward J. Dent. *The Works of Henry Purcell*, no. 14. London: Novello, 1912.

13. _____. *Timon of Athens*. Edited by Frederick Arthur Gore Ouseley. Revised by Jack Westrup. *The Works of Henry Purcell*, no. 2. Borough Green: Novello, 1974.

14. Smith, John Christopher. *Overture to "The Fairies."* London: Oxford University Press, [1972].

SHAKESPEARE PLAYS: COMPLETE EDITIONS BEFORE 1850, SINGLE WORKS, ALTERATIONS

Complete Editions

The Works of Mr. William Shakespeare. Edited by Nicholas Rowe. 6 vols. London: Jacob Tonson, 1709.

The Works of Mr. William Shakespeare. Edited by Alexander Pope. 6 vols. London: Jacob Tonson, 1723.

The Works of Shakespeare. Edited by Lewis Theobald. 7 vols. London: A. Bettesworth, 1733.

The Plays of William Shakespeare. Edited by Samuel Johnson. 8 vols. London: J. and R. Tonson, 1765.

Bell's Edition of Shakespeare's Plays. 8 vols. London: John Bell, 1774.

The Plays and Poems of William Shakespeare. Edited by Edmond Malone. 10 vols. London: H. Beldon, 1790.

The Comedies, Histories, Tragedies, and Poems of William Shakespeare. Edited by Charles Knight. 2d ed. 12 vols. London: Chalres Knight and Co., 1843.

Single Plays and Alterations

1. Bullock, Christopher. *The Cobler of Preston. and the Adventures of Half an Hour.* London: T. Corbett, [1723]. (Loosely based on *The Taming of the Shrew*).

2. Burnaby, William. *Love Betray'd, or The Agreeable Disappointment.* London: D. Brown, 1703. (*Twelfth Night*).

3. [Colman, George, and David Garrick]. *A Fairy Tale.* London: Charles and Samuel Thompson, 1765. (*A Midsummer Night's Dream*).

4. [Cross, John]. *The History, Murders, Life, and Death of Macbeth And a Full Description of the Scenery, Action, Choruses, and Characters of the Ballet of Music and Action of that name.* London: T. Page, [1809].

5. Dryden, John. *The Tempest, or the Enchanted Island.* London: Henry Herringman, 1670.

6. _____. *Troilus and Cressida, or, Truth Found too Late.* London: Printed for Abel Swell, 1679.

7. *The Fairy Queen, an Opera.* London: J. Tonson, 1692. (*A Midsummer Night's Dream*).

8. Garrick, David. *Florizel and Perdita. A Dramatic Pastoral . . . Alter'd from The Winter's Tale.* London: J. and R. Tonson, 1758.

9. [Garrick, David, attr.]. *The Fairies. An Opera.* London: Tonson and Draper, 1755. (*A Midsummer Night's Dream*).

10. _____. *The Tempest. An Opera.* London: J. and R. Tonson, 1756.

11. Gildon, Charles. *Measure for Measure, or Beauty the Best Advocate.* London: D. Brown and R. Parker, 1700.

12. Granville Lansdowne, George. *The Jew of Venice.* London: Tonson, 1701. (*The Merchant of Venice*).

13. Johnson, Charles. *Love in a Forest.* London: W. Chetwood, 1723. (*As You Like It*).

14. Lacy, John. *Sauny the Scot: or, The Taming of the Shrew.* London: E. Whitlock, 1698.

15. Leveridge, Richard. *The Comick Masque of Pyramus and Thisbe.* London: W. Mears, 1716. (*A Midsummer Night's Dream*).

16. Morgan, MacNamara. *The Sheep-Shearing; or Florizel and Perdita.* London: Reeves, 1756. (*The Winter's Tale*).

17. _____. *The Sheep-Shearing; or Florizel and Perdita. A Pastoral Comedy Taken from Shakespeare . . . The Songs by Mr. Arne.* London: Reeves, 1771. (*The Winter's Tale*).

18. "Pyramus and Thisbe." Bodleian Library, Oxford. Malone MS 151. (*A Midsummer Night's Dream*).

19. Ravenscroft, Edward. *Titus Andronicus.* London: J. Hindmarsh, 1687.

20. Rolli, Paolo. *Rosalinda.* London, 1744. (*As You Like It*).

21. Sedley, Charles. *Antony and Cleopatra.* London: Richard Tonson, 1677.

22. Shadwell, Thomas. *The History of Timon of Athens, the Man Hater.* London: Henry Herringman, 1678.

23. Shakespeare, William. *Antony and Cleopatra, with Alterations and Additions from Dryden.* London: J. Barber, 1813.

24. _____. *As You Like It.* Dublin: A. Reilly, 1741.

25. _____. *The Comedy of Errors.* London: Printed for the editor, 1770.

26. _____. [*A Comedy of Errors*]. *William Shakespeare's A Comedy of Errors . . . with Alterations . . . the selections from Dr. Arne, R.J.S. Stevens, and Mozart.* London: Sampson Low, 1819.

27. _____. *Coriolanus or, The Roman Matron. A Tragedy Taken from Shakespeare and Thomson.* London: A. Millar, [1755].

28. _____. *Coriolanus, adapted to the stage with additions from Thomson by J. P. Kemble.* London: Longman, Hurst, Rees, and Orme, 1806.

29. _____. *Cymbeline, a Tragedy . . . with alterations.* London: J. and R. Tonson, 1762.

30. _____. *Cymbeline, King of Britain . . . revised by J. P. Kemble.* London: J. Miller, 1815.

31. _____. [*Hamlet*]. *The Tragedy of Hamlet.* London: Andr. Clark, 1676.

32. _____. [*Henry IV, Part 1*]. *King Henry IV, with the humours of Sir John Falstaff. A tragi-comedy. As it is acted at the Theatre in Little-Lincolns-Inn-Fields . . . revived with alterations.* London: for R. W., 1700.

33. _____. [*Henry IV, Part 2*]. *The Sequel of Henry the fourth, with the humours of Sir John Falstaffe . . . altered from Shakespeare by the late Mr. Betterton.* London: W. Cherwood and T. Jauncy, 1719.

34. _____. [*Henry IV, Part 2*]. *King Henry IV.* London: John Miller, 1821.

35. _____. *Henry VIII. . . as it is acted at the Theatres in London and Dublin.* Dublin: S. Powell, 1734.

36. _____. *Henry VIII . . . With the coronation of Anne Bullen.* London: C. Hitch & L. Hawes, 1762.

37. _____. *Julius Caesar, a tragedy.* London, 1711.

38. _____. *Julius Caesar, a Tragedy as it is now acted by His Majesty's Servants.* London: J. Tonson and J. Darby, 1729.

39. _____. *Macbeth, a Tragedy. With all the alterations, amendments, additions and new songs.* London: P. Chetwin, [1674].

40. _____. *Macbeth . . . revised by J. P. Kemble.* London: Ridgeway, 1803.

41. _____. *Measure for Measure . . . as it is acted at the Theatre Royal in Lincoln's-Inn-Fields.* London: J. Tonson, 1722.

42. _____. *A Midsummer Night's Dream . . . with Alterations and Additions, and Several New Songs.* London: J. and R. Tonson, 1763.

43. _____. *A Midsummer Night's Dream . . . with Alterations and New Songs.* London: J. Miller, 1816.

44. _____. *Othello, the Moor of Venice.* London: T. Witford, 1755.

45. _____. *Romeo and Juliet . . . with alterations and an additional scene.* London: J. and R. Tonson, 1750.

46. _____. *The Tempest, or The Enchanted Island.* London: Henry Herringman, 1674.

47. _____. *The Tempest, a comedy written by William Shakespeare: the music by Purcel and Dr. Arne; with the additional airs and choruses by the late Mr. Linley, Jun.* London: C. Bathurst, 1785.
48. _____. *The Tempest; or The Enchanted Island.* London: J. Debrett, 1789.
49. _____. [*Tempest*]. *Shakespeare's Tempest; or, the Enchanted Island, adapted to the stage with additions from Dryden and Davenant* [altered by J. P. Kemble]. London: Longman, Hurst, Rees, and Orme, 1807.
50. _____. *Timon of Athens, as revived at the Theatre Royal, Drury Lane, on Monday October 28, 1816.* London: C. Chapple, 1816.
51. _____. *Two Gentlemen of Verona.* London: J. and R. Tonson, 1763.
52. _____. *The Winter's Tale . . . adapted to the stage by J. P. Kemble.* London: The Theatre, 1811.
53. Sheffield, John. *The Tragedy of Julius Caesar, altered, with a Prologue and Chorus.* In *The Works of John Sheffield*, vol. 1. London: John Barber, 1723.
54. _____. *The Tragedy of Marcus Brutus.* In *The Works of John Sheffield*, vol. 1. London: John Barber, 1723. (*Julius Caesar*).
55. Tate, Nahum. *The History of King Lear.* London: E. Flesher, 1681.
56. _____. *The History of King Richard the Second.* London: Richard and Jacob Tonson, 1681.
57. _____. *The Ingratitude of a Commonwealth: or the Fall of Caius Martius Coriolanus.* London: Printed by L. M. for Joseph Hindmarsh, 1682.
58. Worsdale, Jeremy. *A Cure for a Scold.* London: L. Gilliver, 1735. (*The Taming of the Shrew*).

PERIOD COMMENTARY

Baker, Richard. *Theatrum Redivivum, or The Theatre Vindicated.* London: Francis Eglesfield, 1662.
Boaden, James. *Memoirs of the Life of John Kemble, Esq.* 2 vols. London: Longman, Hurst, Rees, Orme, Brown, and Green, 1825.
Boswell, James. *Boswell's Life of Dr. Johnson* [1791]. Edited by G. Birkbeck Hill. 6 vols. Oxford: Clarendon Press, 1934.

Burney, Charles. *A General History of Music* [1789]. Edited by Frank Mercer. 2 vols. New York: Dover, 1957.

Caulfield, John. *A Collection of Vocal Music in Shakespear's Plays. . . revised and arranged with an accompaniment for the piano forte by Mr.* [John] *Addison*. 2 vols. London: J. Caulfiled, [1815].

Cibber, Colley. *An Apology for the Life of Colley Cibber* [1740]. Edited by B.R.S. Fone. Ann Arbor: University of Michigan Press, 1968.

Collier, Jeremy. *A Short View of the Immorality and Profaneness of the English Stage.* London: S. Keble, 1698.

Corneille, Pierre. *Trois Discours sur le Poeme Dramatique, 1656-1660.* Paris: Société d'Edition d'Enseignment Superieur, 1963.

Davies, Thomas. *Memoirs of the Life of David Garrick, Esq.* 2 Vols. London: Longman, Hurst, Rees, and Orme, 1808.

Dennis, John. *The Critical Works of John Dennis.* Edited by Edward Niles Hooker. 2 vols. Baltimore: Johns Hopkins University Press, 1943.

Downes, John. *Roscius Anglicanus, or an Historical Review of the Stage.* London: T. R., 1708.

Dryden, John. *Of Dramatic Poesy and Other Critical Essays.* Edited by George Watson. 2 vols. New York: E. P. Dutton, 1962.

Garrick, David. *The Letters of David Garrick.* Edited by David M. Little and George M. Kahrl. 3 vols. Cambridge, Mass.: Harvard University Press, 1963.

Genest, John. *Some Account of the English Stage from the Restoration in 1660 to 1830.* 10 vols. Bath: for H. E. Carrington, 1832.

Gildon, Charles. *The Life of Mr. Thomas Betterton.* London: R. Gosling, 1710.

Hawkins, John. *A General History of the Science and Practice of Music* [1776]. 2 vols. London: Novello, 1853; New York: Dover, 1963.

Kelly, Michael. *Reminiscences* [1826]. Edited by Roger Fiske. London: Oxford University Press, 1975.

Kemble, Frances Ann. *Record of a Girlhood.* 3 vols. London: Richard Bentley and Son, 1878.

Kemble, John Philip. *John Philip Kemble Promptbooks.* Edited by Charles H. Shattuck. 11 vols. Charlottesville: University Press of Virginia, 1974.

Linley, William. *Shakespeare's Dramatic Songs.* 2 vols. London: Preston, 1816.

Murphy, Arthur. *The Life of David Garrick, Esq.* 2 vols. London: J. Wright, 1801.

Raymond, George. *Memoirs of Robert William Elliston, Comedian.* 2d ed. 2 vols. London: John Oliver, 1846; New York: Benjamin Blom, 1969.

Rymer, Thomas. "A Short View of Tragedy [1693]." In *The Critical Works of Thomas Rymer.* Edited by Curt A. Zimansky. New Haven: Yale University Press, 1956.

Wilkinson, Tate. *Memoirs of His Own Life.* 4 vols. York: Wilson, Spence, and Mawman, 1790.

Wright, James. *Historia Histrionica, an Historical Account of The English Stage.* London: G. Croom, 1699.

MODERN COMMENTARY AND REFERENCES

Appleton, William. *Charles Macklin, An Actors Life.* Cambridge, Mass.: Harvard University Press, 1960.

Arundell, Dennis. "Purcell and Natural Speech." *Musical Times* 100 (1959):90-95.

Avery, Emmet L. "The Shakespeare Ladies Club." *Shakespeare Quarterly* 7 (1956):153-58.

Babcock, Robert Witbeck. *The Genesis of Shakespeare Idolatry, 1766-1799.* Chapel Hill: University of North Carolina Press, 1931; New York: Russell & Russell, 1964.

Badawi, M. M. *Coleridge: Critic of Shakespeare.* Cambridge: Cambridge University Press, 1973.

Baldwin, Olive, and Thelma Wilson. "Richard Leveridge, 1670–1758." *Musical Times* 111:592-94; 891-93; 988-90.

Barclay Squire, William. "The Music of Shadwell's *Tempest.*" *Musical Quarterly* 7 (1921):565-78.

_____. "Purcell's Dramatic Music." *Sammelbande der Internationalen Musikgessellschaft* 5 (1903–4):489-564.

_____. "Shakespearean Opera." In *A Book of Homage to Shakespeare.* Edited by Israel Gollancz. Oxford: Oxford University Press, 1916.

Beechey, Gwilym. "Thomas Chilcot and His Music." *Music and Letters* 54 (1973):179-96.

Bingham, Madeleine. *Sheridan, The Track of a Comet.* New York: St. Martin's, 1972.

Broadbent, R. J. *A History of Pantomime.* New York: Benjamin Blom, 1901.

Butler, Martin. *Theatre and Crisis, 1632-1642.* Cambridge: Cambridge University Press, 1984.

Chappell, William. *Popular Music of the Olden Time.* 2 vols. London: Cramer, Bealle, and Chappell, [1855–59].

Charteris, Richard. "Some Manuscript Discoveries of Henry Purcell," *Notes* 37 (1980):8-9.

Cholij, Irena. "Defesch's *Tempest* Songs," *Musical Times* 67 (1986):325-27.

Corder, F. "The Works of Sir Henry Bishop." *Musical Quarterly* 4 (1918):78-97.

Covell, R. "Seventeenth Century Music for *The Tempest.*" *Studies in Music* 2 (1968):43-65.

Cowling, G. H. *Music on the Shakespearean Stage.* Cambridge: Cambridge University Press, 1913.

Cudworth, Charles. "Two Georgian Classics: Arne and Stevens." *Music and Letters* 45 (1964):146-53.

Cummings, W. H. "Who Wrote the *Macbeth* Music?" *Concordia,* 27 Nov. 1875, pp. 491-92.

Cutts, J. P. "Music and the Supernatural in *The Tempest.*" *Music and Letters* 39 (1958):347-58.

_____. "The Original Music to Middleton's *The Witch.*" *Shakespeare Quarterly* 7 (1956):203-10.

Dale, Robert. "Dramatic Music of William Boyce." Ph.D. dissertation, University of Washington, 1975.

Davis, Bertram. *A Proof of Eminence: The Life of Sir John Hawkins.* Bloomington: Indiana University Press, 1973.

Deelman, Christian. *The Great Shakespeare Jubilee.* New York: Viking, 1964.

Dennison, Peter. *Pelham Humfrey.* Oxford Studies of Composers, no. 21. Oxford: Oxford University Press, 1986.

Dent, Edward J. *Foundations of English Opera.* Cambridge: Cambridge University Press, 1927; New York: Da Capo, 1965.

_____. "Shakespeare and Music." In *The Companion to Shakespeare Studies.* Edited by H. Granville Barker and G. B. Harrison. Garden City, N.N.: Anchor Books, 1960.

Dobree, Bonamy. *Restoration Comedy, 1660-1720.* Oxford: Clarendon Press, 1929.

_____. *Restoration Tragedy, 1660-1720.* Oxford: Clarendon Press, 1929.

Ehrlich, Cyril. *The Music Profession in Britain Since the Eighteenth Century.* Oxford: Clarendon Press, 1985.

England, Martha Winburn. *Garrick's Jubilee.* Columbus: Ohio State University Press, 1964.

Faas, Ekbert. *Shakespeare's Poetics.* Cambridge: Cambridge University Press, 1986.

Fiske, Roger. *English Theatre Music in the Eighteenth Century.* 2d ed. London: Oxford University Press, 1986.

_____. "The Macbeth Music." *Music and Letters* 45 (1964):114-25.

Freehofer, John. "The Formation of The London Patent Companies in 1660." *Theatre Notebook* 19 (1965):6-30.

Freeman, Robert S. *Opera Without Drama. Currents of Change in Italian Opera, 1675-1725.* Studies in Musicology, no. 35. Ann Arbor, Mich.: UMI Research Press, 1981.

Gagey, Edmund McAdoo. *Ballad Opera.* Columbia University Studies in English and Comparative Literature, no. 130. New York: Benjamin Blom, 1937.

Gooch, Bryan N. S., and David Thatcher, eds. *A Shakespeare Music Catalogue.* 5 vols. Oxford: Clarendon Press, 1991.

Gray, Charles Harold. *Theatrical Criticism in London to 1795.* New York: F. Blom, [1964].

Greenhill, J., W. A. Harrison, and Frederick J. Furnwall, eds. *A List of All the Songs and Passages in Shakespeare Which Have Been Set to Music.* London: New Shakespeare Society, 1884; Folcraft, Pa.: Folcraft Library Editions, 1974.

Guffey, George Robert. *After the Tempest.* Los Angeles: University of California Press, 1969.

Gurry, Andrew. *The Shakespearean Stage, 1574-1642.* Cambridge: Cambridge University Press, 1970.

Harris, Ellen T. *Handel and the Pastoral Tradition.* London: Oxford University Press, 1980.

Hartnoll, Phyllis, ed. *Shakespeare in Music.* London: Macmillan, 1964.

Haywood, Charles. "William Boyce's 'Solemn Dirge' in Garrick's *Romeo and Juliet.*" *Shakespeare Quarterly* 9 (1960):173-85.

Hill, John Walter. *The Life and Works of Francesco Maria Veracini.* Studies in Musicology, no. 3. Ann Arbor, Mich.: UMI Research Press, 1979.

Hogan, Charles Beecher. *Shakespeare in the Theatre, 1701-1800.* 2 vols. Oxford: Clarendon Press, 1952.

Hotson, Leslie. *The Commonwealth and Restoration Stage.* Cambridge, Mass.: Harvard University Press, 1928; New York: Russell & Russell, 1962.

Hughes, Leo. *The Drama's Patrons: A Study of the Eighteenth-Century London Audience.* Austin: University of Texas Press, 1974.

Hume, Robert D. *The Development of English Drama in The Late Seventeenth Century.* Oxford: Clarendon Press, 1976.

Hume, Robert D., ed. *The London Theatre World, 1660-1800.* Carbondale: Southern Illinois University Press, 1980.

Kelly, John Alexander. *German Visitors to English Theatres in the Eighteenth Century.* Princeton: Princeton University Press, 1936; New York: Octagon, 1978.

Knapp, J. Merrill. "A Forgotten Chapter in English Eighteenth-Century Opera." *Music and Letters* 41(1961):4-16.

Lancaster, H. C. *A History of French Dramatic Literature in the Seventeenth Century.* 9 vols. Baltimore: Johns Hopkins University Press, 1929–42.

Laurie, Margaret. "Did Purcell Set *The Tempest?*" *Proceedings of the Royal Musical Association* 40 (1963–64):43-57.

Lawrence, W. J. "Did Thomas Shadwell Write an Opera on *The Tempest*?" *Anglia* 27 (1904):205-17.

_____. "Early Irish Ballad Opera and Comic Opera." *Musical Quarterly* 8 (1922):397-412.

Leacroft, Richard. *The Development of the English Playhouse.* Ithaca: Cornell University Press, 1973.

Lincoln, Stoddard. "Eccles and Congreve: Music and Drama on the Restoration Stage." *Theatre Notebook* 18 (1963-64):7-18.

The London Stage 1660-1800; A Calendar of Plays. 11 vols. Carbondale: Southern Illinois University Press, 1960–68.

Long, John H. *Shakespeare's Use of Music.* 3 vols. Gainesville: University of Florida Press, 1955–71.

Lowenburg, Alfred. "*A Midsummer Night's Dream* Music in 1763." *Theatre Notebook* 1 (1946):23-26.

McCredie, Andrew P. "John Christopher Smith as a Dramatic Composer." *Music and Letters* 45 (1964):22-38.

McManaway, J. "Songs and Masques in *The Tempest*." In *Theatre Miscellany: Six Pieces Connected with the Seventeenth-Century*

Stage. Luttrell Society Reprints no. 14. London: Luttrell Society, 1953.

Macqueen-Pope, W. J. *The Theatre Royal, Drury Lane.* London: W. H. Allen, 1945.

Martin, Dennis R. *The Operas and Operatic Style of John Frederick Lampe.* Detroit Monographs in Musicology no. 8. Detroit: Information Coordinators, 1985.

Milhous, Judith. *Thomas Betterton and the Management of Lincoln's-Inn-Fields, 1695-1708.* Carbondale: Southern Illinois University Press, 1979.

Milton, W. M. "*Tempest* in a Teapot." *ELH* 9 (1942):207-18.

Moore, J. R. "The Function of Songs in Shakespeare's Plays." In *Shakespeare Studies.* Madison: University of Wisconsin, 1916.

Moore, Robert Etheridge. *Henry Purcell and the Restoration Theatre.* Cambridge, Mass.: Harvard University Press, 1961.

――――. "The Music to *Macbeth.*" *Musical Quarterly* 47 (1961):22-40.

Murata, Margaret. "The Recitative Soliloquy." *Journal of the American Musicological Society* 32 (1979):45-73.

Murray, Christopher. *Robert William Elliston, Manager.* London: The Society for Theatre Research, 1975.

Naylor, E. W. *Shakespeare and Music.* 2d ed. London: J. M. Dent & Sons, 1931.

Nethercot, Arthur. *Sir William Davenant.* New York: Russell & Russell, 1967.

Nicoll, Allardyce. *A History of English Drama, 1600-1900.* Rev. ed. 4 vols. Cambridge: Cambridge University Press, 1952

――――. *Stuart Masques and The Renaissance Stage.* London: G. G. Harrap, [1937].

――――. *World Drama.* New York: Harcourt, Brace & Co., [1955].

Nilan, Mary Margaret. "The Stage History of *The Tempest*: A Question of Theatricality." Ph.D. dissertation, Northwestern University, 1967.

Noyes, Robert Gale. "Conventions of Song in Restoration Tragedy." *PMLA* 53 (1938):162-88.

――――. "A Manuscript Restoration Prologue for *Volpone. Modern Language Notes* 52 (1937):198-200.

Odell, George C. D. *Shakespeare from Betterton to Irving.* 2 vols. New York: Charles Scribner, 1920; New York: Dover, 1966.

Orrell, John. *The Theatres of Inigo Jones and John Webb.* Cambridge: Cambridge University Press, 1985.

Parkinson, John A. *An Index to the Vocal Works of Thomas Augustine Arne.* Detroit Studies in Music Bibliography no. 21. Detroit: Information Coordinators, 1978.

Pereyra, M.-L. "*La Tempête* d'après Shakespeare et la Musique de Pelham Humfrey." *La Revue Musicale* 2 (1927):32-42.

Pocock, Gordon. *Corneille and Racine, Problems of Dramatic Form.* Cambridge: Cambridge University Press, 1973.

Price, Curtis A. *Henry Purcell and The London Stage.* Cambridge: Cambridge University Press, 1984.

_____. *Music in the Restoration Theatre.* Studies in Musicology, no. 4. Ann Arbor, Mich.: UMI Research Press, 1979.

Rice, Paul F. "John Abraham Fisher's Music for the Opening of *Macbeth.*" *College Music Symposium* 26 (1986):7-13.

Rimbault, E. F. "Did Locke Write Vocal Music for *Macbeth?*" *Musical Times* 17 (1876):456-57.

Savage, Roger. "The Shakespeare-Purcell *Fairy Queen*—A Defence and Recommendation." *Early Music* 1 (1973):200-221.

Seng, Peter J. *The Vocal Songs in the Plays of Shakespeare.* Cambridge, Mass.: Harvard University Press, 1967.

Simpson, Claude M. *The British Broadside Ballad and Its Music.* New Brunswick, N.J.: Rutgers University Press, 1966.

Smith, D. Nicoll, ed. *Eighteenth Century Essays on Shakespeare.* New York: Russell & Russell, 1962.

Spencer, Hazelton. *Shakespeare Improved.* New York: Frederick Unger, 1927; 1963.

Sternfeld, F. W. *Music in Shakepearean Tragedy.* New York: Dover, 1963.

_____. "Ophelia's Version of the Walsingham Song." *Music and Letters* 45 (1964):108-13.

Stone, George Winchester. "*A Midsummer Night's Dream* in the Hands of Garrick and Colman." *PMLA* 54 (1939):467-82.

_____. "The Prevalence of Theatrical Music in Garrick's Time." In *The Stage and the Page: London's "Whole Show" in the Eighteenth-Century Theatre.* Edited by George Winchester Stone. Berkeley: University of California Press, 1981.

_____. "Shakespeare's *Tempest* at Drury Lane." *Shakespeare Quarterly* 7 (1956):1-8.

Summers, Montague. *The Restoration Theatre.* London: Oxford University Press, 1934.

Taylor, Gary. *Reinventing Shakespeare.* New York: Weidenfeld and Nicolson, 1989.

Thorn-Drury, G. "Shadwell and the Operatic *Tempest.*" *Review of English Studies* 3 (1927):204-8.

Ward, Charles. "*The Tempest*: A Restoration Opera Problem." *ELH* 13 (1946):19-30.

Warner, Beverly. *Famous Introductions to Shakespeare's Plays.* New York: Bert Franklin, 1968.

Westrup, J. A. "Introduction" to *Timon of Athens. The Works of Henry Purcell*, no. 20. Bourough Green: Novello, 1974.

_____. "Opera in England and Germany." In *The New Oxford History of Music.* Edited by Anthony Lewis and Nigel Fortune. 11 vols. London: Oxford University Press, 1975-. Vol. 5: *Opera and Church Music, 1630-1750.*

_____. *Purcell.* Revised by Nigel Fortune. London: Dent, 1980.

William Shakespeare: His Editors and Editions: A Commentary on the Major Editions of Shakespeare's Works. Milwaukee: Milwaukee Public Library, 1964.

Winn, James Anderson. *Unsuspected Eloquence: A History of the Relations Between Poetry and Music.* New Haven: Yale University Press, 1981.

Index of Musical Scores and Examples

Subject Index

About the Author

RANDY L. NEIGHBARGER, a writer and musicologist, has been a music director for theater and radio. His articles have appeared in *The Diapason* and *Opera Journal.*